BIG THINGS IN TIGHT SPACES

Bram Gunther

To Kate.

PART 1

1. David

ON A CLEAR October day more than half my life ago I first set eyes on Grace. Orange leaves fluttered to the ground in the day's sharp wind and the crows blew back and forth in the air. I stood looking out my livingroom window watching Grace and her roommates haul their suitcases up the hill. They wore tight fitting t-shirts and gestured with their skinny arms. At that time in my life I imagined that it was only a matter of seconds before love called on me and therefore sensed in their female presence my future. Grace was the tallest of them, high despite her hunch, long brown hair, and my eyes followed her as she struggled with her luggage, dragging it along the path until she stopped at the apartment next to ours.

I heard my roommate from inside. I coughed, clearing the air.

Lawrence stood on his bed and put up on the wall a map of America. Opposite this I hung my faded map of Africa. He got down and began to tinker with his stereo equipment and soon it jerked on with loud music. This got us dancing and tangling into each other. He then paused, ducked under his bed, pulled out a bong from his duffel bag, and smiled conspiratorially. He tiptoed to the bathroom, so as not to alert our other roommates, and came back with the bong full of water and the bowl packed with pot. He handed it to me and I took in a long excited breath and went into a coughing fit, red and swollen in the eyes. We put up posters of baseball stars and rock stars, and played air guitar. My throat constricted after another hit of pot but in this fugue state I dreamily pictured Grace's tall frame. I turned to Lawrence and said, "It's unbelievable, as if put there just for us." He agreed. We put the pot away, put on our shoes, and went next door.

We knocked timidly yet heard the commotion that we triggered inside. A pan was dropped and conference ensued. We could only suppose that the ache in their bodies equaled ours. Lawrence leaned into me, hugged me from behind, and I fell forward with his weight, catching myself on their door. It then opened to the pale freckled girl who said, "Not now, boys." The cold air rested on our cheeks, our feet tired from the long day.

We retreated home, watched TV, and eventually separated into our beds. Lawrence asked me if I had ever had crotch rot and I said yes, many times. He told me that his girlfriend Loretta was sick and he was scared to kiss her. I said I loved the taste of a girl's mucus. He said what do you think of the city's new mayor, a Jew? I said, "It's all about the Jews anyway." He closed his eyes. I listened to the walking conversations outside our window and closed my eyes too. I thought of my cats at home and my brother Leo. I thought of my father and how his lips became wet when he was angry. I pictured my mother's face, her heavy jaw, and the charity in the pools of her eyes. I fretted over chemistry class and how hard it was. Despite my best efforts I thought inevitably of Esther and her rejection of me. A summer away from her, a month into my sophomore year of college, just moved into these new campus apartments, this rejection still vibrated my heart.

I looked at Lawrence's map shadowed on the wall and let my eyes trail east to west, the states getting wider and longer, the green spaces of America growing in scale. Lawrence's languorous body spilled over the bottom of his bed, his feet hung like meats in a butcher. I looked through our window at the spotted plane trees. Lawrence choked on his breath and ground his teeth.

I got out of bed, put on gym shorts and a sweatshirt, got a drink of milk, fit my sneakers on, and went out for a run.

The night was startling in its brightness and the air had an elementary chill. I ducked around back of our house and went down a dirt track, past a few lonely cars, and onto the huge grass field that looked over the gym and past into the hillside that was covered with maples and ashes.

I started running around the edge of the field, my knees jarring. Round past the huge sugar maple with its muscular bark, parallel to the road and its streetlights, which lit my body up within the night. I watched my legs move, the skin quivering. Down the hill, I felt strong, full of stamina.

Up the hill, however, a bubble of gas emerged in my gut. I slumped over to my left in pain, slowing down to a near halt. I felt it against my inner lining, stuck. I pushed for its release, and youth still on my side, it dislodged. I found my pace again and ran on.

I dreamed of touching the skin on Esther's arms. I dreamed of kissing her neck. I dreamed of the moment when she lifted her sweater and let me touch her breast.

I ran over the crest of the campus, down the asphalt path, and into the high grasses behind the dorms. I ran to Esther's window. I stood with my chest against the brick and breathed deeply. I inched my eye into view and saw that she was alone. I felt chilled by the night and took another deep breath. I tapped on the glass. She looked around but I spun away. A bubble formed again in my gut and I thought of my father. I pictured him lurching and looming, screaming at me to "Stay alert!" I moved fully in front of her window, tapped again, and caught her eyes as she turned around. My love spun out of control and I felt my forehead get hot. She came to the window, opened it, and said, "Fire, what are you doing?"

"I . . . have come to win . . . your love again."

"You've got to be kidding, right?"

She looked at me to confirm this and I mustered a weak smile.

"Come back tomorrow," she said. "Come back later. I'm tired."

I ran up along the retaining wall down the hill again under the massive canopy of the sugar maple. The night was burst open with stars. I could hear the rustle and sway of the trees. I could hear the night animals. I could feel my heart throb with the sting of loss, its poison. I wanted to be carried away by nature but instead I saw myself all too clearly, success invariably an inch away. I went back to my house. I ate a leftover pancake. I drank hot chocolate. I watched sports, a special on Hank Aaron. I carried myself into bed and listened to Lawrence grind his teeth.

I woke to screeching bluejays, Lawrence still sweetly sleeping. I stretched, got up, showered, dressed, ate more leftover pancakes, and left the house.

There was Grace. We stood suddenly face to face. She stepped backwards. She had a northern body that swirled downwards from her neck. Her eyes twitched back and forth under black eyebrows. Her fingers were thin, and she wore a red threadbare t-shirt, jeans, and suede shoes.

"Hi," I said.

My throat was raw.

"Hi."

"I'm Fire."

"I'm Grace."

"Nice to meet you."

"You too."

She cradled her textbooks against her chest, leaned her head forward, a little intimacy apportioned from the air between us. I could smell her fragrance, like wet leaves, but faint.

"Funny that we are put down next to each other like this," I said.

"What do you mean?"

"I mean it's funny that one day two people are complete strangers and the next day they are neighbors."

"I guess so."

We stared at each other. I wanted to run away. I couldn't think of anything to say that could express how I felt at that moment except perhaps to say please love me without hassle, like my mom. I heaved up some saliva trying to clear my throat. It sat heavy and green in my mouth and I licked it with the end of my tongue.

"Where you headed?" I asked.

I swallowed.

"Class."

I gestured with my arm for her to move, which she did, and I followed her out and into the common, fresh grass and newly planted hackberry trees.

"What class are you heading for?"

"A class on the bible."

"Oh. Everybody talks about that class," I said, looking her over. "Is it as good as they say?"

"It's almost transcendent."

"Nice," I said.

"It is nice."

The path came downwards into a narrow gorge where a tiny wetland had survived the excavators and backhoes that paved the way for our school. In this little patch were cattails and sedges turning a golden brown in the fall.

"King David!" I announced.

"Yes?"

"He was the king. He was blessed."

"What're you talking about?"

"David thought big."

"David was also a murderer of tens of thousands," she said.

"That's true, but it was part of his fate."

"Murder is murder."

"Back then it was a way of life."

"Are you being serious?"

"Yes. They were all a bunch of savages. I mean these guys were fighting all the time, in the name of god . . . Just like now, come to think of it."

"Well," she laughed, "that's kind of true. But all that beautiful poetry too."

"And Bathsheba." I said.

"Where're you headed?" she asked.

"Chemistry."

We finished a short climb and entered the center campus where the brown brick buildings were lined up in a large rectangle.

"Chemistry? Are you going to be a chemist?"

"No. I am going to be an environmental scientist. Chemistry is just along the route. A hard route at the moment."

"Well, I admire you. Nice to meet you . . . I've got to go. But I will see you soon because." She blushed. "We are neighbors."

Chemistry was a blur, as it usually was despite my attempts to concentrate. I had bad dreams about failing chemistry and remembered in high school how every time I thought I had done well on the test my score was in actuality painfully low. I got a 66 in chemistry. Jeff, my best friend then, got a 67. I said to him, "Thank god you suck too." Redux, the numbers on the chalkboard were a blur and meaningless. After class I ate lunch alone in the cafeteria thinking about Grace, and Esther too. In the afternoon I went to history class. I kept picturing Grace in panties and cowboy boots and fell deeper into fantasy. I came back home with the sun nearly gone behind the woods, fended off Lawrence who wanted to talk about politics, and went to visit Grace.

Marjorie, the pale freckled girl, answered the door, which was what I was scared of, and I almost ran off. She had a dramatic overbite and prankish blue eyes.

"Fire," she said, "You! God. Here for Grace? . . . Grace!" She screamed out. "It's Fire."

"Now," she said, "I bet you don't know where we have met before?"

I began to sweat. I couldn't picture her at all.

"Come on Fire, search your memory," she said.

"I presume you don't mean yesterday moving in?"

"Yes, you presume right."

"Shit."

"Don't get frustrated. But if you don't get this right you can forget me."

I laughed nervously. But my mind was a blank on her. This was a huge disaster, I thought.

"Fire, you idiot. We went to I.S. 44 together."

"What? Can't be."

I moved closer to her for inspection.

"Yes." She put her face in front of mine. "How could you forget this face?"

"Never, never could I forget your face."

"Well."

"But I can't remember," I lamented.

"You were up on the third floor in open corridor and I was down with the beasts in the basement."

"You were with those minorities in the basement. Whew, they were sociopaths. I was scared shitless of all of them."

"I was one of them."

"No way."

"Yes. I come from poverty you spoiled boy."

"I'm not spoiled."

"You come from the heights," she said.

Grace came into the livingroom.

"Fire Rosewood. I knew about you," she continued. "You and your friends were interlopers."

"Bullshit."

"Oh come on."

"You are just jealous."

"Yes." She changed her tone. "That you and I survived I.S. 44 is nothing but a miracle. Don't you think?"

Marjorie took me by the hand and brought me over to the couch. Grace joined us, the girls flanking me. Grace massaged my lower arms with her fingers and I fell into a trance. She touched me so delicately I could barely talk. Marjorie said, "My brothers hated I.S. 44. My father of course thought it toughened them up." She snorted. "The old drunk. And my delicate flower of a mother . . .". The words washed over me. Then Marjorie pushed away, got up, and said, "Grace, we have to go." She noticed my wounded look. "You can come over tomorrow." I looked at Grace and she looked back at me hopefully.

A few days later we had a party and Grace and I danced together. She was mesmerizing, swaying her body, her hips rippling, her arms outstretched, her fingers snapping, her face taut. I tried to keep up, but couldn't, so instead watched her, rotating my body back and forth lazily.

A month later Grace was preparing Swedish meatballs for me.

I walked into her apartment, which was lit in blue candlelight, Marjorie and her other housemates gone. The kitchen was chaotic with pots and bowls, the meatballs frying noisily on a pan, wineglasses filled, and utensils set out.

"It smells good," I said.

"It's the only thing I know how to cook."

"Are you Swedish?"

"Half. My mother used to cook this for us."

As she walked back to the stove I watched her ass wiggle through her jeans, a perfect curved pumpkin.

I sat down at the table, my fingers tapping lightly against my leg. There was a Georgia O'Keefe on the wall and a tiny cross hanging just over it. The harsher light over the stove made Grace look yellow. In a white t-shirt that hugged her slim but long back her spine was outlined. She wore threadbare jeans with a hint of white underpants wedged out from the top. I wanted to hug her from behind. I coughed twice.

"America's repugnant, isn't it?" I said.

She turned around.

"What?"

"America sucks so much, doesn't it?"

"That's quite a statement."

"Yeah. Well?"

"You sound ridiculous."

"America's crazy, it's a monster, it gobbles up like seed all in its path."

"A little like you, Fire."

"How can you say that?"

"I know already. You give yourself away. Always ranting, your face all red."

"That's what the thought of injustice does to me, makes me mad."

"You and Tom Paine, right?"

"More like Ben Franklin, really, because I am a scientist too."

"Oh, so sorry, Mr. Franklin."

"All this talk of democracy and freedom and we're down in Central America killing peasants. How do these two ends meet? In a fog of lies of course."

I stopped to see her reaction, but she was turned from me.

I continued. "And the ruling class sucking up along the way more and more pussy and wealth!"

This anger drove my father to rages in that his powers and intelligence were not up to his levels of imagination and aspirations. I was one of the lucky ones. And so why was I not starting the revolution? How could I not seek thanks and distribution for my great luck? I was up at night about this, long sleepless nights.

"I hate them all!" I screamed out.

"My," Grace said, "so righteous. You sound just like them."

"Well, do you agree?"

Her nose was long and tapered and gave her voice a sharp tone. Her flushed cheeks, the heat of her spirit, and her infatuated eyes made it clear, I hoped, that it was possible to sleep with her tonight. I felt tense in the throat and my eyes smarted. She stayed busy in the kitchen. She pushed back her hair from her face as she stared down at the stove and stirred the sauce. She wore a jade necklace around her neck.

"I don't think that much about it," she said, turning away from the stove to face me.

"How can you not?"

"It's just not my way I guess."

"But it's all consuming."

"Not me. I am more inside . . . Why aren't you a political science major, huh?"

"Because, as I told you, it is through enlightened natural resource policy that the world will change."

"Oh."

"But funny you would say that. I think about being president one day. I know that's weird, radical Jew president of the U.S., but I think I could pull it off."

"You do, really."

She turned from me again, mixing sauce into the meatballs, the pasta roiling. Into my nose wafted the frightening smell of onions. My gut would be in poor shape tonight, grumbling and complaining to me, crying out in misfortune; the heartburn like lava flow, my farts descending down the pipe of my gut like an inflated hot ball. This sickness that had haunted me since boyhood, that kept me chained to my bed when I should have been out, a dark inertia that had prevented me from normal growth. I was used to it, but could Grace ever be?

I liked the shape of her back, how her hair fell cleanly over her shoulders, the longness of her chin.

"So," I said, "what do you think about?"

"Lots of things."

"What do you think about most?"

"My school work, I guess."

"You mean getting good grades?"

"I want to do well in my classes and so I study a lot. I love reading."

"Why do you want to do so well?"

"It's what I am good at. Plus," she paused, "I think it might be my career, you know, in publishing."

"That's forward thinking."

"It's from my dad."

"He's in publishing?"

"Yes, academic books."

"Cool."

She picked the pot of meatballs off the stove and laid it down on the counter.

"Dinner is almost ready," she called out.

She came around to the table and picked up her glass of wine. I picked up mine. We clinked, quickly but happily; she balled her cheeks into a grateful smile and we drank our first sip.

"I'm glad you're here," she said.

I put down my wine glass, moved into her, wrapped my arms around her lower back, put my face against hers, the skin so smooth.

"What kind of books do you read for your classes?" she asked me, turning back to the kitchen.

"Biology stuff of course, plant stuff, ecology, forestry, and lots of environmental politics."

"I wish I had a knack for science. I find it fascinating."

"It is, and it's the basis for world justice."

"And you are its spokesperson."

"Yes, I'm going to be a spokesman for justice!"

"You're exasperating."

"Other people have said that too . . . Anyway, what I don't get is how human beings claiming to be so logical can be so self destructive too. Doesn't anyone realize that something's got to give?"

"What do you give up?"

"I give up." I looked at her. "The purity of my soul."

"Oh, what a model you are."

"Yes, that's bad for a person, to sacrifice some of their goodness for the sake of luxury. I will pay for it somehow."

"I was wondering what you gave up in the material?"

"Ah ha! My materialism is kept in check by an inner moral compass. Beyond that there is nothing much else to do."

She smirked.

"What was growing up in New York City like?" she asked.

She moved back into the kitchen, took a metal pot off the stove using a pink and white handtowel, and poured the noodles into the strainer. The steam rose up and engulfed her head.

"It makes you crazy."

"What?"

"New York City. Being born in New York City."

"What do you mean?"

"Trust me, it makes you crazy, all that flesh and ambition banging up against itself."

She laid each plate with spaghetti and meatballs. I smelled the smell of pain, onions. It was like fires passing through my insides. I could smell the fires in foods from way off. She brought the plates to the table. She handed me mine, put hers down, and sat opposite me.

"My explosions," she began, "I guess are more internal."

"What do you mean?"

I sipped at my wine, but yearned for water, but was afraid to ask for it, as if it would indicate my distaste for her meal and her efforts. She drank her wine heartily and tapped her fingers against the table.

"Well, I guess, my dramas are emotional. I've had an emotionally turbulent life."

"How?"

She stuck her tongue to her upper lip, laying it there, glistening.

"My parents had a very nasty divorce and I was sent away to boarding school."

"Why, they punished you?"

"Sort of."

"For doing what?"

"Rebelling."

"What did you do? Not follow orders?"

"Basically."

"Were they insecure?"

"Who?"

"Your parents."

"Yes, I guess you could put it that way. They were too insecure to handle my growing up."

"Don't you hate that? Why become parents if you can't handle the pressure."

"Well, I'm not sure they saw it that way. They were unhappy."

"You can still handle things with grace . . . no pun intended."

"It was hard for them. My father was very disappointed in me."

"An unhappy pappy," I said.

She laughed, but looked hard at me too.

"How, why, what did he want from you?" I continued.

"To be a success where he was a failure." She looked as if she was going to cry. "I tried so hard to please them, and they gave in return no compromise."

"The nitwits . . . At least my father isn't the psychological torture type. He rams right at you."

"Well, that sounds bad too. I wouldn't want to have to be on the lookout for that all the time."

"I was too self . . . focussed . . . to be bothered."

"I was devastated."

"Can't you leave it behind you," I said, "this family business?"

"I am trying. But it's hard. My father went from Jeckyl to Hyde. It was very scary."

"What was up with the dude?"

"He was in an unhappy marriage and he was an unhappy man, he felt he was a failure."

"But he couldn't keep it from you?"

"I guess not."

"What did you do specifically?"

"Got so drunk I was sick. I threw up on a nun."

"Sounds fairly normal."

The wine and oniony meatball had made the pain in my stomach detonate. It rippled in waves through me, and I clenched my teeth to hide it from Grace. I nibbled like a bird at my food, swallowed a burning sip of wine.

"I don't know. I betrayed him, I guess."

"How could daughter betray father?" I said. "It's the other way round. But my father sees it the same way though. Every time I fail to read his crazy mind he feels betrayed and blows up at me. We, my brother and I, are such failures to him, but it's impossible to win a psychotic's mind over quite frankly."

"Us Wasps do it all a bit more tightly. My dad seethed and smoldered."

"Whoa, that's nasty."

"Kids pay for their parents' . . . selfishness. They pay for their parents' rejection of them."

"Damn well said," I said.

My eyes caught sight of the first few flames. In a second the hand-towel burst into fire. I pivoted around Grace and spun into the kitchen. Its white and orange light was stunning. I grabbed the handtowel, threw it into the sink, and doused it with water. It sizzled and let off its oxygenated discharge. I noticed that the kitchen was a mess. The burner was still on, the cause of the fire, and pots were caked and unwashed, glasses half filled with moldy water, sauce stains on the walls, garbage thrown splotches on the tile floor. Turning, I whacked my elbow against the faucet and rose up in anger ready to tear the faucet apart. I turned, went back to Grace, slid into her, and put my lips against hers.

She smelled of meatballs and sweat.

There was a thud at the door. We separated. In came Marjorie.

She looked at us; she was dressed in a blue and yellow sundress, a white jean jacket covering her back, her red hair splayed over her shoulders and forehead.

"Lovers yet?"

"No," Grace said, embarrassed.

"Why not?"

"Because . . .".

"Oh shut up," I said to Marjorie.

"Now, now, Fire, my dear. Don't let me get in the way," she said.

She walked over to me and hugged me, put her hands on my ass. She grabbed Grace's hands and laid them over my ass too, four female hands on my sallow buns.

"Like this, guys. Try some touching . . . Now," she said in her high trilling voice, "come into the bedroom. Get it over with. Don't let it be an obstacle anymore."

She grabbed one of my hands and took Grace with her other. She pulled us out of the kitchen, round into the hallway (I remembered the gray rug swirling in my eyes and the onions passing loudly through my gut), and into their bedroom.

Grace and Marjorie's beds were pushed together as if it were a king size. She threw us down and with that force ended up on top of us. Our faces were all squished together. My eyes beat nervously in their sockets. She opened her mouth, stuck her tongue out, touched Grace's lips with it, and said, "Kids, have fun."

The room vibrated in its now quietness. I was hard already, but nervous, knowing that soon she would see my sickly body. I could be humiliated. However, she began nuzzling my face. We kissed, my body fitting into hers, my sense of my limitations fading, joy filling up my lungs. We rocked from side to side. For a brief moment it felt as if I was in my mother's arms. We kissed again. She sunk her tongue into my mouth, more painful really than pleasurable, but a clear indication of her interest. This, in itself, was quite a turn on. I pulled away a bit, our tongues separating, and instead cupped my lips around hers. Esther had said, in the very few times I had got to kiss her, that my tongue was too invasive. She said, "Let the wet lips brush up against each other, suckle. More lips." I did this with Grace, and soon she got the idea, our moist lips softly rubbing, teasing each other. She pulled back from me and took off her shirt. Her breasts were small and upright, the nipples strained and purple. I began licking them, her eyes receding back into private space, her chin set in concentration. I closed my eyes and let my thoughts fade away, listened to her mumbled sounds, ululations to the night. She unsnapped her jeans and my body tingled with a sense of trailblazing. I was King David in his lair. It was a great gift I was about to receive. Her pants came down over her long legs. I stared at her for a moment, her pale whitehipped rawness. I put my hand over her underwear, the strip hot and gluey. But this blew my cool. Mr. Sex, skinny sickly Fire felt his body's upheaval, the first wave of climax, and at 19 years of age there was no self control, and so the ejection of my desire came fast.

I turned away from her. Grace, however, leaned into me and put my hand over her vagina. She took my index finger inside her, a bog. Her body had released its humus. She kissed me with closed but swollen lips. She lay back and pulled me down with her, but I wanted to go home now. She cuddled her head onto my chest. I pleaded with myself to stay focused, but it felt impossible.

Marjorie burst into the room.

"Hello, my friends," she said, and lay down next to Grace and began rubbing her stomach.

I nearly hyperventilated.

"Don't get so excited," she said. "If I'm going to have sex with one of you it would be Grace. She knows that."

"Leave him alone."

"He's a big boy. You know," she said to Grace, "the arrogance."

"I know," she said. "You have to like his willingness."

"Fire." Marjorie grabbed my dick. "You've got balls."

I didn't stay with Grace that night. Her bed was too small and the presence of Marjorie right next to me was too much for me to handle. I also needed to be alone with my gut pain, which had redoubled. My heron body so like a child's from the outside and so like an old man's from the inside.

I went for a walk. Up to the top end of the parking lot, across the road, lonely and dark, and into the remnant woods of the suburbs. The trees were in age classes: a cluster at 30 years old, some at 50, my father's age, and a few that reached back 80-90 years, one or two at 150. A lattice of bushes tangled me up as I drifted through the understory. I crunched the fallen leaves. I was spooked, but feeling free too, listening for strange sounds, watching for a glimpse of strange eyes. There was an airport on the other side of the woodland where the trees stopped and the land opened up. I whacked through more underbrush and groundcover, thinking about how quiet it was, also remembering, despite myself, all the horror stories of summer camp. I survived the beasts of New York City so the forest can't touch me. Nonetheless, the field ahead settled my nerves. I walked out into the open space of the airport and sat down on a mound of grass next to the mesh fence that surrounded the runway. I tried to clear my head. Did Grace still like me? Was Marjorie telling her to drop this loser? Were they lying in bed mocking me? It was unbearable to think that I might be alone still.

I lay back on the wet grass. I kept sensing the origins of my personality in the dark lights of my night eyes. I interrogated the part of my brain that hummed with the memory of my experiences and reactions, the part of my brain that archived me. My mind worked constantly trying to make sense of it.

A plane started up. From darkness came a burst of light. The sound, the deafening roar of the machine. Slowly, after a lag, it came closer and closer, getting bigger and noisier, the huge monster coming upon me until it lifted up and roared over my head, its metal belly smoky and hot.

When I got home, Jane called.

"Hi, Jane," I said, "I'm heading off to bed."

"Well, did you get what you wanted?"

"I had sex with Grace, yes."

"You were right, oh my goodness, tonight was the night."

"Yes."

"Well, how was it?"

"Great. She is great."

"What does her body look like?"

"Fantastic, gorgeous."

"Really, better than mine?"

"Don't put me on the spot, please."

2. Africa

GRACE AND I finished college together and moved into New York City. I had wanted to move to Wyoming. I saw myself at home with Grace on a mountaintop the pines whistling. I yearned for the country and open spaces. I told Grace this, but she thought that I was being typically unrealistic. She said, "New York is you and you are it." I said, "No way. That'd be like a prison sentence." My brother, in response, said, "You are retarded." My father said, "That's a cockamamie idea."

Diagonal across Westchester County my father's car traveled down the long tubular conduit by the Hudson River, which gleamed with my history, and through the potholed oil stained streets to arrive in my kingdom at 107th Street and Amsterdam Avenue. We hauled our belongings up three flights of stairs to a railroad apartment, pigeon shit on the windowsills, decades of lead paint, musty walls and faulty spigots; Puerto Ricans, Dominicans, Cubans, all the crazy Spaniards above me and below me, closing in, the noise and greasy smells making me sick in the stomach. We moved into our new apartment two months rent paid up by Mom and Dad.

The sun rose like a purple ribbon across the horizon each morning. We settled in, fixed up the place a bit, got some used furniture and gifts from Mom, bought pots and pans, plates, and silverware. I started work at ERDCI, a grunt on a project to plant thousands of street trees in the South Bronx. Grace found a job as a research assistant at an academic press. We came home on the subway after work, stopped at a local restaurant for rice and beans, our newly adopted diet, waved to Rudy our landlord, fat and chunky with a Mussolini mustache. It felt comfortable and stable and we would sit each night in the livingroom listening to the roaring sounds outside the windows.

On these nights she shared with me her feelings of hurt and abandonment, caused, she said, by her parent's divorce. It haunted her; one day they were all together, cohesive and interdependent, and the next it was gone and she suddenly had to fend for herself. I imagined it as chronic lovelessness. She longed for these feelings to go away and hoped that in her work and with me she could find solace.

On these nights too I said to her that I wanted to see Africa. My earliest memories were filled with my father rhapsodizing about the plains, the lions, leopards, Leakey, and ancient peoples. I now wanted to see it for myself. I told her too that I would like to try living out West one day, with its soft curves and open skies. I planned out loud for my life successes and Grace laughed at my ambitions. I dreamed, to myself, of other girl's breasts in my mouth, although each and every time I had Grace in my mouth I felt fulfillment.

Three days after getting cats who we named Felix and Molly, a very special day in our lives, the Puerto Ricanyos calling out from the street, I got stoned as I waited for Grace to come home from work. In the cumulus of pot that engulfed my head I felt the wonder of existence. I was fantasizing about Grace, Jane, and me having sex, the intimacy building and building until it climaxed into a gauzy naked overlap. It was like a mantra for me, over and over the images of sex, and my vision blurred as I watched the kittens chase each other across the apartment, their tiny claws scratching the knotted wooden floors.

The lock unbolted, Grace came through the door, Molly and Felix rushed to greet her, and I got up to greet her too, sticking my tongue into her mouth.

"Please," she said, pushing me away, "a little space. I just got home. It's been a hard day and I'm not stoned like you are. You know that you're a pot addict."

"No I'm not," I said. "I'm in complete control."

"Didn't Nixon say something like that?"

"That lying rat bastard."

"That's right."

"You equating him with me?"

"No. Just saying that he used that phrase too."

"What does that mean?"

"Oh nothing."

"Jesus," I said.

"Just sit still for a while and I will join you soon."

I went back to the livingroom, brought Felix with me, put him on my lap, and rubbed his belly. He promptly clawed me as he launched off to tackle his sister who was walking by.

I listened to Grace go to the bathroom. I prayed that she was sexying up her mind. I wriggled in place and felt my leg muscles go tense. I heard Grace flush the toilet and waddle into the kitchen and open the refrigerator. I heard her fix some food and begin to eat. I heard each bite and swallow as if it were a test on my nerves. The noise outside the window was penetrating my brain and making me go a little mad, all the truck traffic and Salsa music. Grace put her dishes into the sink and walked her heavy shuffle to the bedroom where I hoped she was changing into revealing underthings. Miles and miles of empty green wilderness between me and my desires. Grace turned the corner of our bedroom and walked into the living room. She was wearing shorts and a t-shirt.

"You look nice tonight," I said.

She blushed and said, "Thank you."

"It's nice to see you after a long day's work."

"Yes, it's nice to see you too."

"The cats are insane. These kittens from Brooklyn are insane," I said.

"Last night I wanted to kill them. They ran up and down our bed all night."

"They are night warriors."

"But cute as hell too."

"They have that going for them."

"So, what went on at work today?"

"Nothing," I said.

"Nothing?"

"Nothing worth mentioning, same old thing."

"Nothing worth telling, huh . . . Well, do you want to know what went on during my work day?"

"Sure."

"Achmed, the renaissance man, threw another tantrum when an editor told him that she'd be late with her changes. It's a book on Renaissance Chemistry, you'd think he'd chill out."

"What the guy's deal?"

"Macho and with typically thin skin."

"Yeah, Arab."

"No, you idiot, Iranian Jew."

"That's what I said, Arab."

"No, a Jew, you Jew."

"Those guys over there, no matter Jew or not, are Arab first."

"I have to say that you just don't see it, you don't get that it's not funny, it's just perverted on your part."

"No, it's funny."

"Anyway, I always seem to end up on the wrong end of a touchy and angry man. I was really excited about this job, working on such scholarly texts, but he's making it stressful."

"Not me," I said.

"What?"

"I'm not touchy and angry," I said.

"That's what you think."

"I'm not that angry in the scheme of things."

"That's what you think. You know how often I see Murray Rosewood in your face and behavior?"

"That's ridiculous."

"Why's that? You don't have your father in you like everyone else?"

"A little. Not much. I've worked hard to rid myself of his qualities."

"Only you can do this, no other human, but Fire Rosewood can be rid of his past."

"That's not what I meant."

"Yes, I know, Fire, you are very self made, but you are not from thin air."

"When I hear the ring of my father in my voice I go mute with surprise."

"We all do, it's a weird sensation."

I got up from my side of the couch and came closer to her. Her face had a starlet quality to it, with flirty innocence shining from her eyes. Her body too had that quality, a bombshell, but hidden behind her loose sackcloth.

"I got us a present,"

"What?" she said.

"A sex thing."

She looked away from me, at Molly who was lying on the rug watching us.

"What is it?"

"Do you want to see?"

"I guess I have no choice."

"You always have a choice."

"That's what we think, at least."

"There is always choice when one knows what they want."

"What about those of us who are still figuring it out?"

"Well." I thought for a second. "I guess figuring it out is a choice in and of itself."

"I'm glad you realize that."

"Fair is fair, I guess."

"Let's see them, then."

"The underwear?"

"Yes, of course."

I took them out of the bag and held them up. They were red lace. She reached out her middle finger and touched them.

"Okay, let's give them a try."

She took down her army green shorts and flipped them off over her ankles. Her legs were fleshy and pink, long, tapering down. Her white worn panties came off and she grabbed out and took the new red lacy pair from me. She fit them on, tight over her ass, framing the dimensions and cutting into her skin. Off came her top and she bent forward over the side of the couch, took the underwear down, and said, "Fuck me like this."

This seized my blood and lifted it high into my head pressuring my cranium. I took off my pants, tripped over them, catching myself on the armrest, Molly underfoot. I rubbed myself vigorously and entered what was a wet and ready pussy. I felt myself orbiting into a trance where I felt Grace below me; felt her in my power, yielded to me, her ass up in the air a sign of suspension, of conviction. I felt the sensations of being with her in such an exclusive way, singled out, in love. And I came. I couldn't stay very long under that kind of force. She lifted me off her, turned around, and kissed me.

"That was great," she said.

"Except that I'm a loser, can't seem to hold back my orgasm for more than a goddamn second."

"Don't worry," she said, "you're young and excitable. You'll learn some patience."

"You supercilious queen."

"Just telling the truth."

"I'm afraid to say that you are right."

Grace put her shorts and t-shirt back on and went into the kitchen. She came back with a glass of wine and sat down on the couch.

She said, "So, what's this idea about a roommate you've been chattering about?"

I coughed and sat down on the couch too, Felix on my lap, Molly sitting on the windowsill watching us.

"I think financially it would be helpful, and it could be fun too."

"Who'd you have in mind?"

"I think Jane might be a good fit for us."

The sun had just set over our ghetto, the noises of the night rising up from the stoops of the buildings: high treble music, messy drunken language, the words zigzagging through the matted urban sky, the constant throng of vehicles and their sounds echoing off the windows.

She said, "Why is that?"

"Jane will be perfect. She's fun, and we need some fun, but she knows how to keep her independence too. Don't you think it would be nice to have another person around?"

"I think it's okay just the two of us. Why do we need another person?"

"We need to have another person," I said. "Because we are just getting started in life and we need some diversity. My job pays so little, and so does yours, we need the security . . . Jane is very loyal." I changed my tone. "She stayed with her job far longer than she should have considering how they treated her. That's a mark of loyalty. That's like you, Grace . . . Remember, her mom just died, she's a little unrooted . . . She can be a friend for you."

"I don't need you to make me friends."

"I'm not matchmaking. Just pointing it out. Come on, Grace, it's a harmless move. We have a friend to help defray the rent and to add to our lives. Give it a try."

I could see on her lips the shudder of misgiving. She began tapping her fingers against her thigh. She looked at Molly who was now on the rug arching her back ready scratch it up.

"How did her mom die?"

"Cancer. The slow torture kind."

"How old was she?"

"I think in her 50s. Young."

"It's awful, really."

"I know. Jane has suffered from it."

"How? In what way?"

"I don't know . . . Made her just a little older. I don't know. Made her a bit desperate, I think."

"What do you mean by that?"

I coughed loudly twice.

"I think that she felt she better live now because at any time death can call."

"That's how you feel when you are sick, yes?"

"No, I never feel death will call."

"How can you not? I see you rolling around in pain. I see you holding your stomach after dinner, cradling it. I see you cringe and wince."

"That's just a little battle between me and the gut, it's not a death fight, trust me. My disease has barely affected me."

"Ha! . . . You are such a liar."

"No I am not . . . So, what do you think about the Jane idea?"

"Alright, I guess. I'll trust you on this although I know I will regret it later."

"No way," I said. "I promise."

Jane, stringy long hair and pale skin, moved in and we had a painting party. Our drab dust encrusted apartment, 50 years of soot, needed some restoration. We called in our friends to paint the apartment orange and blue, in part celebration of summer and in part celebration of the emergence of Jane into our lives.

The August morning was stultifying, the moisture suspended in hot particulate matter. I sat up in my mattress on the floor, Grace still asleep beside me and Jane asleep in the room next to the livingroom. I had heard her come in at five in the morning, her sex satisfied steps light down the long hallway. It was just enough for me to stay in bed and not sneak into her bedroom. The heavy trucks going up Amsterdam Avenue this early in the dawn felt like the footsteps of running giants.

I inched out bed, a last look at Grace to see if she were up and perhaps ready for some sleepy penetration. She wasn't. The cats followed me to the bathroom and then to the kitchen where I fed them first and then myself. I got dressed quietly and left the apartment. The heat was like a fortress wall. The rotted fluids of the last 200 years of city living rose from the swamp of concrete. I stretched on the steps, then began jogging east, past all the sleepy tenements and passed out drunks, past the bodega, a morning business of beer and rolls, the decomposed red mansion surrounded by fence and barbed wire, and up into the park. The trees stunk of August ripeness and the pollen was granular. I jogged down into the woods, past the ineluctable locust trees and up around the rocks, onto the trail down through the east meadow and around the reservoir, huffing and puffing, thinking of baseball scores and when my father had thrown me in the snow here at 88th Street. I thought about when Adam got handcuffed to a scraggily cherry tree on the Great Lawn in 8th grade. I ran at fast pace, the mammoth buildings held at bay by the edges of the park, the black dust of the horse trail snaking up my nose. I ran behind some forsythia and let out a long pee between the stems, a red tinted pee that stung as it exited me. Back up north along the drive and through the London planes, down by the pond, clogged in algae. I took a final breath in the park and then reentered the maze of streets, dripping hot sweat.

I came home to Grace and Jane eating breakfast, the cats of course eating their leftovers.

"Mr. Nature is home," Jane said.

Grace laughed.

"How's Mr. Nature? Have you saved the trees today?"

"Ha, ha."

"Seriously, Mr. Nature. I want you to teach me how to identify trees."

"Right, after you put me down."

"I wasn't putting you down, Mr. Nature. I was giving you a compliment . . . Oh my god he's so sensitive," she said to Grace.

"He sure is. Doles it out all the time, but can't take it."

"That's bullshit," I said. "I can take anything."

"That's what you think," Grace said.

"Screw you two."

"Come on Fire, we were just teasing," Grace said. "Don't be so sensitive. Come on, look, Jane and I are sitting here in our panties just waiting for you."

I turned red and my eyes went watery.

"Mr. Nature is blushing," Jane said. "But she's right, Fire, we were making love all morning while you were away. We kept waiting for you, oh my goodness, but we couldn't control ourselves."

"Fuck you, both."

At that, Grace got up, in her red panties and orange t-shirt, emptied her cup of coffee and said, "Time to get ready for the big day."

I looked at Jane and smiled. She opened her shirt and let me see the black bra that was covering her small breasts. I left the kitchen to shower.

Grace and I labored into the municipal humidity. We walked down 107th Street fooling with each other, touching, talking about how Jane was such a picky eater. She ate with satisfied slow bites the food cut into dainty quarters while Grace and I sat fidgeting for desert. I screamed out, "Jane, finish up, will you, I want some ice cream." She said, "You just have to wait." I wanted to strangle her. We kissed leaning against a street tree. We stopped and bought some bagels and tea and ate our meal while sitting on the steps that led into Riverside Park. I stared at the plane trees and beyond to the Hudson River. We finished up and walked back to Broadway. I grabbed Grace's ass in front of some teenagers sitting on a stoop. We went to the hardware store and loaded up on paints, brushes, turpentine, and tarps. I was excited by Grace, by Jane, and by my prospects. We hauled our equipment home. I went back out and bought ten six packs of beer and several bottles of wine. I also bought a bottle of mescal, with the worm in it.

Our friends began to arrive. We passed around a joint and I let the smoke fill up my lungs. Grace lifted herself up and put things in gear. She assigned rooms and color schemes to individuals and everyone dispersed inside the narrow pocketed apartment. We then stole a kiss in the privacy of the bathroom and began to go from room to room, visiting everyone, helping each group out as they worked on a particular section, getting beers, passing joints around, filling shot glasses of mescal for those interested, keeping our cats soothed amid the cacophony, keeping everyone stocked with paint and supplies. We did this diligently for hours until I noticed that we were down to the worm in the bottle of mescal. I announced a worm eating contest. Everyone laid aside their brushes and came to the living room. Grace volunteered to eat the worm. "Seriously, Grace?" I said.

"Why not, it will be fun."

"But will you still be able to function?"

"Fire, you idiot," Jane said, "let her do it."

She grabbed the bottle from me, smiled wickedly, lifted the neck into her mouth, and shook the invertebrate down her throat. I gagged. Everyone sang her praises and Jane grabbed her by the shoulders and kissed her cheek. What a wonderful show, I thought.

I went to talk to Adam, his mustache a black brush under his nose. He was painting alone in a room by the front door. There was a haze of pot smoke and metropolitan dampness. Adam, who didn't smoke much pot despite my constant urgings, a straightly built human being, was enveloped in this fog and he looked like he was going to fall asleep. I said, "You look like you've been lulled with opium."

"I feel very loopy to be honest."

"You like beer more don't you?"

"Yes," he said, "I feel more in control. Remember that time we got stoned and then went to that diner and I thought the walls were swirling?"

"Dude, you are like a baby with pot."

"It hits me hard . . . so now you can understand why I don't do it a lot and so get off my back."

"Adam," I said, "I think I caught the travel bug when we were in Israel."

He started to paint, bold blue strokes on the wall.

"You had it way before Israel, Fire."

"Is that true? Why do you say that?"

"You've always talked about travelling and getting away. Ever since I've known you, to be honest, and that has been since the age of birth."

"Yes, a long time ago," I said.

"Israel was great," Adam said, "despite the Hebrew, which we sucked at, and picking cotton. We didn't get laid once."

"I know. We're losers."

"Face it, you are a loser."

I hung my head.

"It's addicting," I said. "I want to see the world. I want to see it before I get sucked into my profession."

"Go, Fire," he said, "do it now. To be honest, I don't think I will do it again I have to say."

"Why not? Maybe you could come?"

"I don't think so," he laughed through his mustache. "Honestly, it might be too much of a strain. I'd like to stay here for the moment."

"But don't you think it would be fun traveling together, seeing the world, fucking around?"

"You've got Grace," Adam reminded me. "I know you have your problems, but you have Grace. You don't know how lucky you are. Grace is hot."

"Grace is great."

"No, to be honest, I have to say that you don't really know what you have."

"I should be happy, right?" I said.

"Yes, accept what you have."

His cheeks were ruddy and meaty. He was short, stocky (a mutual friend called him phase one obese and Adam took it as a compliment), full of hair that covered his shoulders like epaulets, and skin that tended to be moist with sweat.

Adam said, the words riding on his unsure pot breath, "And by the way, Grace might not want me along."

"Why not?"

"You're not serious, Fire?"

"I guess not, but it would be so cool, the three of us. A threesome is so much more elastic and practical. You share the burden of life amongst three and then increase the pleasure by a third too."

"It could go the other way."

"That's very true."

I coughed three times violently. Adam put the paintbrush down and sat with his back against the wall.

I said, "Nothing sucks more than when it all turns on you. Hell...
You know, Grace and Jane have not become the sexual partners I was
hoping for."

He laughed out loud, a deep squawk, and a bit of his saliva mixed
with the orange paint on his chin.

"What a surprise," he said.

"What?"

"That your girlfriend and your roommate are not sucking pussy
and letting you fuck them at the same time."

"Put that way it does sound a bit unrealistic."

"I'd say so."

"Can't fault a man for trying."

"That's true, I guess."

"So, what's this travel thing?"

"I got to get away. I mean, things are great at work, but I want to
see the world real bad. How do I get Grace to see it this way too? Every
time I step out of that door and head towards the subway I feel op-
pressed by the city."

"So, needless to say you are determined to go."

"How could I not be? How could one not want to see the world?"

He scratched his nose, leaving a mark of blue paint. My eyes burned
from the pot.

"So, what's the plan for Grace?"

"I propose the traveling with a proposal for marriage."

"Whoa. Wow. That's big news."

He leaned backwards in shock and excitement, his palms on his
knees, an opossum smile in his puckered lips.

"That's what you think you must do to get her to come traveling
with you?"

"Yes. But I've been thinking about family lately too. My travel
dreams are accompanied by far away dreams about a family in their
yard sitting around, happy and comfortable, in each other's bosom and
safety, and I see Grace there."

"You are young, Fire."

"Marriage won't age me."

"Perhaps not."

"What do you think Grace will think?"

He thought for a second. "Well, you know her, she's, to be honest, she's cautious. She's very different than you."

"Opposites attract?"

"But they must be ever vigilant."

Adam loved Grace. He too moved slowly, cautiously. I, on the other hand, wanted her to move at my pace, indefatigable. When she said yes the days floated into each other magnificently. But when she said no the pace of my life halted and became derailed. Why the distrust? I distrusted no one. Yet Adam, I suspected, thought I was a jackass to Grace.

"Fire, Grace needs to build up to things," Adam said. "Slow is the key word here. But she's more daring than you think."

Grace walked in. She stared at Adam and then at me.

"What?"

She turned to me.

"Nothing."

"Tell me. What am I being dared to do now?"

"Nothing."

She looked at Adam and smiled. He was covered in orange and blue spots, a clown. He in turn laughed at us, at the nettles of our relationship.

"Tell her," he said.

"I was thinking about us taking a trip around the world."

She bit her lip.

"Where, when, how?"

"I haven't thought the details out yet."

"Just like you."

"Well, I just thought of it, it's still a broad picture in my head."

"When were you going to share this picture with me?"

"Soon."

"When?"

"Actually, today. I was thinking about bringing it up today after we finished painting."

"You are lying."

"No, really. Adam, help me out here."

"No way."

"Seriously," Grace said. "You always do this. Hatch a plan and then tell it to me fait accompli. This is not representative of a re-lat-ion-ship."

"This is the way my brain works, sorry. I just think we can't begin our adult lives before we see the world. It beckons to me everyday now. I see Africa in my eyes. I want to get away, disentangle from this home of mine before it sucks me up for good."

"Why don't you tell me these things? Share these thoughts with me. Make it a dialogue. I want to be involved."

"I just don't think of it. I'm sorry . . . I'm sharing them now."

Adam stood up and left the room. Grace turned to me, ready to say something, her chin set in annoyance, but she left the room with Adam instead.

The sun was wearing down, pink over the river. The apartment was three quarters finished, a tropical orange and blue, making the dreary homestead light and soft with color and faith. It looked great. Jane, who had not emerged from her room all day, painting like an inchworm each meticulous spot, came out of the room and told me she needed more paint to finish up.

"Really," I said, "for that little room. You've been at it all day and you're not done yet?"

"No," she said, "I'm not. I want to do a good job."

"I can see that. How much do you need?"

"Three more cans."

"What!" Grace screamed. "You've done nothing but paint your own room. You can't need three more cans. We're paying for everything."

Jane stepped back.

"Please," I intervened. "I'll get five more cans to finish off the whole apartment. Jane, be conservative with your use, it doesn't have to be perfect. Grace," I turned to her, "Jane is just trying to do a good job."

She turned away from us.

I went out and got more paint from Cohen Brothers. I said hi to Domingo and Rudy, who were bathed in cigar smoke, watched a funeral procession go by, noticed how the four story tenement buildings were being eaten away by acid rain. I weaved in between the people, a sea of humanity, and around the street tree pits that were black soiled pint sized habitats. Towels hung from clothes' lines strung on fire escapes, music played in the apartments, food sizzled, and a person on the street yelled in macho basso. I felt in the city's air a density that was strangulating. I remembered a moment five years before when my friend Danny and I had strolled too far from the Columbia campus where we met to get stoned and into the lawless zone east of Morningside. How we got there was unimaginable now, two white kids well aware of the dangers of the ghetto. But suddenly there we where, surrounded by feral eyes. Danny and I could hear the attack dogs and smell the live chickens, plantains, and beef stew; these were angry subjects with trumpet driven music. Two teenagers approached and we turned pale with fright. They began to angle into us. We looked at each other and bolted, stoned and a bit uncoordinated, but propelled by fear. They gave immediate chase, screaming at us to stop or they'd kick our asses. Okay, I wanted to yell back, I'll purposely stop so you can kick my ass. They screamed, "You white faggots better stop." We moved quickly west, never looking behind us but hearing their voices fade. In that mad scared rush out of unfriendly territory we passed Cohen Brothers and we both looked at each other, sanctuary amid the strangers.

I came back with the paints. I gave one can to Jane and said, "This is it." She looked hurt. I gave the rest out as necessary, and each of us went into high concentration. We moved fast and silently and two hours later we finished and my friends said goodbye.

Jane, when everyone was gone, went back into her room to finish painting. She was lasciviously self focussed and I wanted to spread her ass cheeks apart and fuck her from behind. Grace, on the other hand, was furious at her. Last week she had disputed a few dollars on our electric bill, a show of bad faith and cheapness that was enraging. In fact, things had gone in the opposite direction of my desires since the beginning of this relationship. I had predictably imagined an apartment dominated by female estrus, the three of us awash in nakedness and massages. But a steady progression of slights, misunderstandings, unjivable personalities (although we had fun too), workday stresses, conflagrations, and self indulgences had led to this point now.

Jane stuck her head out of the room and said, "You guys want to come in and help?"

The words hung in the air and I wondered if there was any way I could divert them, create a wind to blow them out the window, make a spell that would make Jane say the right thing instead.

"You must be crazy!" Grace blurted out.

Grace's chin was locked and her eyes radiated.

Jane came out of the room and turned to Grace, her wispy hair flung over her face, her pale skin alight with redness, her arms crossed over her chest in defiance. She looked like she was going to cry.

"Why is that?"

"You have only worked on your own room. All day everyone was doing as much as they could, but you. And you didn't offer to pay for anything."

"What are you saying?" Jane said.

"That you are selfish and don't think about anyone else but yourself."

"I can't believe you are saying this to me."

"I've wanted to say this all summer, but I've kept my tongue, thinking you'd get less selfish as you got to know us and not wanting to disappoint Fire. But this is it."

"Like you are perfect."

"I'm not, but I think about other people."

"So do I."

"No, you don't. If you did you'd act another way. How could anyone dispute $3.59 on a shared electric bill? It's incredible."

"Back to that. I thought that was settled."

"It was. It is. But I have to say it shows how selfish and out of touch you are."

"How? It wasn't my responsibility. I don't have a lot of money."

"You think I am rolling in it? But I don't make a fuss of $3."

"$3.59 . . ." Jane said, but quickly regretted it.

"See," Grace said, "you don't get it."

My fantasies now evaporated, I was merely hoping to get out of this thing unscathed. Still, I had to side with Grace. If my solipsism was a manipulation of the angles Jane's was a blunt object. Grace couldn't countenance this, and really neither could I, in the long run. She would have driven me crazy sooner or later, her pickiness and slow eating.

"I can see that this is not working out," Jane said.

"It's not," Grace replied.

"So, what do you want to do?"

"Why don't you leave by the end of the month."

"Fire, what do you think?" Jane asked.

I looked at Grace and smiled in solidarity. I then shrugged. I coughed three times loudly and tasted some acid phlegm. I looked at Jane, but said nothing.

Jane dropped her paintbrush on the floor, splattering orange on the rug, turned around, and went into her room. She bumped up against the walls, opened her draws violently, opened the closets like thunder, banged and shook. She came out an hour later all packed.

Grace and I sat silently on the couch. Molly and Felix were on our laps. The heavy trucks pounded up the avenue and horns blared.

Jane looked down at me and said, "I'm really hurt," and left.

Grace said to me, "You always screw these things up. I always trust you and then you find a way to breach it. You want too much." She looked at me fiercely with her black acid eyes. "Accept what you have . . . I do."

I wanted to choke her. The endless reams of guilt running through the sands of time. So you are an unhappy victim, I thought, bad parents and exile, betrayals here and betrayals there. Get over it! I can and will leave you too, I thought. And you'll regret it because you can't live without me.

But we stayed instead sitting on the couch, the cats on our laps, the night getting a little heavier and the noises a bit crazier and eventually we got up, fed the cats, brushed our teeth, and went to bed.

After work I walked over on 18th Street past worn buildings with faded gray limestone and dark hallways. I walked to 7th Avenue, dropping out of sight down into the subway. Up to 66th Street. Lincoln Center sat in its whiteness, the fountain frothing, the mall full of commingled humans. West on 66th Street past Julliard its buildings' caught directly in the path of contaminated winds. The small church with its Jesus obsessed ways, the fire station, past the Red Cross complex, and into the well kept gardens of Lincoln Towers, lush and quiet dominion overlooking the Hudson River. I picked a rose off a shrub and trimmed the thorns with my pocketknife. I said hi to Jose the doorman, who had shown me porn mags in the laundry room when I was ten, went up the elevator, walked down the hallway that reeked of my spirit, and through the door to my parents' apartment, always open.

The apartment was the same as it had been for my whole life, discolored white walls and its familiar angles that veered to the right, the folding maplewood dinner table, the blue kitchen tile; the river light filtered through the windows brightening the walls. Mom had paintings of swollen cubist women and abstract greens and purples, stuff she had collected over the years and which I never really gave her credit for. The rug and couch were covered in newspapers and magazines and my father sat amid this mess, his newly rotund stomach resting on his skinny legs, his hair white and lush, cheeks red and inflamed. Mom was in the kitchen cooking, wearing a red, white, and blue apron, despite my father's objections. They had fought about it now for a year. The volume on the TV was deafening and Grace sat at the dinner table smiling distractedly at the whole thing.

"Please turn the tube down!" I screamed at my father.

"Oh, Mr. Important has finally arrived!" he screamed out over the TV volume.

"Yup, that's me. I will save the day. Turn the TV down."

"I can't hear it otherwise."

"Well, it's killing me."

He turned it down a bit.

"Mom's still wearing that apron," I said.

He grunted. "It's shameful. Wearing the American flag in my house."

"It was a present, Murray," my mom called out from the kitchen. "And it's just an apron."

"With hateful symbolism."

"Who's playing?" I asked.

"Yankees and Kansas City."

"You're watching the Yankees?"

"To see them lose, those miserable millionaires."

"It's great to see them lose."

I sat down on the other side of the couch, making some of the newspapers leap up in the air.

"Did you see what the mayor did?" I said.

"I thought he'd be better," my father said. "I supported him at first. I actually collected signatures for him. Now I feel betrayed."

"What'd you expect? The system is all corrupting and it demands that you give in to its ways."

"No it doesn't! I have fought and fought for justice in this country. I have fought for it my whole life!"

"You don't seem to understand that the system is about promoting the elite and wealthy. And they have history on their side. Now America has very good trickle down," I conceded, "but it's still enormously one sided. Once a man is taken in by the luxuries of the system he's a goner. The mayor is just like them all."

"Horseshit," he said. "You don't know anything."

George Brett hit the ball so hard that I thought it would fly forever. Kansas City up three runs over the Yankees.

My father said, "The good guys are winning."

I got up and walked to Grace, avoiding my mother's puckered lips, and handed the rose flower to her. She looked great in her blue button down shirt, a man's dress shirt, her breasts giving it silky uplift, her arms and hands brown from the summer.

"Thanks," she said.

"You are welcome."

"That's so nice," my mom said. "Murray, why don't you do that for me anymore?"

"What?"

"Buy me flowers."

My father groaned.

Grace put the flower in her shirt, which required opening up a button, revealing the top of her unholstered breasts, fitting the flower into her small cleavage. She looked at me with teasing and jealousy.

"I was recruited by another academic press today," she announced. "They'd like me to be an assistant editor there."

"Fantastic. This is what you were born to do. Research and edit."

"And you one day to be president," she laughed, and looked at my father.

"Yeah," he smiled with his yellow teeth, "the putz thinks he can be president."

"And why not?" I said. "One day, later in life, I will travel in a bus around the country, with a pretty vice president, which could be you, my dear," I entreated Grace, "and I will get up on my soapbox in all the small towns and communities across the country and just read from my list of facts how the men in power rape us to make themselves richer. I can't fail to win."

This silenced even my father.

"It's so nice that he's full of confidence," my mother said. "That means I did a good job."

"What about me?" my father asked.

"You were too busy screaming and ranting," I said.

"Screw you you ungrateful schmuck."

Grace said, "I think I will take this new job. Achmed was on my case again, minute after minute. Do this, do that. He's kind of a sadist. He told me that the synopsis I gave him was worthless. I have to say that I did a really good job, and it isn't easy to summarize 'Sleeplessness in the Aztecs,' but then he ruined it all."

"I'll eat your heart out like an Aztec," I declared.

"What," Grace said. "What does that mean?"

"Just what it means, 'I'll eat your heart out like an Aztec'."

"I love what I'm doing," she continued. "But Achmed dismisses me just to show off his power."

"What a jerk," my mother said. "My boss Irving was that way too. I used to get so nervous around him," she said. "I became paralyzed."

I remembered as a boy listening from bed as my mom's old typewriter clanked each troublesome letter onto the page as she tried to get Irving his minutes and papers.

"And speaking of suffering," she continued, "Fire, how's your gut?"

"Mom," I said. "I'm not talking about it."

"I happen to know," Grace said, "that he was in the fetal position in the bathroom in pain today."

"Fire." Mom turned on me. "You must go to the doctor right away."

"No, Mom!"

"Yes. Go now.. I worry so much. I can't bear the thought of your pain."

Grace cracked up.

"Well?" my father shouted out.

"Well, what?"

"Have you seen the doctor? Don't complain about being sick if you don't do anything about it."

"I don't complain."

"You do."

"I don't."

"Honey, see the doctor. Don't be self destructive," my mom

concluded.

My father got up and joined us at the dinner table. My mom yelled at him to shut off the TV, which he did. She brought me soda in a glass with ice. "Can I have one too?" my father asked, so she got him one. She then served us both dinner. I said, "Mom, napkins." Dad said, "You forgot a spoon for me." Grace said, "You men are pigs." I said, "It's good to be the king."

The sun was hanging over the Hudson River, shadowing and reflecting a lifetime of Rosewood existence. I sat next to Grace and touched her leg under the table. After many long conversations in which I sold my ideas to her we had decided two huge things: 1) to travel for six months to Africa and 2) to get married when we got back. In the back of my mind, unspoken, I planned to go to graduate school when we returned, begin the trajectory of my career.

I slurped up my steak and stuffed my mouth with pasta and gulped down my soda like mead.

Between bites I said to my father, "These avaricious bastards lounging about in the golden temple of power built on the foundation of our tax dollars."

"Fire," Grace pointed out, "you want to be president. You might find yourself tempted and compromised too."

"I will crush the whole system and then rebuild it."

"How typical," she said.

Mom said, "Please eat slowly. You eat too fast for a man with a sick stomach. You eat too fast anyway. Slow down and enjoy it."

My father said, "You eat like a slob. It's disgusting."

"Where do you think I learned it from?"

"Yes," my mother said. "Murray you eat poorly too. I've always tried to get my boys to eat well but with your hamburger and cookie diet I didn't stand a chance."

"Ah," my father said, "that ridiculous."

I coughed.

"Mom, Dad, we've got something to tell you . . . Grace and I are going to get married. But first we're going to travel to Africa."

"What about your job?" my father said.

"They said they will take me back."

"They said you can come back. That's good. "

"Yes."

"What about graduate school? You can't get anywhere today without it. You must stay alert."

"I know, Dad. Did you hear the other thing I said? We are getting married."

I felt hot and sweaty, short of breath, as if the walls were closing in on me.

Grace said, "You feeling alright Fire? You look like you suddenly have a fever."

She reached out and felt my forehead.

"I'm fine," I said, pushing her hand away.

My mother rose and hugged Grace and then me.

"This is wonderful news. I have been wondering if you two would take the next step. I was hoping you would."

"Welcome to the family," my father said. "Although, to be honest, I thought of you that way already."

"Thanks, Murray."

He smiled at her, which made me sick, his yellow sleazy teeth.

"So, what's the plan?" Mom said.

"Well, finish the summer at work and then leave for Africa in mid September."

"And get married when you come back?" Mom asked.

"Probably, maybe the summer or fall."

"It's so exciting," my mother said. "But it makes me frightened too."

"Why?"

"Africa is far off and filled with violence. It's a long time to be away."

"Mom, we'll be fine."

"I want you to call every Sunday night."

"You're out of your mind! Every Sunday? Right, I'll find a phone in the Tanzanian bush."

"The boy's right," my father said.

"Then we have to work some type of communication system out. I will be a wreck."

"Why can't you just enjoy our adventurousness and have faith in our survival."

"The boy's right," my father said.

"That would be ideal," my mother said, "but I can't do it."

"Why not?"

"I just can't. I can't overcome the scary image of your death or that you might be hurt and I couldn't get to you, any pain you might have to absorb."

"Jesus," I said.

"Pearl, is that how motherhood feels?" Grace asked.

"No, that's the scary part, and I suffer depending on how far away my sons are from me. The rest," and she looked at me, "is glorious."

My father said, "Your life plans cost money, boy. Where's it coming from? How much have you saved?"

"Well, this is the deal," I said. "I was hoping to work out some loan with you guys." I looked at Dad. "This is a loan to help your son's life be fuller, to help your son become a wiser person. But once I'm settled I will work out a payment schedule with you. Trust me."

"Loan my ass," Dad said.

"I'll pay you back."

"You think we are made of money. Stay alert you kook. We saved, my money. You save your money."

"Stop it, the two of you! Murray, cut it out. Fire, don't push too hard. You are asking for our money and your father has a right to express himself."

I sat back in my chair feeling spiteful. Grace was ashen and stared out the window at the river.

"How much money do you think you need?" my mother asked.

"Money," I said.

Mom said, "Why Africa? Why not Europe?"

"Because I have always dreamed of Africa."

"So have you Murray."

"Maybe," he said.

"Africa has so many snakes," she said.

"I know," Grace said, "it makes me really nervous I have to say."

"Grace, my dear," Mom said, "you feel okay about Africa?"

"Yes, Pearl," she said, "I trust Fire on this one, even though I seem to always end up regretting it somehow."

"That's crazy," I said, "I always follow through."

"Africa," my father said. "The lions."

"The lions and the elephants roaming free."

He looked at me and at Grace and then out the window. He said, "Pearl, it's your decision."

Mom said to me, "Eat slow, will you."

3. Departures

GRACE LEFT FOR Amsterdam a day before I did for reasons I can't remember now. In that day of her absence I met with Jane. When we saw each other we smiled and then laughed. It took that long. We didn't talk about the fight at all. She was seeing some guy but felt relatively low about their prospects, which made me happy. I told her about our trip. She was proud of us, she said, and a little jealous too. Her skin was pale and red and her teeth were pointy. She didn't seem to resent Grace, thank god. When I mentioned sex, about how curvy Grace was, Jane blushed, her eyes veiled coquettishly, and she said, "Oh my goodness."

The next day I arrived at my parents' apartment nonchalantly late for my flight to Amsterdam. I was on my way to see the wide world, reaching higher planes, and I glided about the city streets in great liberation from all that apparently boxed me in. I carried a swollen pink backpack full of everything I could manage to pack: two pair of jeans, three shorts, six t-shirts, ten pair of underwear, ten pair of socks, two long sleeved shirts, a sweater, a windbreaker, a button down dress shirt, an extra pair of sneakers, a hat, four vials of pills for my gut, a razor and ten blades, three toothbrushes, toothpaste, a nail cutter, a washcloth, asprin, athlete's foot and jockrot cream, stationary, three 200 page journal books, binoculars, a Walkman and 11 tapes, my address book, pens, and five books, one hardcover, all forestry and politics books, and one Elmore Leonard. Underneath my pants I wore an inflated money belt filled with traveler's checks and some cash, my New York State driver's license, along with an international driver's license. In my right pocket I had some dollars and quarters, my passport, and an insurance identification card, a gift from my parents' before I left, traveler's health insurance.

"Ready?" I said as I entered. "Let's go."

"The putz," my father said. "The boy has grown a pink hump . . . And," his cheeks swelling up, "why are you are so fucking late? We will never make it."

"Then let's go. Chop, chop."

"Go without me," and he stormed into the kitchen.

I watched him walk away his body flared up from the back. I stood quietly and so did Mom. He grunted, opened up a cabinet and took out some cookies, and slammed the cabinet shut. His white hair was bedraggled. I looked at Mom and shrugged. She was a bit terrified, but also resilient. I put my foot on the organ footpedal, an old organ that sat in the space by the front entrance of the apartment, and it creaked and groaned.

"Dad, come on," I said. "Please, let's go."

The light of New Jersey reflected off the river and made us all glow.

"Come on, Dad, Jesus Christ you're a madman."

He smacked me in the head.

"You both make me crazy!"

Well, he was right. I missed my flight and had to take a later one. I had no way of reaching Grace. I flew over on Air Jordan, surrounded by caterwauling Arabs, highly distressed about Grace's anxiety turned to fear when I didn't show up. I had let her down again she would be thinking, but I hadn't done it on purpose. I had just underestimated the traffic on the Van Wyck Expressway. I knew she would see it as indifference on my part, even rejection. How could I not build in the time to reach an international flight? I was self centered and an impractical dreamer. Nonetheless, I burned with disquiet despite, maybe because of, the joint I had smoked just before I got on the plane. I had run out of the terminal and hid behind a pillar at the end of the building and inhaled a few deep breaths of marijuana before I threw the joint over the ledge and into the shrubs. And now I shivered and swirled with worry. The Arabs were so noisy. The food was rice and chicken and quite good. I fell into a fitful sleep, listening to the Arabic, listening to the occasional announcement, thinking of Grace and how her eyes flickered, thinking of Roberto Clemente, thinking about having sex with Jane, thinking about politics, thinking about my destiny. I did this for a long time in the night sky, the sound of the plane an irritating din, voices filling my consciousness. I was roused from this trance by a fresh yellow sky that emerged over Holland.

I tried calling Grace from the airport, but I couldn't work the phones, and so took a taxi to our hotel. Amsterdam was sunk down into the water. I liked how the canals twisted and turned and the streets fit around them. I liked the long copper handrails on the bridges. My eyes beamed forward and my crotch tingled when we passed the red light district. American prudery, I thought, what a drag! I was exhausted from the flight and the pot high and stank of sweat.

I went up to the room and opened the door. Grace was sleeping. Her clothes were spread over the room, shirts and underwear, socks, and shoes. Her pack was emptied of its contents, much lighter than mine was without a Walkman and tapes, and no prescription pills, no jockrot cream, no razors, less clothes, and only one soft covered book and one journal book. Her money belt was open and leaking its monetary goods. A vial of aspirin was opened on the bureau, three pills dropped to the floor. The pillows from the couch were on the floor too and two towels were splayed on the coffee table. The place looked sacked, and I remembered that it was the first time I truly recognized how messy Grace was. I took off my clothes, tingling with desire, and got into bed with her. She was naked underneath! Her pussy hairs were knotted together with dried moisture. It felt like tangled groundcover in the mud. I entered her carefully through this thicket making it go slow centimeter by centimeter. I felt like I was going to explode, but I tightened my crotch, squeezing my hips, and pushed the come back off. I thought of baseball statistics and the Arabs on my flight. I thought of the red light district and entered Grace deeper. Her arms were splayed over her head, her nipples hard, her stomach rising in fits and starts. It felt so special now, away from New York City, out upon the globe, us amid the strangers. I submerged as deeply as I could past previous limits. I said, "Take it, baby." And she said, "As much as you've got." I came, just as her personality was losing its façade and vanishing back into her primal spot, just when I could have asked for anything in the world and gotten it.

We lay entangled, her breath heavy, the exhaustion of the day coming on strong, the room still and foreign and the sounds from the city muted. Grace moved her body to get from under me and rolled to the side. She said, "Don't give me a lame excuse. You really suck."

"I'm sorry. I missed my flight."

She tapped her fingers against the headrest of the bed.

"You're so selfish. How could you miss your flight? It's unbelievable."

"I know. I know. It's indefensible." I sat up. "But I just thought the whole two hours before an international flight thing was bullshit. I still think it's bullshit, but this time they were right. My father was outraged."

"I don't blame him."

She started to cry.

"Grace, Grace, sweety. I didn't mean it. I was just late. It's not personal."

I hugged her.

"Yes it is, don't you see. Your actions speak louder than your words. I hear what you say, but I feel you far away from me, doing your own thing, not thinking about me. I was scared shitless when you didn't show up. Think of how I must have felt."

I looked at her belly, a trail of hair from her pussy up to her belly button, cutting a black line down the middle of her abdomen.

On the one hand I thought she was being typically melancholic and negative. I was here after all so why not celebrate this fact instead of brood over its opposite. On the other hand I could see her point. This trip was my idea, and even though Grace turned out to be an expert traveler, I needed to be by her side, at least in the beginning.

I got up and went into the bathroom to pee. It burned when the pee came out and I jumped back in pain. "Shit," I said aloud. I thought maybe I had caught VD, although I hadn't had sex with anyone but Grace for years. Adam had had VD and said when the doctor at the Department of Health stuck a swab up his penis slit he cried out in pain. I laughed to myself, wanting to repeat the story to Grace. I checked for jockrot and checked some pimples on my face.

I said, returning, "Sorry, Grace. Sorry to seem so lost and far away. It's my nature, not my intention . . . Do you want to go out to the red light district with me? Sightsee a bit?"

She said, "You've got to be kidding."

I stepped into Africa and ceased to comprehend the world. I thought of David who lived wavering between abandon and self judgement. My

Jewish kings and their blood had dripped over the generations into my blood and all the initial human souls of Africa lay in my blood too.

Grace and I spent 24 hours to get to our destination. Bulgaria, Cypress, Malta, Lagos, each stop a weary seven hours. In Lagos, as Grace and I lay down in the stifling humidity on the airport couches to rest two young soldiers butted their rifles into our guts and said, "No sleeping." Over Zambia a wing of the plane began to shake dangerously. It fluttered and bounced in the wind. I put my hand in Grace's as we flew precariously on over the vast yellow landscape.

We entered Harare, Zimbabwe at night and rode the bus to our hotel along darkened streets, exhaust pipes choking. We checked in, the bright neon lights in the lobby blinding me, and made our way to our room, which was a pink stucco cubicle.

We lay down and stared at the ceiling, its fan's rotation making me dizzy. I was overwhelmed with the thought that I was now on African soil, this triangle continent of mysterious forests and deserts; this map that my father would point out to me as a child and young boy. I snuggled into Grace, feeling safe within the confines of her body, and soon the exhaustion came over us and we fell asleep. I burned, my dreams, my dreams, the dreams of kings, the dreams of men who want to be god. Gods don't like disappointment. Neither did the kings. I woke up. The room and the city were still. I crawled out of bed, carefully so not to wake Grace, washed my face, and went out.

The street was dark except for the strings of illumination from people's windows. The stone houses had fences that were lined with broken glass glued to the top. The cicadas blared and the smell in the air was heavy and musty, a mix of industrial gases and exotic plants. I walked to a thoroughfare, crowded with people and cars, and hailed a cab. I asked the driver to take me to the Intercontinental. The ride was bumpy, as if we had to travel through rocky canyon to get across town. The sounds of Harare commingled in the air, which reminded me of my city, but this one had sheep bleating and donkeys braying. At the Intercontinental, full of lights and people, I found a local paper. I had read in our travel book that Thomas Mapfumo regularly played the Queens' Bar . . . which he was tonight.

Congregated and excited in front of the bar was a throng of people clouded in cigarette and pot smoke. They milled about, Africans and tourists, agitated. The street was potholed and worn and the sidewalk was wet with spit and tobacco. The smell of alcohol reeked from the pavement. There was the universal thumping of music in the bar. The black Africans, by and large, wore frayed shirts and worn shoes. Like the blacks back home I feared their differences from me. As I walked through them I took ginger footsteps and made benign gestures so as not to arouse attention to myself. I could easily vanish into the African ether. I made my way to a group of white people. They were smoking pot. The girls in the group were very attractive, t-shirts tight against their bodies with sweat, breasts the size of coffee mugs, like Grace. I entered their circle and stood looking at them, scanning faces, the whole of the African sky above me.

"Can I smoke pot with you?" I said.

A tall redhead laughed and handed me his joint.

I inhaled, and the smoke went into my mouth as a friendly cloud, sailed past my throat and into my lungs and blood.

I entered the dark smoky box of the bar, Thomas Mapfumo up on stage with his long locks of dreaded hair, sad equine face, and white clothes. The place was packed, from wall to wall. Mapfumo said hello to the audience and began the first song, a marching soft rhythm about eating chicken freely and safely in an African man's land. It hit us in the hips and the whole place ignited into movement, a sea of interchanging fish moving around in their aquarium. I was carried away on the spirit and felt a sublime energy. For me, Mr. Energy, this energy was even more intense, and good natured, opened wide. I swayed around the room, twirling mindlessly. From the corner of my eye I spied one of the women in the group I had just smoked with. I danced towards her. Along the way I was bumped by a large man, who reminded me of Howlin' Wolf, and I could feel his hand in my back pocket. He dug into my ass cheek. However, I had been smart: my money was in my sock, a New York City trait. He moved on and I danced to the woman and held out my hand to her. She came into my body, pressing her chest up against mine. She was wearing a black dress with white polka dots. She smelled tart, like ginger. We danced to Mapfumo, and it was great, in and out, around and around, face to face, back to back, the warmth of our flesh implacable. Then Mapfumo ended. We stood, dazed, waned. My dancing partner turned to me and asked if I'd like to come back to her hotel. I pictured her naked body, felt my arousal, but instead kissed her on the cheek.

Grace woke when I came in.

"Where were you?"

"I couldn't sleep and went out. You won't believe it though. I just saw Thomas Mapfumo play."

"Really." She sat up. "How?"

I told her.

She said. "First late to Amsterdam and now leaving me in the middle of the night in Harare. A pattern is emerging I'd have to say."

"Sorry."

"Was he good?"

"It was incredible, Grace, unbelievable. It was as if I had heard a god play."

"I'm so jealous," she whined.

"He'll play again, I'm sure."

"Right. Not with my luck."

"No, you will see him, I promise. But tonight was a feeling of pure body. That was what it was like tonight, pure body."

"Ah," she said, "you're just too horny."

I rolled into her.

"Oh, no," she said.

"Why not?"

"Because a man who ditches his wife constantly doesn't get laid as much as he'd like."

"Why is that?"

"The nature of the beast."

"This is marriage?"

"This is marriage, yes."

"Constant negotiation, trial, and punishment."

"You could see it that way or you could see it as adaptation, as a blending."

"But then why the struggle all the time?"

"It doesn't have to be. You could see it my way more often."

"You could see it my way too."

"I do. And so you know, every time you do something like this, leave me, insult me, it erodes my love."

Out of the city Grace and I went and up into the bush north. We found a traveling groove, interdependent, sure of ourselves. We journeyed through small towns and over rocky terrain, through burnt deserts. We ran into pygmies and I bought some pot from them, very happy to have found some. The pygmy who handed me the pot in a tied up plastic bag had a hand so rough and calloused that it felt like I was running my hand over rock. Later that day I smoked their pot and I got so stoned that Grace had to help me up to pee at night because I was dizzy.

The earth was sandy with succulent plants in between the cracks of walls and sidewalks and we sat under acacia trees and had our lunch. We ate cheese and bread and waved away the encephalitic flies. Grace and I had stopped talking needlessly and this elementary relationship was making us content with each other. I thought, usually the words kept streaming out over a lifetime. But no one, I imagined, was really listening anyway.

We made our way gradually and deliberately to Victoria Falls. Suddenly, in an instant, we left the sandy bush of the middle of the country where lions sat like golden lumps amid the grass and entered the rain forest surrounding Victoria Falls, which thundered and roared. The forest resonated and monkeys called out loud and birds sang because of the abundance. The plants got greener and thicker and the forest got denser and the Falls was an overriding murmur, skyfuls of water falling through the air and pounding the landscape.

We stayed there for ten blissful days. During our stay Grace developed a crush on an English guy and when in his presence she turned ruddy and shy. The three of us hiked along the Zambezi River one afternoon. It was a skinny switchback trail along the rocks over the water that was home to a large crocodile population. Coming around a bend I lost my footing and felt myself falling over. The crocodiles looked up to see what would happen. I righted myself, cold with sweat. I could feel Grace's crush and I knew that she would be horny. We ended up back at the hotel and took a swim in its pool. The English guy eventually left us and we retreated to our room, lay down in the hot afternoon sun, and made love.

We continued north and took a bus through Zambia to a small town called Kapiri Mposhi where the Chinese had built a long railway from this desert town to Dar Es Salaam. The bus rattled and hit huge potholes and people's chickens squawked. At one small town the bus stopped and a military guard came on and told us all to disembark. He lined us up along the shoulder of the road and gave Grace and me a hard time about being South African spies. I kept saying, "We are Americans." But he kept insisting that we were South African spies. Our seatmate on the bus said that we in fact were Americans and tourists at that.

We holed up in Kapiri Mposhi for three days waiting for the long train to Dar Es Salaam. For three days in this rundown and rough transit point we had intense equator fired sex, drank cold soda (which was rare in Africa, the cold part), wrote in our journals, and went to the lonely depot once a day to check on our train's arrival. The sandy dust blew from all directions wiping the buildings clean of paint and invading the pockets and inner linings of our clothes. On the day our train came hundreds lined up to board and we were ultimately pushed out of our first class cabin and into a zoo cage of humans and their animals, chickens and goats. Grace had to stay in a cabin of women and I was in a cabin of men. This was awful, old Christian sex separation. The African men, ignoring the rules, were constantly going back and forth from fucking their wives and girlfriends to getting further drunk. Out of our element we complied with the rules. During the day, Grace and I rode together with our faces sticking out the open train windows. We watched the endless bush pass by, the yellow grasses and wilted trees. Out of nowhere young boys showed up by the side of the tracks with fruit and rice. Further in the distance, Grace and I saw wildebeest, antelopes, zebra, giraffe. The ride lulled us and we let the days go by, the sun bright and wide, until the plains turned into villages and the villages into towns and finally into the city.

In Dar Es Salaam we walked to the beach, which was empty and strewn with litter, huge rusted ships off in the harbor. The people lived in tin houses that sat on sewage pits, the ground a teeming soup of viruses. We ate spaghetti with meat sauce from a street vendor. Later that day on the bus to the Kenyan border I felt the first tremors of my belly. The spaghetti had been crawling with bacteria and the fragility of my gut offered no resistance. I had probably eaten monkey meat. The pain started to well up in my abdomen.

"Grace, I'm not going to make it."

I laid my head down on her lap and she combed her fingers through my hair. The bus smelled of chicken shit, goat fur, human sweat, rotting fruit, and melted candy. Trebly African music came from the loudspeaker in the front of the bus. Babies cried out and some men snored. The words around me were in languages I didn't understand, and so, with my head on Grace's lap and my hearing muffled, it sounded like chattering wind. I longed to throw up, but it was far off. The waves of pain crashed and I tensed my leg muscles to help distribute it, over and over again as the bus rode north through the night.

When we finally reached the border I went back behind the customs house to the outdoor latrine. The stone roofless cubicle was percolating in fetid earth. Out through my mouth and my anus came the bacteria, Tanzanian spaghetti meat sauce! It was a disgusting show. I kneeled over the sewage mound and stared up at the African sun. It beat down on me unsparingly.

I stood up, wobbly, a piece of used toilet paper stuck to my hand. I walked to Grace and she walked me into customs. The guard took a look at me, sniffed the air. They searched me, my goods, and then stamped my passport. Grace, in the meantime, had hailed a cab to take us straight to Nairobi, 150 miles away, and 50 American dollars, a lot of money on one purchase in Africa, where our hotel rooms were five dollars a night. I slept with my head on her lap. In the city, we went straight to a more upscale hotel considering how sick I was. Grace led me to the room, which was a palace, a livingroom with a couch, chair, and table, a separate bedroom, wide windows and a veranda, wooden floors, and a small kitchen. I went right to bed and fell into a deep sleep and slept, Grace later said, for 15 hours.

When I awoke I felt better, but there was still a nasty slurry in my gut and when I burped I tasted rotten egg.

"Grace!" I screamed.

She came into the room with only her torn white underpants on.

"What? Are you feeling better?"

"I am, but I'm burping up rotten egg. What the hell is going on? What the devil's in me?"

She laughed, her breasts moving up with her chest, so supple and firm they were, like bells. Her hips rounded out just so from the plains of her stomach. Her belly was showing the beginnings of a potbelly. My eyes wandered to the space between her legs.

"Why do you laugh at me? I'm sick here. I'm dying and you're laughing."

"Such impish charm," she said. "That impish charm that you think will get you out of anything." She pointed at me. "I've been doing some research while you've slept.

"Research?"

"First in the travel guide and then at a local pharmacy. I've taken some really nice walks around the city too."

"What's it like?"

"Small and suburban, reminds me of a tropical White Plains. You can walk from one end to the other in an hour. The sidewalks and roads are ripped up, though, and the trash is all over; it's clear that the people are poor, but the heat coming off the buildings warms everything up, gives it a glow. I got to tell you I liked it. It felt safe. There's business going on at every intersection and the cars zoom down the streets."

"My dream town. You know I want to live in the tropics, right? I can't take winter."

"Right, don't let me forget . . . In the meantime, let's get you better."

I burped so loudly it carried me forward. The rotten egg taste rose in a billow and coated my mouth, which I released into the air.

"Wow," Grace said. "That stinks."

"See, I told you. I'm dying here."

"Well, patient," she said. "Here's the doctor's remedy."

"Oh, baby," I whined. "Come here and let me take you. I need the restorative pussy. Please, nurse, please."

"No, no. Let's keep this business, why don't we. My research has revealed that you've got giardia."

"What the hell is that?"

"A parasite from the water. It was probably, I guess, in the water they used to cook your meat sauce." She then cracked up. "Meat sauce from a street vendor in Dar Es Salaam. You're such an impulsive idiot."

"That's true."

"What the hell made you eat that? I told you not to. I had a vegetable samosa and I have a rock stomach and yet I felt a little queasy.

Why do you always act so crazy?"

"Why hesitate? It usually comes out okay."

"Not always."

"Yes."

"Anyway, patient." She moved over to the bed and looked down at me. "You need antibiotics. Simple."

She turned and went into the living room and came back with a vial of pills.

"Here." She handed me the vial. "Antibiotics already purchased."

"How?"

"Here in Africa you don't need a prescription. A woman can medicate herself."

"How enlightened. They have valium, did you see that?"

"No, I didn't look for valium."

"How many do I take?"

"Three now. Then three twice a day for seven days."

"I wonder if they will hurt my gut?"

"I know, I thought of that, but I think you have no choice."

"I sure don't. Bring me something to drink please."

Grace went into the kitchen and came back with a can of soda. I popped the can and took the three pills.

I said, "You take such good care of me. Thank you. I'd be dead out here all alone in the African swamps without you."

"Well, you are my traveling partner, don't want you to die on me and leave me all alone."

"Can I interest you in a poke? It would make me feel so much better."

The black and red clay of the city, which was loosened from the eroded landscape, was carried by the hot wind and got stuck in my teeth. The city smelled of burning acacia and cabbage. We walked down the thoroughfare and there was a school bus expired in a huge cavity. It was sprouting weeds and saplings from its windows and engine.

"All wealth comes from the land," I said, and "look at this place, all torn up and barren."

She stopped, took out her camera, and took a picture of the rusted bus.

"It's a shame, yes."

"Why does it make me so mad?"

"Because you are a hothead. Hotheads get mad at things they can't control."

"See, I was taught the opposite. That logic can supercede hotheadedness."

"I was too, but then it fell by the wayside early on?"

"You mean your Mom and Dad?"

"Yes, when I watched their behavior in front of us, their kids, I realized that logic can only take a person so far."

"Well, some people are more logical than others."

"It's limited, I know this, trust me. It's overrated might be a better way to put it."

"Fair enough, but that doesn't stop me from wanting to make a difference. That's too cliché. I mean I don't want to turn into a fat slob."

"You forget all the good things in your cynicism."

"Like what?"

"Oh, don't be so coy. Come on. All the things that make life good."

"Pussy."

"Yes, you can start there."

When we got to the center of the city street vendors were hawking wares, foods, mortgages, and fortune telling. Minivans drove by with men and women hanging from the sides and splayed out on the roof. The music was everywhere, polyrhythms coming from scratchy speakers from all corners of town. The place was a beehive, a crosshatch of people stomping and shouting, tourists with lanky legs, pockets full, and cameras dangling.

We went to a pizza place.

"Fire," Grace said, after being seated, "I think we should climb Mt. Kenya before Leo comes."

"And I've been thinking too. I think we should split up for part of the time when Leo is here."

"What are you talking about?"

"You know, to travel alone for a bit. I'm only talking about a week. Leo's here for two weeks. I thought it would be cool if one week we got to experience traveling alone."

"Why?"

"To do something new."

"You just want to be alone with your brother."

"No, really. I think it would be good. Make us stronger. More independent. A test, you know."

"What's your test in this?"

"Well," I laughed. "Perhaps this is more your test."

"Ah ha!"

"Still, I think it's a good idea."

"I don't, Fire."

"Just think about it, please."

She looked at me, her fingers clenched around a fork.

"Come on, Grace, it's just a small pilot program. Aren't you curious what a week alone in Africa would be like?"

"No," she said.

"Why not? There is something romantic about being alone."

"Why don't you travel alone then?"

"Because I think it would be cool to spend some time apart. We're going to spend the rest of our lives with each other, how about a week apart?"

She opened her mouth to respond, but said nothing.

I stuffed the pizza slice in my mouth. Not bad for African pizza I thought.

I said, "Mt. Kenya, brilliant idea."

Up Africa's second tallest peak. The air got thinner and my head got dizzy. I huffed and puffed as we climbed, my pack so dense. We saw elephants behind the coniferous trees and the mountain was a wind blown green and yellow. At one point Grace took some of my load and put it into her pack. This got us both huffing and puffing, and we vowed to materially unburden ourselves when we got down the mountain.

On the peak we shivered behind our sunglasses, Mt. Kilimanjaro saying hi from the south.

The next day we walked to the village at the bottom of the mountain to get the bus back to Nairobi. In town, on a central street, we opened our packs and started giving things away. This created fracas, kids grabbing at everything, word spreading along the streets. We quickly reduced our packs to nearly nothing; my large pack now folded over spinelessly. I kept: one pair of jeans, one pair of shorts, three pair of underwear, three t-shirts, three pair of socks, a sweatshirt, a windbreaker, a toothbrush and toothpaste, a nail cutter, my jockrot cream, soap, one 200-page journal, my address book, and one paperback book. Grace kept all the same, except the jockrot cream.

I was at the Iqbal Hotel in my room reading Freaky Deaky when Leo walked in.

"I think I'm gonna die," he announced, and threw himself on a bed.

"Welcome to Africa."

"That trip was killer. I mean those Africans, they are loud."

"I know."

"Where's Grace?"

"Out."

"Out where? Where would that woman be?"

"The post office."

"It's cool out there for a woman alone? Particularly Grace, you know, she tends to get spacey."

"She's fine. She knows what's she doing."

"You guys getting along okay?"

"Actually, we are getting on really well. In fact, this has been very bonding for us."

"Well, that's good because you getting married when you come back. Or is that off now?"

"Why would it be off?"

"You know, you thought it through and it's too early to get married."

"You giving me advice?"

"Not really."

"Well, what do you think?"

"You want the truth?"

"No, lie to me, you dicknut."

"You're getting married just because you think you have to. You like the idea of it. But this is not the right time. Women are difficult and unpredictable you know."

I sat up against the wall and put Freaky Deaky down. In this tiny room were three single beds on shaky skinny metal legs covered in threadbare Moslem quilts; there was barely enough space for a knee.

There was also a small table with a lamp on it, a picture of a rhinoceroses on the wall, and a faint crescent moon etched above the door. Leo put his large pack under his head as a pillow and stretched his legs.

"Well," I said, "I'm not unaware of Grace's issues, but think it is important that I commit to her. In my loins, which have such a powerful hold on me, and you too, I don't want to ever commit. But in my head I think it's something I must do. It's an experiment in intimacy beyond the random. And I love Grace."

"It sounds more like a brain thing than a heart thing."

"No, it's in the heart. I'm using the brain to free up the heart."

Leo stood up and unlocked the top of his pack, fished around, and then handed me a chocolate bar from America.

"From Mom," he said, "but it's nearly melted."

Leo was taller and heavier than I was, strong in the chest and arms. Frequently I compared his carriage to my egret anatomy. He too had the family gut disorder, but mildly, his DNA less disturbed.

"Mom," I said, "she's in love with us."

"Yeah, but can you blame her?"

"What do you mean?"

"Dad, you know, hard to love."

"Yes, but being in love with your kids, it doesn't feel right. It makes me nervous, and makes me mad at her."

"I know, you've got to tone that shit down."

"What shit?"

"Be nice to Mom. She deserves it."

"I know, the most generous being on earth. Without her you and I would be carbon copies of Dad, pissed off."

I listened to diesel trucks snort and the trebly sounds of the music of the city.

"Great place you got here, real luxurious," Leo said.

"Things are different here, dude, this is luxury, clean sheets and clean room."

"Is that chocolate melted?"

I squeezed my fingers into the wrapper, but there was resistance.

"Seems okay."

"Give me some."

"No, it's for me. You just came from the land of goodies and are going back in two weeks. I am here in the land of privation for another several months."

"Just a piece."

"No."

"Come on."

"So, what about Dad?" I asked.

"He's okay, same as always. He's older though . . . I'm starving."

He sat up.

"You want to get some pizza?" I said.

"They got pizza here?"

"Leo, you ain't on Mars."

"I know, but you know, I mean, pizza, it's white food."

"Apparently not. It's here and it's really good, actually."

"Let's go."

I got up and gathered my money belt.

"Man," Leo said, "you look like shit."

"Thanks."

"No, I don't mean ugly, but so skinny. What's going on?"

"Intestinal pests."

"Mom said you were sick a lot."

"Not a lot, she always exaggerates my sickness, just a few bouts."

"A few bouts, come on bro, that's a lot."

"Not it's not."

"Is it safe to leave my shit here?"

"Take the money and the passport. The rest is okay."

"How'd you find this place?"

"Travel guide of course. It's great."

"Muslims, right?"

"Yes."

"Elijah is Muslim too, right?"

"I'm sure there's a Muslim Elijah. I'm sure there's a Muslim Fire."

We stepped out of the room and walked down the steps to the lobby, which was filled with men drinking tea and coffee, reading the paper. The place was coated in cigarette smoke and cooking meats. White travelers leaned against their backpacks smoking and reading espionage novels or their travel guides.

We stepped out into the intense sun.

"Lucky I bought these new glasses," Leo said. "These have extra tint to keep the African sun at bay. Cool, right?"

"Dude, I couldn't give a shit."

"Don't lie, you know these things are cool."

They sat golden, narrow, and slanty over his eyes.

"How much?" I asked.

"A lot."

"Well?"

"$300."

"Mom get them for you?"

"Yeah. But she thought it was the right thing to do too. You know, this is Africa, the sun is a beast here."

"Traveling gift, uh?"

"Yeah."

"Dad know?"

"Nah . . . This is kind of a cool city," he said.

We intersected with Moi street, and I thought of the man himself, his picture everywhere here in Kenya, a king, and a man learned in big capitalism too: keep as much of the tax revenue as you could for yourself. It flared my desire to become president, to change things. We flowed into the heart of the noisy city and we came out from Banda Street into the moving throng.

A man tried to sell us a donkey and another man tried to sell us a haircut. I was tempted to get the haircut, but when I suggested it Leo freaked out.

"Those scissors, what kind of heads have they touched?"

"Mites and lice."

"Just what I'm talking about."

"I was thinking," I said, "that we'd all go down to the ocean for a week and then you and I would go on safari for a week."

"I thought the plan was for us to be alone?"

"Well, we can't ditch Grace for the whole two weeks, that's not fair. But I've been working on getting her used to the idea of a week alone."

"Just a week, this is a once in a lifetime thing."

"She's my future wife, Leo, come on."

"I know, sorry, but it's nice when it's just you and me."

"I know, but half the time is still pretty good."

"What's she going to do for that week?"

"I don't know. Haven't got that far yet."

"You mean to say that this isn't in the bag yet."

"Not 100 percent."

"That's scary. You can't let it go like that."

"These things are subtle. You don't know shit. This relationship stuff takes vigilance. You only fuck."

"That's right. I don't have the patience."

"Well, I'm into this thing and it requires a different pace."

"Don't screw this up Fire, all two weeks together will be rough for everyone involved."

"I know. I know."

"This city," he said. "Feels like a small New York City, but with the blacks in control."

"Just barely," I said, "they are just barely in control of their own land. The place is a mess. The whole thing could blow at any minute."

"What do you mean blow?"

"Everyone is starving and poor, that combination doesn't sit well."

"You mean tribes going at it."

"Yeah, jungle warfare," I said.

"Ugly," he said.

We got to the pizza place and sat down at a table outside. When the pizza came Leo and I vultured it, our family favorite, except for Mom, who ate so well. Our father, on the other hand, was a tainted diabetic in love with sweets and easy foods and we inherited this from him.

"Shit ain't bad," Leo said.

"I told you."

"So what's at the ocean?"

"The beach, the Indian Ocean. Roll that on your tongue."

"They got surfing?"

"I can only imagine yes."

"How do we get there?"

"Train, the old Mombassa Express."

"Those Brits."

"They were good colonialists."

"Remember that movie about Kenya?"

"Those rich expats. The hot tanned flesh."

"My mind goes blank. Thank god Grace is good in bed. And I love her body."

"She's not my type."

"That's a good thing."

"Yeah . . . Dad fancies her, you know."

"Yeah, it weirds me out."

"He is one horny dude."

We finished the pizza, paid, and walked back to the Iqbal Hotel. Grace was back. They hugged. She looked awkwardly at Leo, an alien being as far as Grace was concerned.

"Well, what's the plan?" Grace asked.

I said, "I thought we'd go to Mombassa for now and then Leo and I would go off to safari, as we talked about."

"Actually I'd rather not be alone, but I can see your mind is made up and I don't have the energy to fight you. It's a funny phenomenon, isn't it, you always going away, always wanting it your way."

Two days later we boarded the train for Mombassa. We sat amid the masses, a swirl in third class, jostled and bumped. There were goats and chickens in the aisle, surprisingly quiet and keeping to themselves. The train car had double rows of wooden benches and the windows were opened wide; the three of us leaned out and into the sun.

In the high plains the flowers were small and yellow, discrete in their lonely wait for water and pollination. The grasses, the mustard yellow of the plains (the mustard yellow of a lion tail flickering) and the green joints of the stalks in the short hills. The dust as we got closer to the water went from black to green to red. Gradually, during the course of the day, the train chugging away, we came out from the cool mountains and started downwards towards the ocean. The air got hotter, the tree populations less dense, and then it was all sand.

I turned to Grace and said, "I really think you should just stay in Mombassa for the week and write. It would be a great setting for poetry, don't you think?"

"I'll do what I want since I'll be alone anyway."

"Grace, this is good, really," I pleaded. "Trust me, this is good for both of us."

"Trust you?"

Leo gave me a glance that said, "Are you sure of this? Is this what you want a life of?"

"Grace, it's nothing, just a week. Please."

She turned away from us.

When we arrived in Mombassa, the ocean sun heating up my good feelings, Grace walked out to the end of the platform, turned to me, and said, "Goodbye."

"Where you going?"

"I thought I'd start our separation earlier," she said. "Why not? It's what you want."

"No, I want a week alone, that's it. Please don't do this. What's wrong with me wanting to have a week with my brother?"

"Nothing. I'm giving you two weeks now."

"Come on, Grace, please don't do this."

But she walked away.

"Hold this." I gave my pack to my brother. "I'll be right back."

I caught up with Grace.

"Grace, come on, don't do this."

"What does it matter," she said.

"Because you are my fiancée and I love you and don't want to fight with you."

"This is how you show it? By leaving me again."

"I'm not leaving you. I am spending a week with my brother on safari. It's a week. I'm returning."

"Your brother is so selfish."

"Don't blame him. Leave him out of this."

"You can't say no to anybody . . . except me of course."

"That's not true. I can say no."

"No, you can't. That's from your mother."

"God damn, Grace!" I flipped my arms up in the air like a heron flying off. "Why make such a big deal of everything. There is no betrayal going on here. It's just a week with my brother. One week, seven days, how many hours. It's not symbolic of anything but the desire to spend some time with my brother."

"No, Fire, it's a week away from me. And it's symbolic too. First you are late for Amsterdam. Then you leave me to see Mapfumo. And now you are leaving me for Leo. All three of these departures within three months, on the road, in Africa, where you should never leave my side.

This is not to mention the everyday slights."

"Like what, Grace! Like what? Like what kind of slights am I inflicting on your soul?"

She lunged at me, flailing. I covered up, just like I did when my father came at me, his fists up, his body driven forwards. Grace's opened hands pounded on my uplifted arms, bruising my forearms.

The Mombassans walking up and down the street stopped to watch, forming a loose circle around Grace and me, commenting. Leo, seeing the situation, came running over. He grabbed Grace, who swirled and shot a punch at him, which he avoided and stepped back. She turned back at me, her arms in full rotation, the vectors of her anger and insult.

"Grace, stop!" I said. "Enough. This is crazy."

She gave me one last shot, that I was unprepared for, and it hit me square in the chest, pushing the air out of my lungs. I doubled over, groping for the lost oxygen. I heard the natives laugh. I was humiliated, spinning, knocked out by my fiancée. In my pain, crouched on the dirty sidewalk I wanted to kill her and imagined rising up and choking her to death. But by the time the wind came back to me I had lost my anger and instead sat on the pavement defeated.

In her physical exhaustion Grace lost her anger too.

"I'm you fiancée," she said. "I'm not your mother."

She pulled me up, brushed the dirt and gravel from my bare legs.

The three of us shared a hotel room, shaped in a rondoval, airy, with curtains separating the bedrooms. We left the windows open and the ocean air circulated throughout the space. In the morning we ate breakfast outside in the gardens of the hotel. After this we went to the beach and dug ourselves into the hot sand, closed our eyes, and let the sun take our minds away. Leo went surfing, renting a board from some local kid. Grace and I kissed and hugged, rubbed our bodies against each other, and she read poetry to me in her rhythmic incantations and I felt the words wash me into a stupor. It was sultry and providential, and although I was connected to Grace I was anxious about our separation too, sensing that within this action of mine was lasting damage. We napped in the afternoon the sweat on our brows staining the pillows. At night, the weather cooled, we went out to eat. It was an elongated week under the ocean's tropical sun. The night before Leo and I left we all got drunk and Grace said, "Guys, go. I'll be fine. I've been thinking about it and I think I'll do what Fire suggested, stay here and write poetry. I'll meet you back in Nairobi in a week."

"You're fantastic, Grace, fantastic," I said.

The next day, in the hour before we left, Leo had to dump. He went into the bathroom with the paper. I heard him squeezing and groaning, and looked at Grace and smiled at her. I heard the wiping, the scratching sounds, the jingle of the toilet handle. I heard it jingle again. Then again. Leo called out, "The toilet won't flush."

"Well, fix it, please!" I shouted back.

I heard him try the flusher again and then the door swung open and he jumped out.

"Don't think the thing's going to work."

He went to his bed and continued reading the paper.

Needless to say, I had to dump too and sat there in quandary. If I missed my chance there might be no second one, and for me this compounded my already distended state. I went in and closed my eyes. I heard Leo crack up. I tried not to look, but these things are hard to avoid so I gave a glance. I sat my vulnerable ass down over the pot. Carefully, avoiding splash, I dumped over Leo's dump. I tried the toilet, but the black water's rise was too close for comfort.

As we left I turned to Grace and shrugged.

"What can I do?"

"Asshole."

In Nairobi Leo and I rented a jeep and headed off west towards the bush. The road was bumpy and potholed and we had to remind ourselves to stay left. Leo's head kept hitting the top of the jeep as we bounced along the ravine. I was only half concentrated on the driving instead lost in worry about Grace, hoping she was all right, feeling the sting of my own guilt.

Nonetheless, Leo and I moved around the park for a week, from corner to corner, driving around in the jeep, taking hikes and worrying about snakes. We saw elephants, wild dogs, and lions. The cicadas buzzed like maniacs and the flies swarmed around our faces.

On our penultimate day I was driving looking for leopards but could not get out of my head the image of Grace packing her goods and flying back to New York City without me. In her exodus was my failure and desolation. I felt the jeep go up the embankment; Leo and I screamed as the vehicle flew in the air, floated above the earth for a split second, and landed with a thud, our necks whipped backwards. The jeep was hot and steaming as it sat there in the landscape. Leo punched me in the head. In our distant view was the mountain of Tanzania and it sat in the sky like a sleeping giant. Some buffaloes came to investigate, perplexed by this metal hissing animal. Leo said, "If you get us killed by buffaloes I will kill you." But they stayed away.

Eventually, a car stopped and its driver walkietalkied the rangers, who came and got us and towed the jeep to the closest resort. We stayed there that night, at the fancy resort, another tab on Mom and Dad, got our fixed jeep the next day, and went back to Nairobi where the accident became family lore, to be told a million times in my life.

Grace was not at the Iqbal when we returned. I asked the proprietors if they had seen her. She had checked out a few days ago, they said. I asked Leo what to do, but he said, "What can you do?"

I called the local police, but they had heard nothing. I called the local hospitals, but there was no record of her. I called the Embassy, but they too had not had word of her. I called the airlines, as many as I could, but Grace had not flown out of Kenya as far as I could tell. I even called home, to Mom, but she hadn't heard from Grace. I was shaky with anxiety.

In the meantime, Leo and I ate at the pizza place and had milkshakes. We went to the American Cultural Center to sit in the air conditioning and read the sports. One day we went to the City's animal orphanage. Crippled hyenas, gunshot rhinos, and cheetahs with broken legs.

On the day Leo was leaving Grace came back. I hugged her and she kissed me on the lips.

Grace and I went into the bush for the next several months. We blended with the land, a humid sandy sweat shielding our bodies from the sun. Sitting atop rock outcrops and from our jeep windows we observed the flora and fauna of the plains; New York City faded from my consciousness as my soul calmed down.

Grace and I danced naked under the blinding sunlight. We had been sitting under an acacia tree. Nothing moved except the grasses in the wind and the flies. Grace took her shirt off. In those days she did not wear a bra. I stared at her breasts and midsection. I took my shirt off. Grace took her shorts and underwear off. I took my shorts and underwear off too. We kept our sneakers on, too many small nasty things in the dirt. We came together and danced to an imaginary song in our heads with abandon.

A week later we were in the sky heading west over the Atlantic Ocean back to our cats, family, friends, and fate.

PART 2

4. Meditation

As our plane flew over Brooklyn into Idlewild I was able to locate the large rectangle of my high school and a sadness rose in me as I remembered struggling then with my new sickness, raised from my inner core, importuning my young body. Flying over my high school I also remembered Lightbulb as he grabbed me in a headlock demanding my train pass. Sixteen and 110 pounds, a veteran at being mugged, I elbowed Lightbulb in the balls. His arms around me went weak as he crashed to the ground in pain. I laughed. He reached out for me, but I stepped aside and ran down into the subway.

In August Grace and I got married. It was a small ceremony under a sweeping cherry tree in Central Park. Grace wore a long blue dress with white polka dots and fishnet stockings underneath. Her lips were painted red. I wore my one and only black suit, tapered like a rock star, brown and white twotone shoes. The day was enormously humid. Planes flew overhead and people walked by chattering. I could hear the pling of balls off aluminum baseball bats. We had a new age cantor, despite Grace's Protestantism, and her father's long neck loomed over our Chupa. My parents stood with my brother between them, my mother's arm around Leo's back. Leo, bored, kept following the pretty girls with his eyes. Dad cringed when Grace's hippie friend read James Joyce aloud, "Yes." The sun lit Grace's face. Above the din of traffic the cantor read psalms the words trailing up the branches of the cherry tree. His blue felt hat, more a fez than a yarmulke, was decorated in white Hebrew letters. He gesticulated in the song of David and when he was done Grace and I signed a kituba of fellowship. The cantor urged us to live honestly, and accept each other, and vested us husband and wife. Grace stuck out her leg and pulled her dress up her fishnets to reveal a silver garter around her thigh. I bent down on my knee, took the garter down over her ankle and into my hand.

The minute I opened the door I could feel Grace's mood. Our long hallway was littered with our cat Molly's playthings, straws and toy mice, and in all the corners were dust balls of city particulate matter. The first dim room on the right was my office where I cooked up ideas to save the forests, read books like "Re-Invigoration of Soil Structure," and did research on graduate schools. The window looked out on a shaft, a metropolis of pigeons, but even from this backspace I was disturbed by the noises on the avenue. Our kitchen, right after the bathroom, was a box of a room that looked out on the shaft too and had red painted floors and open shelves that Molly would jump into. Grace was standing up against the sink when I entered. Her t-shirt and khaki pants were covered in cat hair, white and black hairs stuck to her like soot.

"Hi," I said.

"Hi."

"You okay?"

"Virginia and I had fight."

"Why?"

"She disagreed with me on this passage and kept trying to change my mind, but I refused."

"What was the passage?"

"It's a book on the history of mercury."

"Cool."

"Yes, that's why I like it. Books you can't find anywhere else, subject matter from all sorts of perspectives."

"So, you had a disagreement about mercury. What about it?"

"The particulars are not as important as the fact that it just kind of escalated. She pushed and then I pushed back. I could see her getting angrier, but I felt I was right, and I didn't want to get bullied."

"So, what happened?"

"We've been getting friendly. I had been talking to her about my father. She said that her father was also a looming presence. This trust is building. I like it, as you know, the emotional intimacy."

"So, what the hell happened?"

"Virginia turns to me, arguing about the syntax of a passage in a book about mercury, and says that I am passive aggressive because I can't leave the slights of my father behind me."

"She said that? That's not fair. There are rules to fighting, no bait and switch. What did you say back to her?"

"I was too stunned. I kind of said 'don't judge me,' under my breath, but I was too shocked to reply."

"You should have told her to mind her own business."

"Virginia said I was stuck in the past."

"Well," I said, "she has a point."

"What?"

"I need to take this opportunity to tell you that you are too angry at your dad still."

"Bait and switch. We were talking about my fight with Virginia and how she insulted me and now you are insulting me. Dirty behavior."

"Grace, no, this is serious. Your fight with Virginia aside, I think you are being held back in life by your continued focus on your parents, particularly your dad."

"A person who doesn't understand their past will never find true insight."

"I hate to see you so down so often."

"You're a pompous ass."

"I'm the least pompous person in the world."

"You're the most pompous person I have ever met."

"I'm humble."

"You're a blind monster."

"I was blindsided by an intestinal monster."

"Yes, you were. Like I was blindsided by a father monster."

"Yes, you were."

The phone rang.

"Don't get it," she said, putting her arms around my neck, kissing my lips.

"No. I'm waiting for a call from Adam."

"You can call him back."

"It will just be a minute."

"You can call him back."

I disengaged from Grace and said, "It'll be a second."

It was Adam. He was confirming our yoga appointment for next weekend. He had met this man named Vijay and the three of us were going out to his Queen's home for a session.

"Grace, it's Adam," I called out. "He's confirming for next week. The yoga guy."

"Yeah," I said to Adam, "we are on. I'm looking forward to it and I think Grace really needs it. Virginia and Grace had a fight."

"Whoa," he said.

"She said to Grace that she needs to, basically, grow up."

"Whoa."

"I've got to go. But you sure this yoga dude is okay? I mean his basement in his house in Queens? You know Queens is a dreary place. This guy could be meaning to cut our throats."

"You're a dirtbag. Don't worry everything is fine. Honestly, you need to learn some relaxation techniques."

"We all do. All of us here stuck in the city."

"You and the city again."

"Yeah, me and the city again."

"Talk to you later," he got off the phone.

Grace was in the kitchen reading a book about Buddhism. I hugged her from behind. Molly jumped down from a high shelf and leaped onto the table to greet me.

"Virginia is small minded," I said, "like us all, except for me."

"Typical of you."

"I mean, how could she not see that it is not her privilege to make that judgment?"

"Because she's small minded."

"Yes. You got it! Small mindedness is what makes us anxious, paranoid, self righteous, mean, and rigid. Nixon. Reagan. My dad. Yours too."

I leaned into her for a kiss. She opened her mouth and let me wash against her tongue. I pulled her up and put my hand on her ass. I then pushed her up against the sink and rubbed into her belly, my knees bent and my lower back thrusted forward.

"You randy man," she said.

"Oh, yeah. I'm a cowboy."

I unzipped her pants, pulled them over her hips, over her ass, and down to her ankles. I pulled her underwear down. I put my finger between her thighs and into her crotch, moving through her sedge of hairs, submerging in the bog. We kissed, my favorite part; even more so now as an older man. I moved my finger further into her and Grace turned herself around on me, positioned herself over the sink, ass up. I put my penis into her . . . and shot my load right away! It was shameful. I had been getting better at holding it in lately, but this was so strong an elixir that I was rendered out of control. I dribbled come onto the kitchen floor.

"I'm sorry, Grace."

"Don't be."

"I feel like a kid, a loser."

"That's stupid. You were highly charged . . . So was I."

"I know, that's what sucks, I had you going."

"You did, baby, you really did."

She rubbed into me.

"What a fucking fuck up I am."

"I know, not even one hard thrust into my wet pussy and you come."

"I know. You think liking sex as much as I do I'd be able to hold on longer."

"Yeah, why is that? You should be a world champion."

I hung my head in shame.

She rubbed into me again, her wet pussy hairs trailing against my thigh. Grace started masturbating, arched slightly against the sink. I began to suck her tits. I could see through her eyes that her mind was going blank; her energy was turning inwards; she gasped for breath, more and more pressure coming into her veins; up and up until she stretched her long luxurious body . . . and sighed.

"You drive me crazy, Grace."

"I know."

On the morning of the day we were to go Queens for yoga Grace was sick in the stomach. For the past two mornings she had also felt sick. She was into Buddhism fulltime now, part of a group that studied and meditated together, and I thought yoga would be perfect for us, an overlapping of interests, and a means to quiet the soul. But Grace had been sick all morning and I figured the whole thing was shot.

She retched in the bathroom.

"You alright?" I called out.

She came out of the bathroom looking as pale as a sheet.

"What should I tell Adam?"

"I don't know. Can you give me a few minutes?"

She went into the bedroom and lay down.

I paced, down to the front door and back to our bedroom, a six step walk in our dark tenement hallway. Molly and Felix watched me from the armrest of our green couch. I walked into the bedroom. Grace lay face down on the bed, her arms spread behind her. I went back to pacing, five more times before I went to her again.

"How you doing? Can I get you anything?"

"Let me rest a moment longer."

I went to the bathroom to take a pee. The kitty litter was stuck between the toilet and the bathtub. On the floor under my feet was spilled red wet litter, between my toes. I was having trouble again peeing and I stood over the toilet for nearly 20 seconds while waiting for the first drop of liquid. When it came I wanted to scream it hurt so much.

I walked back to our bedroom.

"How's it doing, Grace? You think we can make it or not? Just let me know, I'm fine either way."

"I think I'll be fine. I feel like I am getting my wind back."

"Oh, that's great."

She laughed.

"Seriously, do you think you can make it or should we cancel?"

"I'll be fine, Fire."

We took the Number 1 train down to 42nd Street. We walked the white tiled dungeon of the subway tunnels to the 7 train. On the dirt-caked platform, which was dimly lit and humming with electrical current, was Adam, standing thickly on the concrete and looking back down the platform for us.

When we got to him I said, "Dude, this is making me worried."

"Don't worry, it will be fine," he said.

"How did you meet this guy?"

"Through work, I told you. He's the older brother of Vivek that I work with. Vivek said he does yoga and meditates all day."

"Who's paying the rent?"

"Vivek and his mother."

"Where's the dad?"

"Back in Bangladesh."

"So this Vijay is a guru."

"Grace," Adam said, "you look good."

"I don't feel so good, really."

"Why?"

"Sick to my stomach. The last three mornings to be honest."

"So, you're pregnant," Adam said.

"No, no way," I said.

"Could be. Never know."

"Adam," Grace said, "not funny."

The train roared in and I covered up my ears with my hands as the long lumbering screeching worm came to a full stop. The doors popped open, two people got out, one of them glowered at me, and we slid into the car and found three sticky seats for ourselves.

First through the amazing underwater tunnel that linked Manhattan and Queens. So incredible these engineering feats! Out on the El and over the rotted industrial buildings of Long Island City and up higher, slowly at an angle, the first climb of death, then straightening out over the long highline of Archie Bunker like communities.

Queens was flat landscape and spread wide with clapboard houses and six story apartment buildings, cemeteries, playgrounds, gutted out schools, and green front lawns. There were few woods except for little pockets of oaks and maple trees. The borough sat in its own wetness, at sea level. The sun shined through the subway windows. Queens had big sun, I realized that now. I was exhausted. I wasn't sleeping again. I was up at four each night. My eyes would pop open and sleep would leave me. There was no getting it back. I was thinking about Africa, its open spaces. I couldn't believe I was back in this fucking dirty city again. Being stuck here, especially after Africa, made me feel small, obstructed. Up at night I would feel for Grace next to me, sleeping so well. I rubbed up against her in my horniness, but she wasn't stirred. I thought about work and about the future. I was thinking about graduate school, my career, future adventures.

"We're here," Adam said.

Down the stairs to the street. Flushing, packed with markets and Chinese, immigrant foods, and the smell of fish and beef.

We weaved around stands with spiky balls of fruit, hat vendors, men cleaning the sidewalk, sickly street trees. Adam looked down at the piece of paper he'd written the directions on and said, "I can't read my own writing." I said, "That's because you're a dumbass." We took a left and passed out of the business district and into a wide street with low apartment buildings, all nearly the same size, shape, and color of red/brown. We walked until the neighborhoods turned more open, the apartment buildings turned to houses, and pockets of vacant lot woods. Adam navigated us to the right house, where we hesitated for a moment at the blue door with orange fringe with a Krishna statue nailed to the top.

"This could spell our death," I said.

We climbed the stairs and knocked on the door.

Vijay and Vivek's mother answered the door, an old woman wearing a homespun white sari, comfortable and breezy and covered with food stains. Her eyes were withdrawn, her skin was wrinkled, and she pointed her finger towards the door that led us to the basement.

We thanked her and walked down the stairs. I goosed Adam from behind. He jerked backwards and elbowed me in the gut. He opened the door to the basement and we filed in.

It was a sparse cool room with a gray hard floor. No pictures and no windows. The paint was peeling and the pipes were rusted and stained. Three small red gym mats were laid out on the floor. Vijay was standing at the head of the room. His skin was very dark and his eyes were very white. His nose was disjointed to the right and his teeth were red. He wore a checkered green and yellow polyester shirt, which had stains everywhere.

"Welcome," he said, waving his arms upwards and smiling.

"Hi," Adam said.

"Please, be comfortable," Vijay said. "Each one of you take a mat."

We divided ourselves.

"Welcome. Welcome. This is very good of you to come out. It is a long trip from where you live in the city. Welcome. Welcome."

"Thanks," Adam said, "for having us. We are all looking forward to this."

"Then let's start the lesson, yes?"

"Yes," Adam answered.

"But first please take off your shirts. You." He pointed to Grace.

"Can leave yours on."

Adam took off his t-shirt to reveal a belly and chest full of hair and flab. It rolled like a black seaweed waterbed. I took off my t-shirt to reveal my spindly sick body. Only Grace had a perfect body.

"Now yoga and good meditation come from good breathing," Vijay said. "You must be able to relax and let go . . . Vivek says you are very nice people."

"We are," said Adam.

"What do you do?" he said.

Adam said, "I am a banker."

I said, "I am head of a division in an environmental nonprofit."

Vijay wagged his head.

Grace said, "I work in publishing."

"Good, good," he said. "Why choose yoga?"

Adam looked at me.

"Because we are full of tension and need to relax," I said.

"I see that a lot here," Vijay said.

He stood up straight and closed his eyes and started snorting.

"Watch me and listen. This exercise will help you begin the process of relaxation."

He snorted his breaths in and out rhythmically. Slowly at first, his body still, his disjointed nose making him look like a fool. He filled up his chest and let the air come rushing out through his nose. He started breathing more heavily and quickly. Building up speed. He snorted and snorted, deeply and violently, in a trance. The snot came in and out and clustered around his nostrils like sea foam. His saliva was pooled on his chin. I started to laugh, but Adam gave me a fierce look. Vijay stopped.

"You try it now," he said, out of breath.

We looked at each other helplessly, ignominiously. We started snorting our snotty dusty city breaths. I felt the air rush in and my breath rush out. I suddenly pictured Grace dancing naked under the acacia tree in Africa. King David went to a festival in the desert to dance ecstatically. All the complicated family ties and feelings. To be touched by god, as I was. But Grace was the ecstatic dancer in the family. She danced lithe, round and round. She took the lead in snorting and we all snorted, in and out, making our stomach muscles hurt. For one second I thought nothing. Then Grace shot some snot onto the gym mat and this was the conflagration. The first sounds of laughter, her snotball sitting on the red gym mat like a shiny pebble, and we were in full hysterics. It poured out of us like Vijay's snot. All of a sudden Grace doubled over onto her mat. She fell with a thud and I leaped over to her.

"Grace, what's going on?"

She lay in the fetal position.

"I got this sudden sharp pain to my stomach," she said. "I lost my footing."

"Are you okay? What's going on? Jesus, Grace, this seems serious."

Vijay knelt down and turned Grace onto her back. She obliged in his hands. He spread her body out and ran his hand just over her skin down from her chest over her stomach over her hips and down her legs. He didn't touch her, just traced her.

"Lady," he said, "close your eyes. Breath. Relax."

He motioned to Adam and me to lie down.

"Lady, let the thoughts come to you and then leave you."

He touched her stomach and Grace winced.

"You try this too," he said to us.

We lay back on our mats and closed our eyes. I listened to my breathing, in and out. I heard Vijay in the background talking us through the meditation. I felt the heat as the basement rose in temperature during the hot midday. I felt heavy eyelids and the pull of things inward. Vijay's voice faded, my thoughts disassembled, and I fell asleep.

I woke to Vijay gently touching the bottom of my foot. Adam had fallen asleep too. Vijay stood over us. Adam and I lifted our heads and looked sheepishly at each other. Grace was lying on the mat. She straightened herself and tried to stand up, but she fell immediately backwards. I moved over to her in alarm. She had lost all her color and was shivering. I noticed a dark stain had formed on her jeans over her crotch.

"We've got to get Grace to a hospital," I said. "Vijay, please go upstairs and call an ambulance."

He looked at me helplessly.

"Adam, go with him." I turned to Grace. "Grace, Grace, are you okay?"

"Something is leaking from my vagina, I think."

"I think you are right. You've got a dark stain on your jeans down there."

"I feel all wet and I feel like someone dropped poison in my stomach."

"We're going to get you to a hospital."

"You really think I need to go?"

"Yes. This is serious. I thought you were just fucking around this morning to get out of this, but something is really happening."

Adam was right, I thought, this was probably a miscarriage.

"I'm scared," Grace said.

I lay down next to her and held her.

"You'll be fine," I whispered into her ear.

"Now I am the one who is sick," she said.

"Yes, it's your turn."

I thought of my last bout of angry gut. I had eaten a greasy hotdog and had thrown up all night.

"I won't let anything bad happen."

"It's not your responsibility."

I held her tightly. She was shivering. I could feel her fighting off the pain, trying to get around it. This bodily pain was novel to her and I wished I could convey through the knowledge of my own disabled experiences that it would go away and then you'd never remember it again. Vijay came down the stairs and over to Grace. He looked at her with slightly crossed eyes and then backed away.

"What do you think is wrong?" he said.

"I don't know."

"It could be so many things. There is no way to know for sure. But she will be fine. This is America." He turned to me. "The best doctors here than everywhere else."

"That's what they say, at least," I said.

He left. I rubbed Grace's head. I heard Vijay's mother yell.

"Grace breathe deeply and slowly," I said, "it helps disperse the pain."

She slowed her breath.

I heard a siren and the door open and heavy footsteps on the stairs.

Adam crashed through the door, out of breath. "They are here." He bent over panting.

"Dude," I said, "you're out of shape."

"Screw you."

"Grace, can you stand up?" I said.

"I think I can, maybe."

She moved out of the fetal position and straightened up. Some color had come back into her face. She stretched out her arms.

"Adam, get her from behind while I pull her up."

He took a deep breath, and while I lifted from her armpits he pushed up from the hips. She leaned her head on my shoulder. The Emergency Service guys busted through.

"What are you doing?" one of them said.

"Getting her to you," I said.

"No, no! Put her down on one of those mats."

We turned her around and delicately laid her on the mat.

They asked her questions, touched her belly, which made her flinch, took her temperature, took her blood pressure, and then lifted her just as Adam and I had. They handed her step by step up the stairs. In the hallway was a wheelchair, which they sat her in, wheeled her to the front door, and then lifted down the steps to the ambulance. We followed. They took Grace out of the wheelchair and lifted her into a bed in the back of the ambulance. All three of us clamored behind the truck.

"Just one of you," he said.

I climbed into the back. Adam went around the front and got the address of the hospital from the driver and I watched Vijay and Adam fade away as we rode off.

I held Grace's hand. The ambulance was filled with technology, magic medicine machines, and the ambulance guy was taking Grace's blood pressure again. Things bleeped and hummed. I looked down at Grace who was withdrawn in her pain. I was tempted to small talk the emergency service guy, but was feeling too discombobulated to do anything really. In fact, my mind was too numb to frame the question that haunted me at that moment.

The city of Queens drifted by, its brown streets and sunlit rooftops, paint chipped houses, TV antennae. I stared at the ambulance's gadgets, their blue lights, held onto Grace's hand, and wondered who was going to feed Molly and Felix tonight.

We pulled into the hospital and Grace was put back in a wheelchair and I followed beside to the emergency room: doctors, nurses, cashiers, janitors, and administrators, all in chaos together with the sick; bright lights, electronic noises, puke sounds and blood smells, alcohol and needles. She was wheeled to a bed behind green curtains and a doctor and two nurses awaiting us. Grace's pants were taken off (there was blood all over) and they cut some of her pubic hair down with a razor. They washed out her crotch. She winced and groaned. They hooked an I.V. into her and stuck a thermometer into her mouth.

I was in a daze. I didn't know what to think. The doctors and nurses wrote things down and looked at their machines.

A large bearded man parted the curtains, came in, and put on plastic gloves. A nurse held a bright light over Grace's crotch and the doctor bent down, parted her vagina lips, and started looking around. He moved his finger inside Grace a bit and said to her, "How does that feel?"

"It hurts," she said.

"How bad?"

"Pretty bad."

"On a scale of one to ten?"

"Nine."

He stuck his finger in just a bit more and Grace jerked backwards, clenched her teeth.

He took off his plastic gloves and walked out.

A nurse turned to Grace and said "We are going to take you for x-rays."

They rolled her into a gurney and I followed. We left the emergency room and into the windless white walled tunnel of the hospital. There was my own suffering written on the walls. At x-ray, the nurse said to me, "You wait there."

"Can't I accompany her?" I asked.

"No. You can't be in the x-ray room with her. She will be fine," the nurse said. "Someone will keep you updated."

I bent over and kissed Grace.

I said, "I love you. I'll be right out here. Be strong."

I wanted to smoke marijuana. It was all too much. I paced. My gut hurt, a little rubber knot in the upper left corner. The hospital's electric lights hummed. I worried that Molly and Felix weren't going to be fed that night. I walked the hallway and found a phone to call my parents. Into the phone booth I closed the folding door behind me. But I stepped back out, thinking after all that it wasn't a good idea to call them. I walked back to the waiting room. Adam and Vijay were there.

"Fire, what's going on?" Adam said.

"I don't know. She was bleeding badly from her vagina."

Vijay stared at me with his very black eyes and disjointed nose. He smiled his red teeth.

Adam said, "I have to say that I was right. She was pregnant."

"I think you might have been. But now it seems lost, right?"

"No, we don't know anything yet."

"Remember," Vijay said, "it could be anything. I know a little about medicine. It's all very complicated. But the body is very strong, much stronger than we give it credit for."

"Thanks," I said.

Vijay smiled at me and then sat down on one of the waiting room chairs.

"What's going on here, Adam," I whispered.

"I don't' know. He insisted on coming."

"Why didn't you tell him, thank you very much, but you're not needed now."

"I don't know. To be honest, I just couldn't say it to the guy."

Vijay jumped up and his mother came into the waiting room.

"Holy fuck. The mother is here. How the hell did this happen?"

"I don't know."

"Adam, man, you got to get these guys out of here."

"How? Huh?"

"I don't know."

The mother came to us and said, "Can I do anything for you?"

"No, thank you, we are okay," I said.

"I saw her being wheeled out of my house," she said. "She looked sick, your wife, but she will be fine."

"How can you tell?" I asked.

"Because she had good color the whole time. Plus, she is young.

Being young helps."

Vijay said, "I never felt death around her."

"That's good," Adam said.

"Come, sit down. I have rice and vegetables," the mother said.

I was too sick in the belly to eat, particularly Indian food, but Adam looked up at me excitedly. She took out of a canvas bag a small white sheet, which she laid on a chair, and some paper plates and spoons. In another bag was a Tupperware bowl filled with rice and what looked like garbanzo beans. I would have preferred a burger, if I had to eat. Adam stuck out his hungry jaw for this food and Vijay's mother rewarded him with a heapful of stew.

"Fire," he said, "this is excellent stuff."

"My gut can't take that stuff."

"Honestly, it's good for the stomach. You should try some."

He got a plate from Vijay's mother and handed it to me encouragingly. I put a little on my spoon and stuck the tip of my tongue to it. It made me snap to, the spiced soil alive with bitter chemicals. Surprisingly it hit my gut gently, at an even pace, unlike a burger, which landed in my gut like a giant meaty boulder.

"It's good, isn't?" Adam said.

"Adam," Vijay's mother said, "you work with Vivek, right?"

"Yes."

"Vivek says you are very nice."

"Thank you."

"Vijay stopped working long ago."

Vijay smiled, had heard it before.

"Vivek is out all the time working."

"Vivek," Adam said, "is always hustling. He'll be president of the bank one day."

"He's an American,"

"I guess he is," Adam said.

"The money? What's so cool about money?" I asked.

Vijay said, "Yes. He's right. What's so cool about money?"

"It gives you power," Vijay's mother said. "Power to be left free."

"She's right," Adam said, his mouth full.

"Yeah, but I hate the greed."

"The greed is demoralizing," Vijay said.

"We need a little greed to move forward," his mother said.

"No, we don't," he said, a little aggressive in his tone, and unexpected. "Mother, the more you walk through the portals of prayer to the place where you are one with the gods it doesn't matter anymore."

"Food, Vijay, food."

I said to Adam, "You should have seen yourself back there. I mean, your stomach was all over the place."

"What're you talking about?" he said, indignantly.

"Back at Vijay's, when we were snorting."

"Believe it or not that is a way to free oneself up from your thoughts," Vijay said.

"No, we believe you Vijay," I said, "but it was still funny. I mean, his gut was swishing all over the place."

Adam said, "And your sickly gut was no less appealing."

Vijay said, "Fire, you are no supermodel."

"Ha!" Adam said.

"We are both physical losers," I said. "You fat and me so skinny and only in our mid twenties."

"Speak for yourself," he said. "I have to say that I have a stomach of iron and a constitution of great reliability."

"That's true, you're right. Remember those burritos in Martha's Vineyard."

"How could I forget? You and Leo will never stop retelling it."

"Adam, how could you? What were you thinking? A bean and meat burrito from that greasy food stand. It looked like groundfill. And then a second one!"

"I had never been sick before, honestly."

"Now that's unbelievable."

We lost ourselves to eating. I felt the food enter my mouth, pass my throat, and fall through the long tube of my digestive track. I felt each movement.

"I wonder what's going on, Adam."

"I don't know. It's scary."

"I know. I'm a little freaked."

"Did you call your parents?"

"I went to call them but then thought I shouldn't."

"Why?"

"I don't know, really."

My thoughts were jumbled. Grace was away from me in her suffering and I didn't know her whereabouts. She was alone in there, just what she feared most, being left alone. Could she be losing our baby? Grace pregnant with our child? And I as a father? My father seemed unprepared for it. Was this I too? Was there room for another I?

We waited, all four of us. Vijay suggested meditation, but Adam and I declined. His mother fell asleep. Adam read a newspaper and I flicked through a sports magazine, an article on Frank Robinson. Doctors came in and out and nurses walked around and patients were transported from here to there. Vijay was humming to himself.

A doctor came to us.

"Which one of you is Elijah?"

I pointed to myself.

"Come with me," he said.

"You can speak here," I said.

"Okay." He scanned Adam, Vijay, and Vijay's mom. He looked back to me. "Your wife has had a miscarriage."

Vijay's mother and Adam simultaneously said, "I knew it."

"I didn't know we had a baby."

"Yes, your wife didn't either."

"Is it weird that we didn't know?"

"No, it was only about a month and a half old."

"So no real signs were evident?"

"No, and having never been pregnant Grace wouldn't know the signs anyway."

I felt as if this guy knew more about Grace than I did. It made me jealous.

"But she missed her period," I said. "That should have been a giveaway, right?"

"She missed one cycle really. It had occurred to her, she said, but she said she's never been clockwork."

"That's true."

"You can go back and see her."

"Is she okay?" I said.

"Yes, she will be fine."

Grace lay spent in the hospital bed. She was hooked up on an I.V.

and her head was turned away from us on the pillow. She looked very peaceful now, but I could see the residual strain and anguish in the folds of her eyes and her soaked skin. I came to the head of the bed and kissed her on the cheek.

"Grace," I said, "this sucks."

"I feel torn apart."

She looked up at Adam, Vijay, and Vijay's mom. She looked at me. She let her head back down on the pillow.

"You must stay strong," Vijay's mother said to Grace.

"Yes, this is right," said Vijay, "strong and determined."

Adam said, "Grace, I feel so bad for you."

"This is all your fault."

Adam's eyes popped out of his head.

"Mentioning it before on the train. You jinxed me,' she said.

"Not on purpose I swear."

Grace said, "Fire, I must go to sleep, but don't leave."

I turned to Vijay and his mother. "Thanks for everything. Really, I mean it. Thanks for all the support. And that food was great. But you can go home now."

"We will come back tomorrow," Vijay's mother said.

I didn't say anything. The mother kissed Grace, me, and Adam, and Vijay shook our hands. They left.

I turned to Grace and said, "We are here."

She had fallen off to sleep.

Adam and I slept on two beastly uncomfortable boxy chairs, slumped down, bent necks and crooked backs.

During the night Adam snored.

I kept falling off to sleep and waking back up. I had a quick moist dream where I stood on the corner of 66th street and Amsterdam Avenue and watched a fire truck go by. At some point I woke up to Grace's opened eyes.

"Fire," she called.

"Yes? Are you okay?"

I rubbed my fingers through her matted hair.

"Am I going to be okay?"

"Yes, you'll be fine. I mean that. Modern medicine is great at this stuff."

"I felt the baby go."

Adam snored.

"I don't mean I felt it directly, Fire. Just that in losing this living thing in me I felt its presence . . . and now absence. As if I killed it off somehow. I can't really express it."

"Don't talk like that. Its birth was a mystery and now its death is a mystery too. You're not responsible for it. But nonetheless I'm sad; even though it wasn't on the agenda it is disappointing."

She smiled at me and then fell back to sleep as I rubbed her head.

The next day my mother and father picked us up. Vijay and his mother came back early in the morning and stayed to see Grace chaperoned into my parents' car. Adam looked like an old wolf with his two day beard. His breath stunk. We hugged Vijay and his mother goodbye and made plans to come out for more meditation.

In the car, my father said, "Who the hell were those people?"

Adam and I laughed.

"We went to learn yoga from the man."

"You're a kook," my father said. "And by the way, why didn't you get Grace to a hospital in Manhattan?"

"Dad," I said, "that's naked prejudice. What makes you think a Manhattan hospital is better than one in Queens?"

"Because the doctors are better."

"How do you figure that?"

"The Jew factor, smuck," he said.

We all cracked up, except my mother. Instead she said, "All three of you are pigs."

With Grace's head on my lap I observed the grainy outline of Queens as we drove towards the river. Up the last hump of the Long Island Expressway with the borough beneath us and the wide open billboarded view of Manhattan, the sun bearing down on the road. My father exited at Van Dam Street. Left under the El and over the 59th Street bridge and into the island that I knew so well, its people all striving for faultlessness. Up 3rd Avenue past the cold white apartment buildings and over on 66th Street. Through the gorge of the transverse under Central Park, the cherry branches hanging over the wall, the pear trees of 67th street. Out of the immaculate and into the dirty bedlam of our neighborhood. My parents' dropped us off and two hours later they showed up with bags of food which my mother put neatly into the refrigerator.

I took the week off from work to nurse Grace back into health. I warmed up the soups and pasta dishes my mom had bought us. I cooked her eggs and toast. I got her books from the library. She read me poetry and I read to her from an ecology book. She asked me to read her fiction instead. I read from Rabbit is Rich. Four couples from small city Pennsylvania, including Rabbit and his wife Janice, go on vacation to the Caribbean. It is a sun saturated, golfing, poolside paradise and alcohol soaked wonderland. Near the end of the trip, intimate, the wives make manifest what the husbands' have been dreaming about all along. The women put their names in a bowl and the men close their eyes when they pick. Rabbit yearns for young Cindy, Webb Murkett's fourth in a chain of youthful wives. He tries to will picking her name, so confident that fate has this waiting for him. But he gets his old school buddy Ronnie's homely wife Thelma instead. He is deeply disappointed. But Thelma has had a long and deep crush on Rabbit, and she is overjoyed, and leads him back to her cabin. Poor self pitying Rabbit. But I felt for him. Why enter the extramarital sex stakes for someone you are not interested in? Thelma's undressing, however, gets his attention. She has a surprisingly sexy body. And her confessions of love stimulate Rabbit even more. He's still disappointed with the loss of little Cindy, but he's coming to see that he is lucky too. Thelma comes over to him on the bed and they begin to make love. The sex, slow at first, gets good because of Thelma's passion. He readies himself for entry. But Thelma announces that she is bleeding too much. Rabbit is dumbfounded. Thelma suggests instead anal sex. Rabbit is now stunned. Thelma says that she and Ronnie do it all the time. Ronnie loves it and she thinks it has "its charms." She lubes herself and Rabbit up like an expert and he goes in from the side.

Grace and I took many naps. We watched TV, daytime soaps, and talk shows. I kept reading to her about Rabbit. It was not a book she said she would have read on her own. I listened to all the noise outside the window on Amsterdam Avenue and 107th Street. Adam checked in on us and Mom and Dad brought us more food. Felix and Molly cuddled up beside Grace and kept her warm. Over the week Grace started to feel better.

The day before I was going back to work she got drunk and I got stoned. It was gray and rainy and we felt cozy and cavelike in our apartment. We talked about politics and publishing and nature. We got spacey and lazy around twilight and fell asleep. A deep short sleep. I felt Grace next to me, warm and real, her spirit so incorporated and metabolized into mine. I felt closer to her in my dreamy dark twilight space than at any point before. I felt her roll over and heard her take a breath. She smelled of bread. She sat up and appeared as a sexy ghost, an erotic phantom. She let out a curious moan. She curled into me from the side, her butt against my groin. She said, "Fuck me in the ass."

5. Explosions

IT WAS THE night before my colonoscopy. I was drinking the venomous laxative and gagging as I watched baseball, getting stoned. I had scored some really fine red tinged pot and had been eager to try it; and as its smoky winds blew into my lungs and penetrated my nervous system I began to feel the fraudulence stripped away.

Grace and I were talking about the future. I was working up to confessing to her that I had already applied to a few graduate schools. In its reality, my forward motion, was another division between us, more bad blood.

Sitting on the couch with me Grace said, "Get it over with, you're killing yourself. Drink the thing, please."

I looked at the glass, full of white bubbly chemicals. I put it to my mouth and smelled its briny contaminate. I took a swallow, gagged.

"At this pace you will be drinking until two in the morning."

"You have no idea how bad this stuff is to me."

The Yankees were winning big. They had sucked for years, but were now getting better. It was like evil on the rise for me.

"So," Grace said, "we were talking about graduate school. What's on the agenda?"

Molly and Felix were asleep together on the couch with us.

I took a hit of pot.

I took a sip of the vile juice and burped its rotten taste.

"Disgusting," Grace said, wiping the air in front of her. "P . . . U."

"You'd stink too if you were poisoning yourself."

"Is that the way you see it, as if you're poisoning yourself?"

"Yes, the whole stinking bad toxic gut of mine."

"That sounds awful."

"Depressing . . . Fucking gut," I said, "bad genes from Mom and

Dad."

"Your dad," she said, "what a crazy man. Perhaps his craziness comes from being sick all the time. Or maybe it's the other way around, his craziness makes him sick."

I coughed, as I always do.

"Well," Grace said, "what's the graduate school picture look like?"

"Well," I said, "it's time to change the course of my career with an advanced degree."

"What's wrong with your career now?"

"Grace, that's not a career. It's just a waiting platform."

"Why? You're project manager and it's a big institution. There's a lot of ways for you to move up."

"No, it's small scale. I want the big scale. I have clear ideas on how conservation work should be done and to express those ideas I have to have more schooling."

"Drink more of that thing," she said.

I took another convulsed sip.

"Achhhh!" I screamed. "I hate this."

I took another hit of pot.

"Then what? What comes after graduate school? A lifetime of field work?"

"I was thinking, Ph.D., professor. This is how I can do my own work."

"Fire, are you serious? That's a lot of school."

"I know."

The sky darkened and the cats shifted on the couch and the salsa sounds and loud conversations roared upwards on the strong winds of the trucks on Amsterdam Avenue.

"You're really planning on a Ph.D.?"

"Yes."

"Why didn't you share this with me?"

"I did. We talked about it. I've always wanted to go, you knew that."

"We didn't really talk about it, Fire. Maybe you think we did, but we didn't."

"I'm sure we did. We had to. It's been part of my life for a long time."

"Never explicitly. I feel miserably taken for granted."

"I don't take you for granted."

"You do."

"No. I'm planning for a successful future for us, what's wrong with that?"

"Nothing. I am just trying to figure out what your plans are. They surely only involve me incidentally."

"Ha, very funny."

"I wasn't joking."

"Well, I don't think it's funny. I'm thinking about the future of my family."

"Okay, what're the specifics then? Let me know."

I looked down at the phosphorous soda and took another objectionable sip. It made me gag and spasm, but I took another small sip right away in an attempt to inject some speed into the process. A third of the liquid was still left. I took another hit of pot.

"Get it over with!" Grace screamed.

I took a big swig, coughed violently, heaved, doubled over, then reemerged to say, "That's it!"

"But you aren't done yet."

"That's it! In an hour the shit will be flying out of me, don't you worry," I said.

The Yankees scored another run. I leaped off the couch and screamed, "Fuck the motherfucking fuckmothering pigsucking Yankees!"

The cats flew off the couch.

Grace said, "Jesus Christ! You've gone crazy."

"It's just that the swine sucking Steinbrenner is such an A-1 asshole that I can't stay calm when he's winning."

"This anger you are expressing now I presume is from your spirit of world justice?"

"Yes, as a matter of fact, it is. I root against Steinbrenner because like all his merchant peers he is a blood sucking cow fed parasite."

"You know," she said, "if you really want to take your 'presidential candidacy' seriously I'd leave the ranting behind and start with some well enunciated facts."

I pointed at her.

"You know, you are right. I got to tell the people in fine detail that the means and source of destruction is alone our appetite! We are poorly raised as a nation. Fucking-A, Grace!"

Her jeans were covered in cat hair and her red sweater was nearly white with Felix's fur. She had just emerged wrinkles on her jawline. She looked at me with ache in her eyes.

"I've applied to five schools," I said.

She shifted her position on the couch.

"I just sent them in, just last week. That's what I've been working on at night."

"You just applied to graduate school without telling your wife."

"I only applied, not got in."

"Still, you just changed our life, my life, without any consultation from me."

Through the windows our voices entered the braided city.

"I am sorry," I said.

"It can't go on like this."

"I know. All the pushing and pulling."

"Why are we doing this?"

"I know, it feels like a constant fight."

"So, what do we do? Is there a way out?"

I took a big inhalation of my burned and blackened joint.

"I don't want to break up."

"Then we have to change things."

"Yes."

"You need to talk to me, to include me, take me seriously."

"Okay. But you need to understand that it's not a conspiracy against you. I'm just following the tracks of my personality."

She unexpectedly reached out her hand and pinched the joint with her fingers. Then she took it from me, lit it, took a hit.

"Alright," she said. "Then that's the path we will both travel. I will do my thing and you do yours. But there is one rule: we stay here in New York City."

The first spastic wave of diarrhea hit my gut and I sprung up to the bathroom. I opened my legs to a rush of hot fecal knives and needles stabbing my anus. I held my head downwards; a woozy spirit came on. I swayed my body gently from side to side. Another rush and I braced. I let my head dangle, breathing heavily until the pain receded.

I picked up the Baseball Abstract. I looked up Lou Gehrig. Unbelievable ballplayer! Another rush. I winced, breathed. Lou Gehrig was just an incredible hitter, I kept thinking, just nearly as great as Babe Ruth, maybe even better. The gas faded and the first surge was over. I went back to the livingroom and sat down on the green couch opposite Grace.

Molly and Felix, now awake, were communicating hunger, and Grace excused herself to the kitchen, the cats following in frenzy. I heard the turn of the can, the plop of the food, the scurry of nails on the wooden floor, the vibrato of their meows, and finally the carnivorous groan of fulfillment.

She said, back now on the couch, "Fire, let's try and do this together, okay. Talk about it. Plan it out. Not just run headlong. Is this possible?"

"Yes, I promise."

I leaped up and ran back to the bathroom. It was all liquid from behind now. I was almost numb. I read about Lou Brock. 3000 hits. I waited until this movement was over, reading about Brock's prodigious stolen bases, then wiped hard over my already sore hemorrhoids, and joined Grace again.

"In the mood for a little fool around?" I said.

"You're unbelievable."

"Why?"

"You want to fuck me now after all this?"

"Yeah, why not? We fought. We found truce. And now we make up."

"An intercourse apology."

"An intercourse reunion."

"I offer a blow job."

"Actually, I was in the mood for a hand job."

"Really, anything else?"

"Yeah, can I come on your belly?"

"You are genuinely sick."

I woke up early in the morning for a final cleansing enema the nozzle going through my raw and scratched up ass. I brushed my teeth and got dressed. I went into Grace, who wished me good luck. I walked down the rotted and stinky stairs of our tenement to my mother and father waiting in the car.

The streets were empty except for Rudy the Cuban, our landlord, standing at the corner drinking coffee and smoking a cigarette. I waved to him.

"Honey," my mother said as I got into the car and proceeded to lie down on the back seat. "How are you?"

I growled at her.

My father said, "It's not that bad. I've had many of these things."

He took off toward Mount Sinai, the place of my birth and now the place of the tracking of my burgeoning adult putrefaction. The ruts in the road caused my supine body to be jostled and rolled.

My mother turned her head around and said to me, "Jane called."

I sat up.

"What? Jane called you?"

"Yes. She called and asked for your number."

"Did you give it to her?"

"Well," she said, "you know you hate me to give out your private information."

"Yes, Elijah," my father said, "I hear you screaming at her all the time about this."

"Mom, did you give Jane my number?"

"Fire, you always scream at me when I do this."

"Mom, what did you do in this instance?"

"Fire, dear, I know Grace and Jane had that big fight. I remember how angry Grace was. I wasn't sure if it was appropriate."

"What did you do, Mom?"

"I thought it would be okay in this instance."

I lay back down.

Meanwhile, my father had heavy pedaled the car down Broadway, past the Chino/Latino place, past the shoe repair shop, and the sleazy diner. Past the former movie theater where I had watched The Wild Bunch and Five Fingers of Death with my Dad. Over on 96th Street we traveled past the clothing store with its racks of suits and shirts lined up on the sidewalk.

"Mom, did you by chance get her number?"

"By chance," my father said, "she did."

Through Central Park to the mandarin Upper East Side, left and north on Madison Avenue, out of the cleanliness and into the dirty ghetto. My father let us out and went to park the car. Mom held me around the waist, but I wriggled out of it. "I'm fine," I said. Into the crowded lobby (all the sickies! and me one of them too) and up the elevator.

I checked in with the attendant nurse. We sat down.

"Fire, all that you have to bear."

"Don't."

"I can't help it."

"Mom, it's not your fault."

"I just feel so guilty that you have to go through this."

"Mom, it's not your fault, don't worry about it."

"It's just so awful, really. Who knew that your father and I would both have gut diseases?"

"Mom, it's okay. I'm cool."

"You know those first set of doctors, when you were so young and sick, all thought you were faking it. I hated them," she said, "they were evil."

"Those merchant pussy balling pill popping doctors."

"That's disgusting. Distasteful."

"But seriously, arrogant ass doctors."

"That's still a horrible thing to say, my sweet, but I agree with you. Those doctors made me so mad."

An orderly came, got me, and I was whisked away from my mother, who gave me a loving and anxious look goodbye. I was brought to a waiting room where a nurse fitted me with an I.V. When she left I sat back and felt my tender gut. She came back and fetched me, helped me into a wheelchair. She said, "How you doing?" I said, "Okay, I guess." She wheeled me into the operating room, where my doctor and an anesthesiologist waited. My doctor said, "Champ, you look great. Ready?" I gave the thumps up. The anesthesiologist stuck a needle into the I.V. jack. My doctor said, "Did you see the Yankees? They're getting good again." I said, "Tom Seaver. He was beautiful to watch. He was so beautiful. He was the best . . . pitcher . . . ever."

I woke up in a hospital room. The streetlights gave off a dim gas. Buses honked and cans rattled. I turned and felt sharp pain on my left side, hot and fresh, crippling.

I looked up at Mom and Dad.

"Fire. Thank god," Mom exclaimed.

"Boy, how you feeling?" my father asked.

"Not so good. What happened?"

"Seems that you didn't fully clean yourself out last night and there was a little explosion in your intestine."

"There was an explosion in my gut!"

"The doctor said," my mother said, "that if you are not completely cleaned out there could be some 'friction.' Is that the word he used Murray?"

"So how bad is it?"

"I don't think it's so bad, sweety. I think it's minimal, but they want to monitor you."

"They removed a piece of your gut," my father said, "just like me."

"What!"

"A small piece," he said, "even less than I had removed."

"Yours was removed because your gut collapsed, Dad. Mine was removed because they fucked up."

"I think it's horrible," my mother said.

"They said," my father said. "Didn't you listen Pearl? They said that they told Fire before that this was a possibility. He probably didn't drink the entire laxative. He tried to cheat. He'll be fine."

I buried my head in the pillow. I let the darkness of the room engulf me. I heard my father say, "Pearl, let's go." In the swirl of my pain I still heard the breathing of my roommate, heavy, labored. He was drowning in his own mucus. I drifted away on my own fever instead. Death came to me, whispered in my ear, said, "You won't die."

The door opened and Grace walked in, her heavy footsteps familiar to me even in my withdrawal. She touched my head, leaned down, and kissed me on the cheek. "Fire, I love you." I lifted my arm from under the blanket to hold her hand.

"Grace," I whispered, "what's wrong with my roommate?"

"I don't know," she said, "but he's so sick, listen to him."

"I'm not that bad off?"

"No. You are basically a sound man with a bad gut."

"So by what right do I have to complain?"

"As much right as you want, sweety. You deserve to complain."

"No, I don't see it that way. I am too lucky in life to complain."

"Go ahead anyway."

"How about a footrub?"

She lifted up the blankets and pulled down my socks. I let the rub percolate through my body, turned over in exhaustion, and fell asleep.

I was headed to Columbia University for an interview. Grace hugged me and wished me good luck. It was a wet and dreary day. I walked up Amsterdam Avenue past the church, past the hospital, through the gates of Columbia where I still occasionally got stoned between the statues with my friends. I wore khakis, a light blue button down shirt, and a purple tie with white polka dots. I felt fetching. I had thought of the reason I wanted to go to graduate school: I wanted to become a forester and go back to Africa to teach the people sustainability. This was my ticket in, my big ideas, the clarity and rightness of my energy.

Sitting in a room with two professors I was red hot. I talked eloquently about the changes in the land over time, about ecosystem disturbance, about the importance of forestry and preserving our natural resources. I wanted to work and strive in Africa. They quizzed me about my mediocre grades, but I brushed them aside. I hadn't heard my calling yet, I said, but now I did.

On the day I was accepted to Columbia, nearly eight months after I had a piece of my intestine taken from me, Grace entered graduate school for Buddhist Studies. In addition, I had convinced Grace to let Jane come to dinner. Peace was made.

6. Dances

THE SUN SHONE over the Hudson River, over the hills of Riverdale and the valley of Broadway, into the windows and livingroom of our new apartment in the Bronx. The sun also sliced into the back, which was where I was, gardening.

I was weeding out ivy and Virginia creeper that was bunched up under a thick red oak tree, hacking the roots and stems, cutting it back into a twisty river shape for a garden. I split up the interwoven fibers of the vegetation, loosened up the compacted soil, and mixed in bags of compost. I was topless and covered in leaves and dirt, dripping with the sweat of enterprise, but shielded from the sun while under the big red oak. Fergal, our landlord, stood against the feeble fence he had built that separated my garden from our neighbor Roberta's.

He said, "Did you see Roberta the other day?"

"Yes, I did."

"I like her looks. You can tell she's a fun girl, but scary too. You never know what might happen with her."

"Fergal, the same thoughts have occurred to me. Fun girl, but then hell to pay."

He looked downwards towards her back door. "It ain't worth it, Fire, you are right. She would have me tight. I would have no one to blame but myself."

He had a big jaw, recessed eyes, and pale skin that combined nicely; and he was gentle in spirit for the most part, his brow flat with fairness.

I stopped and looked up at him. There was soil mixed with sweat in my eyes.

"I like to think about it," I said.

"Yes, so do I."

"I am in the thinking about it stage of my life," I said. "I think about it a lot, sex with girls like Roberta."

"Fire," he said, "Grace would tear you apart limb from limb."

"I know, it's a great deterrent."

"Fire," he said, "the wives are hard on their husbands."

I wanted to say, you got it easy, making money and running free. But I said, "Yeah, I feel worn down a bit. Even now, still young. But, you know, I like the stability."

"Yes, the stability. It's what made me crazy."

"I consider myself restless, but you Fergal take the cake."

"Maybe it's worth it," he concluded, pointing his chin towards Roberta's place. "Good luck down there with the plants, Fire. Don't work too hard. A man like you needs his leisure time."

"You are right. I do."

He waved.

Fergal, I thought as I watched him leave, had a faded painting of JFK on the hallway wall and once got a postcard from a friend who was in the Caribbean that said, "Wish you were here. Oh, but you're having a better time laying concrete."

I went into the apartment and found Grace on the toilet bowl with Felix and Molly sitting outside the door watching her.

"I knew it," Grace said, holding a strip of paper and studying it. "We are pregnant. It explains everything."

I felt woozy, then recovered, leaned down, hugged her.

"It's just such bad timing, don't you think?" she said.

She stood up, relaxed into my hug, her pants hung at her knees.

"No, why? Is it ever perfect timing?"

"It's bad timing because your dad just had a stroke, we just moved, and you are going to Africa soon."

"Yes, and you just got a master's degree and a promotion at work so life is good too."

"It's a nice feeling knowing that all my puking was for a purpose."

"Yeah, that's the spirit."

"Don't count the chickens before they are hatched."

She pulled up her pants.

"Should we save the pregnancy test?" I said.

"Why?"

"I don't know, you know symbolic of a new beginning, something like that."

She looked at me quizzically.

We walked into the livingroom, the sun shining from over the river and into our big windows, the space really quite glorious with light.

Grace said, "I'm going to lie down for a while."

I said, "Jane is supposed to come over tonight. Should I cancel?"

"No, she can come."

After Grace's nap and before Jane came over we were going down to Manhattan to check on my father, who was bedridden recovering from his stroke. In the meantime, I watched some TV and read Coming of Age in Samoa, which was on the syllabus of an anthropology class I was taking. "Romantic love as it occurs in our civilization, inextricably bound up with the ideas of monogamy, exclusiveness, jealously and undeviating fidelity does not occur in Samoa." Hmm, I thought. "It is a very brittle monogamy, often trespassed and more often broken entirely." I was completely worked up about a threesome. Grace had accepted Jane back into our life and fairly quickly she had become our intimate. She wanted a threesome, I wanted a threesome, but Grace didn't.

I got up and retrieved my bong and the smoky haze lifted my spirits immediately. The sun shifted in the sky. Felix jumped onto my lap, curled up between my legs, and opened his stomach for me to rub. I sat back, spacey, kneading my feline's white abdomen, and thought of when Jane had laid on her stomach topless as Grace was astride her rubbing her back. I had massaged Jane's legs. I moved my fingers slowly up her calves to her thighs with little streaks grasping towards her crotch. As Grace worked her way down Jane's back I hoped she would allow herself to go further. But at the hip line Grace stopped.

I thought about that night now and the possibility of all out love-making. Grace was pregnant and this was my last chance, it seemed, for this kind of behavior.

I heard Grace move. She breathed deeply, a sigh really, something on her mind. She climbed methodically out of bed, her body heavy on the floor.

"Fire," she said, standing sleepily by the door, "we should get ready to go see your dad."

"How do you feel?"

"The nausea is gone."

"Grace, I'm happy to start a family with you."

Our new neighborhood had a linden tree leaning down into the street its crooked heart leaves kissing the pavement and its roots tucked into the eroded hillside that sloped towards Ft. Independence. People threw their garbage down here and it got caught amid the vines, weeds, and glacial rocks. The sidewalk was cracked and caked in grime. The street trees, sickly locusts and pin oaks, sat in soil moist with warm beer. Fergal had his dump truck and banged up white van in the parking lot he had carved out of the ice age rock. At five in the morning he'd start the dump truck up and it would idle for ten minutes and I'd curse the industrious Irishman. I wanted to kill him, but there was nothing to be done. At five I was usually falling back to sleep after my standard three o'clock wakening. My consciousness rose up despite my attempts to stuff it back in. I hated that moment in which my craziness triumphed. Still do, aged now, slower. Walking down Cannon Place, Grace and I left the refuge of our pretty Bronx apartment, venturing out into the world of boys and their pit bulls and the mugwort taking over the sides of the stone steps.

On the platform of the number #1 line heading down to my parents I said to Grace, "Did you have these pains before your miscarriage?"

"Yes, I did. But the day of the yoga, the day of the miscarriage, the pains were thunder and lightning."

"What a funny way nature made it. The guy just expels his load, a hello and bon voyage at the same time, and the gal gets fat."

"Yes, that's why we hate men."

"Hey," I said, "it's a man's world."

She kicked me in the shin.

"Ah, fuck, Grace, that hurt."

Everyone on the platform turned to us, all their eyes.

I whispered sharply, "Jesus."

She mocked to kick me again, but I leaped back.

"You men are nothing but machines of testosterone."

"That's right," I said. "We are what nature made us. Just like you. See, you want it both ways. Can't be. There's got to be some tension between the sexes or there'd be no interest."

"You are a pedantic idiot."

"Yeah," I said, "that's right."

The train came and we wended our way through the southwest Bronx, over the Spuyten Duvil, past the hills of Inwood Hill Park, into Manhattan, the top part of the island more like the Bronx with its hills and small houses; the obstructing landscape of my Manhattan not really in effect until 116th Street. Grace suggested that we get off early to walk past our old apartment; which we did, east to 107th Street and Amsterdam Avenue where we looked up nostalgically at our former windows, the Tibetan prayer flags Grace had tied to the fire escape faded and worn.

She said, "Remember when we came home from work that day and the window was wide open and Molly and Felix were sitting at the ledge."

"Yes, I was scared shitless."

"I know, they seemed vulnerable to us, but they knew what they were doing after all."

"Yes, I thought that too. They are cats and they know heights. They don't have to be told."

"Remember Richard called it 'Pigeon TV', Felix and Molly sitting at the sill salivating, hopelessly, at the pigeons just on the other side of the pane."

"They were transfixed. It was the only time we could rattle a cat food can and they were unmoved."

"They kept thinking they could kill their own dinner."

"Ah, poor frustrated predators, kept from their nature by civilization."

"Jesus, you're a broken record."

At that we turned south, then west, along the wide block of 106th Street, and over to Riverside Park where Grace and I starting walking downtown by the river.

The sun had partially faded behind clouds, but still illuminated the river and the cliffs of New Jersey. It was a warm September day, sanguine. I heard the birds calling from the trees; my whole existence was written in the trails and paths of this neighborhood. Grace grabbed my hand. We passed the basketball courts, sunbathers on the hill, crabapple and cherry trees.

Grace exhaled, turned to me. "I had an affair."

I withdrew my hand from hers.

"I had an affair with a fellow student," she said, her voice both controlled and filled with fear.

"When?" I asked.

"The past year."

"A year?"

"Yes."

"Really? Not two weeks? Two months?"

"A year."

"Is it still on now?"

"No, he broke it off."

"He did, not you?"

"Yes. I was madly in love with him."

"Are you still now?"

"Yes."

"Whoa . . . This is news." I ran my hand through my hair. "Where does that leave me?"

"As my husband still."

"The rebound guy."

She laughed.

"Husband as rebound guy."

"Yes, I guess that could be true."

"What a fine and uplifting role for me."

People in tank tops and jeans walked past, as well as skateboarders and bicyclists. There was noise on all sides.

"Fire, I am sorry."

"What brought it on?"

"His advances and my vulnerability."

"A horn bone."

"He did use me, yes, if that's what you are getting at."

"Who was he? Did I ever meet him?"

Yes, once or twice, briefly."

"Really, he was just under my nose. A little secret life going on just out of the reach of my awareness."

"Yes."

"A special world that lay just behind the fence of my eyes."

"Yes."

"A secret cabal of sex."

"Funny, Fire, funny."

"Oh, a secret cabal of sex. Just the thought makes me go hard."

"You're a savage."

"I know. Sometimes I think I'm as enlightened as can be and sometimes I think I'm a barbarian, just like King David."

"King David. Only you would compare yourself to King David."

"He's my cousin, same bloodline, why not?"

"King David, as we talked about on the day we met so long ago, was a brutal dictator."

"And the great king as well, with his tender fingers, and his crazy mind as he walked his rooftop palace looking out at the Palestinian desert and down at the city he created. And there was Bathsheba! After all the time looking out at the rooftops and seeing wash hanging, birds nested, smoke from fires, suddenly there is Bathsheba."

"Yes, and then he kills her husband in the process."

"Yeah, that was bad."

"You, Fire, are . . . as close to King David as anyone I know."

"So, who was this guy?"

"He was a fellow student."

"What's his name?"

"His name is Orlando."

"Orlando, conquistador. And so what attracted you to him?"

"He is smart, extremely well educated in Buddhism, and he was interested in me."

"He paid attention to you."

"Yes, and we shared this interest in Buddhism. He's been studying it for two decades. He's meditated in caves in Tibet. I was in awe of his knowledge."

"Well, power is attractive. So, how did he make his move? How did you have the time? How did you fit it in, I mean?"

"Well, it was easy for me. I was at class three nights a week and so were you, we barely see each other during the week. For him, it was a little bit more difficult because he doesn't live in the city."

"He's a suburbanite?"

"Yes."

"Hmm."

"So, when did he make his intentions known?"

"Remember my birthday," she said, "when you took me for dinner at that fancy French restaurant?"

"That night."

"Remember, I came to you crying."

"Yes, in that sexy green dress. I remember. That's what was going on."

"We had gotten intimate, close. We were reading texts together, for hours at a time, and then he turned to me that day and said his brother had a place in the village and would I like to go there with him."

"Ballsy," I said. "So, how did you go from your crying that night to his bed?"

"He kept on persisting and I was in bliss from the intimacy and, you know, I tend to give into other people's desires."

I coughed twice.

"A year?"

"A year. And from the moment I said yes, if this helps, it was painful."

"Well, I am sorry for that . . . How come I didn't figure it out?

"Because, Fire, truthfully, you are too self absorbed."

"I guess I am."

"You can't help it."

She turned and hugged me. I felt like I had been victorious anyway because she was asking for me back. I felt in a position to get what I wanted. I hugged her back.

"I'm sorry this happened and I'm sorry if I drove you to it in some way," I said. "But does this mean that I get to fuck another girl?"

"If you want."

"What I really want is a threesome with Jane."

We were crossing over the Parkway at 79th Street, a crazy intersection where the cars came at you from multiple angles.

I said, "Are we sure this is my baby?"

"I'm pretty sure it is yours."

"What? Pretty sure? Not certain? Not absolute?"

"I'm so sorry. There's nothing I can do."

"When's the last time you had sex with the guy? And by the way I bet I am better in bed?"

"You are definitely a better performer. But remember, I was in love with him."

"Which makes it better, huh?"

"No, just different. Fire, it's so complicated. It's not like I was seeking this out. But he's a strong character and you're always so lost into your new things and ambitions. His advances, wrapped in Buddhist lessons, were too hard for me to fight. I just gave in. But I will never do it again."

"How can you say that?"

"I know."

"No one knows."

We turned and continued walking down the path. The sun had been freed up from the clouds.

"When was the last time you had sex with him?"

"Fire, he always wore a condom."

"So, what's the issue then?"

"Well, condoms aren't perfect."

"Did it break, come off in you?"

"Yes, once recently."

"Once, recently. When?"

"Two days ago. That's when he broke it off for good."

"This is unbelievable! Two days ago his prick was inside you. I was inside you two days ago, come to think of it. You fucked us both on the same day! Holy shit. Me in the morning and Orlando in the evening. Did you wash or were we mixed together?"

"Hah, funny."

"Kind of have to envy the guy, really, all those vulnerable Buddhist students all starry eyed. Kind of easy pickings when you think about it. But two days ago. How many times did you have us on the same day?"

"I don't know Fire, several times, I guess. It was never intentional."

"Well, thank god for little things.

"Fire, stop, please stop. I'm genuinely sorry. I got caught in the rays of love, what I thought was a perfect love, and I got fooled. There is nothing else to be said. The rest is up to you. But I won't fall into this trap again."

The curved buildings on Riverside Drive, in which one of Mrs. Babe Ruth had lived, reflected the sun onto our backs and into our eyes. My mind was looping and twisting like always, tributaries of thought, waylaying islands and compacted dams. We got to 72nd Street and exited the park and walked over to West End Avenue. Now added to my brain was the fact of Grace's affair and what this might all mean for me.

My father lay on the couch with the TV on to a political talk show, his blue and white bathrobe stained from the chicken soup and macaroni my mother had been making him, his skin pale from the hospital and his aging body flattened. His upper lip was curled and loose, warping his face. There were piles of newspapers on the rug. My mother had set up a table by Dad's head that contained a glass of soda, tissues, a book on the Jewish immigration to America, untouched however, and a remote control for the TV. The apartment, I sniffed, had a new smell, antiseptic and medical. The men on the TV were talking about economic policy, tax cuts, fighter jets, corporate subsidies, oil revenue.

"What the fuck are these boneheads saying?" I asked Dad.

"Something woolish," he said.

"What the hell did you say?" I said.

"I said, something 'woolish'."

"Woolish." I cracked up. "What the hell is that?"

"He's not fully back to himself yet," my mother called out from the kitchen.

"Mom, is that good?"

"They say it's normal."

"I guess so."

"So, what's the guy talking about?" I said to him again.

"Something woolish. They are assholes."

"I agree. They are monsters these guys in power. Deviants."

"Ah!" my father screamed. He shifted himself upwards on the couch, stiffly. "You are wull of wit. Stay wocussed, Fire."

"And I say the same thing about you, you know. You don't see it right."

"I do!"

He nearly spat at me.

I said, "How do you feel?"

"Like wit. I ache all over."

"Why don't you turn these turds off and turn on the ballgame," I suggested.

He did just that. He searched for a Met game, but none was on. He found an Atlanta Braves game, my brother's strangely favorite team, and we watched for a moment because Greg Maddux was pitching and he was so good. But it was a blowout. He clicked away from channel to channel, each one growing into the next one in a swollen barrage. Ineluctably there was a Yankee game. A close game with Baltimore. Fuck! We hated these guys but they seemed to be the only team ever on. "They depress me," I said.

"You wean the Yankees? Yes, they are depwessing. Ever since I was a boy I hated the Yankees."

"I wish I could put my finger on it. I wish I could figure out why it's all wrong," I said.

"There is no answer," Grace called out from the kitchen.

Grace and my mother were setting the table to eat lunch. My parents' home quickly separated the sexes, the women to the kitchen and the men to the couch. Grace bristled at this, but was a good girl by and large and helped Mom wait the men. Leo walked in. My mother came rushing to the door, grabbed him, and gave him a big kiss.

His shoulders hulked out from his t-shirt and his jeans hung loosely from his waist. My brother was brown, his eyes moonbeams within dark sockets, delighted and appalled simultaneously.

He said hi to Grace and sat down on the couch with us.

"Isn't there an Atlanta game on?" he said to us.

"Why Atwanta?" my father growled.

"What's the guy saying?" Leo turned to me, smiling.

"Atwanta," my father said.

"Atlanta," I said.

"I like their uniforms," Leo said.

"That's homowexual," my father said.

"That is kind of an effeminate reason," I said.

"This boy has nothing to prove," he said. "Turn the Atlanta game on."

My father flipped the channels searching for the Atlanta Braves game.

"Dad, you can just punch in the number of the station."

"I've tried that," he said slowly, trying to get everything right, "but it doesn't work."

"That's because you are an idiot," Leo said.

My father leaped off the couch to smite my brother, but fell back down. His face was red, veins bursting. His neck muscles pulsed and his eyes were drained. Grace and my mother were buried in the kitchen and didn't know a thing. Leo and I looked at him as he smoldered. We glanced at the TV and the game and then back at him. He slumped over the couch, breathing heavily. Some color came back to his face and he handed the remote control to my brother. Leo took us right to the Atlanta game.

"This is their year," he said about the Braves. "It will all come together."

"They tend to freeze in the playoffs, yes?"

"This is their yoke to wear."

"You still going with Amber ? . . . Amber," I said, "what a name. Makes me think of a porn star."

He laughed. "You could say she is, in a way, but I am not dating her for intellectual stimulation."

My father laughed.

"Yeah, I guess not."

Grace stuck her head out from the kitchen and said, "You men are pigs."

"You heard all that?" I said.

My mother said, "Yes."

Leo asked them for a soda.

Mom gave Grace a soda and she brought it to Leo wearing a sardonic smile that said, In your parents' apartment I am forced to serve you but I think you are disgusting. "Damn, Grace," he said, comprehending the look, "that's cold." She said, "That's right." I said, "Huh oh, my goose is cooked." She said, "That's right." Leo said, "Oh, shit." And my father said, "Werks." There was drool under the fat of his chin and his face was red with embarrassment.

Grace went back into the kitchen and we watched Greg Maddux give up a home run.

Leo turned from the game and started flipping around the channels. He stopped on a station where two women and a man were meditating under a bright ocean light, the man describing the steps necessary to reach enlightenment. I pictured Grace and Orlando away at a meditation retreat sneaking off into the woods to fuck. I pictured his lips against hers. Did she touch him in the same way she touched me? How come I hadn't figured it out? How come I didn't smell it? How come I didn't see it in her eyes? How did Grace pull off what I so desired? Perhaps she was the mover and I was the thinker?

Leo said, "How do they do that? Sit there so still. I could never do it. I'd be bored out of my mind."

"Grace meditates every morning," I said. "She sits there in the livingroom and nothing bothers her. It's quite remarkable."

"She doesn't have a master's degree in Buddhism for nothing," Leo said. "You know," he continued, "I've been thinking of some spiritual quest myself."

"You, Leo? You'd need some chicks along for the ride."

"You're probably right," he admitted, "but I'm still serious."

"Like what?"

"You know, a more peaceful way of life."

I coughed and Leo said, "Cut that shit out."

Dad laughed, and Grace laughed too, nervously.

"Lunch," my mother called.

Grace, Leo, and I filed to the table. My father stayed on the couch and turned the channel to continue watching the Yankee game.

"Fire, tell me about this scholarship to Africa." my mother asked. "Isn't it great?" she said to Grace.

"Mom," Leo said, "later."

"I just can't believe you got a master's degree from Columbia University and now got a scholarship to do research in Africa. It's so uplifting."

Leo said, "Boring."

Mom said to us, "Eat slow. You eat too fast. It's not good for you. Eat slow."

We said, "Leave us alone."

"How long will you be gone?" my mother asked me.

"About three months," I said.

"And what is it exactly that you are going to be doing?" she asked.

"Setting up a forestry program at the university."

"Tell me again, what is forestry?"

"Jesus, Mom."

"I don't know what forestry is, so what."

"I've explained it before. It is the business of trees. But my approach is the business and conservation of trees at the same time. They were once mutually exclusive, but now they can't afford to be. Natural resource management really."

"Leo, are you still seeing Stephanie?" Mom asked.

"That's Amber, Mom."

"Oh, what happened to Stephanie?"

"Didn't live up to the king's standards," I said.

"Did you have a fight with her?" my mother asked.

"No, Mom, we just saw things differently."

"Like Grace and me," I said.

"Like you two numbskulls, which is why I stay single. I mean look at you, enemies already, just like Mom and Dad."

"Well, at least we are the only hope for carrying the blood of this family on. Unless of course you have some illegitimate children hidden somewhere?"

"I might."

"Leo, that's not funny," my mother said.

"You know the guy almost died before," Leo said.

"What are you talking about?" Mom asked.

"Just before. Fire and I got Dad mad and he choked up with rage and almost died."

"You guys should be careful. He's just had a stroke."

"Still crazy as ever," Leo said.

"Can't take the character away from the man," Grace said.

I said, "Grace is pregnant."

"Fire, why are you telling them now? It's a jinx."

"They are family, that's why."

"I hope you don't screw this up."

My mother got up and hugged Grace.

"This is such divine news. I am going to be a grandmother."

Leo said, "Damn, Fire, you are such a blabbermouth."

I had told him yesterday, but told him to not tell Mom and Dad.

"I know, but I couldn't help it."

"I'm so excited," Mom said.

"Murray, did you hear?" my mother screamed at him.

"Grace is pregnant."

"That's great."

My father had always been so skinny, like me, but now, despite his recent affliction, he finally showed some blubber, the natural blubber of aging American flesh.

"How long, Grace?" my mother asked.

"We don't know exactly, we haven't gone to the doctor yet."

"Do you need me to come?"

"Thanks, Pearl, but I will be fine. Fire will come too."

"You better, Fire," she said.

"I am."

"Grace, you can call me at anytime. Remember I took you to Dr. Trachtenberg—I was so sure he was a cousin—when he took your wisdom teeth out."

"I know Pearl, you saved me from that butcher."

"He was kind of savage, wasn't he?"

"I thought he was going to kill me," Grace said, "there was blood all over me."

"I told him that he was being too rough."

"You did," Grace laughed. "You did tell him. She said, 'Dr. Trachtenberg, this is my daughter in law, please be gentle'."

"Who's winning?" Leo called out to my father, but he had fallen asleep. Leo got up and looked at the score. "Seems as if Baltimore is coming back, it's 6 to 5."

"Excellent," I said.

"Fire," Leo said, "you're going to be a dad. And I'm going to be an uncle. It's perfect."

"I know, can you believe it? The generations accumulating."

"It's awesome," he said.

My mother was in tears.

"Jesus, Mom," we said.

"It's so beautiful. I can't help it."

"Grace and Fire bringing a little Buddhist Jew into the world," Leo said.

My mother said to Grace, "Please raise him Jewish first."

"That's your son's job."

"Jesus Christ, Mom. This is the modern world. There is no more religion, except for the dummies."

"Those dummies are in power," Dad said from the couch, now up.

"Evil dummies," Leo said.

"But Mom, lay off the Jewish stuff. It's our kid."

"Don't forget that you are Jewish. This is your heritage."

"Yes," Dad said. "It sounds stupid to you, but it's weaningwul to us."

"Weaningwul," Leo said.

"I'm not saying it's not meaningful. I'm saying we have to figure it out. It's not that easy."

The sun was a disc of orange hanging over the New Jersey cliffs.

"Why Pearl?" Grace asked. "Why is it so important?"

"Well . . . " and she petered off. "I don't know really. I guess it's because I'm Jewish and so is Murray, and my kids are Jewish. I would be confused without it. But beyond that I'm not sure."

"The only meaning to it," I said, "is identification. Reference. Familiarity."

"And brains," my father said from the couch, his arm limp and his chin dropped. "A dwop of Jew blood is both chawm and doom, and they are both essential."

"Dad," Leo said, "that's profound . . . Did you hear that?" he said to us, "the dead guy over there said something truly smart."

Reading Coming of Age in Samoa was eye opening for me. Most of my academic reading was about soil, trees, and environmental economics, but I got a chance my last semester to take an elective called the Sex Lives of Other Cultures. It was a tour of the world's various mores, and it became quite clear, as the class progressed, that our way of being, monogamy, was a choice among many. I liked knowing this. It was an idea of freedom. In the Ivory Coast they gave babies chilipepper enemas. In New Guinea little boys sucked off grown men. So why was it so hard to have modest polygamy here in America, the land of reckless pursuit? It didn't make sense.

Anyway, tonight, Jane, Grace, and I were going to make a video of each other, each one of us doing a dance, and with a bit of luck sexy too. Last time we were together Grace had wrapped herself up in colorful cloths and slowly, to French cabaret music, disrobed one by one. Jane and I had been mesmerized. Grace turned into an angel when she danced. Her naked dance under the acacia tree. She floated just above the ground and as each robe came off the light from her body got brighter. After the dance, we attacked her and started kissing her and pawing her, hopeful, but she resisted. Now was a different moment in time altogether! I knew Grace was willing to do just about anything for me, veiled in guilt as she was, wanting to make me happy and whole again.

The three of us sat in the livingroom, Grace and Jane on the white couch, with Felix on Jane's lap, fast asleep. I sat on the rug and looked up at them. Molly lay next to me. The sounds of the neighborhood were sporadic, a screeching car, a screaming Dominican. It was considerably less than Amsterdam Avenue, but still not the kind of quiet that I dreamed of. I could see the dotted lights of the houses on the hills on the other side of the valley in Riverdale. I held a bong and took a hit of pot. When I was done, sucking back the smoke into my lungs and blood and then blowing it out into the Bronx air, I handed it to Jane.

She said, "How do you do this?"

"Put your finger over that little hole in the back and then fire up."

"It's been since college that I did a bong," she said.

"It's a college thing, yes, but I like the high."

"It's so decadent," Grace said.

"A bong is ancient."

"Doesn't make it less decadent."

Jane took a hit, her eyes bulged, and she sat back winded.

"Wow, that was like a nuclear bomb. Oh my goodness."

"You went quite red."

Grace said, "Give me a small hit."

Jane handed the bong to Grace. She took a hit, closing her left eye and expertly taking in a wee bit of smoke. She held it for a second and let it out.

"That was nice," she said.

We talked about Jane's job, about my going to Africa, about Grace's promotion and the extra worked expected of her now. We confessed to Jane about Grace's pregnancy. Jane moved over on the couch and gave Grace a big hug. Grace started to cry. I joined them for the hug, our faces squished together. I started kissing Grace, just lips at first, but then tongue, getting carried away. Jane stuck out her tongue and joined ours. I pulled back and let Jane and Grace kiss. The wetness of their lips sparkled.

"Well," I said, "how about a dance."

"Who goes first?" Grace asked.

"I'll go," I said.

Jane giggled, her pale skin shining and her face mottled red with excitement.

I got out my old park ranger outfit, which I wore one summer during college, rangering under the sandy dry sky of New Mexico. I put on the green pants and gray shirt. I put on my Sam Browne belt and attached handcuffs. I put on my Smokey hat and fit the badge they let me keep as a talisman into the slot on my shirt breast. I put on my black shoes. I went back into the livingroom and put The Clash's I Broke the Law on. Grace and Jane sat back on the couch, smiles on their faces, cats on their laps. I turned on the music and began to twist and twirl my body, at my hips, slowly turning round and round. I looked at them, flirty glances. I took my hat off and frisbeed it onto the girl's laps. They laughed and Felix looked up at me annoyed. I swung my arms from side to side and pointed at Grace and Jane, wiggling my fingers in time to the music. I turned my back to them and put out my ass. "I broke the law, but the law won." I took off my shoes, bending down awkwardly, almost falling. I shimmed out of my green pants, kicking them out when they were on the last ankle, turning around and flinging them at Grace and Jane. Then my shirt, which I swung around my head. I sang, "I broke the law, but the law won." I took off my socks and moved towards the couch, still singing along with the song, and gave a sock to Jane and one to Grace. The skinny underwear I had chosen made my penis bulge like a big snail. "Look at him," Jane shouted, "oh my god he's so aroused." "I can see," Grace said. "Looks like we have a horny man on our hands." "Whatever can we do?" Jane said. I turned my ass towards them and started to take the underwear down, over my hairy ass and fleshy balls. "Off! Off! Off!" the girls shouted. "Let's see that unit." I bent my knees and wiggled my arms down to take off my underwear, over one foot and then the other. "Who wants the Park Ranger's underwear?" I shouted. They leaped up and tackled me, with the song just perfectly ending. They tickled me in the ribs and under my arms. I twisted in glee. Grace put her hand on my penis and said, "Now that's a hard number to follow." "He was great," Jane said. Grace took Jane's hand and put it on my penis. "Feel that thing." They began to rub it. They both looked beatific, gazing down at me with love. I said, "Why don't you girls kiss?" Grace said, "You don't tell us what to do, pornman." Jane followed up, "Yes, we run the show." Which made me lay back, my mind sandy and stippled, and moist, the seams of thought and desire stitched for eternity. I heaved, nearly crazy. I blinked my eye open to look at Grace and thought, is this too much to ask? Is she going to resent this later? But I was owed this. Orlando, who had stolen my wife, and Grace's lamentations. Was I breaking some universal moral line? I knew the answer. It was stated plainly in my anthropology textbooks. Anything was possible, probable, likely, and known. I wanted them to suck me off. Jane's mouth and then Grace's. I wanted them to moan. As Grace moaned for Orlando, as I moaned for lost things. Grace said, "Trouble, Houston." Jane said, "Throw him a life preserver." Grace got on her knees and began sucking my dick. I tried to will Jane to do the same. I pushed her lower back with my hand to coax the position, but she didn't budge. Grace licked away, dutifully, but I had lost it. I sat up, as soft as a jellyfish, and said, "I got ahead of myself."

"You sure did," Grace said.

"I'm such a fuck up," I wailed.

"No, you just get too worked up."

"I've been waiting for this for how many years and I can't get it up when it finally happens. I'm a total loser."

"You sure are, boy," Jane said. "Mr. Nature. Mr. Relaxed. Mr. Sex God can't get it up."

"It is a poor showing," Grace said.

"I know. I'm ashamed."

"You should be," Jane continued. "Oh my goodness I was ready for anything. I was ready to go all the way, and you went flaccid on us."

I sighed, coughed, and said, "You guys could continue without me."

"No, we can't, you horny porno slime ball."

Jane was in white panties and a maroon t-shirt. Her legs were thin, as thin as a teenager's, but her ass was an adult's, rounded and heavy.

Her stringy hair was pasted on her forehead and her smile hinted at great depths of eroticism.

"You want to see girlie action, don't you? You want the girls to get it on for your pleasure," she said.

"Absolutely," I said.

"Well, Grace, do we give him a show?"

Grace looked down at me, so pathetic on the floor.

"No, let's let him learn from his agony."

Jane looked at Grace in fleeting worry, boundaries crossed without perhaps full permission, then looked down at me and said, "The gig's up for tonight."

She helped me up.

"But, really, you should be ashamed."

I went to the bathroom and sat down on the seat and looked at my spittle wet penis, small and defeated. My swollen semen was blocking the exit route of the pee and so it hurt like hell when it finally pushed out. I wish I could go to the bathroom once without some pain! I read about Frank Robinson. Great ballplayer. 586 homeruns. Damn! The pee. Ahh. I went back to Grace and Jane, who were in the kitchen boiling water for tea.

"Guys, it's so fantastic that you're pregnant," Jane said.

"I know," I said, "it's mind boggling."

Grace smiled into the teapot.

"But Fire," Jane said, "you can't go away now, not now with Grace pregnant."

"I have to," I said. "It's all worked out and it's vital for my career."

"Career schmeer," Jane said. "Time to get rid of the goals and become a family man."

"What? I have to give up my career to start a family? That's absurd."

"No," Jane said, "you don't have to give up your Mr. Nature career, you just have to adapt it to the fact that your wife is pregnant and you are going to have a baby."

"Well, maybe, but not now. This is very important. Jesus Christ," I said, "you nag me like a wife."

"That's because I am your second wife," she giggled.

"Yes," Grace said, "and you need two wives to henpeck you into obedience."

"That's right you egomaniac, you need two wives, and second wife is going to beat you into sense."

"Oh my god," I said, "the true face of polygamy reveals itself."

"The affair's over here, bub," Jane said. "Second wife has arrived."

Grace cracked up.

"Look at him. He's red with fear," she said.

"Serves him right. Couldn't even keep a hard on."

"Pathetic," I said.

"So," Jane said again. "I am serious. You have to cancel Africa."

"No! I am going to Africa!"

I stormed past them through the junk room and out the back door into the garden. There was the impressively tall red oak, its frame taking up most of the sun. I had planted spicebush, which I had stolen from Van Cortlandt Park, from the marshy woods by the pond. I had planted dogwood and viburnum, cotoneaster and euyonmous. I planted holly too. It was a happenstance garden, but I loved it, loved the soft buds and the growing limbs. The lights from the backyards of the houses of the neighborhood were patchwork and seen through stunted junipers and mugwort and rusty fences and cement walls. God damn, I thought, I can't believe that I might have to give up Africa. I won't do it. I will be back before she gives birth, but this is everything I've been planning for, all converging now. I fingered the stem of the dogwood. I touched the soil with my finger and it felt a little dry. I would need to water tomorrow. I liked to wake up first thing, before breakfast, before the neighborhood was out on a Sunday morning and water the plants. I thought, If I didn't do it now there would unlikely be another chance. I would talk to my advisor and see if only staying for two months would be appropriate. I looked up at the burgeoning moon. Figure Grace was at most two months pregnant, probably less. It was September and I was leaving in early January. October, November, December, January, February, March. She might be giving birth in mid March and I could be back just before that.

I went back in and found them sipping tea in the kitchen.

"Are you returned from the mad?" Grace asked.

"Yes. This is what I have thought. I will shorten the trip to two months, if I can, be back a month earlier. You're due perhaps in mid to late March and I will be back the first of March. See, perfect."

"That's cutting it kind of close. Don't be an absent father. I can't afford it. I've got my career and pursuits too. This marriage thing we have will soon turn into a babysitting team and so you've got to live up to your end."

"That's right, bub, don't flake out on us," Jane said.

"Who asked for your opinion?"

"Second wife," she reminded me.

PART 3

7. Babe

LATELY, THE BEER cans had come raining down into my garden from the roof of the decrepit and filthy apartment complex that we sat next to. It was driving me insane! The sun was climbing over the branches of the red oak and the apartments on Cannon Place. The sparrows sang from my neighbor's yew tree. I was out in the garden on this Sunday summer morning, the air restful and the noises in the West Bronx momentarily muted. There were 20 or so bottles strewn between the meshed juniper and mixed in with the pale mulch. I looked up at the rooftop and screamed, "You fucking pigs!"

I went into the apartment, into the kitchen to get a garbage bag. Felix and Molly were lying down on the linoleum floor. Molly had been moving slowly lately and this worried Grace and me. She was a lively cat and this lethargy was out of the ordinary. The Vet said give it time, but I worried about her death; my father's stroke was a glimpse into nearby darkness. However, Felix, still in his prime, fat, unmodest, elemental, all white except for a black spot on his forehead and black paws, got up off the floor and followed me. I stopped in the junk room for weeding gloves and we crossed the patio to the steps that led into the garden. Felix went first, lumbering down and entering a tangled sea of purple green leaves up to his chest. He felt for the wind on his ears. His legs lost in the root mass Felix moved to the edge of the fence where the only slice of direct sunlight was available. He settled down, circling his spot until he was uncompromisingly comfortable.

I started picking up the bottles, amazed at how many there were. Twenty-one beer bottles tossed from the roof and landed with a thud in my soil; each bottled bore the handprints of its uncivilized holder. I weeded Norway maple seedlings and cut back the ivy that was keeping my blue rug juniper from growing out. I spread mulch on the barer spots, combing it out evenly across the soil, setting the ground with an orange brown glow.

I grabbed the bag full of beer bottles, the glass clinking, and went inside. I settled it down next to our garbage. I seethed from this affront, which made me desperate to leave New York City!

Molly lay still on the kitchen floor. I picked her up and kissed her sunken cheeks. She had suckled at Grace's nipples when our son Augie, now four years old, was breastfeeding. Grace said it tickled and Augie liked her by his side, sucking at the same time. I carried her into the bathroom, holding her gently she was so sick, sat down on the toilet seat, and then let her down.

I farted, staring at the Baseball Abstract. Then, surprisingly, because I never shit in the morning, my bowels so tied up after another poor night of sleep, I felt a turd on the way down, eeehhhhhh. I opened the book to Joe Morgan, the great second baseman of the Reds. I pushed at my bowels, hoping for more, but nothing moved. I was suffering, my doctor said, from "incomplete evacuation"; after each shit instead of feeling relieved I felt still heavy and swollen. Just my luck, my own body harassing me. I looked at Jimmie Foxx. Man, the guy was so good, his numbers shining in the sands of time. I pushed once more then gave up. I went to the livingroom to see Augie.

"Love boy," I said to him.

He was watching a video while jumping on the couch. He had straight blond hair, from neither his mother nor father, and he was popping with energy. He was a light unto himself in beauty.

"Good movie?" I asked.

"Yeah, yeah, yeah," he said. "You've seen the pig."

"The pig is great."

I looked to see if it was Babe 1 or Babe 2. We had watched each one about 15 times. It was Babe 1, the scene where Babe is being lectured by Rex after getting lured into the crazy plot of the duck's to steal farmer Hoggett's alarm clock.

"Rex is so serious," I said.

"Dad, where is Babe's mother and father?"

"Well." I looked at him, his body a pogo stick. "They are dead."

"Why?"

"Well, they, you remember, they were taken away on that truck. In the beginning of the movie."

"How come?"

He kept jumping up and down.

"Because . . . we like to eat pigs."

"Why?"

"Don't you like bacon?"

"Yes. Bacon, eggs, toast, and a milk shake."

"Bacon comes from the pig."

"Babe?"

"Not Babe, but Babe's parents. Remember, the farmer won Babe at the fair. Babe is a lucky pig."

"Why?"

"Because he didn't get the fate of his parents."

"What did you say?"

"Babe wasn't killed so he could become our food."

"He almost did, remember, when the farmer's wife wanted to eat him for Christmas. When the farmer was going to shoot him."

"That's right, and what happened?"

"It was not Babe who did bad."

"Yes, exactly, he's a lucky pig, and a smart pig too."

"Why?"

"He keeps escaping death."

"Why?"

"You are driving me crazy!"

I heard Grace grunt in her sleep, eight months pregnant with our second child. The relationship was shaky and we both felt disappointed in each other. Despite a second wife there were no special privileges except some random groping. Therefore I looked maniacally down the backside of a woman's pants or through the creases in her shirt.

"Dad," Augie said, "what are you doing?"

He was still jumping, from one couch pillow to another.

"Just thinking."

"Look Fergie."

"Fergie the crazy duck."

"I like Fergie."

All Grace's hostility, all our wounds. Mombassa, the point at which my true nature was revealed. She reminded me, "Let's not forget Mombassa." When she said this I pictured the blue sky, the yellow wind, and the bleached houses.

I turned to Babe, who was now seriously curious about what was going on outside the gate of the farmhouse, where the farmer and his dogs, Fly and Rex, his surrogate mother and father, went each morning.

Saul's daughter Michal was betrothed to the slayer of tens of thousands, the great poet and harp player. Michal loved him so deeply. She loved him enough to hide him from her angry father. But David eventually turned away to do his things, to fulfill his destiny. They were knit together, but pulled apart too. She came to detest him. She said, "How glorious was the King who uncovered himself in the eyes of the handmaids." David, in his defense, was dancing for God.

I heard Grace grunt again, as if she were rising.

"Bye, Augie."

"Bye, dad."

I went back to the garden. Felix was lying half asleep. He opened his eyes when I padded through the ivy and closed them back down when he saw that it was just me. I settled down next to him. I let the sun shine on my face and closed my eyes too.

I heard the screeching brakes of the subway down in the Broadway valley. I heard the sparrows and the crows.

In three months I was leaving for the International Justice Conference in Amsterdam, going for my second year. I had met Bruno, a dentist from Milan, and he, on the last day of my trip, revealed the pornographic beauty of Amsterdam. I longed for this year's rendezvous. After the conference I was going for two weeks to my research site in Kenya. We were planting our first trees on Nairobi's streets. This was my Ph.D. work, a brainstorm I had one long pot driven night, that my work should be in the city, where the masses huddled in landscapes hard and sharp. My dissertation, over time, became the growing and planting of trees for Nairobi's streets, to give it some clean air and shade. In addition, an anthropology student named Willie who was looking into ancient crop rotations was joining me. I was interviewing her next week.

"Fire."

Felix leaped up, ran through the ivy back up the stairs and into the apartment.

"You scared my cat. And me. Jesus, Fergal, give us a warning."

"You're too skittish."

"Perhaps. What's up?"

I sat up against the fence.

"Going to church."

"You? You've got to be kidding?" I said.

"I know, but it's a ritual."

"Are you a believer?"

"No, Fire, no. But at the same time I want to be. I don't want to make the spirits angry."

"Why?"

"I don't need the hassle."

"What kind of hassle could the spirits give you?"

"Let's say I'm hedging my bets, paying respect."

He was dressed in a green polo shirt and beige khakis. He was clean shaven, which for Fergal was a quick glide over his barely visible blond beard, and had combed his hair neatly to the side.

"You look like a goofy kid," I said.

"Watch out me boy." And he gave me a devious smile. "Fire, I don't want to rock the boat."

"That's the problem with Americans, they don't want to rock the boat so the water stays still and gets fetid."

"Fire, you with this again. This is the greatest country in the world. A man can come here, work hard, and become well off. Like me. Don't knock that, you snob. You have no idea how free it is here."

"Yes, and no," I said. I stood up. "It's free, but within very strict bounds. You talk too much out of line and you feel the pressure. It's subtle. No government man is visiting your home, unless you're unlucky enough to be a black man, but you just don't want to be looked at funny by your neighbor." I pointed to the apartment complex across the way. "No one wants the fear of judgment, or to have to go through the worry of losing your job, not having enough money to feed yourself, let alone not being able to buy a nice meal. Who needs the worry? So you start to conform, make yourself accept things the way they are, with all its stupid anxiety and moneymaking."

I felt presidential.

"Loudmouths like you get it wrong all the time." Fergal said. "The sons and daughters of the spoiled, completely out of touch with the workingman's vision, which, since you obviously don't know, is hard work, independence, rational thinking, and prosperity. All four of these things are fostered here in America and only fools like you complain."

"Rational thinking, my ass. You keep voting for folks diametrically opposed to you. They use your tax money to wipe their asses. No, it's all a lie."

"So, why aren't you out in the streets with the revolution, huh?"

"The simple fact of the matter is . . . The fact of the matter is that my life is too comfortable and I don't want to risk it."

"Ah ha!"

"Yes. Yes . . . So, then, while you are at it, pray for me too."

"Fire, I will . . . Got to go."

"Wait. I have to tell you about last night."

"What?"

"Roberta nearly started a fire last night and I had to go down and rescue her."

"I don't trust that Roberta," he said. "She's a loose cannon. I think I will have to kick her out."

"That's up to you. Anyway, I smell the smoke and go down there to check on them, but no one answers my knocks on the door. I checked the handle and the lock is open and I go in. The place is in a fog of smoke, burnt smoke."

Fergal was shaking his head from side to side.

"I checked on the kid first, but she was fine, on the other side of the apartment behind a closed door. I opened the windows to let the air in. Roberta was fast asleep on the couch, nearly naked."

"What was she wearing?"

"A floppy tank top. Those are nice breasts."

"They are very nice."

"I smacked her in the face, to wake her, but she didn't respond."

"What was she wearing on the bottom?"

"Ah ha. A thong."

"Are you fucking with me?"

"No, Fergal, this is the truth."

"He never speaks the truth," Grace said.

She had stepped out on the patio. She was wearing a nearly see through nightgown, her big round belly pushing up at the sky, the thick trail of hair that connected her pubis and navel like a covered vine behind the fabric, her breasts swollen too.

"He's an untrustworthy type," Fergal said.

"More than you know," Grace said. "Is he telling you one of his girl exploits? You know the girls love Fire."

"Grace, Fire here is a homebody. He's no lady killer."

"I was telling him about Roberta last night," I said.

"He's our hero," she said.

"Hey," Fergal said, "give him some credit. He probably saved my house."

"He tell you she was in her panties?"

"He told me she was in a thong," Fergal said.

"Which is it Fire?" Grace said.

"Panties, thong, same thing. They both barely cover the ass."

"Got to go," Fergal said.

Augie came running out to the patio. He grabbed Grace by the leg and said, "Hi Fergal, what are you doing?"

"Going to church."

"What's that?"

"Ask your parents."

"Bye Fergal," he said.

"Pray for both of us," I said.

We went back into the apartment and into the kitchen.

"Pray for you why?"

Molly was prone, lying off to the side, her eyes on us but her body inverting.

"I'm worried about her," Grace said.

"I am too."

"So why is Fergal praying for your soul?"

"Oh, you know, standard stuff."

"Like what? Tell me?"

"You know, coveting, sloth, greed, avarice, etc."

"Be more specific?"

"What's this the Inquisition?"

"No, I just want to know what's on my husband's mind."

"Many things, like always, like you too."

I felt myself get a little hot, my eyes feeling swollen.

"Yes, but you know what I'm thinking because I tell you. You don't tell me things, I must say. You are too busy scheming."

"Maybe I don't want to burden you with my complaints."

"You always say something like that."

"But it's true."

"No, it's not . . . So what are your sins?"

"I want sex all the time."

"Tell me something new."

"I mean I worry about myself."

"Are you having an affair?"

"No. Unlike you, I remind you. Orlando."

"Thanks for bringing it up."

"It's my trump card. I think of you and Jane all the time."

"Well, you blew it last time."

"I want another chance. I want crazy wild sex with both of you."

"Take a look at my stomach, sex is not foremost on my mind. So, tell me, what're your real sins?"

I looked her in the eyes. I said, "I'm never satisfied. I'm always looking for new things. I lose interest. I wish I could stand still."

"Where does this come from?"

"A nice combination of Mom and Dad, spoiled and entitled."

"And your hot genes too."

She came to me, hugged, opened her mouth over mine, let her happiness be known.

"If you could keep your mind focused on me you'd get lots of sweet treats."

"I know this, but can't do it anyway. Is that dysfunctional?"

"It's just you. But with a little bit of discipline you might find that all you want is right here."

I went to get dressed, gathered up Augie, and we went out.

We hiked around in Van Cortlandt Park, whacking through the shrubs, running down hills, and climbing the rocks. We went down to the horse stables where Augie had me lift him up while he nervously petted a horse's nose. Out into the open grassland, teaming with joggers and soccer players. Augie picked up acorns and pinecones. We walked south out of the park past the ballfields and under some great pin oaks onto and up Van Cortlandt Park South to Lilly's party. Augie and Lilly hugged when we arrived. He proceeded to get high on hot dogs, cake, and candy, running around like a madman with the other kids. When the party was over, he and I went to the playground, slithering around the play equipment, down the slides, general mayhem. We stopped and had a pizza slice and walked under the elevated train, Augie stopping to inspect the weeds in the sidewalk cracks, the broken bottle near the fence of the MTA yards, the dead butterfly on the cement. We walked south on Broadway to 238th street to pick up Jane.

Augie loved Jane as much as I did. He was silenced with stimulation in her presence. Her body was lithe, flat, pale, smooth, her teeth purple.

"Daddy," Augie said, "it's Jane."

She saw me, waved, came to us. She gave Augie a hug and kiss and he blushed. She drew close to me and put her lips to mine. We walked past the shops, over the Expressway, up the hill, through the spot heavy with dog shit, past the sickly locust trees under which boys smoked, by Fergal's beat up white van, through the front door, up the steps past the faded painting of JFK, and into our apartment.

"Mommy, Jane is here," Augie called out.

"Hi, everyone," she said.

Grace and Jane hugged.

"Grace, that stomach of yours is so big and sensual."

"It's a big thing."

"It's so sexy," Jane said.

"Don't start," Grace said.

Augie touched Grace's stomach.

"It's my brother or sister."

Jane said, "What do you think, Augie, boy or girl?"

He thought. "A girl. I have to tell you something. I think it's going to be a girl."

"Me and Augie want a girl," I said.

"I'll take one too," Grace said.

Jane and I played with Augie, wrestling, cards. Felix came waddling past us in the livingroom and Augie, as usual, attacked him with excitement, and Felix fled. We ate dinner, ate cupcakes, and then danced around to loud music, danced into a trance like hora that Augie loved and he let go with easy abandon. We bathed him, his gleaming body coruscating, and Grace got into bed with him to read.

I went into the livingroom. Jane was standing by the window looking out into valley that was dotted with bright yellow lights. I hugged her from behind, turned her head, and started kissing her. I pushed my crotch into her ass. She responded by purring a bit, letting out a confined moan. I engulfed her mouth, but she said, "Oh my god, no, remember, lips, gentle, go slow, seduce." "Yes." Our lips glided over each other's. We were so horny and we wanted Grace to catch the spirit and join us, be overtaken by desire.

I heard Grace stand up heavily, grunting, our second child grown big in her belly. I heard her say "Goodnight Augie." I heard her leave the room and come into the livingroom. There was a wet silence, and she screamed. Augie screamed from his room, and Grace called to him, "Don't worry, honey, go to sleep."

She turned to us and said, "What are you doing?"

"We're just having fun," I said.

I turned out from Jane and let her go. She stepped away from me.

"Fun? What you're doing is not fun."

"What're you talking about?"

"It's cheating on your wife in front of her eyes."

"Like we didn't have a threesome?"

"Fire, that was consensual and many years ago. This is coercion and betrayal."

"No, it's not! It's about having some fun and not letting convention get in the way. Lighten up."

"You lighten up. I don't allow for you to be with other women, I don't want an open relationship, so if you do it it's an infidelity, not fun."

Jane had gathered her backpack. "I'm going home," she said.

"We'll work this out," I said.

"No, Fire, it's best I go."

"Let her go, it's best."

"This is our second wife."

"This is about you and me."

"I am going."

She put her pack on her shoulder and opened the door.

"I'll walk you to the subway then."

We left the apartment and walked down the stairs and onto the street. There was an ambulance siren crying down in the Broadway valley.

"Oh my goodness, Fire," Jane turned to me, "I thought you said Grace wanted to have a threesome tonight."

"I thought she did," I said. "I had been fantasizing about it with her just last week, creating little fantasies about threesomes to get us horny. She said things like, 'it's so hot' and moaned and groaned to my narratives. I said to her, 'You know Jane is coming over next weekend,' and she said, 'I know,' kind of sexy like."

"You took that as evidence? You're such an idiot, Fire. That's not evidence."

"It had been building up. We all knew it. This morning instead of her standard boring white underpants she put on black panties. It was a sign."

"I feel so stupid. You're so stupid. How could you put me in this position? Grace will never forgive me! You said she wanted it."

"I thought she did, really. I felt like she was ready to give it a try again."

"Oh my god, Fire, she was just playing, giving you the pornography you men crave. She was role playing, knucklehead."

"Oh, come on, Jane, you wanted it just as much as I did."

"I really did," she smiled. "I would love making love to Grace, she's so soft . . . But Fire, you really tortured the truth on this one."

"I swear, it really seemed like this was the night. It felt right."

"Fire, Fire, oh my dear you are such a dreamer."

We walked past Bailey and over the Expressway, the cars zooming underneath like angry hornets.

"You're screwed," she said. "You guys have to be careful. This is bad for Augie to see. You know, there is a time when separating is the better thing to do."

"I think about it a lot, but I'm not ready. I can't get Augie's emotional devastation out of my head. Spending the rest of his life reacting to his parent's divorce."

"It doesn't have to be that way."

"I don't know what to do."

"Well, stop fighting in front of Augie."

"We mostly do."

"I finished my book on the trip up here," she said, changing the subject, "and was hoping to get a good book from Grace for the subway ride back. And now you've screwed that up for me too."

"How about the paper?"

"The paper. I hate the paper. I want to read a good book."

"You want to stop in the stationery store and see what books they have?"

"Romantic novels, jerkhead. I want to read Henry James or Alice Munro."

We made it to the staircase to the subway.

"Well," I said, "short night."

"It sure is. Two long subway trips to see a marriage in ruins."

I moved in and grabbed her ass.

"See you."

I walked back home. When I got there my pillow and blankets were on the couch and the door to our bedroom was closed. All for the best, I thought, I wasn't in the mood to fight it out. I went into the kitchen and made myself a peanut butter and jelly sandwich. I made an egg cream. I called Adam, but he wasn't home. I left a message that said, "Things are as hard as ever. But Amsterdam awaits." I had told him about Bruno and he knew I was bristling with anticipation. I went to Augie's room to check on him, leaned down and kissed him. I went out to the livingroom and spread my sheets and blankets on the couch. I lay down. I flipped on the TV. A Yankee game. Fuck. I flipped the channels. I got a gas bubble in my left side, thick with peanut butter. I got up and retrieved my pot and bong. I thought of Amsterdam and the interview with Willie. Two lights at the end of the tunnel. I filled the bong with water and took my first hit. The sad, weary, exhausted habits of my life drifted away. I felt alighted. I thought of the next possible time a menage a trois might be realized. I thought of Amsterdam and what Bruno and I might do. I reeled from horniness. I turned the channels. I heard Fergal come in. I heard Roberta downstairs talking on the phone. I heard Grace stir. I flipped to the public stations to see if any sex shows were on, but none were. My porn, unfortunately, was in the bedroom and hence inaccessible. I flipped to the blue screen and looked up the Playboy channel. I typed in the right code on the clicker and the blue screen turned suddenly into two big tittied girls kissing. It was all melodrama, but those female tongues slithering around each other, gathering their senses, was too much, and I felt the rise in me. I turned off the TV and lay down flat on my stomach. I rubbed and flexed and twisted at my dick while thinking of Jane and Grace getting it on, building up the story in my head. And with the release of my semen my desire for sex left me completely, a silo being emptied. I sat up and wiped off, went to the bathroom to pee, realized my gas pain was gone, and that I was feeling invigorated too. Out I went.

I jogged down the hill, past the night houses of my neighbors, paralleling the quick traffic towards the Expressway and Broadway. I took a right, the night sky lucid, and under the tunnel with the mural of the blue herons, and into Van Cortlandt Park. No one was around, the stillness in the sky and the stealthy animals. I ran through the parking lot to the trail that went by the lake, its path dotted with locust trees and one leaning willow with a knotted trunk. I heard the cars off on the Expressway, but I was hidden to the human world by the vegetation. I zoomed past the drooping birches and over the ferns. I thought of divorcing Grace. Why put up with all her unhappiness and hostility? It was endless, more than a decade, and still she hated me, a repressive satisfaction. Hated me for being myself.

I jogged over the bridge to the marsh, past the muskrat den, through the heavy hanging vines that clamored for space on the branches of the trees. Up the old railroad tracks towards Yonkers, into a tunnel of woods squeezed between the two sides of the golf course. I heard all sorts of noises and smelled the thick taste of gingko. I saw a flicker of light in the distance. The light became clearer, a flashlight. I heard people talking. I slowed up. I thought of turning around. I heard a golf ball get hit. I started running again. I came closer to the light and I could see that it was five teenagers playing a night round of golf. They saw me and stopped their activity. They stared at me for a moment, and I looked at them, thinking we'd share a nocturnal solidarity. Instead, they gave chase. I jumped, landed, and headed back at fast speed, pushing at my leg muscles like a rabbit escaping a predator. I had a good lead, but I could feel them in full throttle behind me. I put it in overgear, racing past the shrubs, under the branches, over the roots, my feet catching the soil lightly as if flying. They shouted, "Motherfucker!" But I was unreachable. In the open, at the top of the marsh, the frogs making their rubbery sounds, and the moon shining on the treetops, I screamed back at them, "You can suck my hairy balls all of you! You Guiness loving losers! Stop fucking up the world with your stupidity!"

I ran out of the park and into the streets, amid people and cars, and lights, past the shops, and up the long steps and under the linden tree.

When I got home Grace was sitting on the couch crying. Molly lay inert on the rug in front of her.

"Fire, she fell. Our acrobatic Molly fell. She tried to jump up on the seat, but she couldn't make it and she fell. I heard it from the bedroom and came running out. There is nothing left of her."

I went to Molly and put my hand on her belly. Grace was right, there was nothing left of her, no meat, no heat, no connection. I buried my face in her thinness and let the pain of her loss fill me up until it hurt my gut and eyes, distending my heart. I kissed her nose but it was dry.

The next week, again a Sunday morning, again clearing beer bottles from my yard, a month before Grace was to give birth to Michelle, Molly was so sick that we went to the animal hospital and put her to death.

Later that same week I interviewed Willie. She had a round face, olive skin with faint freckles, discerning eyes. She kneaded her hands occasionally, her fingers interlaced. She was comprehensive as she told me about her studies and her goals. She was wearing a marriage ring. I didn't bother to ask her for references. Instead I asked her when she wanted to go to Kenya. She said right away. I said, "Really?" She said, "Really." "What about your husband?" "He's in medical school, otherwise preoccupied." I said, "I'm going in a few months actually." "I can join you," she said, "no problem." "Boy, that's great." "Exactly," she said.

8. Anthropology

I COUNTED DOWN EACH day as I neared the promised date.
Augie needed to be taken to nursery school, to visit his friends, and
to play in the park. He was high energy, like his dad, and Grace was exhausted by us. There was shopping to do, and Augie's soccer class, and
a doctor's appointment, and birthday parties, and nightmares to be
soothed, and dinners to be cooked, and baths to be given, and books
to be read. Either one of the kids might get sick. Grace was breastfeeding and wearied. Her tits sagged, her feet hurt, her throat was sore, and
her mind kept telling her that she had chosen the wrong straw in life.
Increasingly, as the days neared my exit from the scene, we treated each
other with hostility. We fought and sulked openly, during breakfast,
errands, and dinner. Augie insisted to be taken to his friends', each
moment planning his escape from the household combustibility. The
baby cried all the time. During the night when Grace had to wake up
to feed Michelle she looked over at me with enmity and lamentation.

To counteract all this I recruited my mother. She moved in the day
before I left. If this Rosewood experiment was going to continue it
needed some breathing space.

On the day of my departure Grace would not say goodbye. Augie
and I hugged and I cried because I knew I wouldn't see him for nearly a
month. I kissed the baby and kissed my mom's cheek even though she
had puckered her lips. I left them together, a wife who wanted to shake
the mother and scream, "You made a monster!"

On the Major Deegan Expressway with its deadly glows I felt sadness as I thought of Grace and the kids. We passed over the East River
with its acid fumes and I sunk even deeper into self doubt. I felt de-
ceitful, unable to control my indiscretions, unable to give myself completely to Grace. From the valley of tunnels and curved roads that

takes you out from the Triborough Bridge I came upon the flatness of Queens with its thousands of absent meadows and my family started to fade. We glided along the white tube within the curves of the low-lands until we reached the marshes of Idlewild airport. I began thinking of my days to come with Bruno, its prospective madness. And then to be in Africa again, working, nurturing our saplings to be planted in Nairobi's sidewalks and roadways. In anticipation of Willie's arrival I felt hot in the temples.

The plane taxied, leapt into motion, and took off into the heavens. I slept well, unbelievably. My dreams came and came, green colored dreams amplified and fierce. I opened my eyes to see the line of distant sunrise coming through the windows. At this first light I felt my gut shift, moving over to allow for this alternate universe. That light, 30,000 feet in the air, was the light of freedom. We inched downwards through the clouds like a snowdrop and into the morning sunlight over the wetlands spotted country to evaporate into the bosom of civilization.

I went to Bruno. His body was like a gorilla's, with tufts of black and white hair on his neck, huge manbreasts, big strong legs, and fine fingers. His smile was like a silver fish amid his beard. We hugged and I laughed. Bruno turned towards the windows of the prostitutes, bowed, and said, "Fire, my friend, you begin."

I scrutinized the long eyed girls in their glass boxes. My heart throbbed. Their nipples so pink. The roundness of their asses each one discrete. Their tongues waterfalls of desire. I felt sick. I grabbed my belly and held my warm hand to it. All these women shed of pretenses, and personality, naked in their wait. I was nauseous.

"Fire?"

Bruno came close to me.

The morning sun shined on the street, but the wind off the water was cold and I began to shiver.

"Are you alright?"

He wrapped his arms around my chest and lifted me up.

"I'm fine. I was just hit with a wave of . . . ice. A chill."

"A sense that you've gone too far?"

"Yes."

"It will go away."

Bruno let go of me and arched his eyes, blinked rapidly, and smiled.

"This is incredible," I said to him.

"Fire, wake up my friend. Wake up. Wake up?"

"Okay. Okay. Okay. I'm getting my shit together."

He turned to a window, pointed at the prostitute, and said, "She looks happy. I like big, you know that Fire. The bigger they are the better. You," he pointed at me, "are too skinny."

The prostitute must have weighed 300 pounds with breasts like spilled mountains down to her ankles.

Bruno said, "The luxury."

I said, "Have fun, my friend."

I turned down the block. The possibilities were overwhelming. My suitcase bumped into the side of my knee, bruising it. The morning sun was cold on my neck and my hands were frozen. The sidewalk was land mined in dog shit and I wondered why such enlightened people didn't have a pooper scooper law. I thought of Grace in the doggy position. In spite of our problems I found her irresistible. I looked at each prostitute and tried to apprehend her feelings. I wanted intimacy. I dreamed of a giantess, like Bruno's, but none were available that I saw. I was curious about a black girl too, but I felt fairly certain that Josephine, the sister of James, my research assistant, and I were going to have sex after many years of flirtation. She was size of a silverback and just what Bruno would crave. I looked up at the girls sitting in their glass enclosures. Each one of them was available to me and I chose . . . randomly, too overwrought to be decisive.

Up the stairs I went to be greeted by a skinny pretty woman. She was wearing just her bra and a schoolgirl's black and white checkered skirt.

I smiled, but felt dry in the throat. I coughed.

"Come in. Please sit here," she said.

She pointed at a gray quilted chair whose cushion was flattened by time and use. I sat down and she closed the curtain over the window that had exposed her to the world.

"America?" She asked.

She had a crown of thorns tattooed over her bellybutton.

"America."

"So, you here for good time?"

"I'm here for the Justice Conference."

"A politician?"

"A scientist. No, more like a natural resource manager."

"A scientist for what?"

"Trees."

"Trees?"

"Trees."

"What do you do for trees?"

"I study them. I am trying to figure out what trees to grow for the streets of Nairobi."

She looked at me blankly and said, "Okay, what you want?"

"What do you mean?"

"Like blowjob or fuck?"

"Oh . . . I see."

She glowed in the red light, the black cotton of her garments next to her white skin, her eyes young and her face strong despite a residue of acne. Her lips were smeared in lipstick. She took down her skirt and revealed pink panties that were tightly framed on her nearly concave ass as if she was a teenager. The room smelled musty, but not pungent. She moved into me, her crotch at my nose.

"You like this?"

It smelled like Chinese food.

She leaned into me and pulled her bra down over her tits and said, "You like this?"

They were small and smooth ivory triangles with buttons.

"Yes."

She turned around and stuck her ass in my face. "You really like this?"

It smelled like sweat and shit.

"You mean anal sex?" I said.

"Yes. Men like it there."

She fingered her asshole over her panties.

I grabbed her ass.

"Okay, now Mr. Scientist, we talk money for a moment."

I sat bolt upright.

"In the ass, how much?"

"200."

"Whoa," I said.

"Precious spot of a woman's body," she said.

"I'll take a blow job."

I counted out the strange currency and handed over what seemed like a lot of my money.

"Take your clothes off and lie on bed," she said.

I did, feeling a bit sick this instant away from my infidelity. My skin was pasty underneath my black body hair. My concave carriage was not that different than hers, although hers was more attractive. We both had bodies of teenagers, but I was 35. My penis hung nearly invisible in my thatch of pubic hair. I lay back on the bed. She took off her bra and underwear and the crown of thorns over her bellybutton heaved in and out. She climbed on the bed, pushing me back towards the headrest, spread my legs aside, and then lowered her mouth and attention onto my penis.

I looked down at the top of her head, her brown hair that was parted in the middle like Grace's, her scalp gray, and head bobbing. Her ass was in the air, and it was disturbingly skinny, as if she was sick. Grace's ass was fleshy and comforting. I loved her rippling cheeks and that her anus was hidden beneath folds of flesh that to get to it I had to feel my way. I grabbed the prostitute's hair in my hand and pulled it aside so I could see her face as she blew me. She stopped, looked up at me, and gave me a mean look. I let her hair go, leaned back, and closed my eyes. But no hard-on emerged; instead I felt myself ready to fart. I clenched my stomach muscles to hold it in, but a little came out anyway. I was a pig. She looked up at me and said, "Maybe you want to fuck? I give it to you for only 50 more."

"Okay," I said, "perhaps that will help."

We traded positions. She lay down on the bed and I got on top of her. This repositioning got me excited; I rubbed myself, got hard. She leaned over, grabbed a condom, and handed it to me. I got onto my haunches and entered her as she held her vagina apart. She was disturbingly unwet, just a trickle of moisture. This nearly finished off my barely measured excitement. I pumped hard to stay alive and keep myself going. She made half grunts. I imagined they were grunts of deep pleasure. I saw Grace as she was when I was inside her, shocked and overcome.

Done, she rolled off the bed and onto her feet. She put her bra and panties back on. I got off the bed too and began to get dressed. When I was done I handed her an extra 60.

"Thank you," I said.

"Have fun at the conference, Mr. Scientist. Maybe you come back?"

I came out into the sunshine and had to shield my eyes. I could see the water off in the distance. I couldn't wait to get to my hotel room, shower, and take a nap. I wanted to call Grace and see how things were. I hoped she wasn't angry. I went down the steps to Bruno who was waiting.

"How was your visit?" Bruno asked.

"Good, actually, good," I said. "I thought I was going to screw it up I was so nervous, but it turned out nice."

"You get sick," Bruno said. "Have you got something and you're not confessing to me?"

"I'm fine, Bruno. Just a little stomach irritation."

"Do you want to see a gastroman? I know a fantastic one in Milan."

"Bruno, you big ape, I live in New York City. I can get a good 'gastroman' there if I want."

"Angry guts. My cousin has one. He's always in irritation. "

"Not me."

"They are talking about a drink of pig worm larvae that is supposed to reestablish a bacterial balance in the immune system. Giving your gut back some parasites that were doing you some good."

"Don't think I can do it, my friend. A drink of pig worm larvae is beyond my abilities."

"The doctor wrote, 'We don't want people going off to Mexico or who knows where else trying to expose themselves to the wrong worm. If people run out and get hurt, I'm not going to feel really good about this'."

He laughed.

"Okay then, ready for action?"

"What do you mean?"

"No time to waste, right, three days is all we got."

"Okay, what?"

"Let's double fuck a girl."

"What?! Are you crazy?"

His hairy fingers drummed against his thighs.

"Wake up," he said.

I turned, feeling at the first turn like a sinner, an overindulged child, and in the second turn like an entitled man who felt that limits were unimportant and false, and in the third turn I thought of how close to death I was at any given moment, and by the end of my full turn it was quite clear to me that this current instant was a speck of dust in measurement to the otherwise loyal, patient, and responsible life that I led every other day.

"Let's do it!"

Within minutes, like in a movie, Bruno was fucking the fat prostitute from on his back and I was fucking her from behind up the ass. She was so huge that all I could see were Bruno's hairy feet sticking out from between her legs. I was a bit grossed out. Her ass spread to the sides like collapsed medicine balls and to get into her anus I had to wrench aside her cheeks. I felt like such a weirdo. What was I doing? How did this act impact Grace? What compelled me? But it felt incredible, my penis up her tightly clenched ass, feeling the long edge of Bruno's shaft through the tissue of her anal lining. I held her at the waist. She kicked and bucked and snarled. Bruno began to pump hard. I felt feverish and chilled at the same time, the murky universe within my head. I went slowly deeper into her, further and further into her intestine. The prostitute squeezed her thigh and ass muscles and grasped the sheets. She felt angry, she groaned; this motion that had set all three of us into the heart of insurrection. She began to move in rhythm with us, up and onto Bruno's dick and then lowering herself into my penis. She started talking to herself in her native tongue. She screamed, quietly at first, but then louder. We rammed and rammed and the prostitute yelled out loud!

When we were done she kissed Bruno and he promised to come and see her again. We walked out into the midday light, which blinded me. I smelled the water in the wind. There was dog shit everywhere, in the street tree pits with their measly and sick specimens. We hailed a cab. I almost fell asleep during the ride to the hotel. Bruno's breathing was heavy. We checked in, feeling worn out and discomfited, at least I did. In the elevator Bruno said, "Wake up." I walked down the hallway to my hotel room thinking about my family.

I called Grace.

"What?" she said.

"How are you?"

"I'm alright. What do you want?"

"To see how you're doing."

"I suck."

I was silent.

"Have you met up with your sex friend Bruno?"

"What makes you say he is my sex friend?"

"He is. I know that."

"From what evidence?"

"From the way you talk about him."

"So what do you think we do?"

"Go to sex clubs, see movies, a deep immersion into porn."

"We do some of that."

"So I was right."

"Somewhat."

"What's with you and sex?"

"I like it and don't think it has to be put in a box."

"Just like arrogant you to think that. No boxes for Fire, but poor Grace must stay in her box."

"I'm not asking you to stay there."

"Oh yes you are. If you don't stay there then there is no one to take care of the kids, to take care of our life, but me."

"How's Mom working out?" I asked.

"Did you hear what I said? While you have sex fun in Amsterdam I'm taking care of your two kids, and your mother."

"She's not taking care of you?"

"She moves like a snail, but she is wonderful, I have to admit, crazy like a loon, but wonderful. She loves Augie so much and he loves her so much too."

"She is my proxy."

"Why are you at that conference anyway, what good is it?"

"I'm here for my career."

"It's all hype."

"That is true."

"Have fun Mr. President. I've got to shower and then take Michelle to the doctor. I have a splitting headache. Your mom is making break-fast for Augie. All the slavish women back home taking care of things."

She got off the phone and then Mom was on.

"Honey, how are things there?"

"Good."

"Has the conference begun yet?"

"Tonight is the opening ceremonies."

"It sounds so exciting."

"Yes."

"Say hi to Bruno."

"Yes, Mom."

"A dentist in Milan. I think we might have an Italian cousin from Trieste that is a dentist."

"Jesus, Mom.

"It's such an honor," she said. "I told Gloria about you and she was so impressed."

"Goddamn, Mom, please don't tell everyone."

"I'm proud of you."

"Too proud. Just keep an eye on Grace, please."

"She's not happy."

"I know. It makes me anxious."

"I heard the mayor is there?"

"The petty dictator? Where did you hear this?"

"I read in the newspaper, or maybe it was your father that read it, I can't really remember. By the way, you father I think is not doing so well. He won't admit it, but he's moving slower, more tired, sits on the couch watching TV a lot."

"Is he getting checked out?"

"No, he's resisting it. I keep telling him to see the doctor, but he re-fuses. He's very stubborn that way, as you know. I don't think he wants to face being sick again."

"I can understand that, but he should go anyway. Is he less angry, screaming less often? Maybe at least if he's feeling slowed down his anger will slow down too."

"You'd think, but no. He's even more angry. He's screaming at the TV, at the radio, at the paper. He and Leo had a huge fight and are not talking to each other. And he screams at me of course."

"Nice to know that some things never change."

"Your father will go to his grave screaming and ranting."

"Anyway, you sure the mayor is here?"

"I'm pretty sure we read in the paper that he was in Amsterdam for the conference."

"You've got to love this world," I began, "where the enemies of freedom are made into the gods of freedom instead. These fuckers are so bloated."

"People are greedy and self important."

"Well, Mom, I can truly say that you are not one of them."

"Thank you."

"Bye, Mom."

I made it into the bathroom in the nick of time. On the phone my gut had started to rumble, my dark internal elves at work. I could feel the acid juices move across the landscape of my belly, splashing my insides, pushing at my bowels, and making my midsection radiate with pain. These movements and sounds resulted in nothing but lost hope and further constipation. But in this case I let loose with such intensity and spray that I thought I was back in Africa with giardia. The hot cranky pain of diseased bowels. It was humiliating, this death descent. I looked at the hotel bathroom, with its foreign tiles, and wished for the Baseball Encyclopedia. I wanted to read Hank Aaron's numbers. His mighty numbers!

I tried to nap, unsuccessfully.

I got up, stared out the window at Amsterdam with its multicolored brownstones, winding streets, spiking white cathedrals, and snaking waterways. The city fanned out amid this archipelago, like New York City, with its lines and rows of stone and wood and personal addresses. The smoke and smells; the waste, the ceaseless commingling. I went into the shower, scouring my dirty ass with soap and shampoo. I shaved, brushed my teeth, dressed in my blue suit, white shirt, and green tie (I thought I looked quite fetching) and went down to hear the opening remarks.

The conference room was bustling and crowded with men and women from all over the world, suits to dashikis, fezzes and yarmulkes. The room was energized, smelled bodily, aroused. I looked at all the people and felt a bit dizzy. All the tiring and crooked introductions. I looked for Bruno, but didn't expect to find him. I looked to see if my colleagues from Yale and Brown had showed up yet. I walked to the side of the room, to the front, and sat down. Up at the lectern was a nearly bald man with gold rimmed glasses.

He said, "I am Ezra Goldbug of The Truth Foundation."

The conversations among the audience were undaunted. He cleared his throat, looked down at the crowd, and began.

"America is a monster and each time she feeds thousands die. Is this what we aspire too? Do we aspire to crushing the world to feed our needs? And what needs too: driving our cars and heating up our pools, and of course firing our bombs and rockets. Do we aspire to having all the resources massed up in less than one percent of the people's hands? Do we aspire to having so many of our neighbors hungry and ignorant? Is this what it all means?"

I jiggled around in my seat.

There were some cheers and whistling. But some boos too. Boo hoo you you reckless capitalist fucks! I will be your president one day so watch out.

"Let me give you some facts," he continued.

He moved his body to the left, the few strands of his thin hair stuck in place by the sweat of his head. He adjusted his glasses. He had a large bulbous nose, big red lips, Buddha ears. He was wearing a flannel shirt and jeans and stood on the tips of toes straining to get it all correct.

"America is the number one producer and seller of military arms in the world. In fact, it spends more on its military than all its other domestic and international programs. More on fighting, in other words, than on education. A lot lot more. Are these the actions of a peaceful nation?"

There was silence now, even shock, but I was hopping with energy and nearly ripping out my hair.

"The same men and women go back and forth between the Congress and lobbying firms and corporations. They see to it that billion of dollars goes from familiar hand to familiar hand. In fact, hundreds of former members of Congress are now lobbyists, and vice versa. Does this sound and smell like corruption?

"This might sound cliché to you, old fashioned, naïve, not in touch with the real life virtues of the free market, but that money could have otherwise gone to feed the hungry, purchase health care for the many uninsured, fix up neighborhoods, clean the environment, educate our people with sophistication and openness."

Behind Goldbug, just coming on the stage, was the mayor. He sat down and looked troubled. Goldbug went on about the grand illusion of America, its false freedoms and warmongering, but finished his short speech on a positive note, saying, "With a little discipline and decency we can live in a clean healthy world, safe, comfortable, and modest, underscored by love."

I went down the aisle to the stage to greet Goldbug. Instead, I was stopped by a security guard. I realized that he was a New York City cop.

"No further," he said.

"Why not?"

"Breach of security to let you near the stage."

"I just want to say hi to the guy who gave the speech."

"You can't go beyond this point."

"You're protecting the mayor?"

"Yes."

"I'm from New York City too."

"I can tell."

"You're not going to let my by are you?"

"Sorry."

Bruno was in the lobby.

He said, "Let's get out of here."

"You missed this guy Ezra Goldbug. He spoke the truth, the righteous truth, but no one listened. And then some thickheaded cop from New York City wouldn't let me talk to him because he was protecting the mayor from subversives."

"My friend, you are full of shit."

"I want these corporate fuckers burned on a stake."

I coughed twice.

"Let's do a quick one and then have some food."

"You crazy ape, I don't have that kind of stamina. I'm exhausted."

"Let's go, wake up."

"I flew all last night and this morning. I then fucked one prostitute and then another one up the ass. Then I had some viscous diarrhea. No, I am pooped."

"Let's have a quick one before bed."

"I wish I had some pot."

"We shall have some pot within minutes. And very good pot too."

"Allons-y."

"Oui."

In a café with black seats and yellow tables Bruno and I smoked hashish. The smoke penetrated my lungs and blood and lit up my insides like the shining desert in its fertile morning. Bruno's hairy face wavered in front of me.

"Bruno, even though the world is run by assholes the truth is I'm extraordinarily happy."

"My friend," he said, "I'm happy too."

"How did a dentist from Milan get to be such an irreconcilable pervert?"

"I was born that way."

"So why not go into porn or something? Dentistry? I don't get it?"

"I have no desire to live on the edge. I'm a mainstream man."

"But dentistry? Jesus, in people's stinking mouths all day. By the way, you are not mainstream."

"Yes I am. I prefer and prioritize my family and will never flag in my responsibilities."

"Bullshit. How many of your clients have you fucked?"

"Nine."

"How does this happen?"

"It doesn't happen in one moment. It builds up. Each time she visits the flirting gets stronger and more direct. We test the waters each time."

"I'm getting a boner just thinking about it."

Bruno scratched his beard.

"Doesn't it make it harder that you are married?"

"No."

"Why not?"

"It doesn't."

"Come on, you've got to give me a better answer."

"Nothing I could say would make sense."

"I cannot shake it. I think of my family at home and think of myself here and feel this jolt to my belly. It makes me sick."

"I see."

"How do I overcome it?"

"You stop altogether, at once and everything. If it bothers you then you give it up altogether."

"That's extreme."

"It's the only way."

"Right . . . So back to the clients. What next?"

"When the flirting feels at its highest pitch, when it feels as if we can barely contain ourselves, the next time she comes she is wearing something that reveals deep into her chest and shows off her ass. When she sits down in that seat looking up at me, I give a bit more gas, and as I lean down with my dentist mirror I instead give her a kiss."

"Holy Jesus! Is your heart racing like a speedcar at that moment?"

"Yes, a million miles a second."

"So?"

"Well, nine out of ten reacted by kissing me back."

"What did it feel like?"

"It felt fantastic, as if this thing that had been slowly building up energy over time was now being released as pleasure."

"I had that once with Grace, at the beginning when it was so heated. I wanted her every minute and in every way. I remember, sadly enough, that I fucked up our first sex. Can you believe it? "

"Absolutely, you nervous man."

"You know, I don't think of myself as nervous."

"But you are."

"Yes, I guess it's my nature."

"I give you credit, though, you follow through."

"See, I'm awake."

"Wake up. Wake up," he laughed.

"Married? How many of them were married?" I continued.

"Some of them."

"What happened with the one who said no?"

"The percentages were against me. I had to fail. And she was number 10."

"Yes."

"She was a knockout. Just my type, big tits and big butt, big fat cheeks, and strong shoulders and legs. A big woman. Her eyes followed me, for months in my presence every time I looked at her she was looking at me. When she came into the office it became very hot. I sweated a lot. My hair was soaked. I thought she was ready, but I was overconfident. That is why I sweated so much. I went too fast. When I leaned in for that kiss I saw her eyes light up in fear. She recoiled and I did too."

"It could have all come apart in that one wrong kiss. The wife and kids and profession all come undone."

"There are risks that's for sure."

"But would your wife understand if you got caught?"

"I think so," Bruno said. "I hope so."

"What do you think?"

"I think that I would probably be doomed, although I can't imagine she doesn't suspect. I would plead guilty."

"I have similar hopes, but I feel doomed too. I want Grace to be as kinky as me. That's the experiment with Jane of course, to see if a threesome can work, but I think Grace sees it as a lack of love on my part."

"Good luck with the Jane experiment," he said. "It could prove, if successful, that there are genuine alternate possibilities in the western world."

"A new paradigm for marriage!" I exclaimed. "That's it, there has to be a new paradigm; it's shifting in these modern lands, and right now the old is so old and the new is so marginal that the current is still shifting. Yes!"

"Fire, wake up," he warned me.

Bruno went back to the same woman and I chose a giant of a woman too, nearly 6'2" and a good 200 pounds, strong on her thick legs and wide waist. Her back went on forever and her breasts filled up her chest with their volume. I was dwarfed by her, a boy next to a woman. Almost like a squirrel under a tree. She told me to undress and when I was naked lifted me up to her face and said, "What you want?"

Her breath smelled of eggs.

"You want to play with tits for a while?"

"Yes," I said.

She put me down.

I put my hands on those big things, as heavy as boulders, and lifted them up, twisted them around, sucked the mammoth nipples, clanged them together, smacked them from the side.

"You are little boy in toy store."

"These things are magnificent."

"To play some more we must discuss money."

I stopped what I was doing.

She listed her prices.

"How about I play with your breasts and you give me a hand job?"

They were forces of nature, continental plates. I stuck my head between them and licked at the sides. I was submerged in their density. She, meanwhile, was jacking my penis up and down, her hand strong, rough, and completely subsuming my penis. I kept my head buried in her cleavage pushing up against her big body until she brought me off in her hand, the semen flowing out between the spaces of her fingers.

"Are you German?" I asked.

"Yes."

"I have always heard that the Germans are good in bed."

"We are masters of the bedroom."

"I hear that you guys are into sick things too?"

"Like what?"

"All the ass fucking and shit eating videos are German."

"No bowel eating for me. If you want my asshole you will have to pay a lot of money."

"No, that's okay."

"You no like?"

She turned around and stuck her large ass out. It was impressive.

"Maybe another time."

"You come back and we talk about my ass."

"Sounds nice."

I started to dress and she wiped my come off her hand.

"I was on safari with this German couple once," I said, feeling talkative, the hash making me gregarious and lucid. "I was just bumming around before I started my field work."

She was so large that I wanted to laugh.

"We were out in the bush and sleeping in tents. One night I got out of my tent to pee. Leopards and snakes I'm thinking. I'm scared shitless. The sounds, the wind blowing through the grasses, the ripple of an animal walking. You can't see a thing. The place is so vast. No people anywhere. No lights. But I had to pee."

"What you doing out there anyway?"

"I work in Africa."

"Doing what?"

"I study trees."

"You study trees," she said. "What you study trees?"

"For science. So anyway, I was standing outside in the plains at night naked taking a pee. Then I notice, just like 20 feet away, this huge male lion. Eyes like the sun. I mean this guy was just sitting there. He's a professional killer, kills hyenas with one bite and wrestles down buffalo. He weighs 500 pounds. I am dead meat, I think to myself, and there is death sitting right next to me in his lion's costume."

"You and lion were looking at each other?" she asked.

"Try to imagine it."

"What does lion do?"

"He doesn't do anything. He just sits there and stares at me."

"He could have eaten you in one bite."

"That's for sure."

"What happened?"

"I peed all over myself."

"You peed yourself."

"Yes, I did."

"You're a funny man."

I paid her, putting the money in the hand that had just got me off. She said, "You come back again, huh? Maybe we pay some attention to my ass next time."

"Maybe," I said.

On the street Bruno told me how he had eaten a banana out of his prostitute's pussy.

"You crazy ape," I said. "I'm going to sleep now."

We went back to the hotel, to our rooms, where I promptly feel asleep.

I awoke the next morning earlier than I had wanted. I had hoped for a deep long sleep. I had a gas pain and so stayed in bed. The sky through the window was steel gray. I thought of yesterday's activities.

It took my breath away. Augie, I thought too, at this moment would be on his way home from school, dressed in his yellow and black down jacket, Grandma holding his hand and trying to coax out of him the story of his day. There was no need to remind myself where I was, away from him. I coughed, sending a ripple of pain through the left side of my abdomen. I went into the fetal position. I hoped I could meet death with grace but I was fairly sure that I was unprepared. What was there to greet me? The ocean? The sky? I straightened myself out, my head buried in the pillow and my feet pointed. What Grace and I needed was a new paradigm. A new paradigm for marriage! I climbed out of bed and began stretching. I got down on all fours and tried in the doggy position to force some of last night's farts out. It didn't work. I stretched for ten minutes and did some pushups and situps. My body was a bit bigger now from exercises and it felt good and I smacked my hand to my gut. I showered, got some farts out in the soapy water, and brushed my teeth. I put on jeans and a white button down shirt.

"Dude," I said to Bruno in the lobby, "you look slick." He was wearing black pants, black turtleneck, and black beret. "We are finding Goldbug."

"Let's go."

I needed to locate the guy: he had the steely facts of America's corruption at his disposal, essential material for my presidential run.

We found out from a conference representative that Goldbug was staying at a hostel which was on a boat in a canal. Bruno and I walked, circling and twisting around small shops and residencies, over bridges, run amok children, the stench of water everywhere. The sky was gray and cold, but the movement of my body warmed me. We walked the streets until we came to an open plaza. Beyond this were the docks, hundreds of white, gray, and blue boats bobbing in the water. I huddled up in my jacket as we pushed through the wind. Up ahead was a white boat with Hostel written on top of it. The people coming in and out were untidy with knapsacks and full of rasta hair. Grace and I had stayed this way when we traveled to Africa, but now I wanted a room to myself with some comforts. I was repulsed by so many commingled smells. Nevertheless, there was Goldbug in the open space at the front of the boat playing guitar. Bruno turned to me and said, "Is that your Goldbug?" "Yes."

We crossed the water on a ladder that led us down into the big boat that was rotted wood and chipped paint, rocking in the waves, covered in hippies. We walked around a post and into the open space where Goldbug sat with a percussionist playing his guitar.

"Goldbug," I said, coming closer to him.

He turned, screamed, "Mother . . !".

"Oh Jesus," I said, "you okay?"

"You shocked me and I twisted my neck."

"I see that."

We shook hands.

"I am Fire Rosewood from New York City."

"I am Bruno Stephano from Milan."

"I am Ezra Goldbug from New Haven."

His hair, so sparse, crossed his head in random tresses.

"Where's The Truth Foundation been all my life?"

"Don't know."

He rested his guitar on his lap, took off his glasses, and cleaned them on his shirt.

"I started it just a few months ago," he said, glasses now on. "It was time to start some type of organization that spread the truth and debunked the lies. The whole ship is sinking and no one seems to notice."

"Oh, yes. It's perfect! Bruno, man, what do you think?"

"That you are a spaced out hippie."

Ezra laughed. He picked up his guitar and played a few chords on it, then got up. We followed him to the back of the boat where it was quieter.

"I have been so frustrated with America," I started. "All its dirty ways. Hearing you last night was awakening."

"Thank you," he said.

Bruno said, "Why do you stay here? It's filthy."

"I don't care about the luxuries of the hotels and I can't afford them."

"Too bad. This is horrible."

"It's the people," he said, "not the furniture."

"So, what exactly is The Truth Foundation?" I asked.

"It's supposed to be a library of facts. A repository of knowledge for anyone curious about how our nation really works."

"That's genius."

"Thank you. I try to make it simple. You can look up say 'Military' and then it will be broken into categories like, 'Government Spending' or 'Corporate Profits' or 'People of Note'. Things like that."

"It's a dream come true, Ezra. I mean I can't tell you how unbelievable this is. There is so much information and to have it condensed in one place is like heaven."

"I tamper with it everyday."

"You have a family?"

"A wife and two kids."

"What does she do?"

"She's teaches women's studies at the local college."

"Dogooders," Bruno said.

Ezra cracked up. "We are classic dogooders."

I said, "You're one too, Bruno, otherwise you wouldn't be here. And by the way the world needs us anyway."

"Wake up," he said.

"Wake up," Ezra repeated. "Wake up. That's fantastic."

I heard the tick tick of my heart and the faulty furnace of my gut.

"All right then," I said, "how did you get invited to give a speech here at this hoitytoity conference?"

"I sent in a request and somehow they sent back an okay. I think they probably thought I was something other than I turned out to be. I was supposed to go nearly last in the schedule, but at the last minute this guy from Burma cancelled and I was there and so they rushed me up."

"So you wanted to show up the hypocrisy of the whole thing."

"In other words."

Bruno said, "Let's go to Anne Frank's house."

"Really?" I asked.

"Then after that I am taking you to the best sex club in Amsterdam." Bruno turned to Ezra. "You want to come too?"

"Not for me," he said. "But Anne Frank's house is moving."

We went to her house, waited in line like all the other mourners of lost time, entered the domain of secrets, and Ezra, despite himself, began to cry. He said, "I get sad easily thinking of the world's grave mistakes." I began to imagine what it was like death hovering so close by, each day, each second, that by the time it actually came it was a relief. Was this how it was for her? Did she know all along that she wasn't going to make it?

Outside, Bruno said, "Now it's time to balance out sadness. Ezra, this place is about life, as it happens in the moment, you sure you don't want to come and see these circus acts of human sexuality?"

"Not my thing."

I got his phone number and address and told him he'd hear from me.

We entered a dark smoky place with the smell of sweat, alcohol, semen, and cleansing detergents in the air. We walked down to a table by the front.

A man was holding a woman upside down as he ate her out. His spittle dribbled down her belly and I could see that her head was turning red from all the blood that was rushing down. The man's muscles were tensed and the woman was balancing herself on her hands. She looked like she was going to faint.

Bruno ordered vodka and I ordered a glass of wine even though I should have been drinking water the wine hurt my gut so.

The hand standing couple was replaced by a lesbian act. One woman was huge, over six feet with hips and ass that filled out the size of her extraordinary carriage. Her hair hung down to her butt like a cape. Her counterpart was a midget, almost too tiny to make out squeezed into her particle body. She too had hair that flowed down to her buttocks, but in her case it almost completely covered her body. The giantess picked the midget up and they started kissing. She held the small woman up from the waist like holding a baby to see into its eyes. The giantess next rotated the midget upside down and starting eating her out. The midget laid her head back and closed her eyes. She began to pant her hair draped backwards like a horse's tail. The giantess stopped, picked the midget back up, and they started kissing again. For a few seconds they lost themselves in this most intimate of acts. A table was moved onto the stage and the giantess lay the midget down on it, turned her over onto all fours, making her look like a pig with long teats. She started eating her out again, from behind, and the midget pushed and pulled under the umbrella of her lover's hair. The giantess stepped back and reached down under the table and came up with a large dildo, which she put in the midget's vagina. The midget bucked forward and then bucked backwards to take whole thing in; the giantess merely held the dildo in place. She rocked like the waves. The giantess took the dildo out, the midget heaving, and began to wedge it into the midget's anus. The midget was so small, and the giantess so big, and the midget's anus so tiny, and the dildo so immense, and it was all being absorbed. The midget was nearly elevated by this, and she was screaming out loud, her wails rippling through the club. Then they switched. The giantess took the midget's place atop the table, butt up too, and the midget wrought revenge by sticking the same fecal dirty dildo straight up her ass. The giantess's butt jiggled from side to side to assimilate the force, but she was too large to be pushed out of position.

I called Grace.

"Hey," I said.

"Hey."

"Was thinking about you guys and thought I'd call in."

"The man who is always on the run calls in."

"Yes."

"The man of my life is always running away."

"I am the 'run away man,' aren't I? It's one of my drawbacks."

"Not necessarily. It's part of what's attractive about you, that independent spirit. I think Augie is full of it, and that's good."

"Thank you. Lately, I have tended to think of my running away as bad, from you and the structure of family. Escapism. I feel guilty."

"I know."

"You'll keep me in check."

"I will. I hope."

"How are the kids?"

"Fine."

"Does Augie notice I am gone?"

"Barely. . . He misses you a lot, actually. There is no one to throw him around."

"Are you okay?"

"Fine. Mainly. But I'm a little horny for you."

"Really?"

"Yes, that old twitch in the crotch came back."

"Maybe I have to go away for it to work."

"Perhaps. Do you want to have phone sex?"

"Phone sex! No, it's too artificial. I couldn't do it."

"More artificial than those sex shows you go to? How many have you been to with Bruno?"

"Just one."

"Huh," she snorted.

"They are boring, for the most part."

"I was thinking of popping over," she said. "Something really impulsive. Leave the kids with Mom and fly over there."

"What?"

"You always say I'm not spontaneous. Well here's spontaneity for you."

"But my schedule is so busy. Workshops, lectures, meetings."

"You can skip one day. Who will know? Who will care?"

"But that's the point. Columbia is paying and I can't abuse their generosity. I must be serious."

"Oh, come on. One day of lusty fun in Amsterdam with your wife on Columbia's tab."

"I have a reputation, a career at stake."

"Who's conservative now?"

"You're right. I'm the conventional one now. Shit, that's bad."

"So, your answer is no?"

"How about when I get back the two of us take a trip, to Newfoundland, where we've always wanted to go."

"Fire, how about if I was bent over the bed and you were to fuck me in the ass."

"Oh my god, I'm dizzy."

"If you let me come over and visit you this is what you will get."

I took a deep breath.

"Do you think it's possible?"

"Not really."

"Really?"

"It's not realistic," she said.

"Why the sudden change of mind?"

"I don't know. I just realized that it is too much to do. Fly eight hours for a whim. I was just being silly."

"Maybe we can pull it off."

"Fire, it's alright. You didn't hurt my feelings."

"But seriously, maybe a quick trip is possible. It sounds fun."

"Don't worry, honey, you still have a chance for anal sex here at home, just a very very small one."

The giantesses were free. Bruno was taking his fat prostitute and I was taking my German behemoth to the final dinner of the International Justice Conference. When Bruno first suggested it I was stricken with fear. I was a married man with two children. I was beginning to become known for my urban forestry work in Nairobi. Full professorship was inevitable it seemed. But then Bruno reminded me of my anthropology textbooks, of the Samoans, of the pursuit of happiness, freedom, and a new paradigm of marriage. A new paradigm of love, he said. I thought, fuck those self righteous capitalist dogs, trying to stick me in a box while they whipped their dicks in every hole they could profit from. And fuck Grace too for making me so guilty. She had the affair with Orlando because she thought it was her liberation that he presented her. So why not me too?

The party hall was lit up by chandeliers, old world relics that had shined for centuries. Blue balloons hung from the ceiling and were occasionally caught on the hanging limbs of the chandeliers. Renaissance paintings hung from the walls. Tables covered with white linen cloth and china were clustered and crowded around the large room, which had a dance floor in the center and a stage in which a band was playing. Waiters and waitresses in black and white populated the eddies and rivulets between the tables. The place was hot with human energy and aspiration, and smelled of sweat, beef, smoke, alcohol, and bread.

Bruno and I walked into this with our prostitutes on our arms, into the throng, past the mayor, past the world's bureaucrats and rulers, and all the many people from around the globe that were enjoying this splendor.

We went to the dance floor. I placed my arms around the huge waist of my date, put my leg in between her crotch, my face in her breasts, and started gyrating. She smelled tart and her skin was a roll of smoothness and elasticity like gum. I let my hand run down her spine and land on her ass, a sandy hillock in the middle of the large mountain of her body. I felt hundreds of envious eyes on me. I felt the voices ringing out in triumph and cheer and the music bringing the messages of the spirits. I could feel the room's absorption of me. She tilted me over backwards then brought me to her mouth to kiss. I thought of Grace and her lithe dancing under the acacia tree.

When done we went to our table amid three other couples, including Bruno and his fat maid.

I said to him, "I feel unleashed. It's because of you. I hope you know that."

"Wake up my friend and pull yourself together," he said.

"I am fully awake and aware. Nothing can escape my eye. I see it all. Every snake that moves in the desert and any woman sunbathing on a rooftop."

"I believe you."

"But a man can't live in total freedom, can he?"

"Not all the time. It's too rough on the soul."

"So we've got to have some limits then?"

"Limits are absolutely appropriate. Even here we have our limits."

"The limits."

"Without limits there is nothing to be reached for. And don't make Grace a limit. Make her a luxury."

"I can't seem to. It's a total shame, but I can't seem to get past my prejudices of her."

I coughed and took a sip of wine.

"Loosen up. Don't create all this worry. You need to have a successful home life. It's good for you. It's healthy."

"I owe it to Grace, I know that. But I can't seem to get past my ambivalence. I think about her and try to stay positive and think about all the good things but then I withdraw anyway. Why? Why can't I get past that? I know that on the other side is friendship and good will, with good sex too. Why do I keep her out?"

"I don't know, Fire. But your descriptions are right. It leads to good will and that is of utter importance."

"It's a limit," I said, "a limit to my personality. I don't want to give up anything and then it's all too much and I need a break."

"And here is where we come for that break. But you must allow for its many pleasant memories to get you through the year."

"I don't have patients I fuck at home, you selfish bastard. Little affairs where you get to touch strange girls. I have nothing but Grace."

"You are wrong. You have Jane, my friend, in a most worthy experiment."

"Yes, can polygamy work in the big modern city?"

"But polygamy of good will and trust."

"It can work, but I doubt it too."

"Don't give up so quickly. Be patient."

"Like you are with your patients?"

"Yes. But don't forget Grace is your priority. Watch what she says and does."

"I should always do that if I can."

"To the right extent."

"I want it to be easy."

"Then wake up."

And there was Grace. Coming through the conference room doors. I turned to Bruno.

"Grace is here. I've got to go. Take care of things."

"What?" he said.

"Grace is here. It's unbelievable but true. She actually did it."

"What?"

"Showed up. Was spontaneous, dramatically so."

"Go. Go. I've got it covered."

I ran off, around the tables, and to the doors. I rushed into Grace and hugged her.

"Holy shit. You came. Unbelievable. You're unbelievable."

"I thought, why not?"

"Why not? It's a ton of money and 8,000 miles away from home."

"So, you're not happy to see me?"

"Oh, I am. I'm just surprised."

"Kind of rash."

"I like it . . . The kids?"

"Grandma, and grandpa too."

"You got my dad to babysit?"

"Reluctantly . . . Where's Bruno?"

"He . . . left already."

"Really?"

"He got bored, to tell you the truth, and went home."

"You're lying."

"No, no. He went home. Got bored."

"So, why does he come in the first place?"

"The sex shows."

"Like you."

"Yes."

"Who are you sitting with?"

"Some boring colleagues from Yale and Brown."

"Let's go sit with them. Have some dinner."

"No way."

"Why?"

"Let's do what you came here for."

Underneath her jacket Grace wore a red sweater that revealed her braless breasts through the tiny windows of her porous garment.

"Let's wait a little. Eat some food."

"Fuck that. Let's go to the room, order up. Screw these people."

"Really? I thought it was significant for your career."

"Oh, it is."

"Really?"

"Got to play the game even if it's bullshit."

I leaned in, kissed her, cupped her breast. I led her to the elevator, where I pushed her against the door and rubbed into her hips. In the elevator I pulled up her sweater and licked her nipples. I put my hand down her pants to a crotch uncovered. Down her thighs trickled moisture. In the hallway we were chaste, but behind the door we met each other with zealousness.

9. Flora

A S THE MORNING rolled in, the blue sun off the water replacing the nightlights, I started to think about Kenya, with its hills that tapered down into the valley of Nairobi.

Grace was beside me still asleep. It was incredible that she had come. (To this day I remember that sex, unwavering, fanatical, no holds barred.) I touched her arm and this got me horny. I moved into the crevice of her ass. She moaned in tiredness and pushed me away.

"What time do you have to go? We can go to the airport together. I still can't believe you are here."

"I'm exhausted. Let me sleep please."

I pulled away from her and sat up in bed. I thought about James and the trees we had propagated, cuttings of acacia, baobab, cedar, and juniper, tree species that I thought could survive in the deadly gorge of Nairobi. We grew them in our greenhouses, but now, eight years old, they were outside spread in rows like toothpick youngsters. On this coming trip we were going to plant our inaugural trees in pits around the city. It was a big moment in my career, solidifying a certain level of reputation and generating movement too. The mayor of Nairobi, representatives of the city's philanthropic and international institutions, and all the scant well-to-do would be on hand to celebrate the first trees into the sidewalk, my unique work.

I got up. There was "incomplete evacuation" in the bathroom. I got back in bed with Grace and this time she let me enter her. I thought of the day long ago where I had showed up late to Amsterdam for our trip to Africa, where her pussy had been similarly wet, the pubic hair tangled in dampness. I thought of Mombassa too, the word, and all its images, ringing in my ears. When done she roused herself and went into the bathroom to shower. I followed her.

"This was great," I said. "Amazing."

"We need more of this."

"We do. The grinding crunch of career and parenting has left us little else."

She turned on the water, let it run, and then disappeared behind the curtain.

"We could make it happen."

"We can. We should. Let's do it."

"We will need to find babysitting."

"There is always Mom."

"Not all the time. She deserves a break. She is getting old."

"Dad."

"Are you insane! I am not leaving my kids alone with that crazy man."

"He was only crazy with us. He'd just fall asleep with his grandkids."

"And Michelle will fall through the window."

"Okay. Let's find a reliable weekend babysitter. Give us time. We can birdwatch, meditate, fuck and suck."

We kissed our lips on opposite sides of the shower curtain.

We dressed, checked out, where I saw Bruno on the other side of the lobby, looking around, and I hustled Grace out the door. We took a cab to the airport, hugged goodbye.

Stepping off the plane in Nairobi the blazing sun blinded me and the foreign smells flared my nostrils. I was numb with exhaustion. In the airport I was attacked by shirtless emaciated children. They grabbed my sleeves, touched and pawed my body as if I was a circus animal. One kid wanted to sell me a hat. Another had some toothpaste for me. They all wanted pens, "Give me a pen, mister. Jambo." They jabbed my thighs with their thumbs and poked my ribs with their fists. Thank god there was James off in the distance. I made my way like a graceful beetle through the masses and landed in James' arms.

"Jambo," he said.

"Jambo."

We went to the SUV that was paid for through my project finances and off we drove into the city. His father Moudra sat in the back seat.

"How was your trip?" James asked me.

"It was long and I am tired."

"How was Amsterdam and the conference? One day I would like you to bring me."

"It was great fun."

"How come you get the fun?"

"This is a specific type of fun. Lots of ass kissing."

"Okay," he said, "but you Americans are always having parties. A party for this and a party for that. How come we Kenyans don't get a party?"

"It's a long story."

"We have close to nothing."

"That's not true. Your life is pretty good now. Stable, with a house, and enough to eat."

"Jambo, sir."

"You are welcome, sir."

"How is your wife and family?"

"They're fine. We have a new baby, you know?"

I coughed.

"I know, you wrote me. This is very happy news."

"Yes it is."

"It must have been hard to leave them behind?"

"It was hard to leave Augie."

"You will be home very soon."

We came into the city that was spotted with contaminated white buildings. The roads were busted up and crumbling and the medians were overflowing with garbage. The cars flew by their engines and bodies rattling with age. The tall glass buildings of Nairobi sat in the dense sun the glass covered by a film of dust.

"How's your health?" James asked.

"Not so great lately," I said.

"You know Josephine thinks she can cure you. You should consider her offer. But I have to admit those drugs of yours work. I got a stomach problem and I took antibiotics. In two days I was up and working."

"Everyone lives to 80 in America, with cancer and tumors and bad hearts, obese like hippos, till 80. The real backwater trash are the only exceptions."

"The blacks."

"The blacks."

"Why we get it so bad? It drives me crazy."

"I don't know the answer. But you blacks have a hard time with it. Where ever one goes you're on the bottom, even in your own countries."

"Sometimes I think it's your fault, the whites taking it all for themselves, but then when I look at my people I feel embarrassed too."

"All those crazy rebels in the bush," I said, "all they want is to steal the pie for themselves."

"You should let Josephine try to cure you."

Moudra moved in the back and made a grunting sound.

Like always, the black and red clay of the city, which was loosened from the eroded landscape, was carried by the hot wind and got stuck in my teeth. A few wilting trees dotted the roads. Sewers were at high tide, car exhaust melded with industrial belch, the carbon suspended in the air. The sidewalks were cracked and peeling. Storefronts were a blackened blue of age, although there were some clean spots in Nairobi too, small immaculate streets with bakeries and tailors. Chickens and goats were led by strings. The women carried loads of children and bags. Vendors enticed costumers to their street lairs. People stomped and shouted and tourists took pictures and crammed their mouths with food.

We drove to Kenyatta Avenue, went shopping.

We bought bags of rice and pasta, cans and cans of fruit and vegetables, tunafish, beef, crackers, biscuits, jelly, peanut butter by the gallon, bottles and bottles of water, butter, mayonnaise, olive oil, cabbages, potatoes, and bread. We bought wine, cheese, and chocolate cake from my favorite bakery. I stocked up on soda. I picked up some forestry books and Elmore Leonard too. I bought film, fertilizer, growing mixes, oil, trowels, gloves, and some local pesticide that we used when the bugs got too bad on the trees.

Moudra settled back into the car seat and stared straight ahead with his yellow eyes.

We started climbing the low mountains that overlooked the city. The houses were large and well kept. Many had front gates and were landscaped. The villages had shopping markets and barbershops, and the people were white skinned and the streets were clean. Up we went out of these towns slowly climbing the hills away from the metropolis. The spaces opened up, the road turning from macadam to dirt, the houses straw and tin.

We were silent in the SUV, calmed by the hot sun. I drifted off, the light a sparkle under my eyebrows. I could smell James and Moudra, who smelled like brick ovens. I could smell the outdoors, sun baked soil. I thought of the Hudson River and of Grace, and my left leg jerked and my mind sank a little deeper into sleep. Sweat pooled on the back of my neck. At the top of the mountain James woke me and there was the vast planet of the veld—the midsection of Africa swept out like a giant's blonde body.

"My god!" I said.

"Yes," James said, "I know, sir. Even though I live here I don't stop to be amazed."

"It's gorgeous! Unbelievable! I forgot how moving it is . . . It feels right, James. Yes, it does. This moment has auspicious tones. You can strive hard to make it right and actually succeed. I believe this."

"Good, sir. I agree. I believe in taking hold."

"Your sister?" I said.

"Yes, sir?"

"Your sister can cure me, you think?"

"She is gifted. She has a talent for curing."

He took off his sunglasses, cleaned them on his shirt.

"What do you think she will do?"

"Who knows?" James said. "We've heard that most people are crying."

Moudra let out a bolt of laughter, his teeth shining.

"What do you mean crying?" I said. "Crying with pain or crying with thanks and admiration?"

"Josephine once treated Moudra. He didn't want to go to her, but she is the great healer and he is the father so he has to. Moudra knows that Josephine must cure him or else she might lose customers, people will think less of her powers. He's scared that she's going to keep him in constant pain to show off. But my father had no choice."

"Why didn't he have a choice?"

"It isn't right for the father of the great local healer to go to someone else. It would be insulting to her."

"So she voodooed your dad?"

"When he came back I asked him how it was and he said it was a 'time for great crying'. Then he showed me all his bruises . . . For you, big scientist, it will be a 'time of great crying'."

"But look at him now. He's strong as a horse and his mind is like a steel trap."

"He knows that Josephine made him strong for life."

James wended his way to our workstation and plant nursery, which were on a twenty acre patch of Kenya that sat on the space between the plains and the green hills. It was a breezy steady spot a few hours from Nairobi. Down one last small hill James stopped the truck and got out to open the gate. He drove through and to the camp.

My house, hut really, was a prefabricated beige and brown box with a bedroom, kitchen, and a patio. In my study were a desk, computer, books, and files. Across the way was a bigger house for James and his wife, Helen, three kids, and Moudra.

I unpacked my stuff, got out of my clothes, and grabbed a towel. On the way to the shower across our courtyard James's son Thomas threw his frisbee to me and in my clumsy thrust to catch it rammed my big toe into a small tree stump. The pain soared through my body! As I went to hold my toe in succor I tripped and went down. I cried out in pain. Thomas ran away as Helen came out of the house shouting at him. She made her way to me lying on the ground. She took my foot in her hand and rubbed my throbbing toe.

She was thin and wiry with skin that turned rose in the heat. Her small breasts pushed outwards from her shirt.

"Fire, the first second you come back you get hurt."

"I shouldn't have chased Thomas' frisbee."

"Thomas will get his. But first thing we must burn that stump out of the ground."

"The boy didn't mean it."

"He did."

She smiled and went back to her house. I limped to the shower and in the warm water tried to calm the pounding in my toe. I couldn't believe that I would be crippled this whole trip now. That delinquent Thomas! I smelled fire, probably Helen burning the stump. I then heard her scream and Thomas meekly defending himself. I smiled. I soaped up my filmy body and let the water slowly pour over my head. The sky above me carried the uncontained breeze of my future. I washed myself, dried up, and limped to Helen.

She was over the stump stoking the flames.

"Thanks," I said.

"No worries."

"You've been good?"

"Yes, Fire. You too?"

"I'm a new father."

"I heard. You must be happy?"

"I am."

"No more stump to worry about," she said. "Come out soon for dinner."

I went back to my hut and lay down in the hammock on my patio. James came to me and handed me a joint.

"You are the best," I said.

"Enjoy it. Don't let Thomas see you smoking it. It makes me too dizzy."

James gave me some matches and I lit one, held it under the joint until it was burning, and then put it to my lips. Inside my mouth went the turbulent smoke down the chute of my esophagus and into the great mid section of my body filling up my soul.

I handed him the joint and he laughed.

"Fire, you've been trying to get me to smoke ganja ever since you met me."

"And I don't plan on stopping."

"That's the American way. An African stops after a good day's work."

"We are a reckless nation."

"That's why you are running for president?"

"Yes, to whip these bastards back into their redneck corrals and keep them there."

"You are crazy, man. Didn't you say your new goal is to not have any opinions?"

"Yes, my man, yes."

"Do you think you are accomplishing your goal?"

I took another hit.

"I do. I think I'm much more tolerant of other views and that I understand how death is the great equalizer and so all opinions are meaningless."

"Mr. Philosopher. If you want to win the people over you need some bare facts, like our study here. What trees work and what don't and will they grow here or not? Keep it simple. Make it personal."

"Others have said that too . . . I met this guy Ezra Goldbug in Amsterdam. He runs what he calls the Truth Foundation, a warehouse of facts about how America actually works. Every government purchase, every stupid new plane, every worthless warship, every baseball stadium, every subsidy paid for by the American taxpayer, me. This Truth Foundation has all the juicy facts. Everything I need to tell the American public that it is being swindled."

"Good luck," he concluded. "You are crazy enough to do this. I've seen other Americans before and they are less crazy than you. You got some kind of crazy disease. Okay, I will see you at dinner."

I put on a nice white shirt and clean white pants. I stepped out from my hut and there was James and Thomas chasing a chicken.

"Catch him, Fire," James screamed out.

The chicken was coming right at me, its legs rotating at super-speed. I hesitated, but crouched down, eyes closed and head turned, and caught the chicken against my chest. It pecked at me, banging its sharp beak into my skinny chest like a dagger. I felt that at any minute it might penetrate my layers and poke my heart out.

"Excellent!" James screamed.

He took the chicken from me and we walked to the chopping block, which was a wide baobab stump that was stained with blood. James stretched the chicken's neck on the wood and held it tight.

"Okay Fire, say a prayer."

I stared at the chicken and then into space.

"We thank you for the food and hope that you are okay in death, chicken."

Thomas, who had joined us, blurted out a laugh and James smacked him in the head.

"Try again, Fire."

I looked up into space again.

"Thank you nature for blessing us."

James gave his machete to me.

It was soft at the handle and its blade shone in the sun. I lifted it up over my head letting it sit there while I felt for the right balance. James said something in his native tongue and I brought down the machete on the chicken's neck. I barely nicked it. I struck again, but missed again, this time thumping his neck in a broadside. I was horrified and the chicken was thrashing. I lifted the machete again, kept my eyes on the bird's open white neck, and came down in a thick slice. The body leaped and made a few panicked steps and fell.

"About time," James said. "I thought you might have lost your touch."

"It's been a while."

"You don't come as often. It's too bad."

"I know. I really miss it here. A lot."

"Too bad you can't move your whole family here."

"I would love to, James, love to, but Grace would never allow it."

"Have you asked her?"

"No."

"Why not?"

"I'm too afraid."

Thomas laughed.

James smacked him again and said, "Take the chicken and get it ready."

"Why?" James asked me.

"Because it's unrealistic, for one. My whole family and network are in New York City. But two, Grace would just say that I am hopelessly restless."

"Tell her that it would be good for everyone, to clean out the lungs with a stay in Kenya."

"I wish I could, but I don't want even more resentment in the house."

"You know what's best, sir."

"I don't."

We heard the gate opening and a car coming down the road.

"Must be Josephine, sir. You must make your final decision now. She expects to be healing you for the next two weeks. She is very focussed on this."

"I really want to do it. I mean how can a sick man not explore his alternatives? But I'm really scared of the pain, I got to tell you."

"I would be too. But she is very good and you sir have been sick more and more."

"I know. I've got to do it."

"She likes you," James said, as Josephine's car pulled up, "she might throw in some pleasure too."

"You think so?" I said.

Josephine was as large as a brown bear. She untangled herself from her rusted car and then straightened up to her full bear height and padded her way to me. I nearly fell from fright and James laid his hand on my hip to settle me. I sought out Moudra with my eyes, but didn't find him.

"Fire, your time has come," she said to me, and picked me up in her arms and hugged me.

"I know," I said.

"You are the father of two children now, you must get better."

"Yes."

"Tomorrow, then, we start."

"Yes."

"Now we party."

At that cue Helen turned the tape player on and out came the dance music. Josephine grabbed me by the wrist and pulled me into her. James was cooking the chicken, Thomas was helping Helen with the vegetables and rice, and his little sisters were chittering in the background. Moudra was tending the fire. Josephine smelled black, charcoal mixed with soil, a lifetime of sweat baked into her pours by the sun. I could hear her heart beat rapidly. Her stomach pushed into my gut and her knee found its way to my crotch and lifted me up onto her belly where I lay like a child. She rocked me from side to side. I felt the warm wind blow on my cheeks. I heard all the noises, crackling, hissing, popping, chirping, talking, crying. I smelled the wood burning and its smoke. The mosquitoes buzzed around us.

"Fire, trust me," Josephine said. "This will help you be healthy. A man needs his health."

I didn't say anything. I was too spaced out and too distrustful of my words anyway.

"I know James probably told you about Moudra, but don't believe him. I never put my father in pain like that. I don't say I didn't do my job, but it's not like they say."

All I could think of was how big her leg was like the base of an oak tree.

"Can you feel my power now?" she said.

"Yes."

"When I am at full capacity it is very powerful."

"I can only imagine," I said, my head rolling along the folds of her stomach.

The song came to an end and Josephine let go of me.

The picnic tables were set out with tablecloths, and the plates and silverware that I had bought for James and Helen were neatly displayed, the food stacked on the end steam issuing into the red and black sky. We sat down to eat, James, Helen, Thomas, the two girls, Moudra, Josephine, and I. James poured all the adults some wine, and Thomas a little too. I raised my glass in the air and said, "Thank you for all this! You guys have no idea how much I miss this place. It's good to be back, even for two weeks."

We clanked.

"So," Josephine said, "you are meeting with the mayor."

"We are," I said.

"Big man. Does this mean that your science is going well? Are you going to get that professorship you always talk about?"

"Yes, Josephine." I smirked. "Our first trees are going into the sidewalks of Nairobi, it's a big step. And yes, I still hope for that professorship."

"And what are your trees going to do for the city?"

"Clean it."

"How?"

"Just like you clean your human bodies, by taking the pollution out."

She pawed at her thick hair.

"I guess that could be true," she said. "And how does this work?"

"Our lungs are black with soot, but the trees are natural filters, taking in the carbons and other irritants and giving us back their clean oxygen. That is why Nairobi is so disgusting, no trees."

"Okay, Fire, no bullshitting, you come tomorrow morning."

"Yes," I said. "I said yes. I will be there."

She smiled, first at me, and then at James and Moudra.

I took a sip of wine, which hurt my belly. Helen passed out the food, the chicken that I had killed now a mixture of soft tendons, petrified bones, and chunks of meat. There was also rice and cabbage. I heaped lots onto my plate. I heard magpies call out before their sleep.

Helen said to me, "Your family, don't they want to come? We met Grace only once. She is very beautiful. But why won't she come again?"

"Grace really did love it here," I said. "She is a great traveler, really, but with Augie and the new baby it is not realistic for us."

"We would love to see her again," Helen said, "tell her that. And when the kids are older everyone will come."

The near dark sky was a buzz with bugs. Moudra swatted lazily.

"Who is this Willie person I heard is coming?" Josephine asked.

Helen rested her hand on the back of Thomas' head.

"She is looking into her thesis about ancient crop rotations."

"Why do you need her help?" she asked. "James is not good enough?"

"One has nothing to do with the other," I said. "It's standard in academia. I am helping her career by offering her access to my data."

"Why not give this to James to do?" she continued.

"Because James is not trained to do what she's looking for."

"Are you paying her?" James asked me.

"What's going on here?" I said. "No, she raised her own money."

"I feel underpaid," he said. "I work very hard for you and keep this place in order."

"It's not that easy. I can't just come up with money like that."

"I don't deserve a raise?"

"Of course you do, everyone does, but it ain't that easy. I raise all this money by myself."

"You live a nice American life from it."

"And you live a nice Kenyan life from it."

"It's not like an American one."

"That's true, but it's good for here."

"Still, see what you can do."

"I will see what I can do James."

I finished my food, took another sip of wine, and said to James, "Tomorrow is a big day. We've got to dig the trees and get Rasul to take them down to the city. We've got to get everything in place."

"I know, boss," he said. "I am very excited."

"Did you contact Rasul?"

"He's ready to go, man. He thinks this is going to be big. He thinks he can get U.N. money for this type of thing."

"I love Rasul," I said. "He's all for the glamour."

"He's been drumming up news," James said. "Telling the newspapers, people at the U.N. and all the agencies. Telling everyone, the tourists too."

"Good," I said, "let everyone know."

Helen brought out the cake, cut it up in pieces, and handed out the slices; when mine came I went at it like a savage until it filled up my crippled gut like cement.

"I'm going to sleep," I announced. "I'm bushed."

"Don't," Josephine said, standing up to her full height, "mistake your priorities tomorrow. Where do you start your day?"

"With you," I said.

Thomas laughed and James smacked him in the head.

I slept poorly, scratching at my mosquito bites like a dog, and woke bleary eyed with the rooster. I stepped out of bed and fell down with the pain in my big toe. It trumpeted to my brain a sharp distress call! I had planned on jogging to Josephine's this morning. Her house was a mile up the mountain, a good soft run in the high African air. I sat on the floor and held my big toe in my hand and rubbed it. It was red, black, and swollen. I wrapped it in bandages and put on two layers of socks. I stepped into the dry air, favoring my left leg.

Helen was already up and a fire was going. She handed me some porridge in a bowl and I ate in silence. She boiled water for tea. The chickens were still up on the roof of our houses waiting for more of the day before they came down trusting that the night predators were gone to sleep. The songbirds were calling across the plains. There were no mosquitoes.

"What do you think, Helen?" I said.

"Don't worry about it Fire," she said. "A lot of it is advertisement, but Josephine knows what she's doing. You can trust her."

"Excellent. Thank you."

"Good luck," she said.

I walked out to the gate, opened it, and started jogging slowly along the side of the road. I was sufficiently padded and felt no sharp pains in my toe. I ran past a field of juniper trees. I looked out at the plains on my left and felt again that sense of wordless awe. It was, I think, the way the sun shone so wide on the flat planet. I heard the feral dogs off in the distance and I heard the magpies call.

Josephine's house was a small wooden box that she had painted white and sky blue and kept in great order. A few thwarted trees sprouted in the sandy soil, but Josephine had gotten James to build her a trench around the house which he filled with good soil from my nursery and she had planted perennials and yellow flowering groundcover and small succulents that were rich green in their moist state. I imagined that when she was alone, no patients or lovers, she ran her fingers through the soil picking out weeds. She had a goat, some chickens, and dogs that were all cluttered in the yard, each animal dirty with brown sand. I waited a moment and knocked, and was soon let in.

"Okay, this is a good beginning, Fire. I think I can help you. You must trust me, though. Nothing works without it. Can you trust me?"

I followed her into the office.

"I hope to," I said.

"You must."

"I will try, I swear."

"I will be able to tell."

"I imagine you will, but it won't be a lack of trying."

"Okay."

She smiled at me and adjusted a bracelet on her wrist.

"Take off your clothes."

Her office was a small well lit room painted in white that had two full book shelves and a big table with rows of vials and bottles of herbs, pills, oils, cotton balls, bandages, iodine, some unguents, a screwdriver, pliers, a machete. There were chairs at the edge of the room and in the middle was a bed.

I took off my clothes.

"Lie face up on the bed."

"Are those sheets clean?" I asked.

"Lie down, Fire."

I settled myself into the rubbery mattress and started to breath deep. Josephine's face turned serious and inward and she looked down at my body. She smelled like a bear come from her cave, but it was pleasing. I tried to catch her eye, to get a sense of what was going on, but she was inscrutable.

I coughed.

Morning in the plains was the most beautiful time, sun slanted and bugless. My toe throbbed. I stared at Josphine's ass, so large like a colossal frisbee. I heard some birds call, shrieking. I wondered if my colleagues from Yale and Brown would come out for my tree celebration. I had invited them, but hadn't heard back, the first step in alienation after my public antics in Amsterdam. Josephine was making me nervous; I was worried that something might go wrong. I closed my eyes. I felt Josephine's hand land gently on my belly and she said, "Stay like that Fire, relax. I am going to examine you." I wanted to stay alert, but I drifted off as Josephine pushed into my gut, her breath up close to my face, my consciousness a fluid space of images and feelings.

I awoke to the sun shining fully in the sky. I felt blissfully alive. It was perhaps the deepest sleep I ever had as an adult! I stretched and felt a wave of happiness enter my lungs. I looked down at my body and it was diagrammed with red circles and dots.

"Josephine," I called.

"I'm out here," she replied.

I got up and put on my clothes.

I went outdoors and she was on her knees pruning and weeding.

"Sit down Fire," she said and pointed at a chair.

"Glorious day," I said. "Are the red circles permanent?"

"No, you idiot."

"That's good. The weather is perfect."

"You should move here."

"It's a deeply seeded dream of mine."

"Well, perhaps one day it will come true."

She stood up. She wiped her brow.

"You are sick, very sick in the stomach."

"I know that."

"I will be honest with you. I don't know if I can cure you, but I have seen this type of ailment before and there are roots and herbs that have been used for ages that work. We will try them. And you must take them."

Like James' nose her nose was a canyon.

"I want you to keep on coming each morning while you are here. I think I can make you feel better. At least you will sleep well."

"Your garden is great."

She went inside. One of her dogs sniffed at my pants. I pushed him away, but he growled. She came back out with a bottle of herbs. It looked like a science lab jar of swampland.

"You must take a handful in a tea each day. I can tell by your face that this is disgusting to you, but you must overcome that and take these herbs. I won't lecture you, now, but do as I say."

I took the bottle from her. She smiled, pawed my cheek, and kissed me on the lips.

"That toe," she said, "what happened?"

"I banged it on a tree stump chasing a frisbee."

"Thomas, huh?"

"Yes. Does he always do these type of things?"

"He's a clever boy."

She laughed. She went into the house. I looked out at the plains.

"Sit down," she said, coming back.

She took off my sneaker and sock. She carefully wrapped the bandage, which felt cold and wet, around my hurt toe. It felt soothing right away. "Keep it on for a week."

"Yes."

"It stinks," I said.

"So what."

"It's overpowering."

"You'll get used to it."

By the time I got back to camp all were up and James was on his way to the office to call Rasul to get things going.

Helen said, "Fire, how was it?"

"Very good," I said. "I was stupid to be nervous."

"I'm glad. I see that she gave you some herbs. Do you want me to put it in a tea for you now?"

"Okay, I guess."

"Fire, it's not so bad. I'll put some honey in the tea and it will mask the taste."

"It looks so disgusting."

"It probably is," she said, "but if Josephine thinks it's going to help you I'd at least give it a try. You seem reluctant, Fire, if I may say so, to get better. You drink it and don't think about the taste. Think about what good it might do for you. Have faith in it."

"Yes, thank you Helen. That makes complete sense."

"You don't have to follow my word," she said, "do what you feel is right."

She turned from me and I turned towards my office.

James was on the phone with Rasul.

When James was off I said, "How long do you think?"

"He said give him four hours."

"Let's go choose some lucky trees."

Helen came to the door.

"Fire, your tea."

James laughed.

Helen said, "Be quiet James. Look at him, he's ready to run away."

"Be a big boy Fire and drink it."

I took a sip and immediately gagged.

"Oh, Fire, it's not that bad," Helen said. "I drowned it in honey."

"Is that allowed?" James said.

"Be quiet," Helen said.

I took another sip and gagged.

"I'll make it through Helen. I promise I'll drink it. But I can't do it fast. I'll take it with me."

"Alright."

We turned away, got some shovels, and walked out into the fields where the trees grew. They lined the landscape with their crooked and bowed branches, and crowned heads, already a little fatness around the flare, king trees of the desert.

"Your foot stinks," James said, "and your body is covered in red circles. What did she do to you?"

He turned and started walking down a row.

I threw the tea on the ground, kicked its contents under the soil, and followed him.

Seven of our trees were being sacrificed on the streets of Nairobi to try and bring some ecological equanimity to the destitute. Even though we were going to plant them in pits of rich soil and cover them with a blanket of mulch they were still being left without any care in a tub of habitat. There was nowhere to go; the roots would break the concrete and heave the joints in search of wider space, and I despaired for them.

We took our shovels and went to the first tree. I traced the edge of the root ball and we started digging slowly on its periphery. Once we had some distance from the roots we dug down. It was blazing hot and I felt the heat fill up my lungs. I shoveled methodically, as James had taught me to do, catching myself when I moved impatiently, and gradually we got down about two feet to the bottom of the root complex when I stabbed my toe with the shovel. I went down on my back as if I had been shot. My teeth clenched and chattered. My blood froze and my eyes rolled. I lay numb staring up at the sky, feeling the sweat that had bubbled up on my neck. I breathed deeply. I got up still half dizzy and softened the soil around the circumference of the root mass, being careful to not cut too many roots, loosening the tree's foundation in the ground, grimacing with staccato pain. Eventually, we pulled the tree out. James cut off some of the hanging small roots. He then spread out a burlap roll like wrapping paper. We lifted the tree and put it on the mesh. I wrapped it around the root ball and tied it tight with string. We did this with six more trees, plucking them out of the ground and wrapping them up, exhausting work, my toe pulsating.

We went back to camp and had some food before Rasul came. Helen asked me where the teacup was and I told her I had forgotten it in the field. I felt flush. I went back to my hut and lay down on the hammock. I heard Thomas in the distance screaming at his sisters. I thought of Augie and Michelle and then thought of Willie, who was to arrive tomorrow. This pulsed my blood and I got up to see Rasul's big heavy truck gurgling into camp. Out of the cab poured five Indian men, Rasul in blue jeans and a t-shirt that said "Pittsburgh Pirates."

"Fire, this is big news."

He smiled, his teeth red, and hugged me.

"The day has arrived," I said.

"The best. I've been looking forward to this ever since you came to me. I know good things when I see them. This is big news."

"I hope so too, you know that. For my own reasons, of course."

"Academic advancement and renown. By the way, you are covered in red circles."

He smoked his cigarette, all his men did, and they carried with them a light hazy cloud.

"You want stardom, like us all," he continued.

"Yes, I guess so," I said.

"How does a man make such success from the planting of trees?"

"When trees come to poor neighborhoods it means things are getting better."

"More money flowing in."

"That's exactly right," I said.

Rasul's men lay themselves back against the truck and continued to smoke. James stood next to me.

"The way we see, it," Rasul said, "those that are bright and ambitious stand to benefit . . . What's that stink?"

James laughed, and so did his men, who wiped the air in front of their noses.

"I jammed my toe last night and Josephine made a bandage of medicine for me."

"It stinks," he said. "I hope you are going to take it off before the event?"

"It will be wrapped in a big shoe by then. No, I am going to keep it on."

"Don't ruin this, Fire. This could lead to good dollars for me."

"Money in trees," I said.

I took a hose and watered each burlapped root ball until it dripped moisture. James and I jumped up onto the flatbed of the truck. Three of Rasul's men bent down, picked up a tree, and hoisted it to us. We caught it, straightened it, laid it down gently, lining eventually seven trees horizontally, their branches interwoven. We laid a green tarp over them, securing it with ropes. We hopped down and Rasul's men climbed up.

I said to Rasul, "See you later. Don't forget to check the roots balls again when you get to the city. They might have lost all their water in the ride. Water them. We can't have thirsty trees for tomorrow's event."

"Don't worry boss man," he said. "They are in good care."

Off he went and James and I went back to camp and packed our bags. I was treating us to a night at a fancy hotel, on the tab of Columbia University, in celebration of our big day. After the event we were going to the airport to pick up Willie. Packed, we kissed Helen and the kids goodbye, and went off in our SUV.

Almost immediately we ran over a civet. We heard it get squashed and crushed under the tire as it let out a terminal moan. I felt a wave of horror pass through me. We stopped the truck and the animal was whimpering for breath.

"James, my god," I said. "How did we not see it?"

"It came out of the grasses and was suddenly there."

"It's going to die, right? It's suffering miserably."

He walked back to the SUV, grabbed a shovel, and brought it down on the animal's head. He picked it up and threw it into the grasses.

We got back in the SUV. I fell asleep during the long bumpy trip and woke as we came out of the hills and into town. We drove around the edge of the city to Rasul's lot. He was there, watering the trees that were still on the truck.

"Good," I said to him.

"We have to keep our assets alive."

"Yes," I said, "exactly."

We left for the hotel, driving through the cracked and potholed streets. At the hotel we gave the SUV to a valet boy while another boy grabbed our bags as we followed him into the lobby that was spilling with tourists, international workers, and local wealthy folks. James beamed and I felt love in that I could open up this world of luxury to him. We checked in and we went to our rooms before dinner.

I unpacked and opened the windows, airing out the room, with its yellow and black bedspreads. There was a desk and a chair, a large bureau, and a TV, which I turned on. It was All in the Family. Archie and Meathead, the incredibly sexy Gloria (who I beat off to as a boy), and Edith. Archie was telling Meathead that Barney had spied some "jigaboos" in the neighborhood. I laughed out loud. Meathead sighed, but Gloria called Archie "disgusting." I thought of Leo, and how he'd love this, watching All in the Family in Nairobi. Barney came over to warn Archie that the "jigaboos" were still around and Archie made a nasty remark that made Meathead call him a "racist." The phone rang, startling me. I picked it up and the operator said, "Mr. Rosewood, you have a call from America."

"Hello," I said into the phone.

"It's Leo."

"What's up?" I said. "Wow, I was just thinking of you. It's All in the Family."

"Dad is really sick."

"What're you telling me?" I said.

"He's really sick."

"About to drop off the planet sick?"

"Near dead."

"How near dead?"

"Emergency room, emergency heart surgery near dead."

"That's near dead."

"I wasn't exaggerating."

"Mom?" I said.

"Nearly comatose."

"You handling it?"

"Barely."

I looked up at the TV. My vision became blurry and my mind went blank.

"You must come home right away."

"I can't. I have my big event tomorrow and it's a whole day affair. I couldn't leave until the day after tomorrow."

"So you're talking probably two and half days from now?"

"That's right."

"You must come home sooner. He might be dead by then."

"I can't, this is the biggest moment of my career, really. I can't just leave, Leo, you've got to understand."

"You must. This is family. It comes first."

"This is my future, Leo, this is what I do."

"Dad is going to die."

"How do you know?"

"Trust me, he's going to die."

"Yes, I know, but how do you know that it is now?"

"I can see. The guy is basically dead. He's white as a sheet and his mind is gone."

"Have you seen him after the surgery?"

"No, but trust me."

"I'll see what I can do."

"Get home soon, Fire," he said and hung up.

I stared at the TV, Archie and Meathead. I went numb and thoughtless, slipping into mystery and listlessness. I couldn't picture my father, his face disappearing from me. I might never see him again, but I felt incredibly far away from it all. He had ignored me, his first son. And I had in turn ignored him. I hoped that this wasn't recapitulated with Augie. I went to the open window and tried to gather my thoughts. I looked out at the courtyard of the hotel, the tourists splashing in the pool, and the hills beyond the compound. The hot wind blew into the room. I thought of the civet cat we had killed. I thought of Molly, who I missed terribly, and then Felix who I was impatient to see again. I had to go to the event itself in the morning, but I would skip the dinner. The mayor would have to understand. I would fly out tomorrow evening, that was the plan. I stared back at the TV, Archie and Meathead now in the kitchen held hostage by the "jigaboos."

James and I had a less than stimulating meal. James was sympathetic, but he wanted to go drink and dance. After dinner I pushed him out the front door and I went back to my room and tossed and turned in a mindless funk, my gut tensed up, my blood acid. My dad kept rolling in and out of my mind, images of him as he was now, old, gray, less stable on his feet, his hands puffy with time, his body weakened, his lips encrusted with the residue of a generation of cookie eating. He was still furiously angry, but it came with less sustain, and Leo and I laughed at him, goaded him. He was a clown to us, but still our father. I fell asleep finally, deep into the night, the city quiet except for a bang here and an engine there.

In the morning I showered, didn't shit, brushed my teeth, and did some exercises. I dressed in my blue light cotton suit, white shirt and green tie. I went down to James, who looked happy as can be, but turned his smile to sadness remembering my father. I told him at breakfast that I would have to leave right away after the event. He said, "What about this Willie?"

"Oh shit! I forgot about her."

"What will you do?"

"We'll have to pick her up at the airport and see what she wants to do."

"What do you mean?" James asked.

"What if she wants to stay?"

"Oh no."

"You can show her the data."

"Not me, boss."

"Shit," I said. "Shit."

We finished breakfast and walked out, waited for the SUV, and drove to Tom Mboya Street, a deteriorated stretch of municipality. Rasul was there with the flatbed and a pickup truck with soil, mulch, fertilizer, and shovels. The pits he had dug a few days earlier were five by eight and three feet deep. His men had already planted four of the trees and I went to check if they had been planted right, the tree's flare at level with the soil. I touched the dirt, dry and sandy. Three inches of mulch was laid on the soil and each tree was given 15 gallons of water. I walked over to James and Rasul, who said, "Okay, time to roll."

We stood around aimlessly for more than an hour waiting for the mayor to arrive. I morphed over that time into an anxious mess, worrying about getting home, worried that the mayor might not show up. But he eventually came, followed by reporters, officials from the aid institutions, from the U.N., from the United States Embassy. A stage of wooden platforms was set up and loudspeakers too. The Kenyan flag flew. Tourists stopped and shopkeepers left their dwellings as the first high notes of the loudspeaker blared across Tom Mboya street. The mayor got up and said that all neighborhoods deserved trees and that he, as a man of democracy, like the great president Arap Moi, was for trees too because they meant that everyone had a chance to succeed. The president of the U.N. in East Africa said he believed in ecological freedom and that these trees symbolized the right path. I looked for my colleagues from Yale and Brown but did not see them. The American ambassador said that, "Once again America has proved its willingness to spread democracy and freedom by supporting a project like this." I walked to the lectern and said, "Thank you Mr. Mayor. Thank you Columbia University. Thank you Ambassador and the U.N. . . . . Trees give us clean air and shade. Everyone deserves clean air and shade. I am proud to be part of this effort to make Nairobi a cleaner and shadier city. There are even early reports that trees decrease crime in neighbor-

195

hoods. Think of it, if these trees clean the air, give shade from the sun, and keep the community safer, they sure have earned their keep. So please, please Mr. Mayor, keep these trees healthy. Water them," I said, "every week. Thank you." I looked for my Yale and Brown colleagues again. I looked at James, who looked angry. I said, "None of this could have been done without my associate James Methu, my tree partner, my colleague. And Rasul Kitenbackensingh, my reliable all purpose contractor. Thank you men."

Rasul waved his hand so everyone could identify him.

After the event was over I went to the mayor, thanked him profusely, and told him my predicament. He said, "Go home. Don't worry about tonight."

I was greatly relieved. I did a little mingling and schmoozing, but then found James and off we went to the airport.

Willie's flight didn't arrive for another two hours. I figured I'd wait to buy a ticket until I found out what she wanted to do. Despite the sorrow I felt at the prospect of my father's death my body still tingled with anticipation for her. I pictured the freckles on her cheeks and how it made her look elflike. I tried to picture the breasts that had pushed up against her shirt during our interview. I listened in my head to the pronunciations of her words, how she had said "exactly" to coming out here to Africa. I thought invariably of the week I had just lost with her.

In the meantime James and I went to Wimpy Burger.

James said, "I am so sorry, sir."

"There is no way to prepare for your father's death."

"Yes."

"You sure you won't show her around?"

"I would feel very uncomfortable," he said.

I stuffed half the burger in my mouth.

"But she flew all this way. It doesn't look good. Come on, just a few days."

"No, boss. I wouldn't know how to act around a female American without you there. It is too awkward around Helen."

"You're right," I conceded. "I will just have to explain to her. These are extenuating circumstances."

"So, boss, when do you think you will come back?"

"Soon. I need to come back and spend some solid time taking stock of the work, thinking about what we need to do. But my pitiful life is not set up for long trips anymore. I have to trust more and more in you."

He said, in a near whisper, "You know, boss, you mentioned at the beginning that once things were going you'd hand over your work to us natives."

I looked at him, sensing the end of my days here. Love is stronger than death, I thought, and pictured Grace's body and how it was now rounded and fleshy by her hips and ass, and I thought of her as a mother, solid and soft.

"You want my project, huh?" I said to him.

"No boss, no. I was just saying that you don't have to worry. I will handle things here. I was saying that if your life doesn't allow for Africa anymore you can trust that things will be okay here. I will make sure of that."

I felt envy for him, living amid the mountains, the sun at his head, taking what I had started and making it his own.

"Yes," I said, "we'll see what takes place . . . Please tell Josephine what happened."

"You know Josephine will eat this Willie alive."

"Yes, that's another good reason to have her come back with me."

I stood up and James followed. We emptied our trash and set out towards the big metal doors that allowed new arrivers into Kenya. We got pushed and pulled by the waiting masses and it felt like the Thomas Mapfumo concert. The gates cranked open and within ten minutes in the middle of this mad rush was Willie. She looked discombobulated, her frizzy hair almost vertical with anxiety. I screamed her name, waved, and she came towards us.

"It's nice to see you," I said. "This is James."

They shook hands.

"It's nice to see you, Fire. I was feeling a little lost after ten hours of flying across the world."

"It's long and hard," I said. "But it's worth it. Wait until you see the mountains and the plains."

James sighed.

"Oh," I turned to Willie, "actually things have changed, dramatically."

"Really," she said. "Can I sit down, please?"

We walked through the immigrant throng to some wooden benches. She threw her pack to her side, sat down, and exhaled. She looked up and said, "Tell me."

"Well," I said, looking first at James and then down at her. "My brother called last night and said my father is on his deathbed and I must come home right away."

She swallowed. She wrung her hands briefly. I kept thinking to myself that she was the most beautiful elf I had ever encountered.

"So that means you are going home? Now? Right away?"

"Right away, I'm afraid. My brother said he's going to die. He had a heart attack, a bad one."

"I am so sorry," she said, "that is awful."

"It is."

She took a deep breath and said, "I guess the right thing to do is turn back around."

"I'm afraid that's your only option really. I'm so so sorry. I know that you were looking forward to this. You can't imagine how much I was. But it's my father."

"Don't think twice about it," she said. "Your father is dying and you must attend to that. Anyone would do the same thing."

She stood up, wiped down her dusty clothes, and grabbed her backpack.

"It would have been great though if you had been able to contact me, but I realize that was impossible."

We went to the airline window to see if she could change her return flight to today. The man looked at her funny, but said that for an extra $100 pounds she could do so. She took out her credit card, paid the bill, and waited for the paperwork. I too bought a ticket with my credit card, in the seat next to hers.

We went to the terminal and I hugged James, who said, "Good luck boss."

In the darkness of the night sky Willie and I talked about each other, our ambitions, our families, our memories, our parents and siblings, our hopes, our secrets, and our desires too. We were invigorated and fully interested, in a mad rush of exchange and intimacy, and thoughts of my father only penetrated briefly. She touched my arm to make a point and I brushed my hand over her thigh. She would lean into me with her large eyes that held great certainty and I would lean into her too our noses almost touching. Our hands interweaved like feathers. Eventually 30,000 feet above the Atlantic Ocean Willie reached above and turned out her light. I did the same. I felt the armrest between our seats rise. I felt her breath, which was warm and excited, moist from turbulence.

10. Returns

DAZED BY THE flight and our feelings we landed in the marshes of Idlewild, hailed a cab, and made our way into Manhattan. I touched her hand as she pulled herself out of the car.

"I'll call you," I said.

I breathed in the dense air and furious spirits of my city and my memories got stirred. Elbert falling down an open shaft from the roof of a building on 70th street. Feeling Julie's just grown tits in the service entrance to building 305. My father injecting himself with insulin each morning.

The cab sped into the lower body of the Upper West Side that had been scrubbed advantageously clean of the last five decades of acid rain and to my parents' apartment on the river.

I opened the door, tripped on some newspapers, got thrown, but got caught by Pearl, my mother, in her arms.

"Oops," she said, "Be careful honey."

"Why're the papers stacked up in front of the door, dammit?"

"Don't be upset. We don't need the added tension. It's been awful." Her heavy jaw dropped in disbelief. "I'm glad you're home."

"Hi, Mom," I said, pulling backwards, straightening up.

She let go of me.

Michelle was in Grace's arms and I kissed them both on their foreheads. Augie was on the couch thumbing through a book. I went over to him.

"Hey, boy. I missed you a lot."

He continued to thumb through the book.

"You didn't hear me talking to you, boy."

He continued to read.

"I think this boy's having a problem hearing," I announced to everyone. "Only five years old and already can't hear a thing."

I leaned in for the big bear hug, sending his book flying into the air and onto Mom's glass coffee table, which made him cackle. He gave me two seconds of pure hug before he started to squirm out of my touch.

"Dad!"

I unleashed him.

"You okay, boy?"

"Yes."

"You're my love boy, you know that. You're my love monkey."

I gave him another kiss.

"Leave the boy alone," Leo said.

"You leave us alone," I said. "So, why's everybody here and not with Dad?"

"He's in for a series of tests so we took the opportunity . . . Remember, dickus," Leo continued, remembering himself, "you've not been here. Your daddy is nearly dead and your baby is just born, but you've been away."

I turned to Grace and she smiled at me sarcastically.

"Right," I said, and laughed. "I'm remiss. How's he doing?"

"He's much better," my mother said. "Just this morning he seemed to wake up . . . It was a shock," she said. "I guess not a full shock considering his diabetes, but still a shock anyway because it was so violent. I called cousin Gloria, you know, and I don't think she fully appreciated how sick Murray is. She sounded impatient, but then again she is always impatient with me. Everyone is, really. Fire, your brother's been great."

I smiled at Grace, who loved Mom's whirling monologues. In her smile to me she was able to communicate the specific memory of Mom taking her to the dentist and asking the doctor, during tooth extraction, if he's related to the Trachtenburgs from Brooklyn, a plea to family to go lighter on her daughter in law.

"It's been hard," Mom concluded, "but everyone's so wonderful. Specially Augie."

I had missed the worst of it, and of course Leo, in his way, and Grace, in hers, would give me shit about this the rest of my life. Mom would never hold it against me.

"When can I see him?" I asked.

"In two hours we go back. Enjoy the moment," Leo said, moving over to the table. "Mom, let's eat something."

"What do you boys want?"

"Food."

"Fire, you must be bushed. How was it? Did you get a lot done? How was the conference?" she asked proudly. "By the way, we finally ordered a new couch."

"Jesus, Mom, you ordered a new couch now?"

"Yes, why not? We needed to get it done and Leo was here so we did it."

"You've been trying to buy a new couch for twelve years, why act now?"

"It's been that long?"

"Eight at least," Leo said.

"Grace," Mom appealed, "has it been that long?"

"I'm afraid to say that it is so."

Mom turned out of the kitchen and popped her head into the dining room and said to Augie, "Does grandma move slowly?"

"Yes," he cried out.

"I am sorry."

"So, what do you have in the refrigerator?" I said.

"Not much. Mom has let the food stocking go," Leo said.

"She sure has," Grace added. "We need Murray here so the refrigerator stays full."

"She's right. Without him here I would just go out to eat with my friends. He always wants to stay at home. You know," she said to Grace, "he really doesn't like people."

"I know, Pearl, you've told me that before."

"Isn't it interesting that I married such an anti social man?"

"Fire married me," Grace said.

Mom thought for a second.

"Yes, but Fire loves people."

"I do not," I said. "I've come to hate them."

"That's not true," she said, "you love people. You've always been social. Everyone loves you. But," she thought further, "when you were younger you did hit kids. Why did you do that? Was it something I did? We took you to a psychiatrist. Dr. Joseph. You remember him?"

"Yes."

"I wonder if that was a mistake? Did it do you any good? Your father didn't think it was necessary . . . But you've always loved people."

"Well I hate them now. And how can you not once you see their true nature: greedy and selfish, aggressive, deceptive, and to top it off self righteous about it too."

"You're so full of shit," Leo said. "Grace, do you believe this guy?"

"He's the most confused and deluded human being I know."

"He truly is so mixed up."

Augie said, "He's a poopy pappy."

"You two have no idea what you are talking about," I said.

"He's gearing up for the presidency," Mom reminded us.

"I forgot," Leo said, "we're in the midst of power."

"He's carrying on the spirit of his father's activism."

"You people are just jealous of my ripeness," I said.

"That's right," Mom challenged them.

Leo snorted.

Grace moved her body, pulled open her shirt, and took out her breast. Michelle turned herself and took the nipple into her mouth. Leo looked at this, had seen it before, but was still nonplussed.

"Mom, don't encourage him."

"I think it's a good thing that he cares."

"He doesn't care for anything or anyone but himself."

"Like you're any different," I said.

"I'm not," he said. "But I have no airs and ideologies."

"That's because you are a cynic, you have a lack of faith."

"That's right," Leo said, "a jackass."

Grace stuck out her jaw at me.

"His whole being is popping around," Grace said, "and it drives me crazy."

"You will be proud to know," I said, changing the subject, "that the event of my life went off without hitches, perfect. Seven darling young baobabs and acacias were planted on Tom Myoba street because of moi."

"Congratulations," Leo said. "I should have come out for that, taken photographs. Next time I'll come with you to photodocument."

"'Photodocument. And I am arrogant?'"

"What the hell is that stink coming from you?"

"Yes, Daddy?" Augie said.

"I jammed my toe and Josephine, James' sister, the healer, wrapped this medicinal bandage around it."

"It sure does stink," Leo continued. "Customs let you through? Take that voodoo thing off."

"Let's see it Dad," Augie said.

"Later," I said, "later tonight."

"Let's see it now."

"Yeah, let's see it," Grace said.

I got up from the table, walked over to the couch, sat down, and took off my shoe. The stink rose up like a volcano now that it was liberated from the shoe and plumed into Augie's and Grace's faces.

"Maybe you should throw it away when you get it off," Augie said.

I undid the dressing, everyone moving backwards, but what I revealed was the return of pink healthy flesh, Josephine's bandage absorbing the wound.

"That's not so disgusting Daddy," Augie said.

"You're right. That bandage was the trick. She's good."

"Okay, I'm hungry," Leo ended things.

Mom fed us and Augie screamed at me to "Slow down!"

"Listen to him," Mom said. "You really eat too fast. It's no good."

We finished our meal, gathered our stuff, walked down 10th Avenue past the high school and the library, past the Projects where the children I went to elementary and junior high school with all lived. To Roosevelt Hospital where I was once a patient of a gastroenterologist who went to jail for sexual molestation. My friend John wondered out loud when I told him this story if the gastroenterologist hadn't molested me too.

Up the elevator and into the blue and white tiled halls of the hospital. Gauges beeped, machines chugged, engines pumped, phones rang, nurses conferred, but the hall was still draped with a pall. Mostly, in my life, I was the patient, the one draped in the pall, but now Father Rosewood, the man with the compromised genes that he had left to his oldest son, was expiring. I stopped at the door, held Augie's hand, and we went in.

He was crossed and punctured by tubes, as to be expected, the room a musty neon light, and his window was facing downtown over the grimy tenements of Ninth Avenue. His roommate breathed noisily in and out and laid with his back towards us his old and wasted rump sticking out from his robe. We surrounded my dad's bed, with me at his head. His face was sagging and yellow, rotted out, and matted in white whiskers. His thin gray hair was looped in all directions and the liver spots on his arms bled into each other. His eyes, however, were illuminated, even pissed off.

"Dad, you avoided the big one again," I said.

"The president is home," he answered.

"I'm back. How are you?"

"I could be better, but I'm not going to die, not right now."

"That's very good news," I said, and leaned in to kiss his stubbly cheek.

"It was the cheeseburger," he said, "that almost killed me."

"What cheeseburger?"

"The cheeseburger the dude was eating when he went belly up," Leo said.

"Dad, how could a cheeseburger cause a heart attack?"

"It was that bad!"

His anger came down like a sharp curtain, completely changing his mood.

"That's crazy," I said.

"That's what you think," he said.

"Murray, all I know," Mom said, "is that you've got to change your diet now for good. Eat moderate, please, honey."

"So what was it like?" I asked, "what was it like to be so close to death?"

"Like a deep sleep. It was like a deep sleep."

"Was it a scary sleep, peaceful?"

"I don't remember . . . Grace," he said, "you look great."

He closed his eyes.

We stood there for a moment to see if he'd come back, but he was asleep. I touched his face with my hand and Grace and Mom did too. We left the room and walked back to Mom's apartment. Grace, Augie, Michelle, and I packed our goods and drove home up the conduit by the river, east through Van Cortlandt Park as the parkway snaked around the marsh with its willows and red maples and to our home on the steep rock in the Bronx. Fergal's rusted truck sat alone in the driveway, the steps icy, my backyard garden covered in layers of snow.

We opened the door and were greeted by Felix. I got down on my knees with Augie and hugged him. He tried to squirm out of it, but I kissed his wet nose and Augie did too.

"He missed you Dad," Augie said of Felix.

"I missed all of you," I said.

I stood up, picked Augie up too, put him between Grace and me, with Michelle on Grace's back in the baby backpack, and Augie said, "sandwich," and we all hugged, my hand on Grace's robust ass, the lines of her underwear framing the dimensions running from the edge of her back to hidden spots.

"Home," I said.

Grace put Michelle down to bed and I gave Augie a bath and sat down beside the tub and looked at his shiny body and watched him play with his toys and sing to himself, occasionally looking at me. His mom fed him fruit and yogurt, I brushed his teeth, and I felt my impatience rise, waiting for Grace sexually, wanting to get there already. Instead, I lay down on Augie's bed with him, side by side, snuggled up together, and I started to read. I read him a jaunty rhyme of dragons, evil knights, and fair maidens, and we fairly sang it together. I looked at the next book lying on my lap and calculated how long it would take to read to him and how much longer before I could have sex. I felt like a horror show, disconnected from the universe and lost in my idiot microcosm. I needed meditation! We read a book about ducks and crocodiles, a good one, where a crocodile would rather be a duck. On the third book, a tale of success among dogs I felt the urge of sex come on so strong that I paused from reading and took a breath. "What's wrong, Dad?" Augie asked. "Nothing, love boy," I said. I thought, will he suffer from this too? I went back to reading and finished up the book. I leaned into him for a good night kiss, sucking in his cheek with my lips and teeth.

Grace passed me in the hallway and I grabbed her buttocks.

I got my pot from the chest drawer and filled the bong up with water and ground some of the pot through my fingers and put it into the bowl and struck the lighter. The smoke entered my mouth and filled up my body.

I went out to the livingroom and sat down on the couch and waited for Grace. I heard her reading to Augie. She finished one book and started another. I thought, If only Grace would consent to be a swinger all would be perfect. How simple. All the anthropology books I had read confirmed this. People fooled around like birds ate berries and mice foraged. The urges were too strong. No one stayed with one thing without exception. And quite frankly it was the message of America: there was so much to choose from. So, I said to myself, stay together, but share each other too. A little give and a little take. Adapt but reach out simultaneously. Don't give up. A new paradigm for marriage! Bruno, I thought, we've got it.

I heard her finish up and I lifted myself up on the couch. She came out from Augie's room and walked away from me, through the dining room avoiding the livingroom, but then changed her direction, passed me in fact—smiled—and went into our bedroom to check on Michelle. My eyes glazed over. She rumbled in there for a while and then came out and sat on the chair next to the couch, sinking into it.

She said, "Welcome home."

"It's nice to be home."

"Nice to have you home."

"Showing up to Amsterdam was fantastic."

"It was. You were very pleased. Got yourself all horny from your sex shows."

"I almost fainted."

"Nothing makes you happier. You'd give up on career and hobbies, even friends, if need be, but without sex you'd go crazy within a month."

"Two weeks. I'd go crazy in a week."

"Kill your whole family with an axe because you didn't get your weekly blowjob."

"Spend the rest of my sorry life in prison being fucked in the ass by some Aryan tattooed Thor."

"You're simply disgusting. Seriously, you're disgusting."

"So, how have you been?"

"Okay, considering the circumstances. It hasn't been easy."

"I can't imagine it has," I said. "But you've been managing, right?"

"Yes, Fire, I can manage."

"I feel bad about going away, but it's my work, you know that."

"We don't need to talk about it now."

"I just wanted you to know that I feel bad about it. It's not like I'm steel. I feel the disconnection."

"You go anyway."

"Yes, I do."

"So now the king is home."

She smiled to show me that she was kidding.

"Yes, he's home. The father of the king is dying. The mother is in love with the son. The king's wife is weary and wary, but the king is horny for his queen nonetheless."

"What a surprise," she said.

"A king can't want his queen?"

"I didn't say that. But the king wants his queen with such regularity and predictability. Even when he's just been in a den of sex clubs for a week."

"It wasn't all sex clubs. There was you too."

"How much conference to sex clubs?"

"Honestly?"

"Honestly."

"70:30."

She laughed. "No way you went to that much conference."

I didn't say anything.

"Okay, tell me something of what you just saw."

"Even better, the people across from me on the plane were giving each other hand jobs when they thought I was asleep."

"Really?"

"Yes, it was unbelievable. I heard these rustlings, and you know I'm such a poor sleeper, and I woke up and saw the blanket over both of them. I could see movement underneath, hands going up and down. Their heads were back with their eyes closed. It was very stimulating. I really knew it was happening when she leaned over and kissed him."

Grace looked at me with her chin out.

"Are you telling me the truth?" she asked. "I don't believe it."

"It's true, really." I leaped off the couch to defend myself. "Seriously."

"How come you see these things and no one else does?"

"Because I am a sexual vortex."

I laughed at myself.

"Yes, you are, a sexual wake of a tornado, all the strewn hearts behind."

"I don't break anyone's heart."

"You break my heart."

"Not on purpose."

"Doesn't matter, it still hurts."

"It's not personal."

"Doesn't matter, it still hurts."

"So, what can I do about it?"

"Probably nothing, but I feel you don't take me seriously. Like I am just part of the furniture."

"That's so untrue," I said. I got down on my knees and said, "I love you as you are."

"Thank you, Fire, even if you mean it in philosophy and not in practice."

"See, you are an underminer." I stood back up. "I said something nice and from the heart and you had to qualify it."

I coughed three times in succession.

"I know you feel I don't care," I said. "We misunderstand each other. It's too bad. I'm selfish, but you and the family come first."

"We both work so hard, both so ambitious, both with exponentially increased responsibilities, and then I come home and you are out, either literally or in frame of mind. That's where the chafing is. Last week things got very pressured at work, two manuscripts were late, but each night I had to come home, feed the kids and give your mom a break, and then go back to the office. I needed you home."

"I've reduced the amount of time I stay away."

"In actual minutes yes, but let me tell you that even when you are here you are usually lost in your office, stoned as an Inca, working away on your projects."

"I feel I can't take a minute's rest."

"From what?"

"From living and accomplishing."

"Being home taking care of your kids and loving your wife isn't lack of production."

"I've got so little time, I mean look at Dad, and I've got to get it all done."

"I've got my own goals too. I understand how much time it consumes, how much we want to get it right, particularly at this age. I know, but you've got to slow down enough to pay attention to your family. Without us nurtured we will wither or fade."

"Perhaps we can come up with a new design. You have a week to yourself, to do whatever you want, and then I get a week."

"Like an internal separation."

"No, like time management. A week on for full intensity of concentration, whatever you're doing, and then a week back in the fold of the family."

"That's ridiculous. Why not just break up?"

"Because I don't want to you. I love the structure of the family, but want to build some freedoms into it also."

"You have a ton of freedom. You were just in Kenya and Amsterdam."

"I mean in a regular everyday way."

"You mean an open relationship?"

"Sort of, but you know with priorities."

"What priorities?"

"Family first, without hesitation."

"If I didn't know you better I would be hurt. You can see that a proposition like this might be seen as hurtful. It's so typically you. The funny thing is I still feel romantic towards you, despite it all, all the absences and false returns. There is something in your "new" design that is pure to this relationship. Maybe a little more time away from each other will bring a renewed closeness. I don't know. I have wanted more time out with friends, just the girls, a few more nights to stay late at work and catch up . . . But I presume you want to be able to have other women too."

"Absolutely not. The only experimentation I want is with you included."

"Last two times you tried a ménage a trios you fucked it up pretty bad."

"That's true. But if I know that you are fully along for the ride I would be more relaxed about the whole thing."

"Well this side of the bargain the jury is still out on."

"You mean you will think about it?"

"A little, but monogamy is hard to ignore."

"It seems intractable."

"That's because you are such a big believer in the power of your will."

"So, what about the people on the plane?" I reminded her.

"You see all these sexy things that no one else does."

"I look out for them is the truth."

"So, is it the truth?"

"You've got to believe me."

"Okay."

"Pretty sexy, huh?"

"Yes . . . If it's true."

"Ah ha! Now you see, it doesn't matter if it's fact or fiction, just whether it's a good story."

She got up from the chair and moved over onto the couch with me.

She said, "How come we never did that?"

"Did what?" I said.

"Have sex on a plane. We've taken so many together."

"I'd be too scared," I said.

"I guess I would be too, but it seems so sexy."

"Why?"

"The fear of being caught."

"That just makes me nervous," I said.

"That's the thrill."

"But what if you actually get caught?"

"No one cares, you know that. They are startled for a second, but then they go back to their lives."

"You're right, Grace, that's the way it is."

She whispered, "I'm a passenger in a plane right now."

I turned to her, nearly blind, and said, "And I'm a passenger too."

A week later my father was released from the hospital. A few days later, Willie still burning in my mind, I took the afternoon off from work and went down from Columbia to 72nd Street to have lunch with him.

We met at Jewish deli, which was buried among the multiple stores on 72nd Street with sawdust on the floor and smelly with beef and soup. My father sat towards the back in a booth.

I walked to him feeling a mixture of familiarity and caution.

"How about we share a pastrami sandwich?" he asked when I arrived at the table.

I dropped into my seat.

His white hair was flipped to the side. His cheeks were fat and sanguine. He actually looked good; the old mad dog, at the brink of death a week ago now eating pastrami with his son.

"How're you feeling?"

"Not bad. I feel pretty good."

"It's amazing isn't it, the technology?"

"What're you talking about?"

"The machines and the medication that can keep a man alive even when death has firmly called."

"Ah," my father sighed. "They don't do a good enough job, that's the real problem."

"You had bad care?" I asked.

"No, that's not what I mean. I mean there is all this high quality for the rich but nothing for the poor."

"It's the way it is."

"It's goddamn disgusting," he said, "and it makes me sick. My whole life fighting for equal rights and equal opportunities and the rich still want more and the poor are still stupid."

"That's naked prejudice."

"What are you talking about? You don't know anything!"

"First, the rich can be stupid and the poor can be smart and second the world can't contain the same opportunities for everyone, it's impossible."

"I believe it's possible. If not my whole life would be a wasted effort."

"The melodrama."

"I nearly just died you ingrate."

"In the hospital you said it was no big deal."

"Ah."

The waitress came up, an old Jewish maid in a black and yellow uniform, her type nearly gone.

He ordered the sandwich and a matzoh ball soup for each of us and then he ordered black cherry sodas.

"Fire," he said, when he had finished the order, "can you manage all this stuff? Can you manage a family and your job, which is not really settled yet, and your money? Are you up to this? Are you staying alert?"

"Dad," I said, "come on. You know I am."

"It's harder than you think."

"It's not easy, I know that."

"It was rarely easy for your mom and me."

"I could see that."

"What do you mean by that?"

"Nothing, calm down. I just meant that Leo and I witnessed all the fighting."

"It comes with the territory."

"I'm not judging you for it Dad."

"What I meant to say is are you okay? Do you need some help?"

"Thanks. I'm fine, for the moment. I take here and there, as you know, but I need to save a big request for the right time, the appropriate time, which is when I'm settled in a professorship and things are more stable and we want to buy a house."

"That seems right, but don't be afraid to ask."

"You'd freak if I really asked for a lot of dough."

"Screw you."

His face lit up even redder than it usually was.

"I was just joking."

He sat back and fixed the napkin on his lap. I looked into his eyes, but he was incomprehensible. I stared at his features wondering how they were etched in me.

The food came and we two gut sufferers lapped at the soup like hungry dogs and devoured our fatty meat like vultures. Our lips and jowls were shiny with grease and our teeth were resplendent with salt and pieces of tendon.

"Fire, can you handle Grace?" my father said after finishing up. "I mean this. She's a hard one, has spirit, doesn't give up."

I coughed. And then coughed again.

"That idiotic cough of yours," he said.

"We both are hard, pushing for what we want."

"That's life, doesn't she know that? Things have never gone my way. Anything that I have accomplished is by my own hand."

"We don't want to give in. Just like you."

I coughed. And he looked at me angrily.

"A person needs to be tough," he said.

"Tough. Tough for what?"

"To overcome all the obstacles."

"You're right."

"But you're spoiled, by your mother."

"Okay. What's for desert? I'm having some ice cream."

"Nothing here?" he said. "Not a pastry here?"

"Na. Ice cream."

"Ice cream in the winter. It's ridiculous."

"What are you talking about?"

"You can't eat ice cream in the winter, it's assbackwards."

"What the hell are you talking about?"

The waitress came by with her hanging face and asked us if we wanted desert.

"No," my father said. "He wants ice cream, in the winter."

The waitress figured out the bill, handed it to my father. We paid and left.

It was snowing, the gray canyon of 72nd Street illuminated in speckled white. The car tires on the road were slippery and people's feet hit the sidewalk like walking in water. My dad fixed his green trench coat over his shoulders and I huddled up in my pea coat, the pea coat he had bought me when I was 14 years old. He was fine, himself, back to life, and I felt suddenly cheated of my time in Kenya and my time with Willie. He stole from me, had stolen from me before, my spirit and my dignity when he seared my courage with his fierce red cheeks and disturbed ego. Ahead of us I could see the space of emptiness which was the river. We passed the shoe store that supplied my child's feet. We turned on Amsterdam, the bank looming above, and we went to get ice cream. I got a black and white milkshake, which made my father shake his head. Out into the cold again the snow falling heavily and collecting on our hair. We walked passed intrepid street trees and pigeon frequented benches. We walked down towards the river past the bakery and past the eyeglass store. The shake was so sweety good and I slurped at it like a hummingbird. At the corner my father said, "Ice cream in the winter. It's cockamamie."

A week later he died. He was eating another cheeseburger up the block at the local dinner and he had a massive heart attack. This time we entered the hospital to identify the body. I went in first, taking the lead, and when they pulled the metal drawer out from its cubby I prepared myself with a deep breath. His face was unmistakable, with fresh whiskers, but his features were frozen, and that freeze told us that he was no longer attending to us, had moved on from the body and left it behind. His clothes were typically his, a checkered shirt, pen in breast pocket, and cheap jeans. I tried to feel for him in the room, and I vaguely did, but I didn't catch on to anything too strong. I tried to think about him, but nothing specific came to mind. I wondered where he was? I wondered what was going on? Was he still conscious of our world? I took his hand and held it. Mom took his other hand. Grace held Mom and so did Leo. Augie held Grace around the leg and Michelle of course dangled from Grace's back in her baby backpack.

Three months later I was sitting in our bathroom in the morning, spring just blossoming and the heat coming back, taking a miserable morning dump. I opened up the Baseball Encyclopedia. I had wanted to look at Willie Mays for a long time, but kept myself from doing it, each time turning to another player. I loved Willie Mays because my father did. His was the only autograph I owned. "To Elijah Rosewood from Willie Mays." I had it framed on my desk. I opened the book to his name, fighting off the urge to stop at Hank Aaron or Joe DiMaggio or Harmon Kilibrew or Willie McCovey or Stan Musial or Carl Yaztremski. There was Willie Mays all of sudden, all his 660 homeruns, and the tears came gushing out.

Five years later, just into my 40s and Augie 10 years old and four more priapic conferences in Amsterdam and five more trips to Kenya behind me (where Josephine refused to treat me because she said I was not serious enough and 30 more trees into the sidewalks of Nairobi), a full professor of Environmental Management and Ethics at Columbia

University, we used a chunk of Mom's (and Dad's) money to buy a house in Riverdale. Mom gave it to us gladly, Leo bristled but said yes, and we could feel Dad at our shoulders hectoring us to stay alert. Nevertheless, much of Dad's capitalist tainted money came to his spoiled son so he could have a house with many rooms and tall trees in the yard and a glimpse of the river!

PART 4

11. Exposed

THE PROMISE OF Willie had slipped from my life after my father died. I was too exhausted by my despairing events to call her right away and then it got longer and longer to the point where a call would have been awkward. Instead she slid into my dreams where thoughts of her brought stimulation and prospect. I kept thinking we'd meet at some gathering of the natural science community, but it never happened. I tried to anticipate mutual events, but she was never there. She became spectral, glowed in my imagination. I dreamed of her most lucidly in the mornings when I would wake before my family and think about our time on the plane, her moist breath and salty fragrance. My house lists down the hill towards the Hudson River and on these mornings I would listen to the birds calling from the branches of the white oak and white pine and wonder if she would resurface in my life. It was a sensual burning in my gut that traveled down to my groin and was stoked by the pot and my general ambitions.

One day there she was sitting under a blue umbrella at an outdoor cafe. The sky smoldered and dripped with heat. The smells lifted from the sidewalk and asphalt into a bacterial tonic. I was thirsty and sun struck from walking the streets of my city. I was inside and outside simultaneously, walking always into the light, which came from over the river. I saw her the minute I stepped up on the curb, and I felt my cheeks get hot. Whatever I was headed to, whatever rituals dominated my current life, faded; I walked to her table, moved out the bulky metal chair, and sat down opposite her.

She was shrouded under the umbrella and a straw hat, her hair spilling out. Her smile amplified her freckles, her eyes hidden under brown and golden sunglasses. She wore a sky blue dress that came down to just above her knees. Her legs stuck out from the dress and past the dripline of the umbrella so that the sun highlighted her calves and ankles and her translucent leg hairs undulated in the hot and dusty wind.

"You look great," I said.

"Thank you."

"It's been a while."

"Yes."

"What happened?"

"We got briefly close and then were whisked away."

"Yes."

"Your father died."

"He did. He's dead now over five years."

"What about your mother?"

"She's alive and kicking," I said, "healthy and still my servant."

She took off her hat and her hair leaped out. She planted her elbows on the table and looked straight at me through her dark glasses, carving out of the atmosphere a space just for us.

"What do you mean by that statement?"

"My mom does what I ask of her."

"Is that what your mom is? Is that what you think moms should be?"

"It is my hope that all the women in my life will in some way do what I ask of them."

"Does your wife do this for you?"

"She doesn't comply nearly enough."

She laughed.

I noticed the large diamond of her engagement ring and thought how gaudy it was, a lump of mandatory rock strangling the finger.

"Well," she said, "perhaps she doesn't agree with your definition of things. Perhaps you are being spoiled and unrealistic."

"You think I possess those traits?"

"They were obvious to me the second I met you."

"In what way?"

"You're a momma's boy."

"What gives you such psychic license?"

"You lack discipline in your human relations. You expect others to mold and ply for you, you think you are blessed in some way, a childish ego in a man's head."

I coughed.

"And you are perfect?"

"I don't suffer from dreaminess."

"I'm a lover. Let's get that straight. I'm persistent in my pursuit of happiness. That's what Grace, my wife, doesn't realize, I am in pursuit of both our happpinesses."

"Really. You have her in mind when you flirt with other women?"

"Absolutely. She's always in my mind even when I pursue alternative things."

"Alternative things," she laughed.

I felt the hot air compress in my lungs. I looked at her chin, her mouth, and sweet thin lips.

She took off her sunglasses.

"You have two kids now, right?" she asked.

"Yes."

The waitress came with a salad and a cheese omelet for Willie. I ordered the same thing even though cheese lately was really hurting my belly. I shifted in my seat suddenly because I had to pee. I was having pains there again. It was very irritating. I stood up, surveyed Willie, and excused myself.

I followed the hallway to the back of the restaurant, waited for the person before me to finish up, holding my cock in my hands to deaden the pain, skipped inside finally and almost screamed out loud when the gooey pee dribbled out. I rested inside the stall for a moment recomposing from my vertigo.

When I got back I said, "I have two kids now. Augie is nearly ten and Michelle is nearly five. Can you believe it?"

"Augie, that's right. You have a ten year old? What's it like?"

"Every minute with him is a joy even when he wants nothing to do with me or whines or complains."

"Pure hippie love."

"Pure godly love."

"Hippie love."

"Right oh . . . What about you?"

"Steve and I have two kids too, four and two."

"That's where you've been, having kids."

"Exactly. All my pursuits dropped away once my kids came along."

"You dropped out?"

"Altogether. I gave up my studies. It was too much, and Steve wanted it that way anyway."

"What does he do again?"

"A psychiatrist."

"A shrink."

"A shrink from a shrink father and shrink mother."

"Oh boy . . . So, you're strictly a mother now?"

"Have been since my eldest daughter entered this world. Kids all day long and TV at night, with a husband who provides little assistance."

"Why doesn't he help with the kids?"

"He works a lot and when he comes home he is too tired."

"I think Grace sees me the same way, as mainly absent."

"Well," she said, "I feel it's time for me to focus a little on myself. The girls are a little older and Steve finally got me a full time babysitter."

I coughed loudly twice.

She said, "What's that?"

"What?"

"That cough, that high pitched cough?"

"I've had it since childhood."

"Really."

I looked out at Broadway, the struggling cherry trees in the street median.

"Don't get me wrong. I love my kids more than anything, and don't really feel compelled to defend myself, but I have felt the strain lately and would like a break from it."

"I'm not judging you, if that's what you think."

"I know that, which is why I talk this freely with you. It feels very good to talk this way with someone, with you."

"I feel totally and lucidly myself with you."

"You're exposed."

"I'm no innocent."

"Actually, I think you are. I'd call you guileless."

"I don't think so."

"You're easy to manipulate."

Her eyes were unwavering.

"Really."

"Really. Exactly."

Her hair hung heavily in the air and when she leaned to one side half her face was engulfed.

My food came and I dove into it like a man who hadn't eaten for a week. I heard Mom, Augie, and Michelle in my head telling me to "Eat slow."

Willie said, "You eat like a Viking."

I opened my mouth to show her my masticated food.

I thought of Jane who drove us all crazy with her deliberate eating, keeping us from dessert as she pointedly chewed her dinner, Augie and Michelle screaming at her, "Jane! Please eat faster."

I leaned back and let the heavy cheese omelet plod its way down my gastrotract.

"It's wonderful to see you," I said. "I thought about you a lot, to tell the truth. I kept imagining that we'd meet sometime . . . I was really upset that Africa didn't work out."

"I was too, but, and I've thought about this, it's for the better. I'm in a better spot now to get to know you."

"How's that?"

"Trust me."

She leaned down to her side, picked up her hat and put it on her head, fit back on her sunglasses.

"Fire." She got up, pushing her chair back. "I've got to go. It was wonderful to see you. It was amazing, really, to meet you after so long. It feels rewarding."

"Me too."

"Do you have a cell phone?" she asked me.

"No."

"Why not?"

"I hate them. More modern distractions from the things that really count."

"Yes, and they are practical and I can reach the babysitter immediately and call the police in an accident. Wake up."

I smiled.

"So, get a cell phone."

She gave me her number.

She leaned down between the umbrella above and the table below stretching out her long torso and face like a giraffe and gave me a kiss on the lips, a little awkward and dry, but a kiss that imprinted me with her nonetheless.

I went crazy! Each and every second I burned for her. I walked on my toes and functioned like a sleepwalker, dropping Augie off at the wrong friend's house, forgetting to give Michelle her breakfast, getting into the first of my eventually three car accidents, none serious, but all wrenching and time consuming, and Grace became furious at me.

In addition, I couldn't work. Instead I walked to the river from the university down the stone steps of Riverside Park and through the London plane trees and down the path out to the water. The sun engulfed me and I was the center of its attention. A tugboat pushed a barge and the George Washington Bridge hung like a colossal spiderweb over the river. The cliffs of New Jersey shrugged their brown shoulders. I held myself steady against the railing over the water and watched the waves splash into the riprap and looked down at the south part of the park that measured my childhood and thought for one brief second about the rats that lived in between the rocks before my brain, stoked by the sun, went right back to Willie.

I bought cellular phones. I felt like I was giving in to the money-making bullshit of America. But I knew that it was necessary now. I came home with the phones and surprised Grace.

"What made you get them now?" she asked.

"I kept thinking of Augie and Michelle and what if something happened when they're with the babysitter and how would they contact us if they get sick at school. You know."

"Well, you're right, but why now? Something fishy's going on?"

"Jesus, Grace, always suspicious. I finally saw how practical and even life saving they can be. That's it, nothing else."

"Still seems fishy to me."

I called Willie the next day as I walked down Broadway from 120th street.

"So you listened to me and got a phone."

"Yes."

"Are you alone?"

"Yes."

"I'll meet you in the park at 106th Street."

She stood under a chestnut tree wearing a pink t-shirt that framed her wide chest. She wore white jeans and white and green sneakers. I could feel the energy as I neared. Before she caught sight of me she kneaded her hands.

"Hey," I said.

"How about we go down to the river. I don't have much time. The nanny and Emma come back soon."

"I was weaned on the river," I said, as we turned south to enter the park.

"What do you mean?"

"I grew up in an apartment that overlooked the Hudson River. I broke my arm looking out at the Queen Elizabeth sail by and I played softball by the shore. It's the light. It has always been in my life."

"What about now?"

"We live in a house in Riverdale where if you sit in one place in the yard and one place in my study you can see the brilliant river."

"We see the river too from our apartment"

We walked down the deteriorating steps to the wide terrace with the weeds in the cracks of the cement and over to a bench that looked out on the river. Her pink Wonder Woman t-shirt was inched up her back so I could see the light hairs on her waist and lower spine and dream about the path that led into parts that were only visited if great intimacy was offered.

"So," I said, "you gave up anthropology . . . I'm attracted to anthropology."

"Like what?"

"Coming of Age in Samoa."

"You would."

"What do you mean by that?"

"Free love in the gentle breezes of the Pacific."

I had to stop myself from touching her leg. I looked at her pink t-shirt and went a bit blind, seeing pink circles. I coughed twice. The color of her skin was a beam of light and the moisture on her lips was nearly fatal.

Her phone rang.

"Hey," she said. "Yeah . . . She's due back any moment now . . .

Sounds like a hard day for you . . . I've got to go, honey. I'll see you later."

We got up, turned back around the bench, over the terrace, and to the stone steps under the locust trees.

"What're you doing on Friday?" she asked.

"I'm supposed to be at work."

"Let's have breakfast. Nine o'clock. That gives us some time because Emma and the nanny are going to the playground, if the weather permits. I'll call you, on your cell phone."

For three days I thought obsessively about the weather, hoping to god that it would be nice. My eyes were red with exhaustion and I took sleep medicine. I went on night runs through Van Cortlandt Park. I trampled ferns and ducked under the pendulous beech branches. I ran and ran, trying to exhaust myself, but I still couldn't sleep so I watched TV late into the night. Sports. I watched baseball until I simply couldn't last another second and Willie finally faded, for a brief instant.

Thursday night, drugged with pot and sleep medicine I fucked Grace hard, leaning in to tongue kiss her. When finished she said, "Why can't you sleep?"

"I'm sick, that's why, sick with middle age."

"Are you having a midlife crisis?"

"I think I am."

I thought of Willie, the way she walked, her ass swiveling up to the left as part of her gait.

"What's it about?"

"I don't know."

"No guesses?"

"No."

I climbed off her.

"You need to sleep Fire, you will get very sick."

"I know. I want to sleep. I just can't."

"Please tell me what's bothering you."

"Nothing really, I swear. I just think it's general malaise. General, uh oh I am over forty and what comes next fear."

"Perhaps," she said. "But I think it's something more specific. You won't even admit it to yourself yet."

"Who knows? I'd just like to sleep."

Which I didn't, going down to the livingroom and putting some pillows on the floor and with my back against the legs of the couch tried to meditate. Grace had been meditating for nearly two decades now, but I could barely make headway. I kept my eyes opened and fixed them on the bay windows on the other side of the room, the white pine's long branches sweeping against the glass. I let my mind go in circles spinning away from my earthly habits and twirling out from words into a cosmos of internal space with milky ways and stars. But this is where it ended and I soared back into my everyday and thought of Willie and what she would wear tomorrow morning and how I wanted to share with her my frustrations with Grace and tell her also a little bit about my devious behavior in Amsterdam; about how I would one day run for president of the United States.

I climbed on the couch and picked up a book called "Love and Sex in Twelve Cultures." I read, "If one had control of death/It would be very easy to die with a Wolf woman/It would be very pleasant." So what if I slept with Willie? I still fulfilled my obligations, the family came first, but after that I was free! This was what Mother Earth offered at her highest and nothing ethical would keep me from it. And after all, Grace had Orlando.

The day was gorgeous and I ate my sugar cereal in the kitchen. Augie sat next to me. Felix sat on the table, lapping at a bowl of milk. I had slept two hours.

"Dad, you're going to die."

"I know," I said, "I can't sleep."

"Are you going crazy?"

"Yes."

"You should see a doctor."

"I'm fine, just a little stressed."

He fixed himself a bowl of sugar cereal.

"This junk I eat Augie, please eat healthy."

"You set a bad example."

"I know."

Grace shuffled above and came down the stairs in her nightgown, rumpled and chunky, her brown hair disordered. Michelle bounded down the steps, the same energy as mine and Augie's, almost knocked Grace down, and grabbed the sugar flakes too.

"The whole family eats junk. Thanks Fire," Grace said.

"Sweet elixir is hard to resist."

"Especially for you my dear," she said. "But I was hoping that our children might be more moderate, like their mom."

"No chance in hell for that," I said. "My genes are too hot."

"I've come to see Mom's way," Augie said. "Mom is more sane."

"Oh, really." I leaped up and bear hugged him, almost my size already so small was I and no sign yet in him of my gut woes and so strong and lean. "You think you can leave the force and go to the dark side?"

"Mom is not the dark side," he said, bent over with me hugging him from behind. "Dad, okay, let go."

"Your father needs to be taken to an insane asylum," Grace said.

"The hospital," Michelle said. "He's sick."

"The hospital," Augie mocked her. "You mean the loony bin."

"Yes," Grace said.

She grabbed her healthy cereal and mixed it with peaches and stirred in a little milk. I reached out and grabbed her ass through her frayed nightgown. Augie said, "Dad, stop that." Michelle grabbed Grace's ass too. Grace said, "You're a perfect role model."

I went upstairs, tried to shit, read about Reggie Jackson and his 548 homeruns, couldn't get a shit out, which depressed me, peed violently and thought I should really see a doctor about this, showered, shaved, and brushed my teeth. I wore my best polo shirt, a dark blue silky thing, brown slacks, and my suede boots. Bye I said to everyone and got in my green car and drove away through the prosperous streets of my neighborhood to the parkway. Down the river, its gleaming surface, past the sewage plant and over to the university. I parked, walked east to Broadway, the day already sizzling in the dawn.

She wore a translucent florid shirt unbuttoned so that her red bra was visible at the top. She gave me a kiss on the cheek. I wrapped my arm around her, touched her lower back, withdrew. We went into the restaurant and when the waiter showed us a table by the window Willie asked for a table further back. I followed her, looking at her body move between the chairs, her swaying torso, her strong back, and fleshy arms. We sat. I moved my head towards her over the table, craning it out, and said, "Nice to see you."

"Nice to see you too."

"You look great. That shirt."

"Steve bought it for me but this is the first opportunity I've had to wear it."

"It's making me a bit dizzy."

She smiled, but at the same time pulled her shirt up over her bra.

The waiter came by and we both ordered cheese omelets and tea.

"Steve already at work?"

"Left at six this morning. But not without asking for his morning ablutions."

"What's that?"

"A bj."

"Everyday?"

"Essentially. That big fish eye staring me in the face, filling up my mouth."

"I gather you don't like it."

"I don't."

"Why?"

She began to knead her hands.

"When he refused to help with the kids. I expected his full participation, I am a modern woman, but he was no where to be found."

"Off doing his thing."

"Off doing his thing. I hate Steve so much at times that I amaze myself."

Her upper lip curled like a caterpillar in movement. Her eyes, like mine, were spilling with want. The food came and I attacked it like a feral dog. I looked up at her chest, her cleavage showing in a wide V. Her lips glowed with the grease from the omelet. Her thick hair was stuck in strands and clumps against her neck with sweat. My phone rang. It startled me. It rang again. I reached into my bag and fished it out and saw Grace's number. I went suddenly hot in the face and chest. I looked up at Willie and smiled awkwardly. I picked up the phone.

"Hi."

"Hi. Are you in a meeting?"

"Yes. What's up?"

Michelle was sick and needed to be looked after. I had to teach at one, but she needed me back at noon, had a business lunch she couldn't cancel. She had tried to find a babysitter, but unsuccessfully. I suggested Grandma, who Grace had already called, but she was busy. I looked over at Willie in self pity. I said, "No, I can't cancel class this afternoon. Sorry, Grace. It's too sudden."

She hung up.

"Well that ruined the mood," I said.

"Don't let it. We've still got some time."

"I think something is happening."

"It is."

"What do you think?"

"That I'm going crazy."

"Me too."

"I'm not without caution, anxiety."

"Me too."

"Do we go through with this? I've been thinking about it even before we remet. Yes, you didn't leave my mind. I've been asking myself, can I have this in my life? Can I live this way? It is right?"

"Of course it's right. Feel it. It can't be resisted. Or if it could it would be a stupid thing to do. It's like the best food, dripping with taste and luxury, the best beach, the sand softly placed there just for you. Why would anyone in their right mind say no?"

"Someone is going to get hurt, and it will probably be you."

I reached out, put my hand under her dress until I found her thigh, damp, smooth; my first touch, a lightning bolt through my heart and groin.

She said, "You have no idea how hot that made me."

I called her the next day.

"On Thursday there's a lecture at the museum on Aztec forestry practices that I'm going to. Can we meet?"

"I'll try. Steve is feeling guilty lately so I think it's quite possible."

"Guilt is the great set of scales in our middle age marriages."

"That's cynical, you know."

"I didn't mean it that way. I meant that it actually helps balance things, keeps a person in check. I'm Jewish. I know about desire and guilt. I also like things in balance."

"I am a Catholic and I know about guilt and judgement. And I like things in balance too."

"Touche!"

"So, I'll call you later and let you know about Thursday."

"Your mere name fills me with excitement. Willie, you uplift me."

I could feel the sudden awkwardness in the air. I worried that my explosion of feeling had brought home to her the danger of her actions.

Nevertheless, she called later that day and said she could make it.

I didn't hear from Willie all week. I became agitated and came down with a cold. My gut hurt. I felt sick and old, but also alive and deeply stimulated. Nonetheless, I continued to feel pain when I peed and finally broke down and called my doctor who referred me to an urologist. I went to see him and peed in a cup. Three days later he called and said that there was blood in my urine and that I would need a penis exam. I asked him if it would hurt and he said yes.

I stood on the steps of the museum and waited for Willie. I looked at the elm and linden trees hanging over the sidewalk. My eyes followed the trees inside the park and I thought of the day long ago when Charlie Sanda had handcuffed Adam to a black cherry on a dusty and sandy lawn. This made me think of Mombassa, how the sand landed on our clothes, how Grace probably felt as humiliated as Adam. I could stand in the same spot on earth over and over again. What moved was time, not I. A man in his city until it progressed to the end. The steps of the museum, which featured in my life, would now include Willie, who was climbing to me at this moment.

When she arrived she said, "Skip the seminar. Let's go."

We walked to my car. She was stunning in green blouse, white skirt, and heels. Inside the car, headed downtown for dinner, we were awkward at first, letting the intensity of the relationship ferment. Once on the parkway, however, our fingers exploded into movement, swarmed with feeling and exploration. I inched my hand upwards along her inner leg. I remembered thinking that her thigh was skinner than Grace's, less to hold. I was awash in desire and my body began to shake. I could feel her body's pandemonium too. She grabbed my hand and shoved it over her crotch, which was humid; I pushed on her, my hand engulfing her vagina, pressing in like an iron.

Suddenly I had to grab the wheel with both hands as I swerved from lanes. I noticed a vanity plate that said "CUPCAKE" and screamed out loud, "Childish exhibitionism! America is a spoiled child."

"What's going on?" she said.

"Vanity plates make me furious."

"This from a man who wants to run for president."

"You've got it wrong. I'm running for president to save the soul of our nation. A person who advertises for themselves on a license plate is the fungus I will root out."

"I could easily see you with a vanity plate."

The parkway dropped downwards to the streetlights on the West Drive. I leaned over to kiss her, but she moved away.

"Not so exposed," she said.

"Who could see us? Come on, don't be silly."

"I don't want to get caught. I'm going to the grave with this, and so are you."

She looked at me severely.

I leaned over nevertheless for a kiss, which she now granted me, a little bit of her tongue touching mine.

The rest of the drive I leaned in for kisses and she measured out little treats with her lips. In the restaurant, I grabbed her under the table. This made her uncomfortable, but she didn't stop me. Drunk finally, we spilled out in passion, the space between us exclusive and unimpeachable. Our mouths were full of garbled words of yearning, coveting, like nature on her hot course towards extinction. On the way home I parked the car along Riverside Drive and we made out, full on, no backward glances.

The day of the penis exam Jane called in the morning to wish me good luck. Grace gave me a big hug and on the way down Willie called to wish me good luck too. Just before I stepped into the office my mom called and said please call the minute I was done to tell her the results. Right after Leo called and said, "Manup!"

In the examination room my body trembled. On the table was stretched out new white paper that advertised Viagra.

I took off my clothes except for my t-shirt.

The doctor motioned me up onto the table and I lay down. He pushed my legs aside. He dabbed a q-tip with some chemical and then daubed it in the slit of my penis making me flinch and grit my teeth. He moved my slit aside and I could feel the scope entering me and it felt like a ship pushing its way through a tiny canal, slicing my membranes as it moved. I held tightly against the table. It drove in further and I could feel it twisting. I was having a sword plunged into me, my blood turned sick, my heart raging. The doctor then turned in his seat and started to bring the scope out until it blissfully left my body.

"That's it. Nothing to it. Doesn't look bad. Wait a few days and you will be riding high again."

From the car I called Willie.

"Well, it's over."

"How'd it go?"

"My penis is throbbing."

"Sounds horrible. Did he say why you have blood?"

"He said nothing was wrong with me."

"Then why the blood?"

"He didn't say."

"You didn't ask him?"

"Felt no need after he said I was okay."

"That's foolish. You need to know what was going on."

I gasped.

I said, "I am going to a conference in Albuquerque in a month. It's a conference on Ecosystems and Culture. For three days. Do you want to come with me?"

12. Sand

THE MORNING WE rendezvoused the night still behind the spectral buildings along the Hudson River we hugged and kissed like lost lovers in our cab. She wore purple and white and I was dazzled by her smell, and charm, and the contours of her forehead, and the way she sat next to me in the cab with a hint of timidity, readiness. It was a gift from god and I needed to treat it with the proper respect and awe. I felt rescued by her, found from among the billions of lost things in the universe. In my touch I wanted to convey these feelings; never, please never, let this come to an end.

We bounded out of Manhattan east, past dark Harlem houses and sagging ailanthus trees. I took a breath from kissing her when I felt us rise up to the bridge. Unfastening the snaps on her corduroy I put my hand down her pants. She looked up to see if the taxi driver was peering at us. She wriggled into my finger, her crotch sharp and pointy, and I pressed her body against the back of the seat and kissed her neck. She kept looking up to see if the taxi driver was watching, which he was. We zoomed past the lakes of Flushing Meadows Park, a little orange light breaking through the black, and to the Van Wyck where the landscape opened up and the smell of the sea mixed with the smell of jet fuel and we arrived at Idlewild.

By the time we checked in the morning light had come up and illuminated the airport in silver and white. She bought a paper and a magazine and we got egg and bacon sandwiches. In her purple and white she looked at me with puckish eyes. I stole the paper from her to read the sports; she read her magazine, legs tucked underneath her lap. The grease of the egg and bacon sandwich smeared my lips and dripped down my belly making it flare. Our flight was called and we filed into the plane, found our seats, put our stuff away, settled ourselves, and held hands.

I wished I was stoned.

When the plane finally straightened in space she released from me and leaned over to her bag and pulled out a CD. She handed it to me with a lover's smile. I opened up the cover to read "Traveling Music." She pulled out a CD player and headphones that were split for two people. It was The Band. The slow march of The Band. I was living the new paradigm of marriage! I was its practitioner now and not just its theorist. What would Bruno say? Wake up.

We thrust down over tan desert mountains into Albuquerque. The city, so early in the morning, felt cold and lonely. The terminal was pink and white stucco and Willie blended in with her purple and white outfit. We hailed a cab, rode down on the mountain that led from Santa Fe into the city that sat in the high brush. Past houses with ghetto stains and tarnished façades and into the area around the university where trees adorned the streets and the pavement was a clean white. At reception we coyly watched each other as we checked in under our different names. My receptionist's face was round and dark, with tight night eyes, big jawbones, and jet black hair. We gathered our luggage, rode the elevator, turned the corners until we got to our rooms, which were opposite each other, and clicked our electronic keys.

I plopped down on the bed and panted. I heard the city outside, muffled unfamiliar sounds; the awkward and mysterious feel of a foreign place. I opened my pack and fished out my pills, emptied them on the table to reveal five Viagras hidden amid. These were violent pills racing the heart to its maximum capacity. I took one. I looked at myself in the mirror, saw my father hidden in the folds and ripples, went into pee, which was still painful from that procedure (a month later), brushed my teeth, and left the room.

I knocked softly, not wanting anyone to see my entry, particularly not my colleagues from Yale and Brown who lurked the conference halls and could very well be staying here on this same floor. Willie came to the door and also looked out suspiciously. I slipped in. I leaped into her knocking her down on the bed and we entangled. We humped and rubbed against each other and kissed with fearlessness. She rolled away from me, looked up, and said, "I have a present for you."

She climbed off the bed. She took off her purple shirt to reveal a transparent brown bra and then took off her pants to reveal transparent thong brown underpants. The brown fabric blended into her lime and olive skin. I stood up, moved into her, put my hands on her ass, and kissed her. I let my wet lips move slowly along hers, like two dolphins swimming together. She tried to force my mouth open, but I kept our tongues separate. Incrementally I metered our mouths until they finally overlapped. I kissed my way down the top of her bra, moving my mouth along its edge, circling inwards along the stream of my saliva until I reached her nipples and put them in my mouth, the morning light streaming into the room. I laid her on the bed and made my way down the straights of her belly where I dragged my tongue through her pubic hair until I felt her clit and rested it there. We calmed down to let the moment elongate and float in its soggy time. Albuquerque was at work and people walked the streets but Willie and I were alone finally, in great closeness. I began to lick around, explore, feel for the subtle and minute signs. I thought for a second that I was going to have a heart attack the Viagra was so strong. She rolled away from me and reached in a drawer. "Here is my present," she said. She showed me a bottle of lubrication and smiled shyly, nearly embarrassed. "Take me from behind." She handed me the lubrication and turned onto all fours. I thought, we don't need lubrication, you're as wet as a swamp. I put it down on the bed and entered her from behind, which made her grunt. She said, her head dangling downwards, "No, in the ass."

"Oh . . . You sure?"

"Are you trying to talk me out of having anal sex with you?"

"I know, it does sound odd, nearly unforgivable. Man turns down anal sex. It's unheard of. But I feel obliged to mention that it might hurt. That's what Grace says at least."

"Well, you turn me on and I want to try it. Steve's dick is far too large for the experiment. So, captain, what do you say?"

I looked down at her brown anus, so different from Grace's red one, and poured some lubrication over the surface of the hole and rubbed it in until my rotations, and pressure, eventually forced my finger to submerge. She was silent; her body barely moved. I pushed in further. I could feel the vapor lock around my finger and wondered how it felt for her. She said nothing, was steely, so opposite Grace who moaned and grunted her pleasure. I took my finger slowly out, taking along in my fingernail a granular of brown sand. I put lubrication on my penis, pushed her cheeks aside, grabbed my dick, pointed at her swollen anus, and pushed. There was resistance, even with such anointing, but eventually my dick slipped into her ass and she continued to be deathly silent as I reached points farther and farther in, until there was nothing left.

I crumpled.

"That was incredible," she said.

"Your first time?"

"Yes, with you, my sex guru. Only with you."

"I don't want to be your guru. I want to be your lover."

"You are, don't worry, but I would never do this with anyone else."

"Not with Steve, not ever? You weren't hot for each other when you were first together?"

"Not this way. It was great with him at first, but this feels different."

"The profanity of it."

"It scares the crap out of me."

"It's unstoppable."

"It feels that way, for now at least."

She got up to pee. I followed her. When she was done I sat down on the toilet.

"Oh, boy, what next?"

"What?"

"I have to witness you poopy? We're that close already? I don't stay in the bathroom when Steve goes."

"I pee this way," I said. "I would never shit in front of you."

"Thanks for that. Why do you pee sitting down?"

"Grace's roommate in college told me when Grace and I became lovers that if I ever forgot to put the seat back down after I peed in the night she'd kill me. I was so scared of forgetting that I just trained myself to pee sitting down."

"You are such a weirdo."

"Why?"

"It's just so woman like. You are so woman like."

"In what way?"

"So skinny, small, and vain."

I began to pee and couldn't help but emit a little grunt of pain.

"Are you still in pain from that procedure?"

"Can you believe it? A month later and I'm still in pain."

"Something's not right."

I peed a little more, grimacing, and then started laughing.

"When I was living with my friend John at college, in my junior year, he used to accuse me of leaving a drop or two of pee on the toilet seat. This drove him crazy. But I denied all responsibility. I said to him, I sit down like a girl to pee so how could I leave any on the seat. But he insisted and we fought about it all the time . . . He used to." I cracked up. "Wash the seat with bleach after I had been in there." She started to laugh too. "I remember once that our other roommate, Lester, had some fat girl come by and when they were done fucking, like bears I might add because both were about 250 pounds, she left a big shit in our toilet. John freaked out. He cleaned the whole bathroom with bleach wearing a mask and rubber gloves.

"But he was right. One day, years later, I stood up from my pee and happened to notice that a few drops arched back and landed on the seat. Two distinct pee drops pooled on the seat. All along John was right."

I got up and pushed her backwards on the sink. I stood on my tip-toes, spread her legs apart, my heart racing at top speed, and slid into her, looking at myself awkwardly in the mirror. For the first time she started moaning. She held herself up on her back stretched arms like spider legs, her face stoic but yielding, absorbing and rebounding each of my thrusts until I pulled out and came on her belly.

We took a shower, dressed, had a Mexican dinner in the old part of the city away from all the conference hubbub, and she laid her spoon into my plate, ate some of my rice and beans. She said, "I don't even eat from my kids' plates."

We got drunk on tequila and I moved over from my side of the booth to sit with her, but she sent me back. "Don't be foolish," she said, but under the table grabbed my leg and squeezed it.

We slipped back into the hotel, she put on a silky nightgown, and we came to bed. I turned over on my side and she rubbed my back till I fell asleep.

We fucked at two in the morning, the sky with just a few dim lights. We fucked first thing in the morning, our bodies still encrusted from the midnight fuck, and fucked again just after breakfast. I did not need Viagra. We went over to the university, the air clear and dry, the streets tended with horticulture.

"Every year," I said, walking side by side, "I go to Amsterdam, for the International Justice Conference."

"You liberals," she mocked.

"When I was in Amsterdam five years ago, just before I was to meet you in Africa, just before our first trees were planted in Nairobi, just before my father died. On that trip, my friend Bruno and I brought as our dates to the final reception some prostitutes."

"You did what?"

"Our dates were prostitutes. I thought, why not be honest, right? I had spent almost the entire time in Amsterdam in the sex world and so why not be honest about it, right? I'm so sick of all the lying. Nigger, please."

"Nigger, please?"

"Nigger, please. I heard an interview with Old Dirty Bastard and this was his response to a profoundly stupid question. I was waiting to use it."

"You can't use it. It's not your right and, I might add, you will get killed."

"Once it's uttered it's public property, and I like the tone and inflection of it. It says so much. It says, fuck the dirty system and it says fuck you for being ignorant and self righteous. It's painfully precise."

"But you're one of the world's greatest liars."

"What are you?"

"Not like you."

"Really."

"Exactly. Do you want to get caught? Do you know how horrible that would be? Do you know how much we would suffer? Why would you risk getting caught?"

"Of course my colleagues at Yale and Brown are here, ever watching my deviations from the norm."

We walked desultorily along, the trees planted in their small street boxes, the wind blowing off the desert.

"I'd love to lick your pussy right now."

She opened her bag and looked at the schedule of conference events and seminars. She read, "Fossils and their Effect on Soil Rates."

I said, "Nigger, please."

She turned around and I followed her. We spent the rest of the day in her room, and I took another Viagra, which almost made my heart leap out the window.

Her phone rang. She fished it from her bag.

She mouthed, "Steve."

"Yes, it was an easy flight . . . Yes, it's a kind of nice city. It's small."

She leaned over and kissed me on the lips.

"Yes, it seems interesting."

She leaned in to kiss me again, with her tongue. I felt her breast.

"How're the girls? . . . Oh, good. Has the nanny been helpful? . . . Sounds difficult . . . Thank you Steve for helping with the kids."

We went out to the old city. I could sense the sandy time line between the past and the present in the patched up adobes. Willie looked stellar in white jeans and a white shirt, black sandals. I squinted and said, "Wow, the sun is so bright I can barely see."

"Why aren't you wearing sunglasses?" she asked. "You need sunglasses."

She had on the golden brown sunglasses that she was wearing the day we re-met at the outdoor cafe.

We walked down the narrow streets filled with lanky tourists, the natives woven in between their strides. We turned a corner and saw an eyeglass shop. We went in. She commenced looking though the cases. She pointed and the salesgirl unlocked the drawer and took out a pair as directed. Eventually Willie distilled her choices to five pairs and I tried each one on. She and the salesgirl looked me over and talked between themselves. Finally Willie said, "This one." The salesgirl nodded. It wrapped around my eyes like an elongated dark chemical slide. We walked back into the sunshine.

"Well?" she said. "Practical. Stylish. What a nice combination."

I said, "I'll be dipped."

Down the street came my colleagues from Yale and Brown. My first response was flight, but then I thought, adjusting my new x-ray sunglasses, why not let them see the real me, emboldened and free. Why was I, the whole world, always hiding behind the bushes? I wanted to scream at the top of my lungs, Willie! Out of the way, love is coming!

Instead, I steeled myself, took Willie's hand for them to see, and promenaded her proudly past.

We went back to the hotel, fucked, and I went to an evening session on horticultural practices in the Anasazi.

The next morning she asked sheepishly to have anal sex again. I took her from the side this time.

At breakfast she said, "I'd get fat if I was with you full time."

I shoveled pancakes and bacon into my mouth.

I went to a morning session, "Hallucinogenic crops in Ancient Mexico."

Afterwards I met Willie and we spent the rest of the day sightseeing, walking the downtown streets, filling our bags with gifts and trinkets.

In the room that night she undressed to a black thong.

She said, "What do you think?"

"That you are unbelievable. Elegant, royal, resplendent, smart, a great lover; you smell so good. That I am in great thanks and blessing to have you. That you are the most perfect being on earth. That I love you."

In the morning I got on top of her and cried, "This is it. I can't believe it, but the greatest three days of my life are coming to an end. I feel like I'm going to die."

She said, "When we get home I want you to think about me every night at 10 p.m., just before bed. I will be thinking of you."

I entered her, pumped with abandon, and started to come before I could pull all the way out. She screamed, "Fire, you came in me!" She wriggled out from under me. "Fire, that was disastrous. What were you thinking? Fire! Fuck!"

13. Wind

WE SAT IN a restaurant in midtown Manhattan and she said to me, "If I'm pregnant it will be disastrous."

"It will be alright," I said. "Trust me, it will all be alright."

"It better be."

She fetched some lipstick from her bag and carefully applied it.

"What's wrong?" I said.

"What do you mean?"

"You feel different. Have I done something?"

"What are you getting at?"

I coughed three times and she looked at me with impatience.

"It feels different. You feel different."

"You're imaging it. It's still the same."

I touched her leg underneath the table, but she pulled it away.

"See," I said, "you pulled away."

"No I didn't."

"Just yesterday you were crazy for my touch."

"I still desire your touch, just not at that exact instant."

"That's the problem. You feel different. There's been a break in your feelings."

"No there hasn't. I don't want to talk about it anymore."

She opened her bag and took out her cell phone.

"I've got to meet Steve."

"Why? Don't go now."

"I've got to. I need to meet my husband for dinner."

"I wish you wouldn't."

"I will see you in three days. We are having lunch."

"That's too long."

"Don't be so dramatic."

"I'm not. I feel devastated. You have moved away from me. It's all my fault of course, but you've yanked your love away and I'm wretched."

"It's just histrionics. Cut it out. I am here and now."

I reached out and touched the meaty part of her calf. She didn't pull away. I moved my hand down to above her sock and gently rubbed her nubby sharp hairs. I thought of the day at the outdoor café and how the sun shined on her undulating leg hairs. My heart turned cold comprehending the gap between that day and today; my rejection, the distance from yes to no. I continued to rub her leg, but in short time she withdrew. She smiled at me, got up, and said, "Let's hope and pray that I'm not with your child."

I stared up at the restaurant ceiling, swirling and tossing in my dark universe. When I imagined Willie's departure from me I felt at the end of the world. Eventually I walked out into a light rain falling from the buildings. The city was bathed in dull yellow light. I watched my feet move along the sidewalk, avoiding the puddles, feeling the mass of energy at my sides. I felt in opposition to my home. As it pulsed away I was lowering my pulse, becoming invisible. "Someone will get hurt," she had said. "And it will probably be you." I crossed Park Avenue. I coughed twice, sicker and sicker. I went west through the 50s and its darkened stores and delis, round past Columbus Circle, the park trees silver. Up Broadway, cross 9th avenue, jogging to avoid the speeding taxis, and up the steps to the plaza. Instinctually I moved towards the back of the complex to the stairs that led to Amsterdam Avenue, to the apartment on the river where Mom would be talking on the phone, looking through the newspapers. Her cats would be asleep on old magazines. The wind from the river rapped against the windows of my childhood room and I was sleepless with fear that they would shatter. She would make me food. She would say nothing when I ranted about politics. She would look grim when I expressed my hatred for her city. Yet I turned away from the apartment. Instead I walked to the subway. When the train came I found a seat in the corner and sat numb as the subway barreled out of Manhattan, elevating, passing over the gray tenements and gas stations until I got off at Van Cortlandt Park.

I crossed the parade grounds, into the dark maw of the woods, and went up the hill to my favorite place in the park, a brown and yellow settlement of grasses; a flat winter meadow in which I found my usual rock, sat down, and looked up at the sky.

The rain fell. All Willie's sweet touches and pinpointed interest, all her passion, disappeared into the air.

I lay back on the rock, feeling the grooves and bumps in its texture. I took off my jacket and shirt and let the air penetrate my skin, its frigid mist searing my chest, the wind blowing against my ears.

When it got too cold I buttoned up my clothes and walked out to Broadway, hailed a cab up the hills to the house I loved so much. I entered, hoping to get magically past my family and to the cover of my bed, but I saw Felix breathing heavily on the couch. He was a very old cat now, and I went over to him and cried into his fur.

"Dad, what's wrong?"

Michelle had sneaked up on me.

"Dad?"

I reached my arm, found her waist, and brought her to me.

"I'm so sad about Felix, sweety. I love him so much."

"I know, Dad. I love Felix too."

I was whimpering.

"He has been with me and your mother for over 20 years."

"How come human beings can live to much older than 20 and cats can't?"

I didn't answer.

"Daddy, why?"

"Because cats are made different than we are and they just don't live as long. Their bodies don't last as long."

"We have medicine too."

"We do, a lot of it."

"Is he going to die?"

"Yes."

Grace and Augie came down the steps.

"What's going on here?" Grace said, "Are you alright?"

"He's sad about Felix," Michelle said.

Grace said, "It's killing me too. I love him so much."

I thought of Willie and it was like poison had passed through my veins. Grace came and draped herself over me. I smelled age in her hot breath and felt the added weight in her chest. I recoiled, thinking of Willie's recent touch, but I tried to hide it. She nestled into me and I told myself that she was coming to me, to help me, to be with me, but Willie was too sharp and raw, and so I flexed my muscles to warn her that I wanted her off. I stood up, looked at my family, and said, "I just can't get over the fact that he's going to die."

Michelle and Augie came and hugged me. I motioned to Grace to join us and she cautiously did. We released into the eight arms of the Rosewoods.

I announced, "I've got a big day tomorrow and I'm exhausted so I'm going to bed."

Grace stepped out of the hug.

"Leaving me to put them to bed and make their lunches?" she said.

"Tonight, Grace, I need to go right to bed. I feel sick and depleted."

"Another asterisk by your name."

"Another asterisk by my name. But I really need to just go to bed."

"Are you really sick?"

"My gut feels stretched and twisted, all knotted up in pain and cramps. I can barely move. My eyes are red, can't you see? I don't sleep. My peepee still hurts." Michelle and Augie laughed. "My throat hurts because I smoke too much pot. My hips hurt from decaying bones. I can't go to Africa this year, again. And Felix is breaking my heart."

This left them silent.

I walked up the stairs to our room and went right to bed. Like a hammer came the weight of my loss. It came at me in a huge thud. I saw the face of Willie's annoyance, impatience, anxiety, and I knew that I had been cut off. This mixed with Felix's eternal departure. Felix, who I worshipped. I was in hell as I lay in bed, staring into space, hearing the trees creak and moan in the wind.

Amid these feelings I fell asleep with surprising quickness. But later on, the house quiet, I felt Grace come to the side of the bed and take off her shirt and pants, grunting softly with exertion, put on her turquoise nightgown, and plop heavily into bed. I opened my eyes briefly. She twisted and turned herself into the blankets until she found her place.

I tried to keep still. I wanted to be left alone in my pain. I wanted her away, but instead I began to sob.

She turned over and hugged me, not so close, but enough to tell me that she was present, and then let go so she could sleep.

I lay awake. When did the change occur? When did I become not magical enough? Was it actually that moment when I came in her? Was it that she could no longer fool herself about the risks? I looked over at Grace and thought, what were the consequences for her? It had been for so long, since Esther, that I had protected myself from blind love. At college, at 107th Street, in Africa and Mombassa, and now at this particular crossroad, Grace still hoped, with time ripened modesty, for blind love. Not so much to ask of your man of two decades. And I thought, now that Willie had opened that place again, of blind love, could I shift it to hold Grace?

I heard Felix come into the room, his long nails scraping the floor. He made his way around the bed to my side. He rested there. He moved his body upwards on the mattress, but his claws didn't catch, and he fell over. I got out of bed, picked him up, and brought him into the blankets with me. I made a pocket for him next to my belly and helped him settle his achy body. This was how he loved to sleep in winter. So fat, warming even more so within of our bodies. But now he was wasted away and I rubbed him until he purred.

In the blurry morning, the sleep deprivation caked in my eyes, Felix, who still wanted to eat, thank god!, made it clear that we should get up and begin the day.

I got out of the house before anyone woke. I felt the chill off the river as I passed through our yard. I needed to be alone and to be away, far away from Willie, and I dreamed of Africa and the winds blowing from the mountains.

I walked the lonely streets that winded down to the subway. On the elevated train platform looking out over the gas station, its red and white sign, I waved to Eddie, who waved back, the sun coming up over the park. On the subway with all the mixed races of New York City I looked down as many female pants as was available, trying to imagine the shapes and smells of these private habitats. I read The Language of the Land. "The Hazda always tell you the truth," he said, "You must eat baboon shit and put kerosene on your balls if you want your dick to grow as big as an elephant's." James always joked that a white man's dick was too small to satisfy an African girl. "'Bocho, come, sleep here,' said Mela, lifting up her blanket, tapping her hand on the ground next to her." I imagined the dark moist center of the universe inside Mela dripping down her thighs.

Out into the cold river sunshine of 110th Street I stopped for a greasy donut, which almost immediately hurt my gut. I walked up Broadway, and there she was in her stellar beauty. Upright, wool pants, a cord white sweater, that self confident sway to her walk.

I hid myself in the entrance to an apartment building and watched her approach. I could feel her power strengthen as she got closer. She was within inches of me, and I stepped out.

"Hey."

"Hey. Wow. What a coincidence."

She stepped back.

"Where are you going?" she asked.

"To see the dean."

"Why?"

"I was called to see the dean. Where are you going?"

"To a doctor's appointment. In fact I'm late." She started to walk away. "I'll see you for lunch tomorrow."

I stood still, heard the pounding of tires on the avenue, the mass of voices, the interlacing notes of competing public music; I thought of work and the day to come, made my way heavily across campus to the dean's office.

He said to me that my reputation preceded me and that before he just thought it was quirky, solipsistic, even funny, but now it was not appreciated anymore, there had been complaints, standards ignored, and quite frankly, job security at risk. Behind closed doors do what you want, don't fuck little girls and boys of course, but in front of everyone, behave. He added, be forewarned.

At lunch the next day Willie said, "You look nice today."

I beamed.

"You do too . . . When's the last time I told you how beautiful you are?"

"Recently, I'm sure."

"Well, you are. The most gorgeous perfect being I've ever encountered."

"Stop it."

"I can't and I won't."

"Try."

"You know," I said. "That we are together for a reason. To balance each other out. We are here to counterpoint our complicated marriages. It's a new paradigm for marriage. We have the central core of the family and that needs to be respected and nurtured, but then we get some alternate realities too. Realities that fulfill very essential human need. It all works out, a wide and layered life."

The waitress came over and we ordered omelets. I ordered some French fries too even though I knew they'd kill my stomach later.

I continued. "We are rebelling against a rigid culture. You and me in this relationship are revolutionary."

"This is the dangerous indulgence of two spoiled people."

"This is the brave quest of two confined beasts."

"You're a fool, and I don't mean it flirtingly. You are a fool to cavalierly risk everything that has been built up, all the pieces in place of family and future . . . The formula has changed."

"I know. That's what's killing me."

"Well, buck up . . . How's your cat?"

"He's dying."

"Be happy that you had him for so long."

"I am, but I can't bear the thought of him dying and never coming back. When his sister Molly died I was devastated. I talked to her for nearly a year in my head trying to persuade her to come back to me. Trying to persuade myself that she was retrievable."

"Did you do this with your dad?"

"No. I was torn up. But I was more dumbfounded, not overcome."

"Why?"

"We were strangers to each other. We weren't intimate. Molly slept in my bed every night. Molly's heart was completely open to me."

"Really."

"Exactly."

Our food came and we both ate like wolves. I lapped up the grease with bread. I could feel the coagulation in my gut.

I said, "How about next Wednesday you and I go a hotel?"

She sighed. "I'm not sure I can."

"Please. Just a quick moment."

"It's too hard to pull off."

"Leave the details to me."

"We still haven't confirmed if we are pregnant or not."

"So? We will never forget a rubber again."

"That's not the point. "

"What's the point?"

"The point is that . . . For you, it seems, it's all of the same fabric, but for me it's a double life and I can't handle it."

I coughed, twice.

"I fear too," I said. "I fear the loss of my family. How could I not? But I feel so drawn to you, find you irresistible. I can't help it. This deserves nurturing and not cutting off."

"This new twist in things has made me nervous, given me pause."

"You mean the pregnancy?"

"Yes, the pregnancy."

"Are you turned on by me anymore?"

"I'm too anxious about being pregnant to feel sexy."

"Just last week you said that what you really wanted was not feelings but a fuckfest. What happened to the fuckfest?"

"It went away when I potentially became pregnant."

"So you admit it. Things have changed. Your heart has left me."

"Shut up, please. I'm just scared that I'm pregnant by a man other than my husband. Do you hear that?" She tapped her finger against the lobe of her ear. "It would be awful for both of us. It would be an explosion that we'd never recover from."

"This monogamy thing!" I screamed.

"Shut up!"

"Everything is twisted up and wrong."

"Stop it. Stop for a moment. I will see about next Wednesday."

She fished out some lipstick from her purse and applied it. She brushed her hand through her hair.

"Got to go," she said.

She called the next Tuesday and said, "Hey. The good news is that I'm not pregnant. The bad news is that I can't make tomorrow. Steve needs to work late. I'm sorry."

I was trying to take a shit after another awful night sleep. Felix had followed me into the bathroom and rubbed up against the Baseball Abstract while I was reading about Willie McCovey, long limbed homerun hitter, 521 of them. I pushed at my swollen anus, but nothing budged. I took a look at Al Kaline, stolid and quiet in Detroit, but more than 3,000 hits. I gave up on any emancipation, my upper gut distended beyond repair. I picked Felix up gently and hugged him. I showered, shaved, dressed, and made my way to the breakfast table.

"My god, you look awful," Grace said. "I'm really worried about you. This sleep thing. It'll catch up with you. Maybe you should go to a sleep clinic and get tested."

"Na," I said, "I don't have the time. I'll cycle out of it."

I took the sugar flakes down from atop the refrigerator and made myself a big bowl.

"I still can't believe you eat that crap," Grace said. "No wonder you're sick all the time you eat like . . . ".

"Poopy," Michelle said proudly.

"Dad," Augie said, "Mom's right. You seem sick."

This morning he was eating some oat cereal, but I saw him eyeing my sugar flakes.

"I'm sick in the brain, I admit this, but my body will hold out."

"I'm not so sure," Grace said.

"I agree," Augie said.

"So," Grace said, "you take Michelle this morning and I'll be back to pick her up."

I turned to Michelle. "You and me this morning, girl."

"You and me, Daddy."

I leaned in and bear hugged her, making the cereal spill.

Augie said, "Is that what I had to put up with?"

"Yes," she said, "he's unbearable."

She left upstairs to get dressed and I played around with the kids, wrestling with Michelle. I felt the soft skin of her back and tiny arms, held her against my belly, smelled her moist head. Augie confided that he didn't like reading and writing that much and preferred numbers. He confided that he'd rather just hang out with his friends than anything else. Grace came down and said, "Let's go Augie my dear." He spun around and grabbed his bag and waved at me, followed his mom. I heard the car start, but then the motor was turned off, and the car door opened. I heard footsteps on our bluestone path. Grace stepped back into the house and motioned for me to come to her. She said, "I was up all morning thinking about a threesome. I wanted to wake you up, my love bone, but you needed the sleep."

"Don't ever err on the side of sleep, Grace," I said. "Wake me up."

"Not now. You're a sick man. You need the sleep."

She went off.

In the car Michelle asked me if girls were smarter than boys and I said yes.

"Then what about Augie?"

"He's like me," I said, "he makes up in charm and wiliness what he lacks in female smarts."

She thought about this.

I dropped her off at kindergarten and she flowed into the stream of kids.

I parked the car at the subway and took it to 50th street; went to my favorite porn joint, closed myself into the peepbooth. There was a pool of cum on the seat, sickly sweet, and I found another booth, disinfected of another man's juices. I sat, fed ten dollar bills into the slot. The screen lit up; swinging tits, asses distended, big cocks, blowjobs, dripping saliva, pubic hair, birthmarks, tan lines, and penetration. The room thundered with grunts, screams, yells, moans, and high pitched activity. I watched their expressions to see if the experience was confidential and private. You could tell through the eyes, of course, whether it was religious or not. I hoped to witness the greatest sex there was and then transport it home to Grace. I searched the channels. Four mini screens and one big screen in this darkened cubicle. I liked when one girl held open the anus of another. I liked when they had to lick the man's cum. I couldn't stop thinking about what Grace had said this morning. Maybe Jane could come up on Saturday night? Maybe Grace would eat her out. I switched the channels endlessly, from reel to reel, from chains to sheep, until I got tired of myself, and left.

I made my way over to the toys and looked at the dildoes. Grace and I used lots of toys now; it was like a third person in the room with us. We owned small pink and blue dildoes, but I wanted something bigger. I wanted to hear bigger noises from Grace. The bigger the toy the bigger the reaction, I thought. Yet some of the dildoes were as big as elephant dicks. As the scale decreased though I started to calculate what Grace would allow, at which largest size was her frontier. I narrowed in on a gold vibrating dildo that was just slightly larger than my penis.

That night, the misery of Willie lodged in my spine, I hurried Michelle off into bed, coaxed Augie through his homework and his TV watching until he was off in his room, and found Grace.

I was throbbing to put that dildo in her. She saw the look in my eye, turned, and sat down on the rocking chair in the livingroom.

"I'm tired," she said. "It was a long hard day."

"Each day is long and hard," I said.

"This seemed longer than usual. This past book has been really difficult. My staff was tense, jumpy. I needed to soothe them, keep them focused, but keep deadline too. However, I can laugh at this age at books called "Botanical Diets of the Royals.""

"Even so, it's your calling."

"It is."

"It seems," I said, "that you get physically exhausted more easily now."

"That's true. With Augie and Michelle, and you quite frankly, and my career, I am exhausted."

"I so thought that tonight we were going to have good greasy sex."

"Why'd you think that?"

"By what you said this morning."

"Oh. I shouldn't have done that. I'm sorry. I was being playful then. But it wasn't an automatic invitation for tonight. Each moment is different."

"Not for me. I want it all the time and then I hear you say something like that, actually coming back from outside to tell me this, and I think, oh yes, it's assured and it's going to be good."

"And what do you mean by good?"

"You know, good things."

"Like what?"

"Like the things I like."

"Like what?"

"Like toys and things."

"That's what I thought. You and your toys."

"I like my toys . . . and you don't dislike them."

"I don't."

"You don't like them as much as I do though."

"That's true most of the time, but sometimes I do."

"Those are the best of times."

"I know you feel that way."

She smiled at me.

"So what are your secrets now?"

"What makes you think I have secrets?"

"You always do. You always have secrets and stories. Who knows where the truth lies."

"I always say what is truthful to me."

"And so what is your truth today?"

"I bought us a present."

"Really."

"Just a little present."

"I presume it's a penis shaped thing that you want to stick in me?"

"Precisely."

"Is it big?"

"Oh, yes, it's big. Perhaps we might try it."

She looked at me sweetly, ambivalently too, turned, and went up the stairs. I watched her butt sway from side to side and pictured her anus puckered out. I went up to my study and filled my bong, smoked some pot. I stared at the white trim of the window and observed my mood shift from heavy to light, the air less humid and my needs more balanced. I put the dildo in my pocket, left the room, passed Augie's room, heard him turning a page in his book. I felt briefly the desire to go to him and just leave sex behind for good. I passed Michelle's room, opened the door to check on her, fast asleep. I went into our bedroom and Grace was naked up on all fours. I almost dropped to my knees. I took out the lubrication from the drawer over our bed, lathered it onto the large golden vibrating penis . . . and shoved it up her ass.

She bucked and screamed and pulled it out in one violent motion. She threw it against the wall. She leaped up and began punching me in the chest.

"I hate you! I hate you! What did you think you were doing! I don't want to be with you anymore! I hate you!"

She punched me again.

"Go! Leave! Go forever! Leave! This is intolerable."

I sunk down to the ground and began to cry.

"How much do you want to hurt me? I don't need this anymore. I don't care how low I might sink on my own, but this is not worth it."

"I have turned into a brute like my father!" I screamed. "I never wanted to be him, but I am. I'm sick. So sick. Sick with indiscretion. My dad's anger in me turned to lust. I don't love you well, Grace. I'm sorry. I've wronged you. I've treated you unjustly. I'm cruel and selfish. I didn't mean to be. Leo and I were always on guard for this. Please forgive me."

She was stone silent.

"Grace, are you talking to me?"

I inched towards her.

"Grace, are you talking to me? Please. Grace. I feel like shit. I'm so out of control that you have no idea!"

I went to our closet in a violent rush and took out the bag of sex toys, dildoes, beads, vibrators, a whip. I found the new golden vibrating dildo and shoved it in the bag too. I declared, "This phase of our sex life is coming to an end! These toys are going . . . Grace, do you hear me. Grace, I love you."

"Go, Fire, leave now. I don't want to see you. Perhaps tomorrow things will feel better. But go now."

I thought of Mombassa.

I got dressed, grabbed the bag of sex toys, closed the door behind me, saw that Augie was sticking his head out of his bedroom, avoided his look, went downstairs and threw away the toys. I pet Felix who was prone on the couch and left the house.

I drove down to my mom's. I was numb. The pain of Willie's rejection and Grace's humiliation combined. I felt like my life was a miscarriage instead of the success I usually thought it was. I drove through the night streets and onto the parkway. My mother was the source of my endless youth. It was a source of water that was blessed, but poisoned too. The Hudson River lay wide and calm on my right. I thought of calling Leo and thought of calling Adam. In the river floated bits of ice. I rode the hump in the parkway at 99th street and the car flew up in the air. My dad did this for us and I now did it for Augie and Michelle. I got off at 79th Street, where Grace had announced her affair with Orlando, round the cobble circle, down on Riverside Drive and West End Avenue until I found a parking spot. Through the lobby and up the elevator to Mom.

But Mom wasn't home.

I ate some toast, watched some sports on the TV, baseball highlights of Harmon Killebrew and the regal Henry Aaron, finally turned the TV off, and went into the back room, my childhood room. I took the foam mattress out from the sliding closets, put it down over Mom's shaggy white rug, found sheets and blankets, made the bed. I got undressed, lay down, read a few pages of the sport's section, and turned off the light. I was dying, that was for sure, engulfed in anguish and guilt, but sleep came to me now. I felt the release. I slept with the wind rattling against the window; the same wind that had kept me up during the night as a child. I slept on the rim of wakefulness. A machine started up, gurgled and choked, breaking my reverie, and it was Mom's fax machine beginning to spit out its contents. I bolted up in anger, the pain of my body rushing to my eyes, and screamed, "Fuck! Fucking machine! These fucking machines! I hate America! All its stupid information technology!"

I heard the lock of the front door unbolted. I heard the heavy step of my mom whose feet were flat. I heard her open the closet door, take off her coat, and fit it among all the other coats of this apartment, some that had been there for half a century.

I rushed out of the room screaming, "Mom, why does a woman of 77 have a fax machine? Why? Why in god's name would you have a fax machine!"

She said to me, flinching, "Because I need to get faxes."

"What kind of faxes do you need to get? It's absurd."

"I get faxes from many people."

She closed the closet door and turned into the kitchen. I followed her.

"Elijah, what's wrong? Why are you here?"

"Because! . . . Because . . . Because . . . I hate this city and I hate America. It's all fucked up."

"Elijah, what's going on?"

"Nothing. I just don't like the city anymore, Manhattan I mean, teeming and aggressive. It needs to slow down, Mom. I need to slow down. The city concentrates the evil of speed."

"I am evil?" she asked.

"You're the least evil person I know."

"So why are you so alarmed? I am worried about you, my love."

"I'm the same as always."

She came in to kiss me, but I moved away.

"You gave me a false impression of the world," I said.

"That's not true. I gave you a sense of love and possibility."

"Don't you see it has made me crazy?"

"It has made you likable, generous, and smart too."

"I'm more crazy than the other things."

"You are not."

"Jesus, you see."

"What? I love you. I'm not ashamed."

"Oh King David!" I moaned. "How about some grilled cheese and chocolate milk?"

"Of course, my love, of course."

"Do you have seltzer? I want an eggcream."

"No, but I'll go out and get you some."

"Mom, you don't need to do that."

"But I want to. Please, I'd love to."

"Alright, but make sure you don't get any of those fruit flavored seltzers, those fag flavors."

"Fire, that's horrible."

"No it's not. It's just a way of speaking. Go. I'm starving."

She retrieved her coat and said, "I'll be right back."

I turned on the TV again to sports and waited out the dreary minutes, refraining from calling Grace and apologizing my way back into her favor and from calling Willie and begging her to change her feelings, and even from calling Jane just to take a break from the other two. I watched baseball highlights, Dave Winfield, Cool Papa Bell, Mickey Mantle, and Satchel Paige. Mom came back. She handed me yesterday's sport's section and I read that and watched sports too until she eventually brought me my grilled cheese, which was destroying my gut, and my eggcream. I blurted out, "Fucking fax machines," once in a while, and Mom read the front section of the paper eating cookies and having tea sitting in the chair that Dad used to inhabit. Eventually, Johnny Bench on the TV screen, I said goodnight to Mom. I slept perhaps an hour the wind rattling the window and my eyes full of grief.

Grace wouldn't talk to me. Mom got the kids on Saturday and the four of us went to the park and then a movie. They didn't say anything or ask anything. At night Mom drove them home. I watched sports. I went to work and looked out my window at the sky. Mom and I went to movies and out to dinner. I ran into Chris and Bobby and we laughed about the day Jeff got punched in the face by the homeless lady.

A week later I convinced Willie into going out to dinner with me. Once seated she said, "I'm here because it's proper to be with you in person. But I can't do this anymore, you know that."

"I know and it's killing me."

"I'm sorry, really. I see how miserable you are. But the magic spell wore off. It's too much for me. But despite all that Fire I'm still crazy for you, you must believe that."

"Why should I believe it? I'm willing to climb Everest for you. I'm willing to do anything for you, but you won't do the same for me."

She said, "You aren't living up to your end of the bargain."

"What bargain?" I said.

"That this was just for fun. That no one would get hurt. That it was just for sex."

"That was not the bargain. The bargain was that we both knew and accepted that this was great risk and that if someone got hurt the other would be there for them."

I began crying hysterically.

She got up from her side of the booth and came to me. I put my head against her shoulder and let the tears flow. I felt almost better just from being able to touch her. She ran her fingers through my hair. She kissed me, giving me a last taste of her spirit and juices.

"I want you back. With all my heart I want you back."

"I don't feel that way anymore. I feel as lucky as if I won the lottery to have met you. To have you in my life. To share what I did with you, but I feel differently now."

"You no longer love me?"

"Not that way anymore. I'm torn apart with guilt and fear. It takes the fun out of it. I want my stability back. Steve is a limited partner, but I'm not in search for a replacement just yet."

She got up and went to the bathroom. When she came out she said, "Ready to go?"

I said, "Really?"

She said, "Exactly."

I called Grace every day but she was stone; she would only talk to Mom. I got the kids on Saturdays and Thursdays, Mom picking them up and driving them home. She didn't ask a thing, just tottered around the apartment making me snacks and dinner, reading the paper, taking Augie out, doing a puzzle with Michelle. I sleepwalked around the city, block by block, all the familiar spaces in the concrete and stained curb. I felt the pulse of my mistakes rise within me as dark waves; holes that couldn't ever be filled. I waited for Grace's signal.

Which came when Felix died.

Mom handed me the phone optimistically.

Grace cried, "He died last night. I found him under the couch, lifeless, wrinkled, full of dust."

"Oh, Grace, we lost the great one."

"Remember the day we got him and the first thing he did was claw into the couch. Right then and there he was announcing his status, the king."

I said, "I want to come home."

"You're an asshole. You push and pull and sulk and whine. You want everything and in that blur of fantasy you forget I'm even there. I'm frankly sick of it."

"You can't believe how horrible I feel. As if I've lost everything that is meaningful. What are your terms for taking me back?"

"Taking you back. Presumptuous, as you always have been. If you want to come home you must go to counseling, you must learn to listen better and modify your shitty behavior. You need to stop pestering me all the time for blowjobs. You need to give a little more to me. I work hard all day and then come home to a man that lies on the couch dreaming of his next adventure. You go fucking around in Amsterdam and growing trees in Kenya and lust after every little bit of ass that wiggles around. You leave me all alone in Mombassa. I bring in the bacon, cook the dinner and make the lunches, and you instead read that stupid Baseball Abstract. Come home, Fire, okay. But I don't live in la la land so just do your best. Don't break my heart so often. Channel your good side and curb the impish devil."

We buried Felix in a box under a tulip tree in Van Cortlandt Park.

I cried desperately, but since Molly's death and my father's too, I was a little less stunned, bathing myself instead in his memory. I said in eulogy, "He was the great fat Buddha of our life and I'm sure that he's eating something right now on his passageway to heaven." We all laughed, Felix, fat and ornery, gnawing on a bone, riding the escalator to paradise.

14. Periodic Table

W E OPENED THE windows to let the warm air circulate through the house. Augie and Michelle were reading and I watched TV. Grace came in from the kitchen and said, "How about we invite Jane up for a 'pagan ritual' on the spring solstice."

We all said, "Fantastic."

We cooked a stew of venison and turnips that we got from the farmer's market, ate like cavemen, had chocolate cake for dessert, and then gathered in our backyard. The sky was fogged with humidity and the stars gave the clouds a silver light. We held hands in a circle around the white oak. We began to turn round and round, a pagan dance, which was really a form of the hora, the pace getting quicker and quicker. The whiskers of the grasses brushed against our clothes. It rained. Michelle danced with abandon, letting herself be lifted up by Grace, Jane, and me, flinging her body, and Augie too danced up and down like a gazelle. We howled at the moon and then flopped down in the grass, rolling around in a scrum, until I pulled apart from them, and stared up at the sky. I thought of Willie and wondered where she was and how easily she had forgotten me. I remembered how she smelled, sweaty, musk. Jane put her hand on my stomach and said, "Let's go down to the river." We rose and walked the streets to the shoreline park. Our heads were all soaked wet. We walked through the poison ivy and sassafras to the river by the railway tracks. We looked at the bridge and over to New Jersey. I held Michelle, who was tired, and Augie read aloud about the Headless Horseman and Grace said a prayer and Jane hugged Grace from behind.

When we got home Michelle went right to sleep and Jane and Augie watched TV until Augie began to yawn and eventually went to sleep himself.

Jane and Grace sat on the couch talking and I went to the kitchen and brought out a bottle of tequila.

Grace said, "What do you have in mind, dear?"

"Just loosening up."

"Is that right," she said, "tequila as relaxation."

"Yes."

Jane said, "I like it."

I took a sip. It burned. I handed the bottle to Jane, who sipped it too. She cringed. She gave the bottle to Grace, who took a sip and let it linger in her mouth before she let it down her throat.

"That is strong stuff," I said.

"It sure is," Grace said.

I went upstairs and fetched my bong and pot. I came back down to the kitchen, filled the bong with water, went into the livingroom, stuffed some pot in the bowl, and fired away. The smoke took away my short term memory and cleared up the day.

I gave the bong to Jane, who took a hit and then said to Grace, "Do you want some too?"

Grace opened her mouth and said, "Blow it into me."

Jane took another hit, sucked it in, moved in closer to Grace, and blew the pot into her opened mouth.

They looked at me and needless to say I was dizzy.

Jane said, "Mr. Nature is reeling."

Grace said, "Mr. Sex is scheming."

I grunted.

"Fire's in our power," Jane said. "But we're in his power too."

"I've been thinking." I stood over them, rocking from foot to foot. "I've been thinking that it's high time I actually run for president. I was thinking that we'd take the summer, all of us, and cross the country and convince the populous to change their ways."

They both laughed.

"Seriously. Think about it. We travel the country with our kids, with their godmother too, and see the great land of this country."

"Somehow it doesn't seem that crazy," Grace said. "Am I that used to you? My god."

I took another hit of pot and another sip of tequila. I handed the bottle to the girls and they each took a little sip too.

"So, are we on for this presidential run?"

The girls looked at me, leaped up, and tackled me to the ground.

"Craziness must be met by craziness," Grace said.

They climbed off me and went upstairs.

I was stunned, expectant. I thought of Willie, where she was, how she was, that she no longer loved me. I thought that I was a good and fair man that deserved my just rewards. I darted up the stairs and into my study, fished out three Viagras, swallowed them. I ran back down to the livingroom to await their return. I took another hit of tequila and smoked another hit of pot. My blood was racing. I heard them upstairs moving around. I thought of Willie again, but was able to free myself of her. I thought briefly of Felix and his burial spot under the tulip tree. I felt the venison and turnips pass heavily down my intestine. I heard the door upstairs open, and there they stood on the landing, looming above me, side by side naked, their entire faces and necks painted in red lipstick, burning sunsets. They each bowed to me, and then started moving their bodies slowly from side to side, in unison, coming down the steps, their hips fitting together like tulip bulbs. They chanted,

Our king. Our king. Our king.

The juice of the rose is like a prostitute.

Our king. Our king. Our king.

The nectar that flows from our pits and our petals.

They sashayed, a mesmerizing waggle, reciting their bedeviling poem. Line by line they moved ever closer and I moved back in intimidation. And then they were upon me and I was reeled backwards through the kitchen and into the livingroom. They stripped me of my clothes, tearing them, turning me around, lifting me up, ripping at me like hyenas until I was naked. Their lipstick got smeared on my skin, slashing my arms, streaking my stomach. They took me down to the ground, held me, painted my face with lipstick. They spread it on heavily and sloppily, red webs like quills.

My heart was breaking. The chemicals, my mind, were too much; I was drowning in them. My receptors were flooded with drugs and worry, too crusted with sickness and sadness. I felt Willie at my side eliminating me. I felt Felix's ghost. I felt my father's too. I felt the venison and turnips turn around as they encountered my angry gut.

Jane and Grace positioned themselves above me on their hands and knees, lowered their necks down, and licked my cheeks, their fiery heads lined with longing.

I didn't respond. My eyes were closing under the pain, which was a growing pressure in my belly. Grace screamed, "Wake up! Fire! Are you okay?" I heard her voice as if buried under soil. I saw their red rose faces looming above me and I remembered Debbie, platinum hair electrified and braided like Medusa, and black pasty lipstick. Debbie escorted me, at our teenage sex party, and laid me down over her already buxom chest. I smelled her stale gum and the vinegary chemicals she used to keep her hair straight up. I felt the dried sweat on her arm. I closed my eyes and brought my timid lips into the open sea of her mouth. The moist strands of her black lipstick saliva settled on my chin and around the margins of my lips like dew. To give this to me was nothing short of sacred love . . . and I faded away and away into my memory packed darkness.

I threw up ten times that night, writhing in agony, twisting up the sheets, stained in sweat, straining my gut muscles, and tasting the acrid mixture of tequila, pot, Viagra, venison, turnips, and chocolate cake.

In the morning, spent and sore, Jane and Grace beside me, I said to them, "I really want to do this presidential thing. I've been leading up to it my whole life."

PART 5

15. Crazy Horse

O N July 4ᵀᴴ, Michelle, Jane, and I set off across America on a two month presidential run. I was going to trailblaze a new ethic of decency and common sense. I was going to offer nothing more than plain facts, friendliness. It was perfectly aligned. Grace was finally seeing, it seemed, that a more open and flexible marriage was a healthier one. I was respected in my field and made good money and was helping the world too. I lived in a beautiful house. The sex was good, if not sometimes great. My eyes comprehended and grasped at all that they saw. When the balance was taken and the variables weighed it was quite clear that I lived a divine life. Thus I headed out with my daughter and her godmother on our mission to save America.

Grace ended up not being able to come because of work. Augie decided to stay in the city too. He said, "On the road with candidate Rosewood is not high on my list of desires." I tackled him to the ground.

Grace added, 'A new paradigm for family'."

The day of our departure from the Bronx was hot with salty water from the river. We all stood in the driveway (Mom, Grace, Leo, Augie, Michelle, Jane, Adam, and I), the white pine behind us. We had purchased a big green stationwagon clunker and it was filled up with our bumper stickers, postcards, resumes, fact sheets, clothes, mattresses, sheets, pillows, books, cds, my computer, cellular phones, toiletries, tent, cooking pots, plates, cups and mugs, silverware, Michelle's toys, food, and pot. I noticed that Jane had brought along some sexy underwear, in particular a yellow thong, and that put me in a very good mood. On the back of the car Grace and Augie had written in yellow: The President. Leo had added on each side of the car, in yellow too: Beware of Fire. Mom took pictures and said, "Remember, the Trachtenbergs in Scranton, the Weisses in Cleveland, the Avrums in Chicago, Dorry in Denver, maybe Nat and Ethel in their ski home in Jackson, Wyoming, that would be nice, and then of course all our cousins in Los Angeles who can't wait to see you." She hugged Michelle, said, "Grandma loves you." She hugged Jane, but looked back at Grace, still confused that Jane was going and not Grace. To me she said, "You promise to call every day?"

"No way, Mom. Once every third day."

"Every day," she said. "That's what cell phones were invented for."

"To track down wayward sons."

Willie would say, "Exactly."

I longed for her particularly in the morning when the day was ripe.

"Every third day to you, Grace, and Augie."

Grace hugged Michelle until she was red in the face and said, "Don't hesitate to call me anytime sweety, and don't let your dad give you a hard time." Michelle said, "Mom, I'll be okay." Grace hugged Jane and said, "Have fun with my husband. Good luck." She kissed me on the lips and said, "May the people love you."

Leo hugged Michelle, kissed Jane nervously on the cheek, and shook my hand. He said, "You're an idiot, always will be. See you in LA, for your grand dénouement "

I hugged Augie goodbye, told him that I loved him.

Adam, his clammy hand in mine, said, "You're an idiot, I've got to agree with Leo here to be honest."

I said, "Adam, help Grace if she is lonely."

His mustached drooped with the humidity.

Mom said, "What do you mean 'if she is lonely?'"

"Mom," Leo said, "wake up. These disgusting hippies mean that Adam can be Grace's husband once in a while when her real husband is out on the road annoying everyone."

Mom said, "Is that what he meant?"

I put Michelle in her seat, Jane climbed in front, and I climbed in too. I rolled down the window, stuck my elbow out, started the car, and pulled it out into the road. We waved goodbye as we sped down the hill.

I swerved, which got a shriek from Jane, who said, "Is this how it's going to be?"

"What?"

"This crazy driving the whole time. I won't put up with it."

"Not ten seconds into this trip and you're killing me."

"That's right because I'm not going to put up with your crazy aggressive driving. I'm not doing 10,000 miles of driving with a maniac."

"Nigger, please."

"Oh, I hate that! You are a cynical racist bastard."

"I'm not. I'm just using a public expression."

"Michelle, oh my god, block this out." To me she said, "Don't drive crazy!"

We went north through Westchester up the Hutchinson to the Merritt. I weaved the lanes and screamed at vanity plates. I screamed at SUVs and started spontaneously singing "F U F U SUV," with Jane and Michelle eventually joining in. The trees on the parkway were large and splendid, spruces and pines mixed with oaks and hickories. Jane continuously yelled at me to slow down, but I didn't. We passed the town where my friend Barbara lived alone in a house by the Sound. We stopped in New Haven for greasy great pizza and I thought of Ezra Goldbug who lived here. In the planning of this trip I had reintroduced myself to him and The Truth Foundation, gathering my facts with his help. We passed Hartford and then passed the Basketball Hall of Fame that made me think of Hakeem Olajuwon and up the low mountain range where the oaks came to an end. To Amherst, Massachusetts where I had decided to begin our run for office.

In front of the motel Jane had me get up on the soapbox Grace and Augie had made for me. It was a strong two foot by two foot maple box and on the front it read, "Fire Rosewood for President." Jane trained the camera on it and announced, "Fire Rosewood's Presidential Run. Staring, Michelle Rosewood." Michelle giggled. "And Jane Violet behind the scenes."

I said, "Nigger, please."

We walked into the center of town. The cicadas chirped and the cars whooshed by at amazing speeds. I could feel the hippie air, which buoyed me, Jane looking hot in her jeans and tank top, and Michelle dressed in a red, white, and blue shirt. I put the soapbox on the cement sidewalk of Amherst, MA, steadied it, and rose up. My gut hurt. I coughed several times.

"People of America," I said.

I felt faint.

"People of Amherst. I am Fire Rosewood and I am running for President of the United States . . . I am here with my daughter Michelle and her godmother Jane to win over the hearts of the people of America to a new code of decency and common sense."

Jane touched me behind the knee in encouragement. I thought of Willie and how her legs tapered down from her sharp crotch.

I took a breath. I looked at my notes.

"American politics is about one thing only: making money. And that money is stolen. From us. You." I pointed down. "And me. You and me. Our tax dollars are stolen everyday by the people we elect into office. How did this happen? Greed bred of anxiety. Of death."

I was dizzy.

Jane said, "Keep going."

"I wonder how we can say one thing and then mean another?" I continued, letting the words ride on my breath. "How we claim we're against criminality, all types of larceny, yet we let our politicians commit it everyday, no whisper from us."

A small crowd had gathered.

"Here are some facts. Our taxes, our money. This, our hard earned money that we have entrusted to the public contract is being spent wildly without our permission. It's like your neighbor asking for some money to feed his family but he instead uses it to get drunk . . . It IS a conspiracy. They are purposely and with discipline stealing the tax revenue to do what they want. The fat wealthy managers stealing our money and bullying us into submission while the black folk eat cement in New Orleans. Is this how you see America? I am getting something wrong?"

I paused for a spasm of pain in my gut. My neck was slick with sweat.

"The leaders of our nation . . .".

Jane grabbed my arm, said, "Cops."

I turned, saw them a few yards away. There was an awkward silence as we waited. Arrived, one of them said, "What's going on here?"

"I am Fire Rosewood."

I stuck out my hand, which wasn't engaged.

"I am running for president."

"Who are you?"

"Fire Rosewood."

"Well, Fire, get going."

He looked at the soapbox.

"Don't I have the right to speak?"

"Not without a permit. Not without permission. And not here in front of all these stores."

"Why not?"

"You're blocking the flow of traffic."

"I'm running for President of America," I said timidly, "and I think it should be allowed."

"Not without a permit, I said."

Jane, her skin flushed and the splotches on her upper chest inflamed, said, "Let him speak."

"Ma'am," the cop said. "I'm asking politely, move on. If you want to speak tomorrow you can apply for a permit. But for now move on."

Everyone hesitantly dispersed, moving away guiltily and fading into the streets.

We went to an ice cream parlor.

"I can't believe it!" Jane said once we were inside. "I can't believe here in liberal Amherst this is how we're greeted. You're right, America is screwed up . . . But it's so exciting that we are doing this, taking the man on."

Michelle said, "Can I have a black and white shake?"Yes, sweety, that's exactly what I'm having too."

"Fire, shakes give you gas," Jane said.

"I need it for my nerves."

"Dad," Michelle said, "eat it slowly."

We had a fitful night of sleep and the next day headed out passed Albany and through Binghamton and ending in Scranton where my speech was ignored by uninterested townfolks.

Nonetheless, as Mom had promised, we had a great hot meal at the Trachtenberg's that night. Howard, the father, teased me for my presidential run, which made Jane defend me by asking Howard if he really felt that in the land of freedom only certain people had the right to speak, which made him austerely agree with her, declaring at the same time that "America is the greatest country in the world," which made me grunt.

Along the flattened roads of the near midwest we traveled to Cleveland and I noticed the sudden emergence of buckeyes amid the maples and elm. On a busy street on top of my box with Jane and Michelle by my side handing out bumper stickers I tried to lure an audience. I said, "Is the heart of the nation committed to leaders who are singularly concentrated on war and riches. . . . Is this what you want? Is this how you imagine your America? Is this something to be proud of?"

Instead, the cops told me to "Move on, quick."

At the Weisses that night, as per Mom again, we had a brisket meal with potato pancakes that made my eyes water with pleasure but hurt my gut later on. In fact, I woke up in the night twisting in pain as the meat stuck in my upper tract and pushed at my raw sides. I had wanted to crawl into bed with Jane and take her from the side, but she was in another room. Mrs. Weiss early on had remarked that she was surprised Grace was not on the trip and was instead replaced by this other woman.

The next day we left Cleveland passed Oberlin where Adam had gone to school long ago and into Indiana and its grimy black industrial towns the air awash with pollution and sticky chemicals. I noticed that there were almost no trees, killed by acid air. Jane rubbed my leg, teasing me. We burst into song, "FU FU SUV," at a monster brown Suburban driving slow in the fast lane, my lane, with vanity plates that read "What's New." West on the expressway and suddenly the skyline of Chicago and its lakefront emerged. We followed the directions Mom had given us to the Avrums, old friends of the family.

Their white house sat amid some maples and Edward and Rita greeted us with wry smiles. From their suburban porch the city hung aroused in the distance. We loaded our stuff down into their basement, and before dinner Mom called; it was the fourth time in four days that we were talking to her.

The evening sun poured in through the windows of the dining room and I glanced at the paintings on the walls, landscapes and family portraits. Rita went around the table and served us our food. We talked about Augie, and their daughters, and my forestry work. Rita asked Michelle about her school, but she refused to talk. I said, "Come on, tell them." But she turned her head away. Jane told Edward and Rita that she was born in Chicago so she considered it her hometown even though most of her life had been in New York City. Michelle kept slinking down and playing with the Avrum's dogs that were positioned under the table.

I said, "Michelle, sit up and eat."

"Leave her alone," Jane said.

Rita said, "Elijah, it's fine."

"Elijah," Michelle laughed. "Daddy's real name."

Jane laughed too. "I forget that he's really Elijah. A retarded prophet like them all."

"We are born into certain things," I said.

The steak tasted so great and I took huge helpings into my mouth.

Edward turned to me and asked, "So, what's this political turn you've taken? What's the purpose?"

"The purpose," I said, "is to right a wrong country."

"What's that mean?"

"To fix a sick country."

"This country is not perfect, but I'm not convinced that it's sick. However, I'm more interested in what you think you're accomplishing."

"It seems to me that America has become the exact opposite of what it thinks it is. Where we think we're generous we're actually stingy. Where we think we're friendly and open we're closed and mean. Where we think we're good we're wicked. How did it get this way? Is it simply human nature?"

"Where do you come in?"

"I hope to be a first wind that will hopefully generate stronger winds of decency and common sense."

"Not if it's not in our nature," Jane said.

"I'm still hoping," I went on, "that the youth or poor folks of the country will start the revolution. In fact, what's needed is very simple: a consumer revolution. When we stop buying they all fall down."

Edward said nothing more, served himself some more vegetables.

We finished dinner. Michelle got to watch some cartoons as the four of us talked, but within an hour Jane and I took her to bed downstairs. We wrestled, Michelle leaping between us, and during this scrim I felt

Jane's ass and grabbed her thighs. Michelle put on her Wonder Woman pajamas. I listened to Jane's fastidious voice as she read to Michelle, who twisted and turned, a piston. Her energy . . . like mine . . . and Augie too . . . like Jane . . . and Willie . . . and my father, and Bruno . . . and Mom and Leo too . . . was coiled. Grace lay on the other side, her energy contained. When Jane was done reading we switched places and I lay down next to my daughter and said, "Michelle, I love you so much." She put her head on my stomach and I read to her about Custard the Cowardly Dragon.

We went upstairs and I called Grace and Augie. They were headed out to the movies and couldn't talk. I called Bruno to confirm that he was still planning to meet us in Los Angeles, with Leo. He was. Edward, Rita, Jane, and I watched some TV, had tea, and then Jane and I went down to the basement, treading lightly so as not to wake Michelle.

I kept a close eye on Jane when she undressed; and in her panties, under the sheet I slipped in with her, moving into the crook of her lower spine, my crotch into that canyon.

"What're you doing?"

"What does it seem like I am doing?"

"I don't think you should be doing it."

I lifted my head and began to tongue kiss her neck. She tried to move away.

"Fire, please. Michelle's down on the floor below us and we're in someone else's house."

I kept licking and she moaned and twisted her body into mine. I put my hand on her chest and tweaked her elongated nipple, which made her go supple.

"Please stop," she uttered. "It's not right, not now."

I ran my hand over her ass and felt generously between her legs.

Michelle stirred and the two of us went inert.

"See. See what I mean?"

I felt a rush of pain go through my gut, which jerked my body.

"What's wrong?" Jane asked.

I burped up the fleshy acid juices of the meat I had eaten earlier and in the flavor I could taste red peppers. How had I missed red peppers? I burped again, cringed, and felt the inflamed pain of my insides. I sat up, put my head in my hands, moved over to my bed.

"Will you be okay?" she asked.

"Yes, go to sleep."

I stepped over Michelle, crawled under the blankets, braced for the onslaught. The city's semi darkness filtered through the small basement windows and I could hear footsteps upstairs and some car traffic. The wooden beams of the house creaked and I listened to Jane as she moved about in bed. I turned onto my side and the pain came with its standard rush, a poison wave crashing down my canal. I straightened my body to absorb it, grit my teeth, and then rolled from side to side trying to dissipate the paroxysm. I pictured the stricture of my gut, the pinholes and scars, the aggravated sliced up and sickly landscape of my gastrotract. My whole life it had been deteriorating, inch by inch, day by day, eating itself up. How long could my gut hold out before it just gave up? I thought of Dad and his diseases and how he had given me sickness. I thought that I was probably sicker than I wanted to admit. The pain lifted me up off the bed with its force, like the devil ready to pop through my ribs. It hit again, and again, and again, like bombs, until hours later I finally fell asleep from exhaustion.

Michelle, the morning light slanting across the basement, crawled into my bed and said, "Hi, Daddy."

Her hair smelled like ginger. I opened my arms and took her onto my chest and began kissing her head.

She pushed into my belly and I grimaced with pain.

"Do you think we can get dogs when we get home?"

"Felix just died, let's wait on dogs. And dogs are harder to take care of anyway. You've got to walk them all the time, even in the deep of winter."

"I'll walk them."

"Right."

"Will you guys be quiet," Jane mumbled from her bed, "I'm still trying to sleep."

"Go get her Michelle."

Michelle leaped off me, ran to Jane's bed.

"Geronimo," she cried.

"Ahhh," Jane yelled.

The dogs barked upstairs.

Landed with a thud, Michelle said, "The dogs, Daddy."

"How are you, Fire?" Jane asked.

"It was a long night."

"I'm sorry . . . But I was thinking that maybe we should turn back. You're pretty sick lately and this trip might be too much for you."

"Did Gandhi turn back? Did Mandela turn back?"

"Mr. President. You've got to think about your health. I'm going to call Grace and see what she says."

"Don't do that. I'm fine. I know what I'm doing."

"You've got to be sensible." She looked at me with frustrated eyes. "I'm hungry so get dressed and let's go."

"I need to rest more," I said.

"Oh no. These are friends of your family and I'm not going up there alone."

"Why not? You're an adult and I really need to sleep more."

"You get up and come with us."

She took off her pajama pants and her legs flowed out from her red panties. Michelle got out of her pajamas and into her shorts and t-shirt. Jane came over to me and said, "Get up you bum. I want you to think about your health."

"Yes," I said.

Chicago, like New York City, was crowded and brimming with workaholics. However, the streets were cleaner, the roads lined with gardens. I was impressed, and imagined Nairobi someday looking like this, although that wasn't realistic. I thought of James and Josephine who I hadn't seen for two years. I really should turn the project over to him, give him my funding, make arrangements with the government to finally take things over. James knew everything there was to know; we had planted nearly 100 trees along the poorest and most barren streets of the city. In truth, it was more his project now; I felt Africa slipping from me.

We walked Chicago, went into stores, bought Michelle a toy, and Jane bought herself some tank tops. I bought myself a blue and white checked cowboy shirt with silver snaps.

Jane said, "Mr. Jewish Cowboy, getting ready for the West."

"That's right . . . Now, let's go and begin the speechifying."

We walked to the car and I got my soapbox. We navigated the

bristling streets passed all the monkey stores on Michigan Avenue to Millennium Park. I felt weary from my hard night, but I was simultaneously excited, feeling in the air some spark of politics. The park was thronged with people sitting on the grass intermingling among the silvery sculptures and people walking through the terraced gardens fingering the succulents. I put my soapbox down on an open spot by running fountains where kids played and adults loitered.

"Hello everyone," I began, a quiver in my voice. "I am Fire Rosewood and I am running for President of the United States."

Adult heads turned and the children paused.

"This is my daughter Michelle and this is her godmother and my old friend Jane Violet.

"I am on a cross country trip to win over the hearts of the people of America to a new code of decency and common sense."

The kids went back to squawking and flailing in the water.

"I wonder how we can profess to want to have respect for others and to teach our children to be kind and polite and want to treat mankind with dignity and then act the way we do? How is such a gap of truth possible? How can we say one thing and then do another?

"Here are some facts. Our taxes, our money. Your money. My money."

I looked at the all people now listening to me, looked into their curious but strange brows. I heard cars traveling and birds chirping and the kids yelling.

"The leaders of our nation see the world in a very particular way. They have taken the tax laws and scripted them very heavily towards themselves and their friends. With this huge pile of money they have made themselves fat and rich. Made themselves untouchable. Pursued their vested interests with great aplomb. Eroded civil rights, private rights, and human rights. And it's all founded on one thing: mindless purchasing.

"Is this the America you want? Is this how you want your nation to behave?"

Michelle said, "Daddy, can I go play in the water?"

"Okay," I said, "but be careful."

I coughed three times.

"Okay, let's start with health insurance. It's a good litmus test of decency and common sense. There are nearly 300 million Americans and yet 52 million of them, in the richest country in the world, don't have health coverage. Why? Why would we not allow for everyone to be protected by health insurance? Anything but is just nasty and mean, at least it seems to me. With all these uninsured the emergency rooms are packed, people are suffering, and guess who pays for these indigent folks: us, the taxpayer. Our money goes two ways, first up to the rich and then to keep the bottom from completely falling apart to the poor. In between we get shit.

"The government with our money spends $5 million a minute on themselves. Is this capitalist efficiency?"

I stopped to look at the kids playing, Michelle splashing herself with water.

"This could all be done so much more sensibly and respectfully," I said.

Jane was filming me in her yellow tank top, her skinny arms under the sunlight.

"You don't know how many people live this way," I continued. "Without safety nets, without protection in a nation that is dripping with money and drips with the rhetoric of equality. Would the men in power ever go a day without full protection? Would you? And here I end: Do you think you deserve more than your neighbor? Do you think that our leaders deserve so much more than you? Rebel: stop buying crap you don't need, be modest, and the whole stinking edifice falls down.

"In fact," I went on anyway. "September 11th was the greatest day of their lives. Built in justification to rob, steal, cheat, make war, make money, send your kids to Yale, tap our phone lines and police check our bags. It is a sad state we are in and no one seems willing to do a thing!"

I finished short of breath, bathed in sweat, dry of mouth, but nearly ecstatic; I felt as if I was flying above seeing it all from the bird's eye, all the tiny people below, moving about, emitting heat, their breath a wind of germs. I stepped off my soapbox and did a little dance step. I said, "Thank you."

An older man wearing a Chicago Cubs hat said, "That's not the mother of your child, right?" He pointed at Jane. "Yes," I answered, "she is her godmother." To which he responded, "Interesting."

Michelle, Jane, and I went on our way, content and tired, back to Rita and Edward and the dogs.

That night we went out to dinner and everyone felt close and homey and that night too I actually slept deeply I was so exhausted. We left that next morning, Rita and Edward waving goodbye.

On the freeway a few miles from the city we were passed by a Navigator with license plates that read "Rozs4some." Right after followed an Expedition with license plates that read "WindyMan." Next came a Range Rover with license plates that read "Esqforhire."

I felt dizzy, turned to Jane, and said, "Did you see that?"

"What?" she asked.

"Three colossal SUVs in a row and all with disgusting vanity plates."

"No, I wasn't looking."

Michelle sang, "FU FU SUV."

The Range Rover was followed by a Hummer with license plates that read "BigToes."

"Please look at this," I said to both of them. "Let's see what comes next."

An Escalade followed with license plates that read "Dicks"

Jane squealed. "Dicks! Do you see that, it says Dicks."

"I don't think it's funny."

"Come on," she said, "Dicks is funny."

Michelle said, "I know what dicks is."

"What?" I said.

"Penises."

"Where did you learn that?"

"Augie."

Jane said, "Look."

The Escalade was followed by a Tahoe with license plates that read "G-D-BL-US." The Tahoe was followed by another Hummer with license plates that read "Saul." A Dodge Neon trailed the pack with license plates that read "Bankstown."

Jane laughed. "Everyone's into vanity plates."

I said, "Nigger, please."

We rode under Wisconsin, where Mom had urged me to go to Madison to see cousin Phillip, but instead we drove through Iowa and stayed in Des Moines where I struck out again with my speechifying and was told "move on" by the cops. We left Iowa and entered South Dakota where you could see straight up to the Arctic, and it was a shock to my system, but a magnificent one, similar to my feelings about Africa. It bathed me in yellow, blue, and white light, and I looked at the grasses that flowed like a river. In those grasses under this light, in this vast space, animals lived in subterranean tunnels and your neighbor was a mile away. In these spaces I could feel the wounded princes in the air and hear the bones that rattled on the frozen dirt. We drove the flat road, empty of cars, drove and drove, silently and endlessly, until we saw a sign that read "Hot Springs," to which Jane said, "Let's go to the hot springs."

Michelle squealed.

We exited, drove for about ten miles past a small town with one store and a few wind smacked houses until there was a State sign that read, "Hot Springs." We followed it, went down a steep hill to a parking lot with two pickup trucks parked.

The landscape was rocky and covered in a thin soil that held the sea of grasses. There were dwarfed aspen, battered by the winds. We put on our bathing suits walked to the end of the parking lot, around a bend, and to a noisy river carrying rocks down on its pace. Hanging over the water were some more jittery aspens. By the shore of the river a square pool had been created by piled up rocks. In the pool were three young women and a man, drinking beers. They stopped talking when they saw us. We scrambled down, holding Michelle by the arms, and Jane took off her shoes, and went into the water.

She said, "It's fantastic."

The man said to us, "Welcome."

Jane said, "This is heaven."

To which he said, "Welcome."

And held up his beer in toast.

Michelle said, "Jane hold me."

I said, "I'll get you."

I took off my shoes, grabbed her, and went into the hot water.

Oh!

I put Michelle down into it and she began wiggling in my arms. She said, "Daddy, it's so hot," but then slunk down into it like an alligator. "It's like a bath," she said.

"Yes," I said, "exactly."

I looked at the women and they were young, skinny, and blond. All three wore wool caps on their heads, pink, gray, and yellow. The guy was also good looking, with a sharp jaw, toned muscles. He wore a black baseball hat that read, "The Pits." I sat down in the water, smiled at all, and said, "Hello."

"Hello," the guy said. "Where're you from?"

Jane said, "New York City."

He sat up and said, "New York City. Did you hear that girls? What're you doing here?"

"Traveling around," I said. "Seeing America."

"Tell them the truth," Jane said.

"What's the real truth?" the guy asked.

"That Fire here is running for President of the United States and we are on a cross country trip to get him elected."

"That right?" the guy said. "Did you hear that girls? So, what do you stand for?"

I was silent.

"Come on, what's your position on things?"

"I don't want to talk about it now," I said. "I just want to relax in this hot water."

"Oh come on, Fire," Jane said, "you can't turn it on and off. Running for president is a full time affair. Speak, Mr. President."

I would have hung her by a noose if we were alone in a room.

She smiled at me, her skin pink.

"That's right, Fire there, you can't just turn on and off," the guy said. "So, are you conservative or liberal?"

"I just want to relax in this hot water. Please, let's talk about other things."

"Like the missiles up the road."

"Are there?"

"Out here on the plains the missiles are like prairie dogs."

"Really?"

"Yes . . . So, what's your stance on missiles?" he asked.

He took a sip of beer and adjusted his hat.

"My stance is they suck," I said.

"Finally, a point of view from the president," Jane said.

"Why do they suck?" he asked.

"Because these missiles added up spell the nuclear death of us all. We should burn them all to cinders."

"What's gone wrong," the guy said, "is that we are flawed beings and doomed to sin. Right girls?"

He took a sip of beer and then proffered the can to me. I said no, but Jane motioned she'd take a sip, which she did, putting her moist lips on the aluminum. Gulping, she said, "Fire is an optimist. He thinks we can be more perfect. I agree with him." Her skin was puckered and nearly blistered, but she looked great in her steamy haze, as skinny as the teenagers, and as ready to leap to sex as they were. "But," she turned to me, "the reason he's such a good candidate is that Fire is truly flawed and he admits to all of it openly."

"That's an honest candidate," he agreed. "But could lead to some troubles too."

"What do you mean?" I asked.

"Admitting your flaws can make you weak. Out here, toughness rules."

"Admitting your flaws makes you strong," Jane said.

"That's a woman's perspective," the guy said, "a man's way is toughness. You can't be president without being made of steel."

The yellow hatted girl asked me how old I was?

"Coming up on 50, an old man."

"He's not old," Jane said. "He just playacts at being old. He's as young and feisty as you and me, and Michelle his five year old."

"His five year old?" the guy said, "not yours?"

"No. I'm her godmother."

"What's your relation to Fire here?"

"Old friends."

She blushed.

"Did you hear that girls?"

Michelle bobbed up and down in the hot water. She bobbed her way to the girls and began to bang against their bodies. I told her to stop but she didn't listen. The pink hatted girl took off her cap and put it on Michelle. The guy said, "She's gonna be as good looking as you girls. Maybe better." To which all three nodded. Jane said, in a high pitch, "Can I have another sip of beer?" The guy handed her the can. I let the warm water heat up my skin and blood. I sneaked a peak at the girls through the foggy mist of my eyes. Michelle was careful to not get the hat wet, then took it off, put it on the girl's knee, and went underneath the water. "Daddy," she said, "this is awesome."

Soon after we said goodbye to all, and the guy said, "Good luck there Fire. Watch out for yourself."

The rusty plains accumulated more human development as we drifted into Sioux Falls. The light hit the metallic roofs and sizzled in the air. We found a motel and unpacked the necessary items from the car and sniffed out our room.

At dusk we walked downtown. The buildings were small, weathered, although some new structures glimmered in the waning sun, the streets small and largely unoccupied. We ate dinner at a bar, Jane's idea, and the burgers were so incredible that even Michelle indulged her usually impatient diet. Jane got drunk and Michelle and I filled up on root beers. The clientele, I noticed, was a mixture of locals, sunburned and run down, and yuppies, pale and restless. I imagined, listening to the wind hitting the side of the bar, Crazy Horse riding in from the north, the winds blowing down so ceaselessly. I listened to the high treble music, looked at Michelle, whose jaws were dripping with burger grease, and felt the first pangs of an alarmed gut.

"I think I'm sick," I said.

"It's the way you eat."

We paid the bill, went back to the hotel, and Michelle and I went off to bed. But when Michelle fell asleep I climbed into bed with Jane, began to dry hump her from the side. My dick grew against the hide of her ass and I pulled her panties down, but she pulled them back up. I slinked my middle finger down the crevice of her buttocks. She moaned, but whacked at my hand. I dry humped her and this time she dry humped back. I pulled her panties down again and took the flesh of her buttock in my hand; only when I moved my fingers towards her anus did she whack me, pull her panties back up, and insist I leave.

I did, sullen, but just in time as the pain of a hamburger and shake diet came on; another rough night, bathed in sweat, gut muscles strained and depleted.

We had breakfast at the diner across the street, eggs, toast, and milkshakes. I started to get excited by the day's speech, feeling in the vastness of the prairie open minds and common sense. We walked downtown, found a WWII monument that was set in the curve of the street and was a perfect sidewalk amphitheater. I put down my soapbox. Jane turned on the camera and Michelle handed out bumper stickers and fact sheets. I coughed three times and rose up on the box.

"Ladies and gentlemen, boys and girls of Sioux Falls. I am Fire Rosewood and I am running for President of the United States of America. This is my daughter Michelle, and on camera is her god-mother, Jane Violet."

Several people stopped to listen.

I coughed again, twice.

"We are on a cross country trip to win over the hearts of my fellow Americans to a new code of decency and common sense."

"That's bullshit," a tall bean pole guy said.

"He's drunk and don't mind him," the man next to him said. "You," he pushed the drunk man, "shut up. Go on," he said to me.

"Thank you," I said.

"Something has gone horribly wrong with this country and now is the time to fix it."

"Screw you," the drunk guy said.

His mate didn't stop him this time.

"Screw you because you guys come in here knowing nothing about us. You fucking preachers. I hate you preachers. Preaching all this shit and then not living up to it."

"I'm not a preacher," I defended myself, shaky in the tendons. "I'm just trying to have dialogue with my fellow countryman."

The sun lay hot over the city, the flags of sidewalk sparkled, and a man on his horse rode by. I dreamed of being home in my garden under the white oak tree.

"Just trying to have dialogue with my fellow countryman," he mimicked me. "Horseshit. I know you types. Knowitalls, cheating, lying, bastard hypocrite knowitalls."

He moved forward and I instinctively moved backwards, but he tripped over his feet and went down, catching himself at the last moment. This made me feel safer. He got back up, looked at me with scorn.

"That's just the point," I said. "I'm sick of all the lying."

"You're a liar too," he said.

"I'm not a liar. I admit to all my faults. I'm far from perfect."

"Horseshit," he said.

"So, you don't think I should be running for president? Who should be president then?"

"There should be no president," he said. "That's horseshit too."

"What do you do for a living?"

"None of your business."

"Seriously?"

The crowd backed up the sidewalk and was swelling into the street.

"Construction."

"You mean you're on a construction crew?"

"Yeah."

"What're you building?"

"Streets."

"Without our tax money most Americans, you, would have no source of income. But instead you rail against government. No social services, no bureaucracy, no infrastructure, and you all are penniless."

"That's cheating, you idiot. That's what you peckers don't see. We can manage without your help."

"No you can't."

At that he stumbled away, his friend following.

My nerves were shot so I got down from the soapbox, unable to go on, and people lingered for a second, as if to talk to me, but dispersed after all, no one saying a thing.

"Goddamn," I said, "that was something."

"Hey," Jane said, "you've been lucky so far. This stuff could happen at anytime. In fact, it could be much worse."

"I know."

"Don't lose your cool," she said. "You need your cool more than ever now."

"What do we do now?"

"Let's go to a different part of town and start again," Jane said.

"Think so? That unraveled me a bit."

"It's still early. I like it here."

"Okay."

We stopped at a bakery and had muffins and tea, and Michelle had a donut (and I had one too), and then we crossed town, a cluster of stores and buildings, some of them rusted and old, frontier and wind blown, and some tinged with the sparkle of newness. We walked to the university section of town, stopped to buy book and cds. We then made our way to a grassy knoll on campus where the students strolled and intermingled. I put down the soapbox to try again.

"I am Fire Rosewood and I am running for President of the United States of America . . . and I am tired of all the bullshit." I said.

"What did you just say?" Jane asked, still operating the camera.

I looked down at her.

"I'm trying a new approach. It just came to me."

"Doesn't sound promising."

I turned to the crowd.

"Aren't you tired of the bullshit too? All the lying? How can a man live in a country where everything that is said in public is a lie? . . . When they say trust me you know they are lying to you, but we do nothing. When they say they want peace and democracy instead we are invading another country. When they say we care about you but then raise your taxes, lower the taxes of their super rich friends, and then cut your social services and health benefits they lie. When they say that they treat people with equality and respect they lie. America, I am sad to say, is full of shit. And there are only two solutions: the gun, which is bad for all, or to stop shopping unnecessarily, all that cheap bullshit crap that no one needs. Stop buying and it all falls down."

I was bathed in sweat. I looked down at Jane and she was smiling behind the camera. Michelle had found a friend and they were frolicking around the trees and bushes. I pictured my father standing against the wall of the local political club saying to everyone gathered that they were all wrong. I heard the heavy steps of the men as they climbed the stairs ready to their speeches. I was at the crossroads. I dreamed of Willie and the smell of her underarms and of how she turned her face into mine with longing.

"Go on," Jane said.

"Okay. Sorry . . . consumer revolution, yes. I lost my train of thought. Anyway, this is America, folks. Your America. My America. A land of mindless purchasing in which that revenue defies gravity and moves up to the rich instead of being spread around."

A man with jet black hair said, "We don't need the moral correction. You killed our civilization. You killed us for no reason at all."

I pictured Crazy Horse coming to the white man's town having given up his spirit and handing himself over to the slights and imprecations of the bureaucracy; the men turned chaotic in this event until someone got killed, Crazy Horse.

I said, "There is nothing I can say to that."

"That's right. There is nothing you can say to that so shut up now."

I felt soreness in the back of my throat and the distension in my gut.

I stepped off the soapbox and said to Jane, "I'm exhausted. I've got to go back to the motel and take a nap."

She turned off the camera and went to fetch Michelle. The man walked away. The crowd dispersed. A professor and some students approached me to talk, but I was feverish and the pain in my gut was tremendous. When we got to the motel I plopped down on the bed and turned over on my side. I listened to the murmuring of Jane and Michelle, heard the motel door open, the sunlight filter in, and then close me into darkness.

The next day we left Sioux Falls and I was anxious to get into the wild so we drove straight across the state to the Badlands. We bought wood and food at a local store and then entered the park. We camped on a cliff overlooking a landscape of boulders, buttes, and flinty peaks.

At dinner that night, sitting around the campfire, Jane said, "That Indian gave it to you."

"I deserved it. There's no apology appropriate for killing off the Indians except that it is our nature."

We put Michelle to bed in the tent, but she was scared and kept calling out to us. Eventually, she fell asleep and I stoked up my bong. I leaned into Jane, began to kiss her neck. I lifted her up, pushed her over to the car, and pushed her up against it. I rubbed myself vigorously. Jane was spread out over the hood, ass up, and this was so sexy, but I couldn't get a hard on.

"Nigger, please," I howled, holding up my arms to the sky.

Jane laughed. "Don't worry, Fire, you've been really sick lately. I think you are sicker than you are willing to admit to yourself."

"Perhaps," I said, "but I'm fine too. The stars are shining bright, we are in the Badlands, and I am morally focused, so why can't I get my dick to go hard?"

"Don't know," she said, and walked back to the fire.

I took off my shoes, unzipped the tent, and went in. I lay down next to Michelle, who woke for a brief second and I got myself comfortable by turning into her and holding her tight. I felt my engorged and sickly gut and mourned the day it went crazy on me, lying in my mother's lap covered by my white blanket as she rocked me back and forth to dissipate the pain. It was a thunderous pain, so new and unexpected, and with these faded feelings the first trickles of sleep came on.

We stayed in that campsite for five days, languishing in the slow sun, staying to ourselves and hiking through the Badlands. We climbed around on the rocks and had lunch sitting in crooks between the mesas or under one of the few trees. I thought of Grace's dance under the acacia tree and how she glimmered in the sun kicking up the brown dust from her feet. I kicked up the sands now like I did when I was a teenager in Central Park, Adam handcuffed to the sickly cherry tree. Between the stones slithering were animals unidentifiable. Ravens called out from above. Michelle and Jane started a collection of rocks, which eventually I carried in the knapsack. I complained about this, but they ignored me. I lugged their rocks each day all day until we came back to our camp in the late afternoon. We listened to mountain music and took naps on our sleeping bags laid out under the sun. I tried to meditate myself to sleep, and had a few surplus moments, but mainly listened to the birds and the low wind. I missed Grace and Augie.

Five days later we set off for Rapid City and Mt. Rushmore. I felt rejuvenated, but also wary. Our stay in the Badlands was so sweet because I didn't have to say anything. But again the words had to flow and this made me uneasy.

After lunch we drove into Rapid City, clean and tidy. We found a little motel in the center of the city and it felt good to me, the landscape bustled and grooved with human energy. After checking in I said, "Let's go see Crazy Horse."

The roads were crowded with pickup trucks and SUVs and we all sang, "FU FU SUV." We snaked through the big avenues past the malls until we climbed out of the commerce into the hills and eventually to the memorial. We parked and when we got out of the car I noticed a few Indians standing on the far side; that we were the only white folk. I noticed their stares and got anxious about trespassing, hoped Jane wouldn't make a snide remark to them about my presidential aspirations.

We walked up to the statue and I wondered if my father and Crazy Horse were in touch in the afterlife.

Michelle said, "Should we put rocks here like at Grandpa Murray's?"

"Yes," I said, "that's a fantastic idea."

I looked at the Indians and felt paranoid.

Jane said, "It's a great idea, Michelle."

Which made Michelle blush and scurry off to get some rocks. She came back with her little hands full, put the rocks at the base of the monument, and said, "Mr. Crazy Horse."

I tried to remember the kaddish, but couldn't.

Jane began, "The Lord is my Shepherd; I shall not want

He maketh me to lie down in green pastures

He leadeth me beside the still waters

He restoreth my soul.

He guideth me in straight paths for his name's sake

Yea, though I walk through the valley of the shadow of death

I will fear no evil

For thou art with me

Thy rod and they staff, they comfort me

Thou preparest a table before me in the presence of mine enemies

Thou hast anointed my head with oil; my cup runneth over.

Surely goodness and mercy shall follow me all the days of my life; and I shall dwell in the house of the Lord forever."

She blushed and turned pink all over.

I said "Amen."

I saluted Crazy Horse, turned, and walked to the car. Jane and Michelle waved at the Indians, and they waved back.

In the car I asked, "How the hell did you remember that bible passage? Impressive."

"I surprised myself too, but I was a catholic school girl for many years."

"I forgot you were a catholic school girl. You must have looked great in those uniforms."

The next day we went to Mt. Rushmore.

We parked the car and walked to the monument. I looked up at the presidents carved into the rock.

I said, "Jane, how perfect, we visit the presidents on my presidential run."

"Oh my god, it's perfect. I never made the connection," she said.

I said, "I'm scared shitless. So many people and they all look so patriotic."

"You might be tarnished here," Jane said, laughing at me. "Yet this might be the place where you hit your true stride. Mt. Rushmore was fated."

A sea of people spread in front of me, a vast sea of faces, eyes, and opinions. The cameras dangling, the video equipment rolling, sunglasses glaring, diamond rings flashing, pockets full, and bellies bloated. I put down my soapbox and stood upon it.

Jane turned on her camera and I said to Michelle, "Don't wander. It's crowded here and I don't want you to get lost."

"I know," she said. "But Daddy, I'm tired of this. I have to sit through these things and I can't run around. Daddy, let me run around?"

"No, it's too crowded here. Please, Michelle, this is what the trip is about."

"I don't like it anymore."

"Well, you're just going to have to wait. So sit down or stand up but wait patiently. Please."

She scowled, went to Jane, and stood with her back to me.

"Jesus," I said, "later, we will find a playground and you can run around like mad."

I turned to the crowd and they were laughing, which I took as a good thing, and then began.

"Hello fellow Americans. Here at this great site, at the site of our great past, with four great presidents carved into the Black Hills, I introduce myself. I am Fire Rosewood, from New York City, and I am running for President of the United States. By my side are my daughter Michelle and her godmother Jane Violet . . . I am here today to convince you all to become, with me, better citizens and to readopt the ways of decency and common sense."

The smiles in the crowd turned to frowns and confusion and I felt in this change of feeling antipathy towards men like me.

"We are a nation gone wrong," I continued. "We have lost sight of the real things, the things that make us decent. Treating our neighbor as ourselves. Being fair and generous. Respecting other's privacy and self determination. Where has all this gone to? Why has America abandoned these things?"

I stopped and wiped my brow.

But I was feeling the trance of the talking come on. I lectured about poverty, discrimination, closed minds, racism, corruption, and corporate subsidizes. I lectured about bad behavior and arrogance, inefficiency and waste. I lectured about profligate shopping. I said, "Monster TVs, alarm systems, bottled water, pods in the ear, perfect teeth, gold plated trash cans, and missile systems. How much shit do we need?"

"SUVs," Michelle said.

"Yes, SUVs. Is there no more perfect symbol for what we've become: big fat gas guzzling road hog self exhibiting slobs."

A man dressed in a purple football jersey and khaki pants stepped up to my soapbox.

"You're in the minority, my friend, Americans that don't like their country. It's self hatred."

"You're missing the point. The point is free speech. That shit you blather on about on sports radio and the nightly news, that shit you think you are sending your sorry asses overseas to defend. This is it right here in your face now. I have free speech."

"Not if you are full of crap."

"Even if I'm full of crap."

"You're a pussy."

"Shut up," I said. "Go back to your white trash cabin."

He rushed at me, tripped over the soapbox, and we both fell.

He smelled of beef and onions mixed with pungent odor of his aggression. He was slick in sweat, his body was heavy, and I felt suffocated, my nose stuck between the folds of his belly. I pushed up at him, but he was a whale. He laid on top of me, choking me, his spittle dripping. "Get off!" I screamed. He pushed upwards and off, but gave me a quick shot in the ribs.

I went inert on the pavement, blurry and disoriented, the voices a commingled chaos, the smells of tar and soil, staring at the ankles of the gathered crowd. I heard the siren of a police car. Two Rangers, in their Smokey the Bear hats, pushed their way through the crowd.

"What's going on here?"

Jane said, pointing at the man, "He beat up my friend."

I stood up slowly, feeling the pain in my ribs.

"So who are you?" a Ranger said.

"I am Fire Rosewood."

"What were you doing?"

"Speaking."

"About what?"

"Politics. America."

"Did you have a permit?"

"No . . . Aren't you going to ask what happened? Why I was lying on the ground?"

"First things first. Did you have a permit?"

"No, screw the permit. Either arrest this guy or get him away from me."

"Speaking here without a permit is forbidden."

"I said screw the permit."

He grabbed me fast, twisted me around, and cuffed me.

"What the hell are you doing?"

"Undo him!" Jane screeched.

The guy said, "He's a menace."

"What are the charges? Huh? Let me go."

"You're a pubic nuisance. Disorderly conduct. Speaking without a permit."

"You've got to be kidding."

The cuffs hurt tremendously.

"Please," I said, "reconsider. I was just exercising my right to free speech. I didn't do a thing. I was attacked."

"That's right," said Jane. "And I am telling you that if you don't let him go not only will I go straight to the press I will have a team of New York City lawyers swarm all over this place looking just for you. I've got it all on video, buster."

He laughed out loud.

But he let me go, unleashing me, the pain throbbing in my wrists, and in my ribs too.

"No speeches here," he said. "This is a public recreation space, not a political arena, and either way you need permission, which you don't have."

Michelle, who was wrapped around my legs said, "See, Daddy, all this does is get us in trouble. I want to go home now."

"Good advice," the ranger said. "Follow it."

I brushed myself off, the pain in my ribs resonating, grabbed Michelle by the hand, and walked away.

The next morning we left for Yellowstone. Off in the western distance the mountains rose. The longfaced plains were behind us. I could feel the air change as we began to climb in altitude, the pines and spruces forming continuous ecosystems up the mountains, chains of arboreal communities all the way up to top of the earth. In this silence, Michelle fell asleep and I drove along the empty Interstate, through Gilette and towards Buffalo where we were going to stop at the Big-Horn National Forest.

I reached out, ran my hand from Jane's knee up to her crotch.

I said, "How about a blowjob?"

She looked back at Michelle, who was deep in sleep, unzipped my pants. She fished around for my penis until I finally popped out and she said, "I see." She held me in her hand for a moment and then giggled, her skin turning even more red and mottled than usual. She moved her body down the seat and lowered her head. At that moment I lost my nerve and said, "Stop. Stop. I'll crash." She said, "You're such a wussy."

In BigHorn the next day we hiked to a secluded hot spring. The sky was blue and big. Michelle spun around and around.

The next morning we shopped for a week's worth of food and supplies. We had pancakes at a diner, and Michelle and I split a black and white shake. We drove out of town and the last stretch into Yellowstone. We paid our fees at the gate and drove to our campsite, along burnished roads bisecting the wilderness. We pitched the tent, put everything in order. Jane then decided to take a nap and unexpectedly so did Michelle. I said good dreams to them and went behind a tree with my bong, sat down in the bristly soil, and smoked until my head was awash with stimulation. I put the bong away, and went off onto the trail that led up the hill to the lowland. I breathed hard, the marijuana a bit heavy on my lungs, a few pains in my leg, but whisked myself up and into the golden bowl of the valley. It felt like I had stepped inside a foreign planet where I would never be seen again. I hiked through the grasses and wind stilted trees until I found a low flat rock that curved up from the ground. I climbed onto its center, lay back in the sun with a view of the dirty canyon walls, took out my cellular phone, and called Grace.

"Hi, there."

"Where are you?" she asked.

"I'm sitting on a rock in some incredible valley in Yellowstone."

"Sounds fantastic."

"It is. It really is. I wish you were here."

"It would be nice, but Augie and I are city folk."

"I know. I've come to see that, even though it's depressing to me."

"Why depressing?"

"Well, I want to live far away in the country, not in the city."

"Well, I don't."

"Yes, I know."

Several squawking ravens flew above me.

"You hear that?" I said. "Ravens. Smartass birds."

"They are the wise ass animals of the sky."

"What did you do yesterday?" I asked.

"Augie and I went to the museum . . . Something you would never do."

"Yes. Yes. Did you have fun?"

"We did. We saw Van Gogh, which he really liked, and then we went out to lunch in the museum and he got some chocolate pudding."

"I love when Augie is pleased with himself."

"So do I."

"Why Van Gogh?"

"He's such a sad character. From birth to death he was so serious."

"You wanted my son to be exposed to that?"

"Yes," she said, defensively. "We have all these sides to us, not just happiness and impulsiveness, your only two emotions."

"That's right. I'm happy."

"And impulsive and in denial of your true feelings."

"This again. As if only sadness and depression are true feelings."

"I didn't say that. I said that a person could have a full realm of feelings."

"No, you accused me of denial and in that meant to say that I'm denying my depression."

"Yes, you deny it."

"I don't have it, that's the simple truth."

"That's ridiculous."

"I called," changing the tone, "because I missed you and wished you were here with me now. This spot is so beautiful."

"It would be nice, but Augie really didn't want to go and I, to tell you the truth, couldn't bear to be with you as you ran for president."

I laughed, but also said, "Screw you."

Off in the distance I heard a low grunt and lifted my head, but saw nothing.

"How's that going, Mr. President?" she asked.

"Good, very good."

I heard grunts again, sharper and closer, and the breaking of vegetation, and I sat up and looked out, but still saw nothing.

"How about when I get back you and I take a little vacation. To the beach, where you can wear that thong I bought for you."

"Yes, that's good, but no guarantees on that thong. It hurts my crack."

I heard several heavy grunts in a row and twigs being snapped and saw about 50 feet away a grizzly bear and her two cubs.

"Shit," I said to Grace, "it's a grizzly and her cubs."

"You better get away from there quick," she said.

"But isn't running the wrong thing to do?" I said.

"I don't know, but I would be running."

I hung up.

I looked at the bears, watched their hind muscles rotate and their limber fleshy lips suck and squeeze. I leaped out from my spot and hit the soil running through the uneven grasses and pebble laden soil. I raced and raced, feeling sick actually, until I got to the head of the trail, looked back to see that I was not followed, raced down and back to camp.

Jane and Michelle were still sleeping and I crawled into the tent with them, snuggled up behind Jane, pushed my crotch into her, and Michelle rose, wiping away the bad taste of her mouth with her tongue, and I said, "Daddy just saw a grizzly bear!"

A week in Yellowstone, and then to the Tetons, where we had lunch with Nat and Ethel in Jackson, Wyoming. It was great to have a big steak at a good restaurant and I lapped up the juices with my mashed potatoes. I gave a speech in Pocatello that went quite well until I said, "In Afghanistan a person can truly be unconnected to government, but here in places like Pocatello the jobs are government and the money generated is all from the tax revenue and without it you folks would all be living in tents and have no health insurance."

Jane said, "I don't think this is the way to win folks over to decency and common sense."

I said, "They piss me off."

Down the eastern end of Nevada where we saw bull elks and mule deer. I gave a speech in Ely in which I said that only a blind man could not see that America was so thoroughly corrupt it was nearly dead. I said "We've got it so assbackwards, we're so stinking greedy, that soon we will we be licking our own sorry asses as the Chinks come in and chaos abounds." To which Jane shrieked and the men walked away laughing.

We stopped to eat burgers and fries in small towns and at night now my gut pains frequently erupted into nausea and puking. In fact, I began to throw up so much that I wondered if I had bacteria or something. I gave a speech in Caliente where a guy baited me into saying that "Hunting is usually practiced by sadistic slobs" and then lifted me by the collar, this man whose forearm was larger than my neck. In his face, still mad I said, "Viva the consumer revolution!"

It took us a week or so to wend our way from Yellowstone to Las Vegas, burning up in the hot sun, and in that time I puked up my food on three separate occasions. By the time we neared Las Vegas I had vowed to give up burgers and shakes and try to eat more lightly.

In the flatness of the sands rose the towers of Las Vegas and I channeled the decadence of its spirit and became even angrier at Americans. I hated it all, FU FU SUV! On the strip I got out my soapbox and with a mighty righteousness began with "America sucks! We are worse than the Romans and worse than Napoleon because we actually think that we are better . . . I mean, you fools, throwing away your goddammed money on gambling in this godforsaken philistine desert. No wonder

America is such a mess, everyone's red in the eye and smoked out with intemperance." Needless to say the cops descended and we were hauled to the station (Leo had warned me about the nasty police here) for disturbing the peace. They searched me, harassed us, and made Michelle so sick and unhappy that she cried for her mom. In the end, though, seven hours later, they freed us and we fled as fast as we could to Death Valley.

That shimmered in the distance.

We spent two quiet days there, hiking up the dunes, hearing the ferocious winds, watching the vultures glide around in circles.

On the way to LA, still in the remnant of desert, we pulled into a gas station. Jane and Michelle got out to stretch, and then went into the shop for some provisions. I filled up our green stationwagon with the Beware of Fire slogans on the side and felt the heat on my shoulders. I thought of Grace and Augie and wondered if Willie was perhaps thinking of me once in a while. I heard the ravens cry. I heard the door of the shop slam and saw three biker guys come running out. They were carrying guns. They whizzed past me, stopped for a second, looked at me, fired their guns into the side of the car, which made me leap backwards and hit the ground, ran to their car, a big 1950s thing, and squealed away.

Jane came running out holding Michelle screaming, "Fire! Fire! Are you okay?"

I stood up, dazed, and said, "Yes . . . But they shot our car."

"They did? Why?"

"I don't know, but they did."

We walked to the side of the car and saw three bullet holes penetrating the B and F of Beware of Fire. The proprietor came out and stood with us. He shook his head and said, "Drug addicts." Nothing though was leaking from the car. We lifted the hood and nothing seemed to be out of the ordinary. We waited until the police came and we all gave our witness and then continued on.

Out of the desert and the hills start to roll under your feet, tan marbles draped in coniferous groundcover, a jagged underneath of plants with sharp edges and waxy leaves; this landscape that will turn sandy and take you eventually to the ocean. We stopped, however, at my cousins in the valley. We were greeted by big a hairy dog, two kids (ages 9 and 14, and Michelle went right to them), and my aunt sat in the background, old now, withdrawn. She did not resemble my father in her face, but her demeanor was tough and reserved and I felt in her the vestige of him. They served us fried chicken, and Jane got a bit drunk on wine, and Michelle was so happy to be in the midst of home and succor, with her cousins tending to her five year old needs. That night I slept soundly and long, in one of the kid bedrooms with just Michelle and her hot smooth tiny body. After breakfast, we packed the car, hugged the cousins goodbye, exchanged vows of familyship, pet the dog, and went off in our shot up car to get Leo and Bruno, who were flying in at the same time.

First thing Leo said when he saw the car was, "Dude, who'd you piss off?"

"Can you believe it? Three Hell's Angels shot up my car."

"You probably pissed them off," he said.

"I didn't say anything to anyone at that moment."

"Jane," he said to her, "he pissed them off, right?"

"Well," she said, "he has been pissing off lots of people lately."

"See, dickbone," he said, "it's your fault."

Bruno said, "Jane. Jane. We finally meet."

"We finally meet."

"Jane likes Italian guys, Bruno. Play it right," I said.

Jane blushed and said, "Fire, shut up."

Michelle had meanwhile leaped into Uncle Leo's arms and she was crawling over his body like a ferret. She was shy with Bruno, but did whisper to me that she liked his beard.

"Michelle likes your beard, Bruno," I said.

"Daddy," she hissed at me, "why did you tell him?'

"Because it's a nice thing to say."

We all got into the stationwagon, packed and squeezed amid our stuff, and Leo said, "Damn, it stinks in here. Did you guys ever bathe?"

The ride into the city was hot and tiresome as the traffic built up along the freeways. The landscape was tawny hills covered in waxy plants and the wide and flat expanse of the LA metropolis. Leo complained bitterly that there was no airconditioning in the car. Bruno and Leo bumped their heads every time we hit a bump and they both complained about it. Michelle told them about the many hot springs we went too. She said, "We usually went naked." She giggled. Bruno said, "That sounds wonderful." Michelle told them about me almost getting arrested at Mt. Rushmore and in Las Vegas too. Leo laughed and Bruno tugged at his beard and smiled. She told them about the biker guys. "They were very big and mean," she said, "and then shooting Daddy's car." Bruno and Leo listened with disbelieving chins and ready to laugh cheeks. I said, "They were inbred hillbillies." Bruno said, "Jane, you are so much more beautiful and sexy than I could have imagined." She turned pink, and I said, "Bruno, cut it out in front of Michelle."

In Hollywood we drove down the strip and I looked at the all the sexy girls walking in their flamboyance until we came to our hotel, a fancy thing off the strip, a luxury stay arranged by Uncle Leo through his business. It was fabulous, a large suite with three bedrooms, a terrace, and a kitchen. The western sun shone through the windows onto our beds, onto the carpet, off the television screen, and onto the gleaming kitchen tiles and it was all illuminated in wellbeing. We, the cross country revolutionaries, were in bliss and we lay back on the firm leather couches with relief.

"So, how's it going, Mr. President?" Leo said when we were all ensconced. "Pick up any votes along the way?"

"Yes, as a matter of fact, I think I did pick up some votes. Jane, Michelle, don't you think so?"

"Not a one," Jane said. "Not a one."

Leo and Bruno laughed out loud.

"Don't you think we scored some points in Chicago?" I pleaded.

"Yes, I think Chicago was perhaps your only near success."

Bruno said. "Think positive. You know this is very Dutch of you. This grassroots common sense thing is very Dutch. Needless to say, I agree with all that you say and are doing, the decency and common sense. Anything a person wants unless it's criminal can fit into the space shaped by decency and common sense."

"Well thank you," I said, "but Jane's right, the people have a different definition of decency and common sense."

"I give you credit nonetheless. These things are subtle. You never know when and where change starts to happen. And where is your LA speech going to be? I can't wait."

"I'm going to Watts. I'm going to speak to the blacks."

Leo said, "There is no doubt in my mind that you will get us all killed."

That night Jane and Bruno went out, and I felt the pangs of jealously as they left without me. They came back late in the night, their voices low but intimate, bonded.

In the morning Michelle and the sun rose together and she raced from bedroom to bedroom waking us all. I grabbed her and brought her to me.

"You're a crazy monkey," I said.

We opened the blinds to let the light into our quarters, and washed, brushed our teeth, farted. We had breakfast down at the hotel's dinner, salty eggs and bagels, and we walked a few shadowed blocks to our shot up car that sat alone on the street. Leo cracked up and said, "You got shot, I still can't believe it." I had come to love this car and had convinced the cousins to keep it in their garage until I could send for it. Leo climbed in front and Bruno and Jane squeezed tight next to Michelle.

Half an hour from the hotel the squalid decaying houses were lined up in rows and the sidewalks were black with gum residue and grime and the stores were behind bars. The few street trees were beaten and beerlogged and they barely gave out any life. The streets were noisy with yelling and music and cans rattled in the curb. The unemployed washed their fancy cars and mothers sat on their porches and gasped. At a busy junction we stopped and parked.

Leo said, "Fire, you sure about this?"

"No, but it seems that it's the right thing to do. It seems that I can't have talked to everyone else on this trip and not the blacks too."

"All righty then," he said, "but don't be surprised if we die."

We climbed out of the car, Leo holding some of our pamphlets and Bruno holding the soapbox, and Jane with her camera, and Michelle trooping along for one last speech.

I set up in front of a liquor store, breathed deeply, coughed four times, wondered why I was doing this, wondered what Willie would have thought, wondered why humanity was so barbaric, wondered why I was having such gut problems, wondered why my genes were configured the way they were, wondered if Grace would ever let me fuck her up the ass again (since the birth of Michelle she claimed her ass wasn't as flexible), was astonished by Henry Aaron's accomplishments, thought of Mombassa, and the quiet unambitious life I so wanted to live . . . and began.

"People of Watts I am Fire Rosewood and I am running for President of the United States. I have just come across the entire country speaking to people about how America has gone wrong, how it's lost its way, and how we need to adopt an ethic of decency and common sense."

A small crowd gathered, some drunks.

"I have spent the last two months traveling America on this presidential course with Jane Violet, my daughter's godmother, and Michelle, my daughter."

Someone said, "Where's your wife?"

"Joining us today is my brother Leo and our old friend Bruno, from Italy."

I pointed at them and Leo cringed.

I coughed twice and cleared my throat.

"And what I want to say . . . is that America is a nasty tangle of lies and suppression. Our blood poisoned with greed. It's dysfunctional and rotten. It doesn't care about its people. It says it does on the TV and in the papers, but we all know that they don't care. Do I need to say anything more than Katrina . . . Katrina? Where the whites watched on their TVs as the blacks drowned and ate broken glass. A real action snuff film for the entertainment of the leaders in Washington. The injustice of our system is mindboggling. But I don't have to tell you, right? It's as clear as day. Your people populate the prisons and ghettos. . . ." I looked around at the gathered and stunned crowd, more people stopping to listen, cars screeching past and mothers yelling at their sons. I continued, "If the climb to riches and success is tough in general to you people it's almost impossible, except as minstrels and circus acts. There's no room for you in the elite. Jesus Christ. You people should be out burning and looting."

The drunks laughed and some teenagers exclaimed solidarity, but the sober adults looked at me like I was a demon, a strange being landed in their territory. I could see their confusion, the skepticism on the edges of their lips and eyes, the defensiveness but also the supplication.

Michelle was wrapped around Leo's leg, which he held stiff and tense. Bruno stood next to him, amused, not quite sensing the awkwardness, admiring of my resolve. Jane filmed and a bottle was broken on pavement and a plane flew overhead.

"Now, the problem is," I said, "that America thinks it has shaken off the patterns of history and is a totally unprecedented country. That all this talk of freedom and liberty and justice has actually made us a historically unique nation of fairness, decency, and equal opportunity. It's a lie, of course. We all know that, you all in particular know that. Do I even need to give you the facts? Do I need to say that the percentage of blacks that go to college is exceedingly small? Do I need to say that no whites live within miles from here and that they go up in arms when you move to their neighborhood or invade their schools? That all the money goes from our pockets to the men and ladies that run the country." I felt a rush of pain hit my gut. "The tax . . . All this talk of freedom and democracy and it makes me want to throw up! In fact, September 11th was the greatest day in the lives of the folks who lead the country. It gave them full excuse to run wars and burn oil and make you folks toil even harder."

The drunks laughed.

"Let's take torture," I said, bearing my forehead down.

"Let's start with the legacy of slavery. Do I need to even use another word? You folks make up the biggest ratio of those in prison today. Folks in prison for ten years because of a few joints. A few joints! Folks that are usually black and that are by and large uneducated bottom dwellers. How many folks can we lock up in these places before they just bust out? How many folks can a big rich society let rot?"

I looked at out my audience and they were becoming edgy. They swayed on the balls of their feet and rubbed at their chins, looked at me with pressurized eyes. Leo too was agitated, but Bruno was fascinated, and Jane filmed.

"Guns, and killing, and heads rolling, lynching, and electrocution. We kill the enemies anyway we can.

"We are the world's biggest seller and maker of arms. What does that say about us? That we think weapons are more a priority than health care or education. What do you think about this?

"The question is, what are you going to do? You've got the most to gain if the revolution finally got underway. What's stopping you? Don't tell me it's the hope of an SUV and a diamond ring?"

Three large men dressed sharply in black suits and white shirts joined the restless crowd. They placed themselves behind the first row of people, prominently in my view.

I said to them, "I am Fire Rosewood and I am running for President of the United States."

Leo was twitching and pacing from side to side.

"I have come across the country speaking to communities about the need to change the way we govern ourselves and this is my last stop."

"Where do you come from?"

"New York City."

"Are you a politician?"

"No, I'm a forester. And as a forester I favor diversity. And I believe in nature, in the force of nature, and so I came out here to speak the truth, to break the inertia, to move things forward, to talk man to man with my fellow human beings."

"That is noble of you, but we don't need you here," said one of the well dressed men.

"You want to censor my speech because I'm white?"

The drunks laughed. Leo cringed, Bruno laughed, Michelle stood tired against a car, and Jane kept on filming. The sun was excruciating. I felt a few sharp gas pains hit my belly.

"It has nothing to do with your color," he said. "You're not from here and not invited so go home."

"This is censorship. Why not hear what I have to say instead of banishing me?"

"Okay, what is it that you have to say?"

"That Katrina was the worst nightmare of current America. They say it is 9/11, but it's Katrina. The city drowned in front of our eyes and few people were stirred. It's not hard to figure out. The money had already been targeted for the arms and oil business and so there was nothing to spare of the tax revenue for the poor ni . . . blacks in New Orleans . . ." I stopped myself and wiped my brow. "Respect yourself and your neighbor. Pay attention. Be open minded. Be humble. Be decent. Use common sense. Stop buying all this genie in the bottle crap being sold down our fucking throats. Stop following the rules.

"I mean, look at these neighborhoods," I pointed down the block. "Run down, full of guns, bad food, bad hygiene, bad education, bad health care. No one should have to live like this . . . And yet I see such extravagance too. Why? . . . You folk." I looked at the three well dressed men, their neck muscles in friction. "Should be leading the way, punching holes through this free market bullshit. But instead, sadly, it seems that it's all the same here too."

"What are you talking about?" he said. "Be careful what you say, sir."

I felt so sick in the stomach, the gas building up to such high pressure.

"What's up with the all guns?" I said. "Why do we love these fucking guns . . . You folks are shooting each other dead instead of shooting the enemy. What's up with that?"

The men moved a step closer to me. I half noticed. I felt like I was going to throw up.

"I mean, you folks play right into the white man's hands. Rise up. Wake up."

"You come here," the man barked, "and insult us and tell us what's wrong with us! You're a monster. An infestation. You eat us all. But no more! We don't want to be eaten anymore. We are going to step off to the side, bide our time, and then all of a sudden take the power for ourselves. Rosewood, huh? Rosewood sounds fishy to me . . . You talk about good government. This is a government that has found explicit and successful ways to continually undercut the black man. A government and ruling elite that is run by Roosevelts . . . and Rosewoods."

The sun shone down on the filthy and potholed concrete and the pigeons congregated in the locust trees. I chuckled to myself. I looked up at the men in their suits, nearly blinded by the sun, and said, "Nigger, please."

The men stepped up to the soapbox and two grabbed me by the arms with great speed and the third man punched me in the stomach. He rammed his fist into my belly and kneaded it violently into my intestinal lining. It felt like a car had run into me and I threw up in a huge heave. It sprayed the suits of the men who held me. They screamed out loud. I was punched once more, which forced another episode of vomit, and then I went down unconscious, the sun making its way past my eyes and filling my head with spinning orbs of light.

The next thing I knew I was spread out on the dirt caked sidewalk looking up into the sun and squinting at Leo, Bruno, Jane, and Michelle. They carried me to the car and we drove back to the hotel. At one point Leo said, "Dude, you're unbelievable" in a not friendly way. "You have no idea how much trouble you cause." Jane said, "Oh my goodness." Bruno said, "Wow, my friend, what a show." And Michelle said, "Daddy, what happened?"

When we got to our hotel room they put me in bed where I moaned in pain all night, retching continually, my abdomen in great shock and terror from that mighty blow. Bruno came to me in the morning and said, "You were valiant and brave. You fought for your ideals, but now you must go home and see a doctor."

At the airport Bruno and Jane kissed on the lips.

I twisted in agony as I watched the great country pass underneath on our way back to Idlewild. In the cab on the Van Wyck I continued to throb, contorting my body looking for relief. I said, coming into Manhattan, "Get me to the emergency room. I can barely breathe."

16. Punctures

A NURSE USHERED ME through a swinging door into the crowded noisy beeping germ mingling emergency room and I was given a bed in between two others. I lay back numb. I had told Jane to take Michelle home and Leo had stayed with me until the nurse had called me in. I looked up at the ceiling and listened to the sounds of the other patients and the doctors conversing on their cellular phones and the maintenance staff discoursing. I listened to all the technology. In these strange surroundings, engineered for the sick, I began to recede into my body. I had lived a life of preternatural decomposition, my existence a rope being steadily drawn from me. The pains radiated as my friends yelled in cheer. My arms were bruised from so many needles. I watched once as they carried my hospital roommate out of our room, a sheet over his head. Now, I curled my knees into my belly and closed my eyes. Usually the pain came in spasms, but since the punch it was constant.

A nurse came and took my blood pressure and temperature. She told me to take my clothes off and put on the hospital gown, which exposed my backside and my meatless flanks. Another nurse came ten minutes later and said, "I need to take blood from you." She turned me over, stretched out my arm, looked at my veins, smacked my forearm, which hurt, and stuck me with a needle. I watched the tube fill up and I wondered what messages the liquid carried and how incredible it was that we had learned to read the information of our blood. They were looking for signs of my death. Fifteen minutes later another nurse came by and said, "I am setting you up for an I.V." She inspected my arms, chose my left wrist, and pushed the needle up my vein. I tensed and watched it go into me as if being invaded by a mysterious life force; it was the line that skirted my past and present, the line that could direct me to continued good fortune or to a dramatic change in luck. She taped the contraption down on my wrist hair, which got caught alarmingly in the folds of the tape. I curled back up into a ball when she was done and tried to snooze but was woken by two inaugural doctors. I turned over, looking up at them as if they were giants, and told them about my bad gut, the family history, my medication, and the recent blow to the stomach. They felt my belly that was bloated with gas pains and I flinched each time one of them pushed at me.

Half an hour later a team of three doctors came by and asked the same questions, except did my eyes hurt, which I said yes lately they did, and did I have a cough, which I admitted to. They touched my belly too and made concentrated faces. They listened to my heart and lungs, and left.

I turned over and looked at the old woman beside me. She could have been Mayan, tiny and wrinkled. She coughed up horrible phlegm and I turned the other way. On that side was a young black woman who moaned in pain, balled up and nearly naked in her gown. I too was nearly naked, my gaunt ass showing and my spindly legs exposed, and I felt for her. I turned away, onto my back, and looked up at the ceiling again. I thought about when my mother took me to Roosevelt Hospital when I had broken my arm as a boy. I remembered being whisked down the hallway, into the lobby, and into a cab. I remembered passing my elementary school, the trash in the yard being whipped around by the winds off the river.

A surgeon came by to visit. He asked the same questions and I gave the same answers. He touched my belly and I flinched. Soon after he left I was whisked off for a chest x-ray. The nurse had pumpkin sized boobs and maneuvered my toothpick body up against the wall. I wanted her to touch me forever. After this I was taken back to the emergency room. I tried to sleep again, but was taunted by my thoughts. I was retrieved for a cat scan; into a freezing cold room, the white machine like a monstrous donut. The technician told me that there was a slight chance that my kidney might give out because of the dye that was about to be injected into me. What were the percentages? What were my percentages? I took the dye into my blood, had a hot metal flash, lay back into the loneliness of the machine, held my breath when I was told to and let it free after being fully scanned.

Back to the emergency room, where I stared back and forth from the Mayan lady to the black woman.

A doctor came and told me I had to be admitted to the hospital. He looked grim and serious. He told me that a portion of my intestine had been ruptured but was also obstructed. "The obstruction has been happening over time," he said, "because of your disease, but the rupture is from the punch . . . There's a good probability that you will need a colostomy bag."

I didn't say anything and he left.

Another doctor came by and he stuck his lubricated finger high and hard up my ass. He was a sullen pimple faced sadist. A moment later a large black man carried me like a football from my bed to a gurney. He took me through the crowded viral hallways and up the elevator to my room.

The window by my bed looked out at the Hudson River.

A nurse came in, linked me to the room's I.V. unit, went out, came back with a bag of saline which she then connected to the hook above the machine. She took my blood pressure and temperature. She showed me how to operate the button to call for her.

I turned over on my side, the sun from the river shining through the window, my back and legs bare, and closed my eyes, put my arms over my belly to give myself some warmth, and fell asleep to dreams of my body floating away through space.

I was woken by two doctors calling out my name. "Mr. Rosewood. Mr. Rosewood." They hung over my bed like giraffe. I shimmied anemically up the pillows.

They introduced themselves; one was a surgeon and the other a gut specialist.

The gut guy said, "We have looked at your bloods and looked at the cat scan and considering your history, Mr. Rosewood, you need to have a bowel resection."

He waited for a reaction.

"We're going to surgically take out the part of your gut that is obstructed and ruptured. A portion of your intestine," he went on, "is completely inflamed and we need to remove it."

I sighed.

He said, "The small intestine is a very long organ. You can afford to lose this sick bit of it. However, you will probably live the rest of your life with a colostomy bag."

I closed the blinds and shut myself into darkness. I heard the murmurs of my roommate, his breath filled with disease and hardship. I thought of Crazy Horse who had been shot in the face by his rival and lay for months as he slowly recuperated.

I woke to the door being opened and a stream of light entering the room. Grace came over to my bed and sat down, fitting herself in the space by my belly. She rubbed my forehead and kissed me there too.

"Fire, sweety, how are you?"

I didn't answer.

"Fire, speak to me," Grace said. "Don't keep me out. Not now. This we need to go through together. Tell me how you feel."

I refused to speak.

Her hand lingered on my forehead and it felt heavy. She moved her hand to my leg and there too it irritated me. She tapped her fingers for an instant on my thigh. She moved her hand into mine and said, "Fire, I love you. You take your time, but you must eventually let me in. You need to let us all in, those of us who love you."

I fell asleep, but was woken sometime later by the nurse wanting to check my blood pressure and temperature. I kept my eyes closed and when she was done fell right back asleep. I dreamed that I had a large mastiff dog and that he protected me when the devil came to get me. The night still thick, the orderly came in and woke me up for my blood pressure and temperature again. I heard all the talking between the nurses, saw the light of the hallway where machines chimed and beeped, phones rang. When she left I dreamed again, about being in a post apocalyptic world where the wild had turned into ashes and the city into smoldering fires. In this barren and dying landscape I searched for Willie. I turned and twisted, continued dreaming, the I.V. in my arm limiting my movement, my buttocks sore, my arm bruised. But morning still came, the sun glowing behind the blinds, and the nurse was here to take my blood!

Soon after Grace, Mom, and Leo walked in.

"Hi Elijah," Mom said.

She wore a bright blue t-shirt that said, "Eat Well."

"Fire," Leo said, "what's going on? What did the doctors' say?"

I refused to talk.

"Wake up, dude."

"Elijah, what's wrong?" Mom said.

"Fire," Grace said, "you have to tell us what's happening."

"Your dad," Mom said, "had his gut operated on when he was in the Navy and he never had problems after that. And your great uncle Nabby also had a part of his intestine removed, you remember that, and he's in great shape now. Just last year he swam across the Hudson River."

"Uncle Nabby, what a freak show," Leo said.

Mom said, "That's not nice."

Leo asked, "What effect did that punch have on this?"

Grace said, "I can't believe you got punched. How could you have said that nasty racist thing? You are, I really have to say, totally insane."

"Why," Mom asked me, "did that man punch you in the gut? What did you say?"

Her heavy jaw was set in confusion.

"It's hard for me to imagine that someone would want to punch you in the stomach, sweets."

"Mom," Leo said, "trust me, he deserved it."

"I can't believe that. Grace, can you believe that?"

"Oh yes, Pearl. You live in delusion about your Elijah."

"How did a son of mine become a racist?"

Leo said, "Because he's an arrogant son of a bitch."

"Hey," Mom said, "watch your mouth."

"Speak to us," Grace said.

Leo said, "You have to man-up Fire."

They left.

I fell asleep and dreamed of meeting my father on 72nd Street.

"Dad," I said, "What're you doing?"

"Walking the streets of the city," he answered.

He looked good, his cheeks ruddy.

"Dad, can the dead do this?"

"Sure," he said, "it's what I like to do."

The next day I submitted to the doctors' will. The door opened and I heard the heavy unmistakable footsteps of my wife. She came to my bed and sat down.

"It's nice that you have a view of the Hudson River," she said.

She opened the blinds and the morning sun came rushing in.

She leaned down and hugged me.

"Don't keep me out," she said.

I let my anger flow through my head and around my body, but said nothing.

Grace brought Augie and Michelle.

I lifted myself up.

Michelle jumped on the bed and Grace screamed, "Be careful Michelle, don't knock Daddy's I.V. out."

She made her way to the top of the bed and hugged me.

She said, "That guy hit you really hard, Daddy."

"Your daddy went down like a tree hit by lightning, according to your uncle Leo."

"Dad, what did you do?" Augie asked.

"Let's say," Grace said, "that he said something very inappropriate to the wrong people."

"What's inappropriate?" asked Michelle.

"Something that's not right," Augie said to her, with impatience.

"He said, 'Nigger, please'," Michelle said.

"You said what?" he said. "I can't believe it."

"He did," Grace said. "Your father, the world's man of freedom and equal rights."

"Dad, that's a terrible thing to say. You got mad at me for calling our neighbor black. You said we're all the same blood. So how could you say what you did?"

"Your father thought he was doing the right thing. He just went about it the wrong way."

I shrank in the face of these growing giants.

Annie my night nurse leaned her small body over mine as she checked my blood pressure and cleaned my shit bag. I felt it on my side like a warm tumorous pimple. I could feel Annie's warmth and desire and it was exhilarating. She tried to show me how to clean my bag, but I didn't pay attention. Her skin was like velvet, so young and unbruised, and I wanted to run my fingers down her arm.

Jane and Adam came to see me.

I took a glimpse at the bag, but turned my eyes quickly.

I watched a lot of baseball, thinking about Tony Gywnn and Cal Ripken Jr.

Mom, Leo, and Grace were in constant rotation. My dean came by, said we needed to talk when I was back to health. Bruno called from Milan and said, "Wake up." James called from Kenya.

Augie, Michelle, and Grace came by again.

Michelle immediately jumped up on the bed.

"Hi, Daddy," she said.

Grace and Augie sat down in the chairs.

Augie told me about his friends and how they had found some skeletons in Van Cortlandt Park. He said he thought they belonged to a horse. Michelle, jumping up and down on the bed, told me about how she could swim. Augie and Grace shook their heads. Michelle saw them and said, "I can swim!" Augie asked if he could have the polar bear book he'd seen on my shelf. Michelle said she had gone to a birthday party yesterday. Augie said he had started a rock collection. Grace said that her boss was a pain in the ass and that her father had again insulted her. She said that several street trees had been cut down in the neighborhood and that all our neighbors were up in arms. Michelle got bored and Augie wanted to leave too. Grace looked at me, smiled, and said, "We want you home."

The nurses, and Annie, who I waited for, cleaned out my shit bag.

On the day I'm released Grace comes to get me. I step out of the hospital doors to the warm sun coming off the river and I smell the greasy city air.

Grace leans in to kiss me, brushing up against my bag.

We get the car from the garage and drive north up the river parallel to the park through the toll and into the suburban woods of the Bronx to my glorious home with the white pine and white oak trees.